THE LOVE LIBRARIAN

OLIVIA SPRING

HARTLEY PUBLISHING

March 2025

www.oliviaspring.com

Follow Olivia on Facebook/X/Instagram: @ospringauthor

TikTok: www.tiktok.com/@oliviaspringauthor

AUTHOR'S NOTE

Please note that this novel includes references to a toxic family, controlling parental behaviour, racism and the challenges of having a parent suffering from Alzheimer's disease.

Rest assured that these topics were approached with the utmost care, and in consultation with individuals for whom this was a lived experience.

I hope that I have treated these topics with the thoughtfulness they deserve. If they are delicate subjects for you, please read with care.

To everyone who believes in love.
May you get your own happily-ever-after.

1

___

JANE

'How bad is it?' My heart thudded against my chest.

'It's not good, Jane.' Bill winced as he stepped off the ladder propped against the library wall. 'It could've been worse, but—'

'Will it be difficult to fix?' I jumped in.

'Difficult, no. Expensive, *yes*.'

My stomach tightened, knowing my boss was going to be so upset.

When I'd arrived for work this morning at The Romance Library (which, as the name suggested, was a library that specialised in romance books), I'd noticed a massive puddle on the floor in the main hall and realised that the ceiling was leaking.

Luckily it hadn't damaged any books, but if I'd come in any later, it could've been a very different story.

A leak for any business was inconvenient. But having to fix the ceilings and the roof right now would tip the library's finances over the edge.

We'd only been open for six weeks and although my

boss, Jess, had tried to keep her spirits high, I knew that money was tight.

A kind lady called Mrs Davis had left Jess a million pounds to buy this building and create a romance library, but making that dream a reality had been more expensive than Jess had budgeted for.

The money was running out fast. Especially as Jess had to shell out a big chunk to pay for work to start on the library's new cafe next weekend. Plus, we desperately needed another employee, which meant covering another wage.

There'd been a huge buzz when the library opened and we had a lot of members, but that wasn't enough. We were self-funded, so if we didn't start generating a bigger income soon, we'd have to close. Which would be a huge tragedy for all the romance book lovers who flocked from far and wide to visit.

And, I'd be unemployed.

Working here was the best job I'd ever had. That was why I had to do everything I could to protect the library's future.

'Once I've worked out all the costs, I'll email a proper quote,' Bill said.

'Okay,' I sighed. 'How much will it be for today?'

When Bill told me the call-out charge, my eyes watered. I reached in my bag, then handed over my card.

Technically I shouldn't pay for company stuff with my own money. But this was the first morning that Jess and her boyfriend, Theo, who also worked at the library, had taken off in weeks, so I didn't want to disturb them. Especially with bad news like this.

After Bill took the payment, then left, I stepped back through the library's solid wooden double doors.

Every time I wandered down the corridor, my worries melted away. This library wasn't just where I worked. It was my happy place.

Cool bookish quotes like 'I'd rather be reading' and 'Just one more chapter' had been carefully stencilled onto the warm rose-painted walls.

When I entered the grand hall, which was the main library space, my heart bloomed.

Rows upon rows of tall pink-and-white bookcases, complete with rolling ladders, lined the shiny wooden floors. Colourful book chandeliers hung from the ceilings, and the seats were all so comfy you could literally fall asleep in them.

And, yes, I was definitely talking from personal experience.

On the evenings when I closed the library, I'd curl up on one of the pink sofas with multiple cushions, a warm fluffy blanket, a steaming cup of tea and a plate of biscuits, then read for hours.

My parents thought it was ridiculous that I spent so much time here surrounded by books, but there was no place I'd rather be.

Plus, the more time I spent at the library, the less time I'd have to spend with them. The sooner I could move out of their toxic house, the better.

Just as I picked up the mop to give the floor another once-over, I heard footsteps racing down the corridor. That was weird. It was only just gone nine and the library didn't open until half past.

'What happened?' Jess burst into the hall. Her thick,

curly black hair was thrown into a ponytail. Normally she wore lip gloss and sometimes mascara and some tinted moisturiser, but today her brown skin was bare and she had dark circles under her eyes.

'I thought you were taking the morning off?' I frowned.

'I was, but Theo went to get breakfast and saw Bill's van pulling out of the library, so he asked if I knew why he was here. I told him I didn't, and then when I couldn't get through to you, I got worried and sprinted down here.'

Crap. Even though I wasn't responsible for the leak, I hated that Jess's lie-in had been ruined.

'I must've left my phone on silent, sorry. When I came in, I saw the leak and—'

'Morning, Jane,' Theo said as he entered the hall. Every time I saw him I thought of Superman because with his dark hair and piercing blue eyes, he was the spitting image of Henry Cavill. 'What happened?'

'I was just explaining to Jess that I saw a massive puddle, so I called Bill. He says there's a big hole in the roof that leaked through to the room upstairs, then down to the ceiling here.' I pointed up at the wet patch.

'Shit.' Jess squeezed her eyes shut.

'That's strange.' Theo's face crumpled. 'The building was checked over thoroughly before we opened last month and the roof was absolutely fine. We're not even at the end of September yet. It's not normal for tiles to deteriorate so quickly.'

Hmm. Bill also said that it was odd to have a hole like that, particularly because the tiles seemed new, but said he'd look into it.

'This is the last thing we need!' Jess blew out a

defeated breath. 'We've only got enough to keep us going for a few more months, so this will really set us back. Maybe I should put the cafe and hiring someone on hold.'

'No,' Theo said firmly. 'We'll lose the deposit if we don't go ahead, and we need help—otherwise we'll all burn out. The candidate I have in mind could help us generate revenue. We have to speculate to accumulate.'

'We've been doing a lot of speculating. When does the *accumulating* start?' Jess asked.

'It's still early days. It'll happen. Don't worry, we'll be fine.' Theo wrapped his arm around her waist and kissed her softly on the forehead. I wished I could find a man who loved me like Theo loved Jess. 'Was there a call-out charge?' He faced me.

'I took care of it,' I replied quickly, not wanting them to worry.

'You paid it?' Jess's eyes widened.

'Yeah. I know things are tricky financially, so—'

'That's really kind,' Jess cut in, 'but it's a company expense. I don't want you to be out of pocket.'

'Exactly,' Theo added. 'Let me know how much it was and I'll reimburse you straight away.'

'Okay,' I replied, knowing they wouldn't take no for an answer. 'We can't do anything until Bill sends the quote, so go home and relax.'

'That would've been nice, but I've got an interview in ten minutes,' Theo said as he glanced at his watch. 'It was scheduled for this evening, but he messaged earlier to ask if he could come now, and seeing as I was up, I agreed.'

So it was another man they were interviewing.

If he was anything like the last two men, he wouldn't get the job.

The guy they'd interviewed a couple of weeks ago had the personality of a wet fish. I was hardly the life and soul of the party, but at least I didn't grunt like he'd done when I'd asked how he was.

They'd interviewed another guy last week who was the complete opposite. When we showed him around, he spoke so much that we barely got a word in. And he tried flirting with two members. He probably just wanted the job because he thought a romance library would be a good place to pick up women.

Oops. I shouldn't have thought that.

Jess and Theo hadn't hired him because the library wasn't a place for a rowdy chatterbox, not because he was some sort of Casanova. Clearly I still hadn't got over what had happened at my last job.

Of course I knew that all men weren't terrible. Theo, for example, was amazing. But as bad as it sounded, given the choice, I'd prefer them to hire another woman. That way I wouldn't get humiliated again.

A sharp pain ripped through my chest as a mortifying memory invaded my thoughts.

Anyway, it wasn't going to be an issue. Considering Theo had said this guy had messaged at the last minute to change the interview time, I doubted he'd get the job. Jess and Theo were busy people. If this man wanted to work here, he should fit around *their* schedule, not the other way around.

'Now that I'm here, I was gonna make some calls,' Jess said.

'I'll start the interview, so just join us when you can,' Theo replied.

As Jess stood on tiptoe and kissed him quickly on the lips, another pang of yearning shot through me.

I was happy for them. I really was. As a certified romance junkie, I loved the idea of love. Jess and Theo proved that for the lucky few, romance didn't just exist in the pages of a good novel. It happened in real life too.

Just not to someone like me.

'I'll leave you to it.' I blushed as I picked up the mop and bucket. 'I'll bring up the new books from the stock-room and start restocking the bookshop.'

After emptying the bucket and putting away the mop, I headed down to the stockroom, organised a stack of new steamy romance novels into a tall pile, then picked it up.

As I struggled up the stairs from the basement to the main corridor, I realised I was carrying way too many books.

The tower of novels obscured my vision, but I had loads to do this morning and once my colleague, Celeste, arrived, she'd need to stay in the bookshop, so the more stock I brought up for her now, the easier it'd be.

It seemed like a logical idea until I hit a wall and all the books tumbled to the floor.

'Shit!' a deep voice boomed.

My head snapped up, then I saw that it wasn't a wall I'd crashed into.

It was a very tall and *extremely* handsome man.

Wow.

My eyes popped and my lips parted as I took in the sight of the guy, who looked like he'd just walked straight out of one of my romance novels.

He had brown skin and short black hair that was

shaved at the sides, and he wore a white shirt that clung to what I imagined was a very muscular chest.

'You okay?' he asked.

'I… I'm… sorry. I…' I stuttered, touching my brown hair to check that my bun was still intact whilst desperately trying to remember how to form a sentence. I was softly spoken at the best of times, but seeing this god had literally taken my breath away.

'Wait.' He frowned. 'Jane?'

Nope. Now I was convinced that this couldn't be real. What were the chances of meeting a hot guy here at work and having him know my name?

Literally zero.

'Yeah…?' My face crumpled with confusion and I adjusted my tortoiseshell glasses on the bridge of my nose, hoping that somehow it'd help me to see better. 'How do you…?'

'It's Jackson.' His face broke into a smile. 'We used to go to school together. At Northwood.'

No. Bloody. Way.

My jaw dropped so hard I was surprised all of my teeth didn't shatter.

'Jackson *Campbell*?' I frowned, still trying to get my head around the fact that it was *him*.

'Guilty as charged!' He laughed.

'But you look…'

'*Different?*'

'Yeah.'

'A little.' He laughed again and goosebumps erupted across my skin. He might look different, but the low rumble of his laugh was exactly the same. 'Let me help you.' Jackson bent down to pick up the books.

'It's okay,' I said quickly as I spotted a postcard that had slipped out of one of the novels.

'*Okay…*' Jackson looked up at me, then raised an eyebrow as he picked up the postcard.

Whilst a devilish smile spread across his face, my cheeks heated with embarrassment.

This wasn't an ordinary postcard with pretty pictures of the beach opposite this library.

This was a *very steamy* postcard, with custom artwork that was so X-rated that most retailers said it was too spicy to offer to their customers.

It had an illustrated scene of the female main character sat with her legs spread wide open on a kitchen counter whilst the male main character was on his knees going down on her.

'It's, erm…' I sank to the floor and started hastily organising the books into a pile. 'It comes with the book. Like a free gift… I don't think you're supposed to send it to anyone. I'm not sure the Post Office would even *allow* that. It's for… actually I don't really know what you're supposed to do with it.'

Sweat pooled under my armpits and I wished that I'd stayed in the stockroom longer so I wouldn't be up here now having this awkward conversation with the boy I used to have a crush on at school years ago.

He might've been a boy back then, but he was *all man* now. Which was why I was still struggling to string two words together.

'Maybe put it on the wall and use it for *inspiration*?' Jackson smirked.

'Oh.' I blushed, feeling like an idiot. 'Er, yeah. Ha-ha!' *God.*

Ground, swallow me up.

Of course I knew that's what people could use it for.

That thought probably would've popped into my head a lot faster if I'd actually had sex before.

Yeah. That's right.

I'm a virgin.

Thirty-one years old and I *still* hadn't popped my cherry.

People thought unicorns were rare. But these days, I reckoned the average adult probably had more chance of seeing a unicorn or meeting Taylor Swift in real life than knowing someone in their thirties like me who still hadn't *done the deed.*

I was a joke.

If my cheeks were burning before, now they were so hot you could fry a dozen eggs on them. I hoped my porcelain skin hadn't turned bright red, but something told me it was already too late.

'Jackson?' Theo's voice sounded behind me.

I spun around, then jumped up as I saw him approaching us.

Thank God.

The sooner I could extract myself from this situation and avoid putting my foot in my mouth again, the better.

'That's me! You must be Theo?'

'I am indeed. Good to meet you.' Theo stretched out his hand and gave Jackson a firm handshake. 'Jane, this is Jackson.'

'Yep. The one and only Jackson Campbell!' My voice went up several octaves like I'd sucked on helium, and I groaned internally.

As I fiddled with the cuffs of my silk blouse, I

wondered if there was a chance I'd stop embarrassing myself anytime soon. Never had I wanted to crawl under a rock and hide for eternity more than I did right now.

'You two know each other?' Theo looked between us.

'Yeah,' Jackson helpfully replied, giving me time to attempt to compose myself. 'We went to the same school. Jane was always top of our English class.'

'And Jackson was always great at IT, maths, science and basically *everything*,' I gushed.

God. I sounded so pathetic.

'Small world,' Theo said.

'I should…' I stuttered again. As my eyes locked with Jackson's, my stomach flipped like a dolphin on happy pills. I really needed to get out of here. 'I have to take these to the bookshop. Really nice to meet… I mean, *see* you. Bye!' I sprinted down the corridor before remembering that I'd left the pile of books on the floor.

Doh. What the hell was wrong with me?

I shuffled back towards them, embarrassment coursing through me, then saw that Jackson had the books in his arms and was already heading in my direction.

'You forgot these,' Jackson said.

'Yeah…' I laughed. 'I'd forget my own head if it wasn't screwed on!'

Jackson smiled, instantly putting me at ease.

'You sure you don't want me to help you carry them?' My heart fluttered. He was always kind to me at school. I was glad he hadn't changed.

'Thanks, but I'll be fine.' I took the tower of books and tried to balance them. 'I'll let you get to your interview. I've already held you up enough.'

'Sure?'

'Absolutely! Great to see you again,' I said before remembering that I'd already said the exact same thing two minutes ago.

'You too.' Jackson smiled, then followed Theo to the office.

I hurried to the bookshop, almost dropping the stack again before eventually plopping it down on the counter, then leaning against it.

Jackson Campbell.

I hadn't seen him in years, and my God, what a transformation.

My mind raced, wondering if he was single. Then I slammed on the brakes, ordering my brain to stop creating ridiculous fantasies.

Although I'd always thought he was cute, Jackson was never the popular boy at school. But things had no doubt changed since then.

Now, Jackson must attract women like bees to honey, so he'd never be interested in someone like me. Whilst he'd blossomed, I was still *Plain Jane*, just like the bullies used to call me.

Anyway, it was irrelevant.

Didn't stop me from being curious about Jackson's life, though.

Last I'd heard, he'd gone to Cambridge University, then landed a high-flying finance job in London.

But if that was true, what was Jackson doing here in a small seaside town like Sunshine Bay, interviewing for a role at The Romance Library?

2

___

JACKSON

J ane Riley.

Wow.

I hadn't spotted any photos of her on the library's social media pages, so she was the last person I'd expected to see here.

When I'd noticed the main library doors were open, I'd decided to go in and ask for Theo. But just as I'd headed down the corridor, a text had come through from the agency about the job this afternoon and I'd got distracted.

Next thing I knew, I'd crashed into something and saw a woman scrambling to pick a pile of books up from the floor.

And as soon as I saw those pretty brown eyes, I knew it was Jane.

She had the kind of eyes you couldn't forget.

Jane hadn't changed much. She still wore her chocolate-brown hair up in a neat bun.

She still wore glasses, although I noticed these ones

had a tortoiseshell pattern instead of the plain thick black-rimmed ones she had at school.

She still seemed sweet and softly spoken.

And she was still so damn beautiful.

'Did you find the library easily?' Theo asked as he stopped in front of a pink door and stepped inside an office.

As I followed him, I snapped out of my thoughts. I didn't have time to think about how good Jane looked in that pencil skirt and silky cream blouse. I was here for an interview and I really needed this job.

'Yeah, thanks.'

'Please.' Theo gestured to the chair in front of the desk he was now seated behind. 'So…' He pulled out a printed copy of my CV and put it on the desk. 'You used to work in finance in the City? Why'd you leave?'

'Needed a change of pace,' I answered quickly. I knew this question was coming. There was no way I could go into the real reason. That shit was still triggering. 'It got too intense and started to have a negative effect on my mental health.'

It was true. That job had fucked me up.

'I can relate.' Theo nodded sympathetically. 'I used to work in a high-pressured job too. My quality of life is much better now.' That was good to know. So far I liked this guy. I could tell that he'd come from a privileged background, but he still seemed down to earth and genuine. 'So why would you like to work at The Romance Library?'

'I love books. They've helped me through some diffi-cult times. I used to mainly read thrillers and non-fiction, but I recently started reading romance and I'm really enjoying it. I like knowing there's going to be a happy ending every time, because that's not what always happens in real life.' My stomach tensed. 'And from a commercial perspective, I'd like to work here because I'm confident I can help you make more money.'

'Sorry!' A woman I instantly recognised from some online articles and the library's social media pages burst into the office.

'Jessica, right?' I stood up and stretched out my hand. 'I'm Jackson. Nice to meet you.'

'Nice to meet you too, Jackson. And please, call me Jess.' She smiled. 'I had to make some calls, but I'm here now. What did I miss?'

'Jackson was saying he could help generate income for the library.'

'I like the sound of that!' Jess pulled a chair from another desk and sat next to Theo. 'Tell us more.'

'The Romance Library is a cool concept, so for starters you could capitalise on that by selling branded merch. It'd be good to do some social bookish events and charge an entrance fee. And if you can start selling drinks and snacks that will help straight away.'

'Great ideas!' Jess grinned. 'We've always wanted to sell branded stuff and organise events, but we haven't had the time. Work starts on our new cafe next Sunday, though.'

'That's good to hear.' I nodded. 'If I got this role, I'd also like to contact publishers and let them know they can rent the library for romance book launches, events and signings.'

'Brilliant!' Jess said. 'And who are your favourite romance authors?'

'I was saying to Theo that I'm new to the genre, so I've got a lot to learn, but I started the *Bromance Book Club* series by Lyssa Kay Adams, because the books are about men who read romance and I can relate. My mum used to read a lot of Beverly Jenkins…' My voice trailed off and my chest tightened. I shouldn't have brought Mum up. I hated that she couldn't enjoy her favourite books anymore. 'I want to read more romance, so working here would be perfect.'

'And you know this will initially be a part-time role?' Theo asked.

'Yeah,' I confirmed. 'That's great for me.'

Although they hadn't advertised the salary, I knew it wasn't going to compare to what I used to earn. But the other job I'd started recently did. I didn't enjoy it, though. And I knew that if I didn't have something to balance it out and distract me from the pressure I was under, I'd crack.

Working with books would be an ideal distraction.

Books fed our minds and enriched our souls. And based on what I'd read so far, romance novels gave me the joy I needed right now.

'Are you flexible with your working days and hours?' Jess asked.

'In the daytime, yes. But I can't work evenings.'

Jess and Theo's faces instantly fell.

Shit.

'Why's that?' Theo asked.

'I…' I paused. This was a question I hadn't prepared for. I didn't like hiding the truth of what I did, but it wasn't the kind of thing you mentioned in an interview, so I needed to think of something else to say, fast. 'Because I have to… clean,' I blurted out.

What I did had nothing to do with cleaning, but it was the first respectable job I could think of that people did in the evenings.

'Oh! I had a cleaning job too before I started the library. I'm sorry we can only offer part-time right now, but hopefully we can offer more hours soon. I know that cleaning can be tough.'

'I actually enjoy it.' That was also true. Although doing housework was different to cleaning for a living.

I probably had an unhealthy obsession with it, but when your world got turned upside down like mine had been, you needed all the distractions you could get.

'Thanks for coming in,' Theo said. 'We have everything we need for now. We have a couple of other candidates to see, but we'll let you know our decision in the next few days.'

'Thanks again for seeing me early.' I stood up. 'I'll wait to hear from you.'

As I stepped out of the office, I scanned the corridor, hoping to catch another glimpse of Jane. It was for the best that I didn't see her, though. I couldn't afford any distractions in my life right now.

After getting the train back to Shamwick, a small town close to Sunshine Bay which was where I grew up, I walked to Mum's house, then raced upstairs to get dressed.

As I stepped into my tuxedo, my chest tightened. I really didn't want to do this job. But Mum needed me. I couldn't let her down.

My phone rang. It was the agency.

'Jackson! Hi!' Fearne answered. 'Thanks for replying

to my text earlier. I just wanted to brief you on the client you'll be meeting at the luncheon.'

'Okay.' I tried to sound enthusiastic. Normally they booked me in the evenings, but today I was working earlier, which was why I'd asked Theo if it was possible to change the interview time. I couldn't afford to miss the opportunity to earn some cash.

'Mrs Buckingham is one of our most important clients. Impress her and you'll be set. She'll book you for at least two nights a week.'

'That'd be… good,' I said. *Financially at least.*

'You received the address?'

'Yeah.'

'Fantastic! Enjoy!'

Once I hung up, I slipped on my shoes and caught the train to central London.

A text came through from my best friend, Marcus, asking how the interview had gone. Even though I was sure I'd blown it, I tried to stay positive, so told him it was okay. I also casually mentioned that I'd bumped into Jane, who I knew he'd remember me mentioning from my days at Northwood.

When I looked up from my screen, I saw we were pulling into the station, so put my phone in my pocket, got off the train, then caught the bus to the posh Mayfair hotel.

Before I'd had a chance to find the client, someone touched my arm.

'You must be Jackson,' she purred.

The lady who I assumed had to be Mrs Buckingham, considering she already knew my name, was a tall, slim woman with white skin, dark hair and bright red lipstick.

She was wearing a silver dress, and if I had to guess, I'd say she was in her mid-fifties.

'That's me. Mrs Buckingham?'

'No need to be so formal, darling.' She flashed her perfect white teeth. 'Call me Helen. Or sweetheart.'

'Okay, Helen.'

The thought of calling a stranger an affectionate nick-name made me cringe, but it probably made sense if we were supposed to be dating. I'd only been working as an escort for a few weeks, so I was still getting used to this. I had to put my thoughts about how uncomfortable it made me feel aside and do what was necessary to pay the bills. It was as simple as that.

'And if people ask how we met, what would you like me to say?' I whispered.

'Oh, I don't know, darling!' She patted my bum and I flinched. She knew that touching wasn't part of the arrangement, right? I was very clear when I signed up that I wasn't prepared to offer any sexual services: just companionship. 'Just say we met at a dinner party. Darling!' she called out to a woman who'd just walked into reception and waved her over.

'Lovely to see you, sweetie!' The redhead air-kissed Helen before scanning me from head to toe. 'And who is *this* handsome fellow?'

'This is Jackson,' Helen said, stroking my bicep suggestively.

Bile rose in my throat. I didn't like her touching me. It made me feel sick.

Think of the money. You can't afford to lose this job. Think of the money. Think of the money.

'*Ding-dong!*' The woman licked her lips.

'Nice to meet you.' I stretched out my hand and plastered on a smile.

'Oh, come on, sweetie.' She lurched forward and planted a kiss on my cheek and then a second one on the other side. 'We're all friends here.' She stretched behind me and squeezed my butt and it took all the strength I had not to swat her hand away and walk out. I hated this shit. '*Very* nice.' The woman smiled at Helen approvingly. 'I like this one. Might have to book him myself.'

This one?

She made me sound like a piece of meat she'd picked up from the supermarket counter.

I'd known this was a bad idea when Marcus had suggested it. After what had happened before, I shouldn't put myself in situations like this, but right now, I didn't have a choice.

I fought the urge to grind my jaw and reminded myself to suck it up. This was just a job. And the fact that it wasn't a secret that Helen used escorts was good. Especially as her friend was interested in booking me too.

More bookings meant more money.

More money meant I could pay for the care Mum needed.

That was what was important.

For the next three hours, Helen paraded me around like a shiny new trophy. I did my best to smile and charm everyone she spoke to and I tried not to flinch every time she squeezed my arse. I knew my job was to make her happy, but the physical contact made me uncomfortable. I'd speak to the agency tomorrow about that. Let them know that if she wanted to book me again, that wouldn't be part of the deal.

Finally, the event came to an end.

'I'm going to head off now.' I glanced at my watch. I was booked until six, but it was now twenty past.

'So soon?' She cocked her head to the side. 'I thought maybe you'd like to continue the evening back at my place?'

'No.' I shook my head. 'I only offer companionship services.' I lowered my voice, trying to keep things discreet.

I knew that for some escorts, sexual services were part of the package. If those guys were fine with that, it was their choice. No judgement. But it wasn't for me. Even though I knew I could earn a lot more, I couldn't cross that line.

'Oh, come on, darling.' Helen stepped forward, smiled, then casually grabbed my dick.

'What the fuck?' I shouted, jumping back in horror. 'That is *not* okay,' I snapped, my nostrils flaring. I'd put up with her pawing and groping all night without saying a word, but grabbing my cock was taking it too far.

I couldn't deal with this. Not again.

'Don't be such a spoilsport!' She rolled her eyes.

'*Unbelievable.*' I shook my head. 'I'm leaving.'

'Wait!' She grabbed my arm. 'You can't! I paid for eight hours and it's only been five. You owe me. I demand that you come back to my house!'

'You paid for six hours and it's been almost six and a half, so I think you'll find that *you* owe *me*.'

'This is your last chance, Jackson,' she warned. 'If you leave, I'll make sure the agency never uses you again. You need money, correct? I've got plenty. We can come to a little arrangement. Keep me satisfied and I'll take care of you. All of your debts could disappear, just like that.' She clicked her fingers.

Helen was right, I *did* need the money. But despite my financial troubles, I wasn't even tempted. I'd been black-mailed before and I wasn't going to let someone do that to me again.

'No,' I said firmly.

'Don't say I didn't warn you!' she hissed. 'You've just missed out on the opportunity of a lifetime. Don't come crying to me when you're forced to sell your body on a street corner or have to strip on the internet to make ends meet. Good luck. You're going to need it!'

As Helen stormed off, reality suddenly hit me.

I'd just upset the agency's biggest client. What if that meant I didn't get paid for today?

And if what she said was true, I had bigger problems to worry about. Like how I was going to clear those overdue invoices and pay for Mum's care this month.

And next month. And the month after that.

I couldn't go back to what I'd done before. Not after what it had done to me.

If I got the library job, it'd help my sanity. It'd be amazing to do something I really enjoyed, and I really felt like I could make a difference there. But it wouldn't be enough. I needed money. A lot of it. *Fast*.

And after today's shitshow, I was fresh out of options.

Fuck.

3

JANE

After saying bye to Jess, I left the library, immediately deciding to take the long way home.

The town I lived in, Shamwick, was only a few stops away from Sunshine Bay, and it was just a short walk from the library to the train station. But I wasn't ready to go home. Not yet.

Instead, I headed down to the beach opposite the library. Although it was September and the weather was cooler, I still enjoyed going for walks here during my lunch break or after work.

The beach had gorgeous golden sand, and watching the gentle waves as they rippled against the shore was so calming.

After I slipped off my shoes, my feet sank into the sand. I breathed in the salty sea air and exhaled.

That's better.

As my mind relaxed, my thoughts wandered back to this morning, when I'd bumped into Jackson.

I'd like to say that was the first time I'd thought about

him since we were at school together, but that would be a lie.

I was desperate to ask Theo and Jess how his interview had gone, but they'd been busy all day liaising with Bill about the leak and organising stuff before work began on the cafe, so I hadn't got a chance. Hopefully tomorrow I'd find out more.

Anyway, I couldn't think about Jackson. It didn't matter how sweet he was to me or how hot he looked. He hadn't been interested in me at school, so he *definitely* wouldn't be interested in me now. Especially if he knew how inexperienced I was.

Didn't matter anyway. I probably wouldn't see Jackson again, which was for the best. I was doing well at the library and couldn't let anything mess that up. I needed to focus on helping Theo and Jess keep it open, not thinking about my silly childhood crush.

I skimmed a few stones in the sea in frustration. When I looked up, the sky was a beautiful shade of orange, yellow and pink. Apart from reading, watching the sunset here was one of my favourite things to do.

It'd be dark soon, so I couldn't put it off any longer. I had to head home.

Once I was on the train, I took my book out of my bag. I was reading *Office Delight*, a steamy workplace romance Jess had recommended.

I only managed to read a chapter before it was time to get off the train and make the short walk home.

As soon as I put the key in the lock, my stomach tightened. I took a deep breath and stepped inside.

The TV blared from the living room. As I poked my

head around the door, I saw Dad with his legs over the edge of the armchair, watching the news. Like always.

'It's bloody ridiculous!' he cursed. 'This country's going to the dogs.'

'Shocking,' Mum murmured in agreement as she handed him a cup of tea, then looked up and saw me. 'Hi, love.'

'Hi, Mum. Hi, Dad,' I said nervously. He didn't hear me. After sliding off my shoes, I walked into the room, then stood by the TV to get his attention. If I didn't greet him, he'd go into a lecture about how disrespectful it was, so before I disappeared into my bedroom, I had to make sure he heard me. 'Hi,' I repeated.

'Get out the way!' he snapped. 'Have you seen this? More immigrants trying to get into the country! We should ship every single foreigner out of here. It's out of control!'

Nausea rose in my throat and my face twisted in disgust. This was exactly the kind of toxic talk I hated. The energy in this house was full of it.

Dad was always bitching about something or airing his narrow-minded, ignorant views.

I'd tried so many times to get him to open his mind. Tried to tell him that not everyone was the same. Attempted to balance his views by talking about the people that came to England to do good and who helped make it better, but it was like talking to a brick wall. Actually, I'd probably get more sense out of a brick wall than him.

'I'm going to make a sandwich for dinner. Anyone want anything?'

'I've already eaten,' he replied, his gaze still fixed to the screen. Mum shook her head.

After I'd wolfed down my sandwich and showered, I headed to my room, then shut the door.

My shoulders instantly loosened. Being around my dad zapped away my energy. Mum wasn't much better and neither was my older brother, Wayne.

Most of the time I was convinced that they must've taken home the wrong baby from the hospital, because I'd never felt like I belonged in this family. They were always so angry and bitter. Being around people with such negativity and hate in their hearts was exhausting.

The best times of my life were whenever I was away from them. Like when I'd spent a few summers working in a library in Hastings in my late teens, until Dad had demanded I give it up to help at my parents' shop.

I'd escaped them properly for about a year when I'd tried living in London. I got a job in a bookstore there and felt like finally I was free of them and could start living my own life.

But then some bad stuff had happened at work and I'd had to leave. I'd wanted to stay to find something else, but the rent in London was too expensive, so I had to return to Shamwick and my parents' house.

Dad took great pleasure in telling me he'd told me so and that I shouldn't get ideas above my station. He'd insisted there was nothing wrong with Shamwick and said I was lucky they'd let me come back home. At one point I thought he was going to ask me to kiss his feet to get my room back. Wouldn't put it past him.

I knew that if I didn't get a job quickly, Dad would try and rope me into whatever his latest *business venture* was. That was why, when I saw the job for The Romance Library pop up on Instagram, I jumped at the chance.

Not only was it my dream job, it was a start-up, which meant Jess would need a lot of help to get it off the ground. That was ideal because I loved being helpful and I'd have to spend more time away from the house.

Hopefully in a few months, I'd have enough saved up to move out. But if the library had to close, not only would I lose the best job I'd ever have, I'd lose my only chance of escaping this house and having a proper life.

I pulled out my paperback from where I'd hidden it in my handbag, took out my highlighter pens and tabs, then slid under the duvet. Usually I only read steamy romance on my Kindle, but Jess had bought me this paperback copy as a gift because it was her favourite book.

If my parents knew I read spicy books, or the kinds of books available at the library, they wouldn't approve. They took so little interest in my life that I was sure they didn't even realise it was dedicated to romance.

Like everything else, they had very narrow-minded views about sex. As far as they were concerned, it was only for procreation. Not for enjoyment.

TV shows or films with even a hint of kissing or intimacy were banned from our house when I was growing up and nothing had changed. If anything like that ever came on, Dad would brand it as 'disgusting' and immediately change the channel.

That was why I had to bury this book deep in my handbag whenever I brought it home so he wouldn't see it.

This definitely wasn't how I saw my life panning out. I was thirty-one years old, but living here made me feel like I was a child and had no control over my life. But hopefully it'd only be temporary. If the library started making more money, everything could change.

I opened the book and started reading the next chapter. Rocco, the male main character and billionaire boss, was in his chauffeur-driven limo with his assistant, Virginia, who he was now romantically involved with, and had just suggested that they have sex on the back seat.

My cheeks heated and a tingle raced between my legs.

So far, they'd already had sex in his office and he'd gone down on Virginia multiple times.

I wondered how it'd feel if a man did to me the things that Rocco did to Virginia.

I'd been kissed by a few men before, but it was sloppy and wet. Never anything enjoyable.

With a couple of guys I'd gone a bit further. A little bit of touching over clothes, but nothing more.

When I moved to London, just over a year ago, I got my first vibrator. I could never have one whilst I lived at my parents' because I was too worried Mum or Dad might find it if they were snooping around my room, which I knew they did when I wasn't here. It wasn't worth the fall-out. They'd see it as dirty. Shameful.

Given my parents' views on sex and how strict they were about me going out, I'd always known I probably wouldn't get to lose my virginity at a similar age to my peers. But I hadn't expected to get to my thirties without ever having sex. It was embarrassing.

On the one hand, that was one of the reasons reading romance novels was my sanctuary. If I couldn't have a relationship of my own, reading about fictional characters getting intimate was the next best thing.

But on the other hand, I felt like a fraud. I was a romance fan and a love librarian, but I'd never even experienced sex or true romantic feelings myself.

I used to hope that one day I'd at least lose my virginity. Every year I'd tell myself, 'Maybe this year it'll happen'.

But I'd been doing that since I was eighteen and so far, nothing.

I bet Jackson didn't have this problem. Right now, he was probably in bed with his girlfriend or some other hot woman, doing all the exciting things that Rocco and Virginia did.

Another tingle of desire shot between my legs and I quickly scolded myself.

Stop bloody thinking about him. It'll only lead to disappointment.

I sighed and brought my attention back to the page, trying not to let the fact that Rocco was now fucking Virginia on the back seat affect me.

Virginia might be a fictional character, but she was one lucky woman.

As I reached for my pen to highlight every single line of this steamy scene, my mind drifted again.

Would I ever get to pop my cherry and do anything thrilling like this with a man?

Or was it time to finally accept that having wild, passionate sex was just what other people or characters like Virginia experienced, not people like me?

4

JACKSON

Reluctantly, I closed my book and got off the train. I was reading a new friends-to-lovers romance and it was just getting to the good part.

And by *the good part*, I mean the male main character had just confessed his feelings for his best friend. It could've ended in tears, but luckily she'd admitted she felt the same and they were just about to kiss.

I'd only started this novel last night to try and take my mind off the shit show that was my life right now and I was already about halfway through, so it was definitely helping.

I was starting to realise that the fifty per cent mark in romance books was when the characters started to get it on, so as much as I was enjoying it, now was a good time to get off the train. The last thing I needed was to get a boner in public.

These days I was more likely to be reading about sex rather than having it. It'd been over a year and a half since I'd dated anyone, and with everything that was going on with Mum right now and struggling to earn enough to pay for her care, I had zero time or desire for a relationship.

Once I got off the train, I walked to Marcus's house. He lived in North London, so it wasn't easy to get to from Shamwick, which was in south-east England. The journey took almost two hours door to door, but I hadn't seen him for what felt like ages, and after that disastrous escort job two days ago, I needed someone to talk to.

'Hey,' Marcus said as he opened the door.

His short, dark brown hair was slicked back and his white skin looked freshly shaven. Marcus was wearing a pair of jeans with a smart shirt, so I was guessing he still hadn't changed since getting in from work.

'Hey.' I stepped inside and gave him an affectionate slap on the back. 'Good to see you.'

'Same! It's been too long. I just made dinner. Come and eat.' He said.

After I'd taken off my jacket and shoes, I followed him into the kitchen, which looked like a bomb had hit it.

I loved my friend, but he was the kind of guy who never used the same glass twice and used multiple pots to cook when he could just use one or two. So the sink and worktops were covered with dirty dishes and pans.

'How's your mum?' he asked, dishing the stir-fry onto two plates.

'She's okay. Has her good days and her bad ones. But it's hard, man.'

I blew out a breath. Mum had Alzheimer's and was currently in a residential home. I hated the fact that I couldn't look after her myself, but I'd tried and eventually realised that staying at the home allowed her to get the kind of expert care she needed.

'I can imagine.' Marcus sighed.

'Seeing her like that, like a shadow of the person she used to be, is tough, and then there's the bills.'

I'd tried to get support for her care but was told Mum didn't qualify because she owned a property. So if I wanted Mum to receive the best care, I had to pay for it myself.

'Shit. But the escorting must be helping, though, right?'

Marcus was the only person who knew what I did. It was actually him who'd suggested it after seeing one of his clients at an event and hearing on the grapevine that the man wasn't her boyfriend like she'd claimed.

I'd dismissed the idea at first. But when Mum's care bills started stacking up and I'd realised that to cover them I'd either have to try escorting or go back to working in the pressure-cooker environment that had nearly caused me to have a breakdown, I knew I didn't have a choice.

'Yeah. It *was* helping. Until their best client fucked me over.'

'What?' His face creased. 'What happened?'

As Marcus pushed a stack of dirty plates to the other side of the island, I filled him in on my last job.

'When I called the agency the next day, they said they didn't have any more work for me, so she clearly followed through on her promise to make sure I didn't work again.'

'Didn't you tell them about what she did?'

'Yep. I told them about the groping, touching and that she'd basically blackmailed me to sleep with her, but they brushed it off. Even though they're supposed to be an agency that doesn't offer extras and I was clear that I wouldn't do anything sexual when I signed up with them, she's one of their best clients, so they turn a blind eye. If it's a case of choosing between her and me, of course they're going to choose her.'

'That's fucked up.'

'Tell me about it.'

'Can't you try another escort agency? There must be loads.'

'I tried. But they all seem to like to offer their clients the full service…'

'And you're not down for that?'

'I don't think I could do it. It's not for me. I couldn't even stand her touching my arse, so I probably wouldn't be able to get my dick up.'

'I know what you mean. The attraction has to be there.'

'Exactly. But I don't know how I'll survive. I think it's so messed up that she knew that I was desperate and didn't care. She said if I didn't come home with her, I'd end up stripping online. It was all a game to her. She got some kind of twisted pleasure from knowing I was going to suffer.'

'Actually…' Marcus paused, holding a forkful of noodles mid-air. 'That might not be a bad idea.'

'What?'

'You hate the physical contact with these clients, right? Like you said, you flinched every time she squeezed your arse.'

'Yeah?' My eyebrows knitted together.

'So maybe doing something online could be a better option. You can give these women a chance to fantasise about you and get themselves off, but without having to see them in real life. I was reading an article the other day about a new content subscription website service called

Only For U. Basically, people pay to watch sexy videos and the performers get a decent split of the royalties. You could make a shitload of money from it.'

'So you want me to be an online stripper?' I said, my eyes bulging.

'You don't have to take *all* your clothes off. You can just do a little show, like a sexy dance or something. Listen, you're a good-looking guy and I've seen the way you can move those hips!'

'You hitting on me, bro?' I smiled.

'Nah, man!' He laughed. 'I'm secure enough in my masculinity to appreciate a handsome dude when I see one, and I saw the way you turned heads with the ladies when we used to go out. Even if you did something basic in front of the camera, I'm sure you'd get a ton of subscribers. It'd need to be something a bit different, though, because there's probably loads of people dancing or stripping on there already. You'd need a USP.'

Marcus worked in marketing, so I was used to his fancy acronyms.

'Like what?' I said before sliding a piece of chicken into my mouth. 'I don't know what my *unique selling point* could be.'

'I've got no idea either, but something that fits your personality would be good. Back in a sec.' He slid off the stool, then left the kitchen.

As my mind drifted, thinking what I could do to earn money quickly, I scanned the dishes piled up around me and winced. I knew Marcus had no intention of cleaning them any time this century and my hands were twitching. I hadn't been lying in that interview when I'd said I liked cleaning.

Speaking of which, it'd been two days since I'd gone to The Romance Library and I hadn't heard back from them yet. I reckoned me not being able to work evenings put them off. I wished I hadn't said anything because now the escorting was off the table, my schedule was wide open again.

If I didn't hear from Jess or Theo soon, I'd get in touch and let them know evenings wouldn't be an issue anymore.

Marcus returned to the room clutching his laptop.

'Thought I could do some research and a bit of job brainstorming,' he said, sitting back down and putting the laptop on the only clear space on the counter.

'Whilst you're doing that, do you mind if I wash up? Seeing all these dirty dishes is giving me palpitations!' I joked.

Marcus and I had known each other since we'd met at school when we were four years old, so I knew he wouldn't get offended.

'Be my guest. Dishwasher's broken and I haven't got round to sorting it out yet.'

Even when his dishwasher was working, Marcus rarely used it. That was just the way he was. He hated housework. Lucky for him, I enjoyed it. At least if I tidied up for him, it'd take my mind off my troubles.

'Got any more washing-up liquid?' I asked, looking at the almost empty bottle.

'Ah.' He scrubbed his jaw. 'Must remember to put that on my shopping list.'

Looked like I'd just have to make do with what was left in the bottle. After carrying all the dishes to the sink, I started rinsing them off.

Whilst I washed up, Marcus tapped away on his

laptop, googling different jobs and filling me in on how things had been going for him at the marketing agency where he was an account director. He worked long hours, so that also explained why housework wasn't his top priority.

Half an hour later, the washing up was done. Seeing the clean dishes stacked up gave me a real sense of satisfaction, so I decided to continue my clean-up mission. I reached for the duster I'd spotted in the cupboard under the sink, which unsurprisingly looked like it'd never been used.

'Thanks for that.' Marcus continued tapping on his laptop. 'How about this?' He turned the screen to face me. 'It's a website for naked cleaners. Maybe you could try doing that? Looks like it could pay well.'

'Cleaning someone's house in the buff?'

'Pretty much. I think you can wear an apron, though. Apparently sometimes the clients get naked too.'

'That's just asking for trouble. I want to *stop* clients touching my butt, not do stuff that'll encourage them! Anyway, I thought you were researching online options?'

'You're right. Sorry. I got sidetracked.'

'No worries.'

Marcus turned his attention back to the screen as I dusted the cupboard tops, then started cleaning the stove.

'I've got it!' he shrieked. 'That's it! You love cleaning, right?'

'Yeah…' I said cautiously.

'So *that* could be your USP!'

'I don't follow.' I frowned.

'You could dance on camera in your underwear whilst you clean! Or dance with cleaning products. Yes! You wouldn't have to show your face or strip. Just wear tight underwear that shows the outline of your junk.'

'That's nuts.'

'*Exactly!*' he sniggered. 'If your pants show the outline of your *nuts* too, I reckon that'd be even better! Think about it. This would solve all your problems. You'd get paid a load of money for customers to ogle you without touching you. So you could get the cash to pay for your mum's care and you could still fit it in around your work at the library. It's genius!'

'I haven't heard back from the library, so I probably blew it.'

'No way, man. They'd be crazy not to give it to you. And I'm sure *your sweetheart* put in a good word for you!' He smirked.

As I realised who Marcus was talking about, my insides lit up and a small smile touched my lips.

Jane.

I wondered if she'd thought or talked about me to Jess and Theo since I'd come in? Nah. Like me, I was sure she had more important things to think about.

When I saw the mischievous grin on Marcus's face, my smile instantly dropped. Shit. I shouldn't have told him that I'd seen Jane.

After I'd left that nightmare job on Monday night, I'd seen that he'd replied to my text with a load of kissing emojis, which I'd obviously ignored because I was worried about the fact that I'd just fucked up my only source of income.

'Up until two days ago, I hadn't spoken to Jane in years, so she's not going to vouch for me,' I said, hoping that would shut the direction of that conversation down.

'Course she would! You two were inseparable. And you didn't tell me, how'd she look?'

'That's irrelevant,' I said quickly.

'Was she hot? Does she still wear those glasses and tie her hair up in a bun?'

'Yeah,' I said.

'I *knew* it!' He grinned. 'I knew she'd be hot.'

'I didn't say that!' I protested. 'When I said *yeah*, I meant, yeah, she does still wear glasses and have her hair up in bun.'

'So she's *not* hot?'

'She looks really pretty, but—'

'You totally fancy the hot librarian!' he teased.

'How old are you?' I rolled my eyes. 'I'm trying to have a serious conversation about getting out of my shitty situation and you're talking about whether or not a woman is *hot*? Seriously, man.' I shook my head like a disappointed parent.

'Sorry.' He cleared his throat. 'So, like I was saying, the more I think about it, the more I'm convinced you should definitely try the dancing side hustle. The earning potential could be astronomical. Maybe down the line you could get sponsorship deals from cleaning product companies too.'

I paused as I thought about the idea.

'Nah. Maybe I should think about going back into finance.'

'Are you joking? You've only just crawled out of the hole that job left you in. There's no way you could go back to that.'

He was right. Just the thought of being in a high-pressured environment again made my chest tighten.

'There must be something else I can do that doesn't involve me taking my clothes off or fucking manipulative rich women.'

'Yeah, there is. You could always rob a bank!' Marcus laughed.

'Not funny.'

'I know. I couldn't resist! But seriously, I think the whole dirty dancing thing could work. It's easy money. God gave you that body for a reason. And seeing as you've sworn off dating or screwing right now, it'd be a shame to let it go to waste.'

'I work out to stay healthy, not to flaunt my abs on the internet.'

'Nothing to stop you from doing both…' He raised an eyebrow.

My phone pinged. I pulled it out of my pocket, and when I saw who it was from, my eyes widened.

'What's up?' Marcus asked. 'Who is it?'

'It's Jess from the library. She's asked me to call tomorrow morning.'

Here's hoping it's good news…

5
___

JANE

I glanced at my watch and groaned. I'd woken up much later than planned because I'd stayed up late, reading.

Experience had taught me that whenever I told myself I'd only read one more chapter, I always ended up reading more, so I knew I shouldn't have, but I needed a distraction.

Even though it'd been days since Jackson had come to the library, for some reason, I still couldn't stop thinking about him and how good he looked. Silly, really, considering it was obvious I'd never see him again.

Although the pay was fair at the library, I doubted it compared to what Jackson was used to getting as a City high-flyer. Plus, I'd overheard Jess and Theo mention he couldn't work evenings, and I knew that wouldn't be good because the earliest the library usually closed was seven. And we wanted to do more events after hours, so whoever they hired needed to be available for those too. That was why Jackson wouldn't get the job.

I felt bad because he'd obviously applied for a reason,

and even though we hadn't spoken for years, I still wanted him to do well. But at the same time, it was probably a blessing in disguise for me, because if I was thinking about him this much after speaking to him for a few minutes, imagine how hard it'd be if I had to see him every day.

So to take my mind off having ridiculous thoughts about a man I hadn't seen for ages, I'd escaped into a book and it'd worked.

Jess hadn't been joking when she'd said *Office Delight* was addictive. I'd been highlighting and annotating the pages like crazy. I'd told myself I'd just finish the chapter, then I'd go to sleep. But one chapter turned into another *seven*.

Things were certainly heating up between Rocco and Virginia and I couldn't wait to find out what happened next, but at the same time, I didn't want it to end.

After letting out a long yawn, I hid the paperback at the bottom of my handbag, jumped in the shower, got dressed, then went down for breakfast.

I was still fine for time. Technically I didn't need to get to the library until around nine fifteen, ready to open up by nine thirty, but I always liked to get there around eight thirty so that I could get ahead of the day or snuggle up on the sofa and enjoy some relaxing reading time.

When I got to the kitchen, Dad was sitting at the table, his favourite talk radio show blaring.

'Good morning!' I said, attempting to sound cheerful.

'Good?' he barked. 'What the bloody hell is good about it? The unemployment rates are up again. What's this country coming to? It's going to the dogs, I'm telling you. Someone needs to do something!'

I rubbed my temples. This wasn't how I wanted to start my day.

'Is Mum around?' I asked.

'She's at the shop. Although who knows how much longer we can keep that open with all these big discount supermarkets opening up all over the place, trying to kill off the little man. It's outrageous!'

Mum and Dad ran a corner shop a few streets away. It was one of the few business 'ventures' Dad had come up with that actually lasted more than just a few months before he got bored and moved on to something else.

'I'm… I have to get to work,' I said, deciding that eating at home would be too stressful. I was about to wish him a good day, but knew he'd just say something negative, so once I'd grabbed my jacket and bag, I left.

After catching the train to Sunshine Bay, I considered going straight to the library. But when my stomach rumbled for the twentieth time, I knew I had to get breakfast.

I walked to Sweet Treats, a cute bakery and cafe, and stepped inside. As usual it was heaving with customers. It was one of the most popular places in town.

Once I got to the front of the queue, my mouth watered as I took in the display of cream cakes, pastries, muffins and colourful iced fingers. It was hard to choose what to get because everything looked so delicious.

'Jane! Hi!' Maddie, the owner said enthusiastically. She had olive skin and dark hair which had been tied into a high ponytail. Underneath her branded Sweet Treats apron she was wearing a blue T-shirt and jeans. 'Sorry to keep you waiting. What can I get you?'

'Can I have a double-chocolate muffin please? Actually, make it two,' I said, thinking I'd get one for Jess. I knew she loved them as much as I did.

'Coffee?' she asked.

'Please.'

'I'll bring it over in a sec,' she said.

I tapped my card on the reader, then scanned the cafe for somewhere to sit.

Luckily a couple got up from one of the cute white tables towards the back and I quickly nabbed it.

A few minutes later Maddie came over with my coffee and muffins.

'So, how've you been?' I asked.

'Good. Just busy, what with this place to run and getting everything prepared for the new cafe too.'

'I bet! We're so excited about the new place,' I said.

The cafe opening in the library was going to be a joint venture with Maddie.

Sunshine Bay was big on community, and when Jess and Theo decided to open a cafe in the library, they didn't want it to take away business from Sweet Treats. So they suggested that rather than competing, it became an extension of Maddie's brand.

Although it'd be the library's cafe, which meant they'd fund the building work, Maddie would be paid to supply all of the homemade cakes and biscuits, plus provide the staff, so it'd be mutually beneficial.

'I can't believe it's happening so soon! And we still haven't thought of a name for the place,' Maddie said.

'Oh! I thought it'd just be called Sweet Treats just like this place?'

'No. Jess was thinking it would be better to have something that reflected not just the cakes and stuff but the bookish element too.'

'Makes sense,' I said. 'Well, I can chat to her later and maybe we can do some brainstorming to come up with some suggestions.'

'That'd be amazing, thanks! How are you getting on at the library?'

'Best job ever!' I said, meaning every word. 'We just need to find someone else to join to help with the work-load, y'know?'

'Pretty sure that Jess has found someone.'

'Really?' I frowned. 'They've been interviewing for weeks, but I didn't think they'd hired anyone yet.'

'I think it literally just happened. Jess was here about an hour ago and said she was heading in early to meet the new recruit. At least I thought that's what she said.'

'You could be right,' I replied, thinking it was strange she hadn't mentioned it. Jess was probably planning to fill me in this morning. If she was at Sweet Treats an hour ago, she'd be at the library now. 'Actually, I might take these to go.'

'I'll pack them up for you. I need to get back too, but we should catch up properly soon. Maybe have a girl's night at the Seaview Arms?'

'I'd love that!'

I didn't have many friends who lived locally. Shamwick wasn't like Sunshine Bay. In general, people tried to leave Shamwick as quickly as possible and never came back, so the friends I'd had before were long gone.

When I lived in London, I used to hang out with people from the bookshop, but after what had happened, I hadn't kept in contact with anyone.

'Great! Ask Jess if she'd be up for it too. I'll speak to Kara.'

'Perfect!' I said, excitement rippling through me.

Kara was the town's favourite hairdresser. I hadn't spent much time with her, but she seemed nice.

After collecting my coffee to go and two paper bags with the muffins, I headed over to the library.

As I stepped inside, I heard voices coming from the office. The door was open and when I caught sight of who was inside, my stomach plummeted.

'Here she is!' Jess beamed. 'Jane, let me formally introduce you to your new colleague and our new librarian, slash bookseller, slash events manager: Jackson Campbell.'

Shit.

6

———————

JACKSON

J ane's jaw was literally hanging on the floor.

Clearly she was shocked to hear the news, and I couldn't blame her. When Jess had offered me the job, I'd been surprised too.

After I'd got her text, I'd replied to say that I'd call in the morning like she'd asked and would keep my fingers crossed that she'd consider hiring me because I'd be honoured to join the team.

Jess had replied straight away and asked if, instead of calling tomorrow, I'd mind coming to the library instead. And so I had. I'd been here bright and early at eight thirty, ready to meet her.

'Theo and I really like you,' she'd said. 'But we're just worried that evenings might be an issue for you because—'

'Change in circumstances,' I'd jumped in. 'I can do shifts whenever you need me.'

'In that case,' Jess had added, 'welcome to the team! How soon can you start?'

'Now?' I'd replied.

Jess said that the role would be a mixture of working in the bookshop and library, plus helping to organise events to generate revenue, which was pretty much what it'd said in the ad. The pay was surprisingly fair too.

She explained that Theo would have to organise the paperwork etc. but I didn't have anything else to do today, so I'd suggested I could shadow her or do some training in advance.

It had nothing to do with wanting to see Jane again.

Honest.

'W-wow!' Jane finally spoke. 'Congratulations! What a… surprise. A good one, of course. I just… I wasn't expecting… I didn't know you'd made a decision yet.' She turned to Jess.

'It all happened so quickly,' Jess said. 'I confirmed it half an hour ago. I'm so excited! And Theo said you two have met before, right?'

'Yeah. We used to go to the same school,' I said.

'Perfect! You guys will be working together a lot, so it's great that you already have a relationship.'

'It was like fifteen years ago, so…' Jane said.

'Cool!' Jess replied. 'That means you've got *lots* to catch up on! Theo's checking the dehumidifiers to make sure they're helping to dry out the ceilings and the floor upstairs and then he's seeing Bill. He thinks there's something fishy about the hole in the roof.'

'Oh?' Jane frowned.

'Apparently the type of hole that caused the leak is a bit suspicious.' Jess shrugged. 'I know nothing about roofs or leaks, so I have no idea.'

'That makes two of us,' Jane added.

'Make that three!' I smiled.

'Not a DIY man, then?' Jess asked.

'I can put together IKEA furniture, but that's about my limit.'

'Wow.' Jane's eyes widened like I'd revealed I could walk on water. 'That's impressive. Just looking at the instructions intimidates me.'

'Same!' Jess said. 'Anyway, I'll take care of things in the library. Jane, can you give Jackson a tour and show him the ropes? It should be quiet for the next couple of hours.'

'Oh, okay, sure,' she stuttered.

'I'll leave you to it!' Jess smiled, then left.

'So, this is kind of…' I paused.

'Weird?' Jane said.

'I was going to say *unexpected*,' I laughed.

'Oh! Um, yeah. That's kind of what I meant. It's just… it's been so long and I, given what I'd heard, I just didn't expect…'

'Heard?' I frowned, curious to know what she was referring to.

'Sorry. Forget I said anything.'

'No, tell me.'

'It's just, the last I heard you were at Cambridge studying economics, then working in the City.'

My gut twisted. I hadn't expected Jane to know anything about my past. I wasn't on Facebook. The last thing I wanted was for those school bullies to start contacting me. And the last time I'd checked, Jane wasn't on social media either.

Once we'd left school, I'd tried to keep in contact, but her dad was really strict, so even though she was sixteen, he still banned her from going out. In the end, I stopped asking and we drifted apart. I went to a college outside of Shamwick, and once I went to Cambridge, I rarely returned.

There was no way I could tell Jane the full story, though, so I just needed to keep it light to stop her from probing.

'Sounds like you've been keeping tabs on me...' I raised an eyebrow and the corner of my mouth twitched.

'No! It's not... I didn't... I just heard it from Laura when I bumped into her a few years ago and she was talking about old times. She wasn't gossiping. She was just saying, y'know, how good it was. Like you went to our shitty school and that you'd become a big success, that kind of thing.'

I wasn't sure if hearing that made me feel better or worse.

At the time it was a big deal.

So many of the teachers at school had written me off and never expected me to make something of myself. But I proved them wrong when I got a scholarship to Cambridge, then, after graduating with a first-class honours degree in economics, landed a role working in mergers and acquisitions at a high-profile investment bank in London.

After working my arse off for years doing gruelling hours including late nights and weekends, I was earning a six-figure salary, renting a fancy apartment and spending crazy amounts of money on designer clothes.

Despite the significant pressure because of the high stakes involved in negotiating and completing successful deals and how competitive the industry was, I'd thought I was living my best life. Until it had all come crashing down.

'Yeah. Laura was right, I went to Cambridge, then worked in the City, but it was intense. I needed something less stressful and more fulfilling.'

'I understand.' Jane nodded, not quite meeting my gaze. I think she was embarrassed. Or worried that I thought she was prying.

I knew she didn't mean anything by her questions. Jane was always a good person. During the difficult days at school when I was bullied, Jane was one of the few people who showed me kindness. I'd never forget that.

'So, do you want to give me the grand tour?' I asked, thinking it was probably best to change the subject.

'Okay!'

'Oh, wait.' I looked down at the coffee cup and paper bags she'd put on the table. 'Is that your breakfast?'

'Yeah,' she replied.

'Sorry! I don't want to stop you from eating. Why don't I have a look around the library and start famil-iarising myself with everything whilst you have your breakfast?'

'Are you sure?'

'Certain.'

'Have you eaten?' Jane asked.

'I had a slice of toast before I left.'

'Is that all? You'll need more than that if you're going to last until lunchtime!' She smiled. Jane always had a nice smile, and seeing it again made my insides light up. 'Do you like chocolate muffins?'

'Love them!'

'I bought two. I was going to give the other one to Jess,

but Maddie, the lady who runs Sweet Treats, which is our favourite cafe, said afterwards that Jess had already been in for breakfast, so you can have it if you like. Consider it a small *welcome to the team* gift.'

'Thanks,' I said as she sat down and handed me a paper bag.

'And if you're worried about the calories, I mean, not that you need to because clearly you're in great shape—I mean, you look fit—sorry, *healthy*.' She winced. 'What I'm trying to say is, eating this muffin is also market research.'

'Yeah?' I asked, trying to hide my grin at the fact that she'd just said I was in great shape.

'Yes, because we're partnering with Sweet Treats for our in-house cafe. Work starts soon, so seeing as it'll be an important part of the library, it'd be good for you to sample the goods.'

'In that case, I think I'd better try something new there every day!' I laughed. 'Maybe you could show me where this cafe is later too?'

'Course I will. Have you been to the beach yet?'

'No.' I shook my head.

'I'll have to take you there too.'

'Sounds great. But first, let's eat.'

7

———

JANE

'And that's it!' I said as I completed Jackson's tour of the library.

As well as obviously taking him down all of the different aisles of the library to show him that we had books from every romance genre you could think of, including contemporary, historical, paranormal, new adult, LGBTQ+, steamy and closed-door romance, I'd shown him the bookshop and stockroom.

I'd even taken him upstairs to the first floor to see the space that Jess and Theo hoped to develop one day into a rooftop book bar with sea views. But that was a long way in the future. Before we could even think about that, we had to work out how to keep the library and the bookshop on the ground floor open.

'This place is amazing! It's even better than I'd imagined.' Jackson's lovely eyes sparkled.

'It is,' I said quickly, trying to keep my thoughts professional. 'You're going to love working here.'

How *I* was going to cope was a different story.

When we'd walked around the library, I'd try to stay focused and not get distracted by how gorgeous Jackson was. But it was hard.

I still couldn't get over how much he'd changed. Just like adults cooed over babies and gushed about how much they'd grown since they last saw them, I wanted to study every part of Jackson to try and understand exactly what it was that made him look so different.

Maybe it was his height? He was always tall, but he'd added an extra inch or two since school.

It was clear from his muscular chest and arms that he'd discovered the gym.

Before, he'd worn glasses, so I assumed he used contact lenses now. He still had those gorgeous deep brown eyes and ridiculously long lashes.

His hair was cut a lot lower than the small Afro he'd had at school, and obviously he had more facial hair. The immaculate beard he was sporting now made a big difference. So did the clothes. I was no expert, but his shirt, trousers and super shiny shoes looked expensive. Those evil bullies that used to laugh at his second-hand uniform and damaged glasses definitely wouldn't be teasing him if they saw his outfit today.

Thankfully, though, just like I'd noticed when we bumped into each other earlier this week, his personality hadn't changed. He still seemed like a great person.

'So you've had the grand tour?' Jess said as we returned to the library. There were about a dozen members milling around in the main hall. Some lounging on sofas with a book, others browsing down the aisles.

Theo was working in the bookshop and was very happy when one customer from the US came in with a suitcase because she'd heard about the library and bought the entire Windy City series by Liz Tomforde, Lyndsey Gallagher's Sexton Sisters series *plus* the Twisted *and* Kings of Sin series by Ana Huang. If we could get more people doing that, it'd definitely help our situation.

'I have. What you've created here is amazing. You should be really proud,' Jackson said.

'Thanks! It was a team effort, though. I couldn't have done it without Jane and Theo's help.'

'She's being modest,' I said. 'And now we have the cafe to look forward to. Speaking of which, I was chatting to Maddie earlier and she was struggling to come up with a name for it. Do you have any ideas?'

We'd been so busy getting the library up and running that we'd never got around to giving the bookshop a proper name or creating a sign. It was always just known as The Romance Library Bookshop, which wasn't very catchy. So it'd be great to give the cafe its own name.

'My brain's so fried these days I've got zero creativity. Tell you what: how about you two have a brainstorm? This afternoon, Jackson, I'd love you to start working on some event ideas, especially for the cafe. But maybe you could help Jane think of some names until lunchtime whilst it's still quiet? You could use the events room.'

'I'd love to help!' Jackson said enthusiastically.

'Great,' I said, trying and failing to convince myself that it was no big deal. 'Follow me.'

I led Jackson to the events space. It used to be two classrooms, but when Jess had bought the old school and done the renovations, they'd knocked down the wall to make it into one big space.

'So.' Jackson pulled up one of the chairs and his scent

wafted through the air. It was hard to describe. It smelt like very expensive shower gel, mixed with a rich, woody aroma with a hint of citrus. Whatever it was, it was bloody delicious and extremely distracting. 'Do you have any ideas?'

'I made a few notes on the walk over from Sweet Treats.' I pulled out my notebook and turned to the page where I'd scribbled down my thoughts. 'So I've got Coffee & Books, Books & Biscuits and Books & Brews.'

'Hmm.' Jackson rested his finger on his chin. 'I like that they're simple. They say exactly what we're offering, which is great, but maybe we could think of some other options, just in case.'

Most people would've just said my suggestions were too basic, but Jackson had always been diplomatic. Even when I'd struggled to answer simple questions when we did maths homework together, he was patient.

'How about One More Chapter?'

'That's cool.' I nodded. 'It could apply to all book genres, though. Maybe it'd be good to have something that relates more specifically to romance. You know, like the happiness it brings. I know! How about Happy Endings?' I said enthusiastically.

Jackson's eyes widened.

'Um, yeah… good idea, but that name just on its own kind of makes me think about something that *isn't* related to books.' He smiled. 'Then again, it'd probably fit well with some spicy novels.'

'Huh?' I asked.

'Happy Endings… y'know. It has another meaning…' His voice trailed off. 'Like a *sexual* meaning.'

I frowned, then the penny finally dropped.

'Oh! Of course!' I slapped my forehead. He must think I was such an idiot for not knowing that. Then again, if he knew how inexperienced I was, he'd understand why a massage ending with a blowie or handjob wasn't the first thing I thought about.

Jackson was probably inundated with women desperate to give him a *happy ending,* so no wonder that thought had popped into his head.

Head was an inappropriate choice of word given the context of the conversation. But I supposed I should be pleased that I'd spotted a double entendre without being given a signpost.

'Ever After could be a safer option?' Jackson suggested.

'Could be. But it doesn't convey the happiness. How about Happy Ever After?'

'Let's put it on the list.'

'Okay. So what do we have so far?' I glanced down at my notepad. 'Happy Ever After, Books & Biscuits, Books & Brews… anything else?'

'How about Love & Lattes?' Jackson added.

'I like it!'

'Or the Library Cafe? No. That's too safe. Cupid's Cafe sounds better.'

'Great! I'm sure we can come up with more ideas. It's always harder to do it on the spot.'

'Yeah. I'll ask my friend Marcus. He's in marketing, so will probably have some ideas.'

'Perfect! Jess's friend Sarah helps out with our social media, so I'll ask her too.'

'Good thinking. The more ideas we have, the better.'

Jackson and I continued brainstorming for another half

an hour before Jess called him in for a meeting to discuss the cafe opening.

It was crazy. As I watched him leave (desperately trying not to shamefully ogle how good his arse looked in his trousers), I was filled with disappointment.

Initially when Jess had said we'd be working together, I was nervous about spending time with him. But when I stopped staring and focused on our brainstorm, I started to relax and really enjoy it.

Fifteen years had passed, but somehow it felt like only yesterday that we'd chatted during class as we tried to solve whatever task the teacher had set.

I thought that maybe Jackson and I could get lunch together at Sweet Treats, then I could show him the beach, but he spent most of the day either being briefed by Jess or in a meeting with Theo, and just as I was putting away the library returns, he came to say goodbye.

'You're off already?' I blurted out without thinking. 'Sorry, I didn't mean… I just didn't realise it was so late, that's all.' Time always flew here.

'Yeah. I'm going to… I'm meeting someone.'

'Oh.' My stomach sank. Sounded like he was going on a date. 'No worries!' I said as enthusiastically as I could. 'Thanks for your help today.'

'No, thank *you* for showing me the ropes and making me feel welcome.'

'My pleasure. When are you working next?'

'Tomorrow.'

'Great!' My stomach fizzed with excitement. Maybe I shouldn't sound too enthusiastic. I didn't want him to think that I liked him. I mean, okay, maybe I did, but just as friends, nothing more. The last time I'd got involved with a colleague it had been a disaster, and ultimately it cost me my job.

Luckily for me, I landed on my feet and got to work here, which was a million times better. But that was precisely why I couldn't allow anything, including a stupid little crush, to mess up the best opportunity I'd ever had.

Jess and Theo really valued the work I did here. I loved everything about this job and provided we could keep the library going, I reckoned there would be a lot of opportunities for me here.

I had to nip whatever lingering feelings I had for Jackson from years ago in the bud.

'Enjoy your evening.' Jackson smiled and my stomach flip-flopped.

'You too,' I said, thinking it was a good thing he was going on a date.

If Jackson was off the market, it'd be another point to add to the list of reasons why I couldn't like him.

And given how much I'd enjoyed working with him today, the more reasons there were and the less temptation I had, the better.

8

JACKSON

'Please!' My chest tightened as I leant forward across the desk. 'If you could just give me more time, I promise I'll get the money.'

I was at the office in Mum's residential care home, pleading with Hilda, the manager, not to kick my mother out because I hadn't paid the last few invoices in full.

'I'm sorry, Mr Campbell,' she said firmly. 'Like I told you last month, we can't keep allowing your payments to be incomplete and late.'

'Did you get the money I transferred last week?'

I'd done another balance transfer of a thousand pounds on my credit card, which was now maxed out, and I'd hoped that'd be enough to keep them off my back. But from the look on Hilda's face, it wasn't.

'We did, and whilst I appreciate your efforts, it's not acceptable. We have overheads, Mr Campbell. We have to pay the carers who diligently look after your mother. If we allowed everyone to pay late, we'd be plunged into chaos.

The rules are the rules. If you're not able to pay the fees, perhaps you'll need to consider moving your mother elsewhere or attempting to care for her at home again.'

'No!' I protested.

I'd tried that. For months I was adamant that I wouldn't put Mum in a home. I'd had to quit my job before she was diagnosed, and I was too messed up to look for a new one, so time wasn't an issue. I'd vowed to look after her myself. Just like she'd taken care of me for years.

The doctors had warned me it'd be difficult. Particularly as her memory seemed to be fading fast as was common with Alzheimer's. They said she'd probably had the symptoms for a while, but because I'd been so wrapped up in my work and didn't visit as often as I should've, I hadn't seen the signs.

But as soon as I knew how serious things were, I vowed I wouldn't let her down. I was determined to be the most devoted full-time carer that there was.

But then it became obvious that I'd bitten off more than I could chew.

The first sign was when Mum left the house whilst I was in the shower. It wasn't that she'd left the front door wide open that worried me. It was the fact that when I rushed out onto the streets, desperate to find her, Mum was seconds away from stepping out onto a busy road, oblivious to the cars speeding towards her. I knew that was a red flag, but reasoned that as long as I kept the front door locked, she'd be fine.

But one day I'd popped to the corner shop to get some bread and milk and when I came back, I was hit with the strong smell of gas. I found Mum staring out the kitchen window and it was obvious that she'd forgotten she'd turned the old stove on.

That was when I really started to worry.

I realised that the house wasn't safe for her to stay in. She was a danger to herself, and as much as I'd wanted to, I didn't have the skills to take care of her.

At that point, even though the cost of residential care was high, I had savings, so I thought that would be enough to cover it until I'd found something else or sold the house.

I was wrong.

'I'm sorry, Mr Jackson. Wickstead Residential is one of the most prestigious care homes in the South-East. We have a long waiting list of individuals eager to join us, and like any business, we have overheads to cover to enable us to maintain our high standards. Per the contract, if you don't bring your account up to date within twenty-eight days, we'll have no other option than to start eviction proceedings. Now if you'll excuse me, I have another meeting to get to.'

'Can I at least see her before I go?'

'She's sleeping. As you know, visiting hours ended forty minutes ago.'

'I know, but I was working! Trying to earn the money to pay your fees.'

'I'm sorry, Mr Campbell. Like I said, the rules are the rules. We can't disrupt your mother's routine.'

I blew out a frustrated breath, admitting defeat. Hilda wasn't going to change her mind. The bottom line was, if I didn't get the money together in the next four weeks, Mum would be kicked out.

As I trudged down the corridor, the heavy disinfectant scent flooded my nostrils.

My head hurt. What the hell was I going to do? I had the job at the library, which was great. That income would definitely help, but it wasn't enough.

I stepped out into the cool air, then pulled out my phone. Marcus answered on the third ring.

'Hey! How was your first day at the library?'

I'd texted Marcus at lunchtime to let him know I'd got the job. He'd replied with a simple *I told you so.*

'Good.'

'Did you get to see the hot librarian?'

Jane.

I'd been so focused on racing here to the meeting that Hilda had called unexpectedly that I hadn't had a chance to think about anything else. But as soon as I pictured Jane's face, my shoulders instantly loosened.

Once she'd got over her initial shock about me working at the library, Jane had been sweet. Just like she always was.

It was kind of her to give me the muffin she'd brought because she'd worried that I hadn't eaten enough for breakfast.

And she'd patiently shown me around the library, answering my millions of questions and not laughing about how little I knew about romance novels compared to her. The brainstorming was fun too and it reminded me how smart Jane was.

Sounded stupid, but I'd been disappointed when Jess had called me away. But I had important work to do at the library. Based on the meetings I'd had with both Jess and Theo, the library was in trouble. They were relying on me to turn things around financially, pretty quickly.

And they weren't the only ones. If I didn't get some money coming in soon, Mum would have to come back home. And there was no way I'd be able to take care of her *and* work. The carers' allowance wouldn't be enough to live on. Not with the bill repayments I had to make after maxing out my credit cards to pay towards the care home fees.

Whichever way you looked at it, I was fucked.

'Jane was there, yeah,' I finally answered, snapping myself out of my thoughts.

'So were you able to concentrate on work or were you trying not to imagine taking her up against a bookcase?' He laughed.

'Do you ever think about anything else but sex?' I snapped defensively to hide my shame, because when Jane had given me a tour of the library and my gaze had dropped to how good her arse looked in that fitted pencil skirt, I *had* fantasised about pushing it up around her waist, dropping to my knees and burying my head between her thighs.

I wasn't proud of that thought. And I'd pushed it out of my mind seconds after it'd appeared. She was my colleague and I'd promised myself I wasn't going there again.

Plus Jane was a sweet woman. Like her dickhead older brother, Wayne, liked to remind me at school, girls like her weren't for boys like me.

Jane had probably settled down with a nice guy, with a stable job. That was what she deserved.

When I'd looked at her hand, I hadn't seen any sign of an engagement or wedding ring. I'd wanted to ask if she had a boyfriend, but it was inappropriate and it was also irrelevant. It didn't matter either way. I wasn't interested in a relationship or hooking up.

I hardly ever thought about sex these days. I couldn't even remember the last time I'd wanked. Which was probably why I'd had those inappropriate thoughts about fucking Jane earlier. I just needed to release, that was all. Once I got myself off, I'd be fine.

'Occasionally,' Marcus replied. 'But when my best mate tells me he's got a job at the same place that his childhood crush is working at and that she's blossomed into a hot librarian, naturally I'm here with my popcorn, waiting for the inevitable show to happen!'

'She's not my crush.'

'Just because I didn't go to Northwood like you and Jane doesn't mean I didn't know you had a crush on her. Whenever we used to speak it was always *Jane this* and *Jane that.*'

'We were in the same classes together, so of course I'd mention her!' I protested.

Marcus and I had gone to school together in London until I was thirteen. Up until then I'd had the perfect life. I'd lived in a comfortable three-bed house, in a nice area, with two great parents who were madly in love.

But when Dad died unexpectedly from a heart condition we didn't even know he had, our whole world was shattered overnight.

We survived on his savings for a while, but when the money ran out, Mum was left shouldering the burden of paying for the huge mortgage single-handedly.

In the end she couldn't manage all of the expenses on her salary. So we had to sell the house and move out of London. A small two-bedroom house in Shamwick was all she could afford. That was how I ended up going to Northwood.

I went from being in a London school where I was accepted and had great friends like Marcus to being the only black kid in the school and being subjected to racist slurs.

Mum said to ignore them, keep my head up, work hard and make Dad proud, so that was what I tried to do.

It was hard, though. School was tough for most teenagers, but when you added in the fact that I'd lost my dad so young, so was grieving, had to listen to Mum crying herself to sleep every night, and had been ripped away from the home, school and friends I loved, all whilst dealing with puberty, bullying and the pressure of exams, it was almost unbearable at times.

I missed not having Marcus to hang out with. Everyone else was already settled in their own friendship groups. No one wanted to invite the nerd with the shitty second-hand school uniform and broken glasses into their little cliques.

Jane was different, though. She wasn't part of any of the cool groups either. She didn't fit in. A lot of the girls wanted to attract the boys' attention, but like me, Jane was a boffin. She was more interested in learning than her appearance. So when no one wanted to sit next to us in class, we paired up and found the solidarity we'd been missing.

'Yeah, yeah, whatever. I saw how your face lit up when you spoke about her the other night.'

Shit. I was hoping he hadn't noticed.

'She gave me a tour of the library and helped show me the ropes, y'know, as part of her job. That's it. You of all people should understand why I have no interest in getting involved with someone from work again. If I hadn't done that the first time, I wouldn't be in this mess now.'

The phone went silent. I knew I'd struck a nerve.

'Shit, sorry, man. I didn't mean to… I shouldn't have said that. But Jane isn't like… never mind. Anyway, did it go well? At the library?'

'Yeah. I like it there,' I said as I made my way to the station to catch the train home. 'I'm screwed, though. I've just left the care home—'

'How's your mum?'

'I didn't get to see her. I got there too late. But Hilda called me in for an emergency meeting. Said that if I don't bring my payments up to date, she'll kick Mum out.'

'Fuck,' Marcus gasped. 'Listen, I can help you out if you—'

'No,' I jumped in. Marcus had already helped me out a few months ago. I couldn't keep running to him for loans. He had his own bills to pay. 'I need to figure this out for myself. I've maxed out my credit cards, sold my watches, jewellery and most of my clothes and the bank won't give me another loan. This idea you mentioned, the other night.' I paused and took a deep breath. I couldn't believe I was about to say this. 'Do you really think posting videos on that website would work?'

'Definitely!'

'And would I get paid quickly?'

'Yep! That's one of the great things about this site. You get paid weekly.'

'And I wouldn't have to show my face?'

'Nope. Just dance for a few minutes. I'll help you set it up. Just give me the green light and I'll start putting the wheels in motion.'

I blew out a breath.

I couldn't believe I was about to agree to cavorting half naked and posting videos online for strangers to leer at. But I was desperate. And desperate times called for desperate measures.

'Okay.' My chest tightened as I prepared myself to force the words out. 'I'm in.'

9

———

JANE

'Bye!' I said as I whizzed past the dining room, shoving the warm toast and jam I'd wrapped in foil into my bag.

Dad had gone to the bathroom and I'd used that time to slip into the kitchen to make breakfast to go. But now he'd returned to the dining room, I needed to leave before he roped me into another one of his depressing conversations.

Bill was coming back to finish fixing the roof this morning, so I'd offered to go in early to give him access, which meant I couldn't afford to be late. Actually, that reminded me. I should ask Jess if she'd found out what Bill and Theo had meant when they'd said the roof leak was suspicious.

'Wait!' Dad called out. 'I need to speak to you.'

I sighed and my whole body slumped as I turned around and trudged back to the room.

'Good morning.' I tried to sound upbeat.

'You came home late yesterday, so I didn't get to talk to you.'

'I had to work,' I said. Admittedly, I could've left a couple of hours earlier than I did, but I had to finish *Office Delight* and it was easier and more relaxing to do it at the library.

'You spend too long at that bloody place. You might need to cut back soon so you can help me out.'

'What?' I frowned.

'I decided yesterday. I'm sick and tired of the state of this country. And you're right. I shouldn't complain. I should do something to help.'

My eyes widened. Had my words finally penetrated his thick skull? Hmmm. Something told me that was wishful thinking.

'What are you going to do?'

'I'm running to become a local MP. It's time changes were made, and I'm the man to do it.'

Oh. Dear God.

The man was deluded.

When I'd said he should help, I'd meant do something to help support people in need, like volunteering to help refugees so he could learn more about their plight, for example. Not becoming a bloody local politician.

The last thing this town needed was someone like him inflicting his bigoted views on everyone.

'Dad, I don't think that's a good—'

'And you'll need to get married. Or at the very least, engaged.'

'Sorry, *what*?' He'd shocked me before, but now my jaw was hanging on the floor.

'If I'm going to talk about the importance of family values, I can't have a spinster for a daughter. You're in your thirties. You should be married with kids by now, not wasting your time reading sodding books!'

What the actual fuck?

Throughout most of my teens and early twenties, Dad had constantly harped on about the 'dangers' of mixing with boys. When one of my school friends got pregnant at fifteen, he didn't stop banging on about how disgusting it was.

He constantly ranted about the perils of sex and 'loose' women. And now he was chastising me for keeping my legs closed, which was exactly what he'd insisted on?

What a twat.

'And what about Wayne?' I asked, still trying to process the latest crap to come out of Dad's mouth.

My brother seemed to be able to live to a completely different set of rules to me. He didn't work, only helping out in the shop whenever he felt like it. He rarely got out of bed before noon, didn't lift a finger around the house and seemed to spend most evenings down the pub with his mates. If I did the same, I'd never hear the end of it.

'He's a man. That's different.'

Anger bubbled in my stomach. I opened my mouth to speak, then closed it again. Just when I'd thought this man couldn't shock me anymore with his narrow-mindedness, he said something that proved me wrong.

I wished I could tell him what I really thought about him.

'I'm going to be late for work.' I stormed out of the room, then through the front door.

Once I was halfway down the road, I let out a long, frustrated exhale.

I didn't know how much longer I could take living in

that house. Dad was awful at the best of times, but if he was running to become a local politician, it'd be unbearable. Especially if he expected me to stand beside him and support his stupid opinions.

I couldn't do it. I disagreed with everything that came out of that man's mouth, but I had nowhere else to go.

Anyone I'd ever known here had moved away. I'd cut contact with all of the friends I made at the bookshop after I left because I was too embarrassed about what happened, so there was no one I could stay with. And my other relatives were just as toxic as my parents.

Jess and Theo had a spare room in their cottage, but I knew Theo had recently transformed it into a home library as a place for Jess to relax and unwind after work, so there was no way I could impose. Plus, I was their employee. It wouldn't be right.

I had no one.

I just had to suck it up for a little bit longer. After all, I wasn't the first person who had a rocky relationship with their parents.

Jess said that before her mum passed, things were tricky, and she didn't even keep in touch with her father. I knew Theo and his dad didn't get on. Jess even mentioned that Mrs Davis, who was clearly a kind lady, hence why she'd given Jess a million pounds to set up The Romance Library, seemed to have a difficult relationship with her son too, so it wasn't unusual.

The only person I really knew that had a great bond with their parents was Jackson. I remembered him saying that his dad was amazing and super supportive and I knew how much his mum doted on him, but maybe that was the exception, not the rule.

As soon as I got on the train, I pulled out my Kindle and escaped into a new romcom. By the time I arrived at Sunshine Bay, I was feeling calmer. Books always made me feel better.

When I arrived, the library was already open and Jess and Theo were standing by the side of the building, where Bill was climbing the ladder.

'Morning!' Jess chirped as she saw me approaching.

'I'm not late, am I?' I glanced at my watch, certain that Bill was coming at eight in the morning. It was five to.

'No, no,' Jess reassured me.

'It's my fault,' Bill called down. 'I phoned Theo to ask if I could come earlier just to make sure I'd finished before the library opened.'

'And it was short notice, so I didn't want to call at the last minute to ask you.'

'I wouldn't have minded,' I said.

'It's fine. We were already up and at Sweet Treats anyway. Speaking of which…' Jess paused. 'Theo, you okay to take care of this whilst I have a chat with Jane?'

'Sure.' He nodded.

'Is everything okay?' I frowned.

'Course! Maddie mentioned that she was thinking of organising a girls' night?'

'Sorry! I meant to ask you as soon as I got in yesterday, but then you told me you'd hired Jackson and with the training and brainstorming, it slipped my mind.'

'No worries! Anyway, Kara is up for it and so am I, so Maddie suggested maybe next Friday night at the Seaview Arms. Are you free? Theo can lock up here.'

'Sounds great!' I said, happiness instantly flooding my chest.

Like I'd said earlier, I no longer had a friendship group, so it'd be good to change that. The idea of a night out with the girls seemed like just what I needed to take my mind off life at home.

'Perfect. Maddie's coming over later to discuss the cafe, so I'll let her know.'

'Speaking of the cafe, Jackson and I came up with a list of names yesterday…' My voice trailed off as my thoughts drifted back to how good it felt to sit beside him, listen to his ideas, stare into his eyes, inhale that delicious scent…

'Great!' Jess said, snapping me out of my fantasy.

'I've typed them up, so I can email it to you if you like?'

'Yes, please. If I could have a read before Maddie arrives, that'd be even better.'

'I'll get straight on it. Oh, and I wondered if I could ask Sarah for her input too? I thought she might have some ideas.'

'Good thinking! You've got her number, right?'

'Yeah. I'll text her. What time's Jackson in today?' I asked, trying to sound casual.

'Nine thirty.'

'Do you want me to help him with anything?'

'No, it's okay, thanks. I need you in the library today. Jackson will be in the bookshop with Celeste. She'll be showing him the ropes before she leaves.'

Celeste had started as a volunteer, but after Jess had seen how great she was at recommending romance books, she'd insisted on paying her to work part-time, which was really decent. She'd be going back to uni in a couple of weeks, though, hence why we desperately needed an extra pair of hands. Trying to run the library and the bookstore between just me, Jess and Theo six days a week was proving almost impossible.

'Oh.' I tried to mask my disappointment. 'Okay.'

My stomach twisted. Celeste was confident, outgoing, pretty and fun: the kind of woman I reckoned Jackson would date. And for some stupid reason, I was a little bit jealous that she'd get to spend the day with him. It was ridiculous. I had no claim on him, so I needed to get over myself.

'Actually, I might ask Celeste if she wants to join us on Friday night.'

'Great!' I said. I had nothing against Celeste. She was nice. In fact, she was kind of an inspiration. She was twenty, so eleven years younger than me, but she had the confidence of a woman twice her age. If I had ten per cent of her self-assurance and assertiveness I'd be happy.

Rather than focusing on Jackson and Celeste spending the day together, I was going to think about the fact that next week I'd hopefully be making new friends.

I had something fun to look forward to and another reason to spend more time away from my parents' house.

And that was a win in my book.

JACKSON

I felt like a fucking idiot.

I was standing in front my bedroom mirror, basically naked, except for the tight shiny gold leopard print thong Marcus had ordered and recommended I wear to film my first video.

He'd also suggested I watch Magic Mike films to get 'inspiration' for my sexy moves and slather about ten litres of baby oil over every inch of my body to make me look more 'defined and shiny'.

Jesus.

On the bed was a pile of different cleaning tools he'd also bought as 'props', including a mop and bucket (what the hell I was supposed to do with the bucket, I had no idea), a pink feather duster, yellow rubber gloves, a broom and a selection of brightly coloured cloths.

I'd set up my phone on a tripod (also courtesy of Marcus) and had lit the room so it was bright enough to show my body clearly, but still dim enough to create a 'sexy atmosphere'—whatever that was. So technically, I was good to go.

But I had no idea how to *perform*.

Don't get me wrong. I'd had a lot of experience in the bedroom. Once I'd started earning good money, one of the first things I'd done was spend a fortune on nice clothes. I'd gone to the best barber in London once a week. Plus, I'd started working out at the gym.

To other people, it might sound superficial, but after being taunted by the bullies for years because of my clothes, hair and gangly frame, it felt amazing to finally feel like I looked good.

Soon after changing my appearance, I noticed that the kind of women that'd always ignored me started making it *very* clear that they were interested. Including a woman who was fourteen years older. And she taught me a *lot* about how to please a lady in the bedroom.

We were only together for seven months, but being with her was like being enrolled in an intensive sex masterclass and graduating with honours. After that, my confidence with women rocketed. Barely a week went by without me sleeping with someone new.

Sometimes I did repeats, but more often than not, I'd meet a woman at a bar, on the street or at the gym and we'd fuck. I may not have lost my virginity until I was twenty-two, which was pretty late compared to my friends, but once I did, I was like a kid in a sweet shop. I made up for lost time and then some.

I spent most of my twenties sowing my wild oats (safely, of course) and having pretty much any woman I wanted, until almost two years ago when I screwed the wrong one and got totally fucked over.

Anyway, my point was that I wasn't shy in the bedroom. I'd tried a lot of different things. Role play, threesomes, all sorts. But one thing I'd never done was film anyone or perform in front of the camera myself. So knowing that I was about to make a video that could be seen by hundreds of people freaked me out.

I needed to get over my fear, though. Mum was depending on me.

Marcus said I just needed to do a short video. A few minutes. That was all.

As much as I hated the fact that I was standing here dressed like a greasy Tarzan wannabe, I was grateful that Marcus had been so supportive.

He'd set up my profile on the website, chosen my name—the Filthy Cleaner—and was taking care of all of the admin. And he'd paid for the props, including a set of dodgy male thongs. I was lucky to have a friend like him.

Thinking about that gave me extra motivation. Buying this stuff couldn't have been cheap, so I couldn't waste his money or let him down either.

I took a deep breath, then scanned the items on the bed. My eyes were drawn to the pink feather duster. That'd look great on camera.

After picking it up, I blasted Ginuwine's 'Pony' from my iPad to get me in the right mindset. This might be my first rodeo (pun totally intended), but I knew that no one would want to watch my video with a flaccid dick, so I had to find a way to get hard.

I contemplated going onto one of the ethical porn sites I knew, but then an even better source of inspiration flashed into my head.

Jane.

When Jess had said I'd be working with Celeste in the bookshop earlier today, I'd been gutted. I'd hoped that I'd get more time to chat to Jane. There was so much I wanted to find out about her.

Had she gone to UCL to study English literature like she'd always hoped? I bet she graduated with a first-class honours degree.

Where did she work once she'd graduated?

And was she dating anyone?

No, scrap that last question. Like I'd said before, it was irrelevant. I wasn't available. Which was something I'd had to mention at least twice whilst Celeste was training me in the bookshop.

Celeste had made it very clear that she'd be open to becoming more than just colleagues. Multiple times. All the eyelash fluttering, playing with her hair, biting her lip and touching my bicep became a bit full on after a few hours.

And when she suggested we go down to the stockroom together after work and have some 'fun', I had to nip that shit in the bud and tell her that I wasn't down for that.

A couple of years ago, if Celeste was a few years older, I might have considered her offer. She was pretty, but I was a different man now.

I had to hand it to her, though. She was a woman who knew what she wanted and went for it. And she hadn't taken offence or seemed too bothered when I'd turned her down. All she'd said was, "Oh well, your loss. So, do you reckon you can use the till by yourself now? I'm going on a break."

Anyway, as pretty as Celeste was, it was Jane that I was interested in. Correction: if I *was* interested in dating someone right now, which I wasn't, I'd prefer someone like Jane.

I loved her big brown eyes, how effortlessly sexy she looked in those silk blouses she liked to wear, how good her legs and arse looked in those skirts. And I'd love to tug on that bun she always wore and watch her hair tumble past her shoulders. And she was so smart. Intelligent women were my kryptonite.

What Marcus had said the other day wasn't wrong. I really would've loved to pin Jane against that bookcase and…

No. I shouldn't be thinking about fucking Jane.

She might've been my childhood crush, but we were colleagues, and like I just said, I couldn't date anyone right now.

My brain might understand that, but another part of my anatomy hadn't got the message.

When I glanced down at my cock, it was hard as steel.

I wasn't proud of the filthy thoughts I'd just been having about my new co-worker, but on the plus side, right now, this boner was a good thing. It meant that it was showtime.

After switching off the music (Marcus said he'd add a track during editing that was copyright-free), I set the timer on my phone, placed the feather duster in front of my dick, then when the countdown ended and recording started, I thrust my hips back and forth suggestively before whipping away the duster to dramatically reveal the massive boner straining against the hideous shiny gold fabric of the thong.

I ran the duster suggestively over my chest, then along my six-pack, before rubbing it against my hard-on repeatedly whilst winding my hips in a circle, then flicking them like I was grinding against a woman on the dance floor.

Next I slid the feather duster between my legs and attempted to push my embarrassment out of my mind as I started riding the cleaning tool like a cowboy.

As I thrust, I imagined it wasn't a damn pink feather duster beneath me but that it was Jane I was fucking instead, which made me even harder.

Jesus. Dancing on camera like this was one thing, but I wasn't going to come in my pants on camera, no way.

I was pretty sure I'd been doing this for a few minutes, so now was a good time to start winding down before I lost control.

After skimming the duster over my thick thighs, I turned slowly to show my arse to the camera, brushed the soft pink feathers across my butt cheeks, then spun back around to give the camera one last look at my raging boner before sliding my hands inside my pants and squeezing my cock.

I held still for a few beats like Marcus had told me to do at the end to make it easier for him to edit the video, pulled my hand off my dick, stopped the recording, then plucked the phone from the tripod before flopping onto the bed.

I blew out a breath.

I'd done it.

I'd made my first video.

I knew it wouldn't be perfect, but the important thing was, I'd pushed myself out of my comfort zone and given it my best shot.

When I watched the video back, I was surprised.

Whilst I was doing it, I'd felt awkward, but on camera, it actually looked like I was really into it.

Sure, I knew how to move my hips. But I knew it wasn't my dancing skills I had to thank for the authenticity that came across from the video: it was the woman I was thinking about whilst I was grinding my dick against the duster.

As a vision of her bending over to pick up the books on the floor that first day I'd come to the library flashed into my head again, my dick twitched. I knew Marcus had said I should send him the video as soon as I finished filming, but I needed a few more minutes.

Scrap that. Given how hard I was right now, I'd be done in seconds.

After dropping the phone on the bed, I dragged down the hideous thong and gripped my dick.

And as I moved my palm back and forth whilst I thought about the hot librarian I was growing dangerously attracted to, I exploded into my hand.

11
———

JANE

'Ready?' Jess whispered as she stood in front of the meet-cute desk in the main library hall.

The meet-cute desk was our library's special name for where books were checked out and returned.

Jess and I came up with the name because we thought it was a fun way to describe that moment when a reader first starts a 'relationship' with a brand-new book. Every time a member came to the desk, they were about to be whisked away to start an exciting romantic adventure, so the name fitted perfectly.

'Yes!' I lowered my voice to make sure I didn't disturb the members who were reading in the comfy sofa several feet away. 'I've just put away the last of the returns.'

It was now Friday. We were about to head to the local pub, the Seaview Arms, for our girls' night out, and I was actually excited.

Generally speaking, I preferred hanging out with book characters instead of interacting with people in real life (unless they were bookworms like our library members).

But it'd been so long since I'd gone anywhere other than work and back to my parents' that I'd been looking forward to it.

Jess and Maddie were both great, Celeste seemed fun and I reckoned Kara, the hairdresser, would be nice too.

'Great. Jackson's taking over in five minutes.'

'Brilliant. Excellent. Yay!' I stuttered like an idiot. 'Actually, can I just pop to the loo?'

'This place might be based in an old school, but you don't have to ask permission to wee!' Jess laughed.

'Sorry, I know, I just…' *I just get tongue-tied whenever Jackson's name is mentioned…* 'I just didn't want to leave the desk unattended.'

'You're fine!' Jess said.

I grabbed my bag and walked quickly to the toilet. I didn't actually need to wee. I just wanted to check that I looked okay and change into a top I'd brought to wear tonight.

As soon as I stepped inside, I headed straight to the mirror and pulled out my tiny make-up bag. I didn't generally wear much make-up. Just mascara and a neutral gloss. Dad always said that bright-coloured lipstick was for 'hookers', and whilst I knew that was absolute nonsense (like literally everything that he said), his toxic thoughts had been seared into my brain so deeply that every time I considered choosing a bolder colour, all I could hear was his voice in my head reminding me to stay 'pure' and 'decent' and not draw 'unwanted attention' to myself.

I sighed, then pulled out my mascara. After removing my glasses and placing them on the ledge under the wide mirror, I applied a fresh coat to the tips of my lashes, swiped on some more gloss, then unbuttoned my blouse, ready to change into the sparkly V-neck top I'd bought.

Normally I never really showed my neck or arms, preferring to wear long-sleeved silky blouses that either buttoned all the way up or had a neck bow. But I'd worn this top before to an after-work drinks gathering when I worked in London and I liked how it made me feel.

God. If wearing a simple V-neck top which wasn't even low-cut made me happy, clearly I needed to get out more.

Just as I was about to slide my arms out of the sleeves of my blouse, I heard the door open and spun around.

'Oh shit.' Jackson's eyes widened. When his gaze dropped to my chest, then flicked back up again, I realised that I still had my blouse wide open and was basically flashing my bra.

Crap.

My cheeks flamed and I quickly pulled my blouse together.

'Sorry!' Jackson said. 'I didn't realise you were in here.'

'It's… I… It's my fault. I should've changed in the cubicle. There was just more room out here.'

What on earth was I thinking? I knew the toilets were unisex. The library was still open, so anyone could've walked in, including one of our members.

'I'll come back later.' Jackson turned his back to me, then darted out the door.

I squeezed my eyes shut with embarrassment. I couldn't believe I'd just exposed myself to him. And of course I didn't even have on a decent bra. It was just a basic white one with a pink bow at the front. I instantly regretted not wearing something better. Then again, who was I kidding? It wasn't like I had a drawer full of sexy lacy underwear.

If I ever put anything like that in the wash, my parents would have a fit.

Yes. This was the kind of crap I had to deal with. Thirty-one years old and even the underwear I wore was based on what my bloody parents would approve of. I hated my life.

I gathered up my things, slid inside the cubicle and shut the door, shame still coursing through my veins.

It was hard enough looking at Jackson without getting tongue-tied and now I'd embarrassed myself again.

He was probably laughing at how pathetic my underwear was and the fact that I had small boobs. He probably preferred women with bigger breasts.

Anyway, enough of feeling sorry for myself. I couldn't keep Jess and Celeste waiting.

After slipping on my top and giving myself one last glance in the mirror I headed towards the library, where Jess and Celeste were waiting.

'Shall we go?' I asked, deliberately avoiding Jackson's gaze. He was stood behind the desk and I could feel his eyes on me, but I was still too mortified to face him.

'Yep!' Celeste said loudly, causing multiple members' heads to snap up.

'Shh!' Jess's eyes widened and she ushered us out of the library hall.

Once we were outside, Celeste slid her arm through mine and did the same to Jess.

'*Finally* we can talk freely!' she said at the top of her voice. 'Honestly, I don't know how you guys keep so quiet all day long in there. I much prefer working in the book-shop. At least there you can chat to the punters!'

'I like the silence,' I said. 'And if we chatted too loudly, people wouldn't be able to concentrate on reading.'

'I guess.' Celeste shrugged her shoulders. 'But the customers like to chat too. I had one woman in earlier who wanted recommendations on the smuttiest books we had in stock. I told her she'd come to the right place!' Celeste cackled.

She was a self-proclaimed smut lover. And it wasn't just steamy romances that Celeste enjoyed. She loved erotica too. The raunchier the better. The other day Celeste had written a list of at least a dozen erotica novels she thought we should stock.

She was a big fan of monster romance, dark romance and why choose? too, which came in handy because I hadn't got a chance to read any books from those genres yet and a lot of our members loved them.

'What did you recommend?'

'I went straight to the erotica, but then I got the feeling she needed to be eased in a bit first, so recommended some steamy romances to start her off—y'know, like Meghan Quinn and Hannah Grace—then suggested after that she tried a bit of Elodie Hart, Sierra Simone and Penelope Douglas.'

'Did she go for it?'

'She bit my hand off! Walked out of the shop with ten out of the twelve books I recommended. Boom!' Celeste raised her hand triumphantly in the air.

'Brilliant! You're an excellent bookseller,' Jess said. 'Thank you.'

'Cheers!' She beamed. 'It's a shame I have to go back to uni. I'm really enjoying working there.'

'And we love having you,' Jess said.

She was right. Celeste might be pretty full on and loud, but she was great at her job.

'We had a member who came in earlier singing your praises after you recommended a book to her last week,' I said.

'Cool!' Celeste replied. 'I love when that happens.'

Just because I was a tiny bit jealous about how much time Celeste had spent with Jackson alone in the bookshop this week, it didn't mean I couldn't give credit when credit was due. I believed we should all support each other. I couldn't let my personal feelings get in the way.

As we pushed open the door to the Seaview Arms, laughter and chatter filled the air.

The traditional British pub had deep burgundy patterned carpet and worn-looking dark wooden tables and chairs. My favourite place to sit, though, was on the comfy banquette seating at the back of the pub.

The bar, which was in the centre, had the same dark polished wood with brass beer taps.

Whenever I visited, I loved looking at the old framed photographs of fishermen and local residents, sea-related memorabilia and old Sunshine Bay postcards which lined the walls.

'Sweetheart!' Bob, the landlord, beamed as he caught sight of Celeste.

'Hey, Dad.' She smiled. 'How's it going?'

'Good, hon. We've reserved the table for you in the corner so you can have your girl talk in private. Your mother will be back soon. She's just touching up her lippy.'

'Thanks,' Celeste said, then waved at Maddie and Kara, who were already seated on the banquette in the corner.

'Jess, Jane, how are you?' Bob said. 'You two are looking beautiful tonight.'

'Dad!' Celeste rolled her eyes.

'What?'

'You sound like a perv!'

'I beg your pardon!' he shouted. 'Nothing wrong with complimenting two beautiful ladies. Your mother's always saying how gorgeous Theo looks.'

'That's true.' Jess grinned. 'And he loves it! Thanks for the compliment, Bob. I know you meant well. Your dad's a decent one.'

'Thank you!' Bob blew out a relieved breath. 'So what can I get you ladies to drink?'

'Shots!' Celeste said enthusiastically.

'Erm… I'll just have a glass of white wine, please,' I said.

'Come on, Janey!' Celeste said. 'Let your hair down! It's Friday night, baby!'

'How about I organise a round of shots, on the house, *and* a couple of bottles of wine?' Bob said gently.

'Sounds perfect,' Jess added. 'And if you don't want a shot, it's totally fine,' she added with a reassuring hand on my shoulder.

'Thanks,' I said, really meaning it. Celeste was so domineering sometimes, it was hard to say no.

As we headed over to the table, Maddie and Kara stood up to greet us.

'Hi!' Maddie said as she hugged Jess, then did the same to me and Celeste.

After giving Kara two cheek kisses, we all sat down.

'I'm so glad we finally made this happen!' said Kara. She was dressed in black jeans and a black slogan T-shirt and had wavy burgundy shoulder-length hair. Even if I'd never met her before, her hair was so glossy and perfectly styled that I'd instantly guess that she was a hairdresser.

'Same!' Maddie replied. 'It's been so full on at the cafe, I need to de-stress.'

'How's things at the library?' Kara asked.

'Good. We're getting new members every day, but we still need a bigger income.'

'Hopefully the cafe will help when it opens.'

'I really hope so. Especially after shelling out to get the roof fixed.'

'Oh no!' Kara gasped. 'What happened?'

Jess filled her in on the mystery leak, which apparently Theo and Bill were still puzzled about, then said how grateful she was that it was all sorted.

Bob brought over the wine and shot glasses. Whilst Jess, Maddie and Celeste downed their shots, I poured the first bottle of wine into the glasses, then took a large glug.

'And we've got a hot new guy working with us now!' Celeste smirked. I swallowed hard.

'Oh yeah!' Maddie said. 'Jackson, right?'

'Yeah!' Celeste replied. 'Dad! Can you bring another round of shots, please!' she called out and Bob nodded.

'Jess introduced me yesterday when I came to go through some paperwork,' Maddie added. 'He's very easy on the eye.'

'He is! It's a shame I have to go back to uni soon,

otherwise I'd be tapping that on repeat!' She laughed and my stomach bottomed out. 'Oops. Sorry, Jess! Is it wrong of me to say stuff like that because you're my boss and me and Jackson work together?'

'No, no. You're fine.' Jess smiled. 'Mrs Davis— y'know, the woman who left me the money to set every- thing up—always said she wanted people to find romance between the walls of the library, so I wouldn't stand in the way of love.'

'Oh, honey,' Celeste laughed. 'It wouldn't be *love*! Just sex! I'm too young to settle down!'

My chest tightened. I *knew* Celeste would fancy Jack- son, I mean, who wouldn't? He was gorgeous. So was she. I wondered if anything had happened between them yet?

I had no claim on Jackson, but just the thought of him hooking up with Celeste made my stomach churn.

Because secretly, I wished it was *me* he liked.

I know, it was a ridiculous thought and we worked together, but I couldn't help it. And just because it would never happen didn't mean that a girl couldn't dream.

Bob placed another round of shots on the table, and once he was out of earshot, conversation started again.

'I'll have to make a special trip to the library to check him out… oops, I mean to *check out* some more of your finest romance novels!' Kara giggled.

'You won't regret it!' Celeste added. 'Trust me. The man's a god. Bet he's hung like a horse too!'

My eyes widened. Celeste always spoke so freely. I could never imagine being able to do that. Especially not with my dad just a few metres away like Bob was right now.

Hopefully with all the background noise and chatter, he wouldn't be able to hear our conversation.

'What do you think, Jane?' Jess asked me.

'Huh?' My eyebrows shot up.

Surely she wasn't asking me how big I thought Jackson's penis was? I'd never even seen one in the flesh before, so I was hardly an expert, but if I had to guess, it was probably beautiful, just like the rest of him.

'What do you think of Jackson?' she repeated.

'Oh…' I replied, bringing my fantasies about his dick to an abrupt end. 'He's, er, nice.'

'*Nice?*' Celeste gasped dramatically.

'A cup of tea is *nice*! Jackson is more than just *nice*. He's freaking sex on legs! He said you went to school together. Did you two ever snog behind the bike sheds or whatever people did in your day?'

I wish.

'No.' I shook my head quickly.

'In *your day*?' Jess's face wrinkled with horror. 'How old do you think we are?'

'Sorry!' Celeste laughed. 'Slip of the tongue. Speaking of tongues, I wouldn't say no to slipping mine in Jackson's mouth. Or over his cock!'

Kara, Maddie and Celeste erupted into a fit of giggles.

'That would certainly brighten up the working day,' Maddie said.

'Oi!' Jess said. 'There'll be no kissing or blowing colleagues in the bookshop or library during working hours! I know I'm a relaxed boss, but I have my limits!'

'*Yeah, right.*' Celeste rolled her eyes. 'Like you and Theo have never shagged at the library!' A mischievous smile tugged at her lips.

'I can neither confirm nor deny anything…' Jess said sheepishly.

My insides were shrivelling like a prune. I could never imagine asking my boss whether she'd had sex at work. I'd be too afraid of getting the sack and it crossed boss-employee boundaries too.

'You *totally* have!' Maddie laughed.

'I can guarantee it!' Celeste added. 'Ooh, I know! Let's play a game! Where's the wildest or coolest place you've had sex before? The winner gets an extra shot!'

As Celeste picked up her shot and downed it in one, my heart thundered against my chest.

These kinds of games were the worst. They often played them at work parties and whenever the subject turned to sex, it was always so awkward because I had nothing to contribute and I couldn't exactly confess to being a virgin at the age of thirty-bloody-one.

Look at how people laughed and ridiculed the main character in that film *The 40-Year-Old Virgin*. I supposed I couldn't blame them. Being a virgin in your twenties was considered by the majority of society as being weird enough, but these days, reaching your thirties or beyond without popping your cherry was literally unheard of.

I remember doing some research online and I think it said something like between ninety-five and ninety-nine per cent of thirty-year-olds had had sex at least once. Who knows whether it was accurate or not, but either way, I knew I was in the minority. Especially because I wasn't a virgin because of religious reasons, or because I was waiting to get married.

Okay, sure. In the beginning I held out mainly because my parents brainwashed me into thinking it was wrong and that if I had sex, I'd become a teenage mum and bring shame on the family, so I needed to wait until I was married.

But after I realised that it was fine to do it if I wanted to, it just never happened. I just didn't feel ready.

One year just rolled into the next and now here I was, sitting in a pub, mortified about how I was going to wriggle out of answering this question because I still had my virginity firmly intact.

'In the back seat of my ex's parents' car!' Maddie chuckled. 'He forgot to throw away the condom packet and his mum found it and accused his dad of having an affair!'

'Oh my God!' Jess gasped. 'Nightmare! Did he fess up?'

'Nope. He was an idiot. We broke up soon afterwards. Last I heard their parents did too.'

'Noooo!' Kara said. 'Because of the condom packet?'

'Think it might've had something to do with his mum running off with her personal trainer.'

'Classic!' Celeste said and once again my insides shrivelled as I thought of what to say. I knew precisely zero people whose mothers had an affair with their personal trainer.

'The wildest place I've had sex before was on a sun lounger on holiday in Ibiza!' Kara said.

'I fucked a guy on a train before,' Celeste said casually.

'What? On the actual train seat?' Jess frowned.

'No! In the toilet,' Celeste clarified. 'Although I let a guy finger me on a train seat once. No one even noticed!'

My eyes were bulging so much far out of my sockets, I

was sure they were seconds away from flying into some-one's face.

'Theo and I may or may not have got a bit frisky on the beach...' Jess added.

'Knew it!' Celeste pumped her fist triumphantly in the air. 'I bet you've done it in loads of other places too.'

'Like I said before. I can't confirm or deny... as he works with you guys, it wouldn't be professional to go into details, so that's all you're getting from me.'

'How about you, Jane?' Celeste asked and I instantly felt Maddie and Kara's eyes on me, causing my cheeks to flame.

'Oh, er...' My brain froze as I struggled to think of a response. 'Nowhere particularly special. I'm, erm... I'm just gonna pop to the loo.'

I jumped up from the table and raced towards the toilets. Once I was inside the cubicle, I pressed my back against the door.

That was so awkward.

How was I supposed to go back out there now?

For all I knew, Celeste would start suggesting we answer more sexual questions, and I couldn't keep running off to the toilet every time. They'd either think I had a drug problem or cystitis.

I'd been looking forward to a girls' night out, but now I remembered why I'd shied away from them in my old job and why it was safer to find enjoyment through books.

There was nothing wrong with the topic of conversa-tion. I probably wouldn't mind it if I'd actually had sex. But I hadn't, so it was frustrating and embarrassing not being able to contribute anything to the discussion.

It was my own fault. Because I'd built it up in my

mind for so long, it'd become a massive deal. If I'd just shagged someone ages ago, I would've been able to avoid all this awkwardness. I'd be part of the 'club', a 'proper adult', instead of being a weirdo outcast.

I'd lost count of the amount of times I'd thought about just logging onto Tinder, finding someone to hook up with and getting it over and done with. After all, what the hell was I waiting for?

But on the other hand, now I'd waited so long, I kind of felt like I wanted it to count and be worth the wait.

Then again, who was I kidding? From what I'd heard, the first time was always rubbish and painful, so expecting it to be some magical and memorable experience was asking too much. But after all this time, I wanted it to be with someone decent instead of just a drunken fumble that was over in ten seconds.

But that saying *beggars can't be choosers* was true, so I needed to lower my expectations. At this stage, I'd just have to take whatever dick I could get.

There was nothing I could do about it right now, though, so after taking a deep breath, I stepped out of the toilets and headed towards the table.

'Jane! There you are!' Celeste said. 'I just asked these girls whether they'd ever sucked a guy off in public before! Can you believe Maddie has only ever done it in the bedroom?' She cackled and my stomach crumpled.

'I, er… I'm gonna head home,' I said quickly.

'Oh no.' Jess touched my arm. 'Are you okay?'

'Yeah, I… I just got my period and I'm getting really bad pains,' I lied, praying I wouldn't get sent to hell. I had to get out of here, though. If I kept dodging Celeste's questions, eventually everyone would realise I was a virgin and I'd be ridiculed. Just like I was in my last job.

'I think I've got some paracetamol.' Maddie's face creased with concern, then she started rifling through her handbag.

'Thanks. That's really kind of you, but it's probably best if I go to bed with a hot water bottle.'

'You okay getting to the station?' Jess asked.

'Yeah, I'll be fine, thank you.'

'Okay. Well, text me when you're back home, and if you're not feeling better in the morning, let me know.'

God, I felt awful about lying. Jess was being so kind to me.

'Don't worry. I'll be fine tomorrow.' I picked up my jacket, then pulled my purse out of my bag. 'How much do I owe you for the drinks?'

'I'll sort it with my parents.' Celeste waved her hand dismissively. 'Feel better, yeah?'

'Thanks,' I said, surprised at her concern.

'And if the cramps get too painful, just masturbate. Orgasms are great for period pains!' She laughed and I winced internally. 'It's true! Look it up if you don't believe me!'

'I… okay,' I said, thinking that I probably wouldn't. 'Well, enjoy the rest of your evening and see you tomorrow.'

After racing to the door, I stepped outside and inhaled the fresh air.

That was intense.

I couldn't go on like this. I had to do something about my sexual 'situation'. I planned to work at the library for as long as Jess and Theo would have me. And that meant more social nights out.

So I couldn't keep running off every time the conversation turned sexual. Plus I was working in a romance library: y'know, a place which sold and lent books where the characters had sex. How could I do my job properly if I'd never even done more than kiss a guy?

I needed to find a way to get rid of my virginity. It was holding me back.

Forget making it special or waiting. I just needed to get it done.

As quickly as possible.

But the question was, how?

And most importantly, with who?

12

JACKSON

Before I stepped into the library, I paused and checked my phone. I'd looked at it at least ten times since I left the house this morning to see if Marcus had replied about when he planned to post the video.

When we spoke yesterday evening, he said it'd been full on at work, this week, so he hadn't had a chance to edit it yet. At first I was worried that he was editing it on his office computer, but he reassured me that he'd intended to do it at home.

As desperate as I was to get it online so I could hopefully start earning some extra money, I understood that I had to be patient. Marcus was doing me a massive favour by taking care of all this stuff.

Just as I was about to go inside, my phone pinged.

MARCUS

Here's the edited video. Let me know if you're happy with it and I'll get it uploaded.

My heart thudded against my chest. I quickly walked away from the entrance, then pressed play.

As I watched myself thrusting my hips and stroking myself with a pink feather duster, embarrassment washed over me.

How had it come to this? I shook my head with disappointment.

Although I still thought the leopard skin thong was hideous, I supposed the video fitted the brief Marcus had given me to try and look like I was getting off on touching myself with a cleaning tool. And the music he'd added fitted the mood. It was just… really hard to watch.

'You okay?' Jess's voice sounded from behind me and I almost jumped out of my skin.

I quickly paused the video, which was at the point where I was riding the feather duster between my legs like a cowboy competing in a rodeo. I hoped she hadn't seen it.

My head bolted up, and when I saw that she wasn't close enough to see my screen, I exhaled.

'I was just about to come in, but a message came through.'

'No worries! There's still fifteen minutes before we open. I was just seeing if you were okay, that's all.'

'Yeah, great!'

'Celeste is going to be in late this morning. She's currently got her head hanging over the pub toilet throwing up.'

'Shit. What's wrong with her?'

'Hangover, I suspect…'

'Oh yeah! How was it last night?'

'Good,' she said without much enthusiasm. 'Will you be okay to man the bookshop on your own?'

'Sure. I've got the hang of the till now.'

'Cool. I'm just popping over to Sweet Treats. When I get back, can we go over your ideas for the cafe opening? I was thinking we could do one of those silent reading events you mentioned, so we could talk about that too.'

'Course, boss,' I said.

'*Jess* is fine. *Boss* makes me sound too… I dunno. It's too formal.'

'Got it, *Jess*.'

'Want anything whilst I'm there? Coffee, muffin?'

'Nah, thanks, I'm good.'

'Okay. See you in a bit.'

I waved her off, then messaged Marcus to give him the green light. I'd already watched the video after I'd filmed it, and from what I'd seen, the edits seemed fine. I really didn't want to watch it again.

As soon as I stepped into the library and walked down the corridor, my shoulders relaxed.

There was something about this place that was so calming. It was like some sort of magical bubble. It felt as if whenever I was here, the real world and all of the problems I faced somehow didn't exist anymore. It might not pay the kind of salary I needed to cover Mum's care, but being at this library was like eating a warm bowl of chicken soup. It really was good for my soul.

'Morning!' I said as I entered the library hall, where Jane was sifting through a pile of books.

'Oh, hi!' Her face brightened. 'I didn't hear you come in.'

'Hope I didn't scare you.'

'No, no.' She shook her head. 'I was just focused, that's all.'

Jane looked beautiful as always. She had a pink silk blouse and a grey pencil skirt. A strand of loose hair had fallen from her bun onto the side of her face and I instantly wanted to reach up and brush it away.

'How was last night? Jess just said Celeste is throwing up, so wouldn't be in until later. Sounds like it was a wild one!'

'Not sure. I went home early. I... I wasn't feeling great.'

'Oh?' I frowned. 'What's wrong? You okay?'

'Yeah.' Jane waved her hand dismissively. 'I'm fine now. It was just...' She paused, her gaze flicking away from me. 'Y'know. *Girl stuff.*'

'Period pains?' I asked. 'Sorry. I didn't mean to pry. It's your business. It's just... Mum used to get bad cramps, so I know how hard it can be. When it was her time of the month, I made sure I had the paracetamol, hot water bottle and some chocolate around.'

'She was lucky you were so understanding. How is your mum?'

My stomach clenched. I shouldn't have mentioned her. Very few people knew about Mum's condition, and talking about it was hard.

'She's...' My voice trailed off. I wanted to say she was fine, but she wasn't and I hated lying. I just couldn't go into that now, though. I needed to focus on work. This library had already become my safe space. A place where I could escape reality. I needed to protect my mental health. If I crumbled again, I'd be no good to Mum or anyone. 'I've got a meeting with Jess in a minute, so I wondered if I could get your opinion on something?' I said, quickly changing the subject.

'Course!'

'It's for the cafe opening. At first, I was thinking we could do a party, but then people would just come to get free food and drink, which could be expensive. What I really need is some kind of incentive to get people to spend money. So I was thinking, maybe for the opening day, we could offer anyone who buys a coffee or a hot drink a free bookish biscuit. And for people buying soup or sandwiches, they could get a free bookish cupcake. What do you think?'

'I think it's a great idea!' Jane smiled and my heart swelled. 'Nothing beats curling up with a good book, a cup of tea and a biscuit. Especially if the biccy's got a bookish design.'

'I'm going to speak to Maddie to see what's possible design-wise, but I think all the biscuits we sell should have some kind of bookish theme because it'll be something unique to our cafe and help us stand out.'

'Definitely! I reckon loads of people will take pictures and post them on Instagram or TikTok too. I mean, who doesn't love a good biscuit?'

'So you're still a biscuit fan, then?' I asked.

'Yes!'

'Still a die-hard rich tea or digestives stan?'

'You remembered?' Her eyes widened.

'Hard not to!' I chuckled. 'I remember that time we helped out at parents' evening and as a thank-you, Mrs Clements said we could have the biscuits that were left over and you inhaled that packet of rich tea like you hadn't eaten for years!'

'I did *not*!' she gasped, then the corner of her mouth twitched as she tried to stifle a smile.

'You *did*! I didn't even get a look in!' I laughed.

'Because you said you didn't like them! How anyone could *not* like rich tea biscuits is beyond me. They're completely inoffensive. And they're perfect for dunking!'

'I'll give you that at least. It wasn't that I didn't like them. I just preferred the more *exciting* biscuits. I'm more of a Party Rings, Jammie Dodgers or chocolate digestives kind of guy.'

'What about Jaffa Cakes? You used to love those!'

Now it was my turn to be surprised.

'Wow.' I raised my eyebrow. '*You* remembered.' I smiled and our eyes locked.

Jane really did have beautiful eyes. I used to love when she took off her glasses so I could get a closer look.

My gaze dropped to her mouth and she bit her lip. Her lips looked so soft and for a second I wondered how they felt.

Then my mind flipped back to last night, when I'd accidentally walked in on her changing her top in the toilets.

When I saw her in her bra, my breath caught in my throat. Jane never exposed her body. At school she always wore the most conservative uniform options. Even in the summer months, she didn't go for the open-neck school shirt. She went for the buttoned-up one with a tie.

Lots of the girls in class liked to flout the rules and wear skirts that were shorter than the school's approved length, but Jane's skirts were always long. And she was rarely seen without her thick tights underneath.

Even now as an adult, from what I'd seen over the past week and a bit since I'd joined the library, she liked to wear blouses buttoned all the way up, and her pencil skirts were never above the knee.

So to see her bare torso and neck and the curve of her breasts in that white bra instantly set my body on fire. But as much as I wanted to stay and admire how beautiful she looked, I knew I had to leave. We were colleagues.

'Oh my God!' Jess raced into the library, breaking the spell. For a second I thought maybe she had some kind of mind-reading super powers and was shocked about the fact that I'd just been picturing Jane half naked. Those fantasies were nothing compared to the ones I'd had when I was filming that video last Sunday night, though.

'What's wrong?' Jane said.

'I've just heard the news! It's official!' Jess gushed.

'What is?' I frowned.

'The *Office Delight* sequel is coming out! It's called *Illicit Delight*!'

'No way!' Whilst Jane seemed to mirror Jess's excitement, I had no idea what they were talking about.

'I'm guessing *Office Delight* is a novel?' I asked. Seeing as they were both massive book fans, I'd put money on it being that instead of a film.

They both looked at me like I'd just suggested readers shouldn't buy any new books until they'd finished reading the ones on their TBR, which I'd already learnt was a crazy suggestion.

'*Office Delight* is only one of the greatest steamy romance novels ever written!' Jess shouted before scanning the library in horror, then remembering that we weren't open yet, so she hadn't disturbed any members.

'I finished it last week and it's *so* good,' Jane added.

'It's the best! Anyway, I just saw on Instagram that the

author, D.D. Desire, is doing a book tour. So far she's confirmed she'll be doing a signing in Manchester and London, probably at Waterstones, but we need to find a way to get her here: to *our* library.'

'How?' Jane asked.

'That's what I need Jackson to figure out!' She turned to face me with a glint in her eye that told me failure wasn't an option. 'I'll leave you to it! I'll come to the bookstore in ten minutes, Jackson, to run through your ideas.' Jess smiled, then left the room.

'Why do I get the feeling that getting this Desire author woman to do a signing here isn't going to be straightforward?' I looked at Jane and raised an eyebrow.

'Because D.D. Desire's been out of the limelight for a while. She wrote *Office Delight* a few years ago and it blew up on TikTok.'

'That's great, right?'

'Yes and no. She sold millions of copies. But along with the success and millions of fans came a load of haters. People thought it was cool to slag off her books and after that she became a recluse. The negativity messed up her creativity and she stopped writing.'

'Damn.' I shook my head. 'That's a shame.'

'Yeah. Especially for her fans, who were desperate to know what happened with Rocco and Virginia. They're the main characters.'

'Got it.'

'So the fact that she's written a sequel is a big deal. But I'm guessing that after all the hate she got, she'll probably want to limit her tour and only stick to big cities.'

'Maybe.' I rested my finger on my chin. 'But if she's worried about haters, then a small, intimate venue at a library dedicated to love and the romance genre could be the perfect location. We could have a curated selection of readers—her biggest fans all here ready to give her a warm welcome.'

'I like your thinking!' Jane said.

'Do you know where she's based? Is she American?'

'No, she's British.'

'Even better. That means she won't have to worry about travelling thousands of miles to get back home. It'll be easier to squeeze in an extra visit at a certain romance library.' I grinned, my mind racing as I tried to think of ways I'd convince her to come here.

'Definitely.'

'And I'm guessing that because she's such a big deal, we have her *Office Delight* book in our library?'

'We have multiple copies, but as soon as they're returned they go straight back out again. Someone checked out the last copy yesterday morning. I think I overheard Celeste saying we'd sold out in the bookshop too. Hopefully the new order will come in next week.'

'Shit. If I'm going to work on this, I'd like to start reading it sooner, and I'd rather buy or borrow it from here than get it somewhere else. I could get the ebook or audiobook instead, but I prefer reading paperbacks.'

'Well, I could…' Jane paused. 'Never mind.'

'What?' I frowned.

'I have a paperback copy I could lend to you, but, it's kind of…'

'*Worn?*' I smirked and Jane's cheeks turned pink.

'No!' Her eyes popped. 'I don't mean… not like that! There's no sticky pages or anything!'

'I'm only joking! I know you love books too much to

soil them. Even at school you were horrified whenever you saw someone dog-earing the textbook pages. Do you still carry spare bookmarks in your bag?'

'How did you remember *that*?' She looked at me like I'd just performed a complex maths calculation without using a calculator.

What Jane didn't realise was that I remembered everything about her from school. How smart she was, the way she used to bite the end of her pen when she was thinking or couldn't figure out the answer to a question.

The way when we had lunch, she always ate her vegetables first, then cut up her meat into tiny pieces before taking the first bite.

How she carefully snapped her rich tea biscuit in half before dunking it into her tea.

And how she never invited me to her parents' house because she knew they wouldn't approve of our friendship.

Yep. I remembered everything.

'It's all up here.' I tapped the side of my head. 'Photographic memory. So anything you say or do may be used as the source of an embarrassing story in the next fifteen years!'

Jane laughed and a warm feeling flooded my chest.

Hearing Jane laugh used to be one of my favourite things and even now, I couldn't resist smiling at the sound.

'I know it sounds lame, but books, even textbooks, are beautiful. I couldn't stand the idea of people damaging them intentionally. Books must be protected at all costs!'

'*Hear, hear!*' I lifted my fist in the air in solidarity.

'Anyway, what I was going to say was that my paperback is… *annotated.*'

'Perfect.' I smiled. 'Then I can understand what

sections and chapters have the juiciest parts and quote the popular ones in my pitch to Madame Desire.'

'*D.D. Desire!*' she corrected me with a smile.

'That's what I meant! Note to get the author's name right before I contact her.' I laughed again. 'Do you have your copy here or is it at home?'

'God, no! I could never leave *that* at home!' Jane said before her gaze dropped to the floor.

'Huh? What do you mean?' Did her boyfriend not approve of her reading romance?

'I… I live with my parents and they're… well. If you remember about my biscuit preferences and bookmark obsession, I'm sure you'll remember that my family aren't exactly open-minded.'

I ground my jaw. I should be relieved that she wasn't living with a boyfriend (not that it mattered if she was), but knowing she was still stuck with those bigots made me sad for her.

Normally I didn't speak badly about other people's relatives, but I made an exception for Jane's family.

Her older brother, Wayne, was the biggest dickhead in school and from what I'd seen and heard of her mum and dad… just thinking about how they treated Jane made me want to put my fist through a wall.

'Yeah.' I ground my jaw. 'I remember.'

'Er, so, I have the book here.' Jane spoke quickly, clearly wanting to change the subject. 'It's in my drawer in the office. I'll bring it to you later.'

'Thanks,' I said.

Our eyes locked again.

I knew I was supposed to go to the bookshop now, but

I didn't want to leave. I really enjoyed being with Jane. She was so easy to talk to.

'So,' I broke the silence. 'I should go…'

'Okay. I'll come and see you soon. To bring you the book. Not to look at you,' she stuttered. 'I mean, obviously I'll need to look at you to give it to you, but, I… I better go and put these on the shelves.'

As she grabbed a pile of books, then rushed off towards the bookcase, I couldn't even focus on why she'd got flustered because I was too busy taking in the prime view of her arse in that skirt.

Damn.

I was trying to keep my thoughts about Jane professional, but I was failing.

Big time.

13

———

JANE

It was now almost lunchtime, and as I started shelving the pile of books in my hands, I replayed the last part of my conversation with Jackson for the hundredth time, then winced. Why did I have to say that stupid thing about not coming to look at him?

On the one hand, talking to him felt so natural. It was like we were just those two teenagers back in the classroom, chatting like we used to. But then I'd look into his eyes and then my stomach would do that annoying flip-flopping thing, my brain would turn to mush and a load of crap would fall out of my mouth.

I shouldn't have suggested that I lend him my copy of *Office Delight*. I was mortified when I thought that Jackson thought I'd soiled the pages whilst reading it because I'd got myself off.

Okay. Full disclosure: I'd be lying if I said I hadn't touched myself when reading some of the spicy chapters in bed at night, but I always kept the pages clean.

As well as keeping a box of tissues nearby, I made sure

my tabs and highlighter pens were also always on my bedside table next to the lamp, ready to mark my favourite parts.

And as a result, that novel now had more tabs than a hundred internet browsers. I'd annotated the pages like crazy, colour-coding not just the parts that I found funny or romantic, but also the many sections that were super spicy. I *may* have also written some comments in the margins that might not be suitable for other people's eyes…

Crap.

If there was another bookshop nearby, I'd go there in my lunch break and buy Jackson a copy. But there wasn't, so I was stuck with giving him mine.

I'd seen Jess's copy, which looked very *worn*. And it wouldn't take a genius to work out how it got that way…

I'd agreed to give the book to Jackson now, so there was no going back. He needed it for research before he contacted D.D. Desire. If we got her to the library, that'd be major, so I'd just needed to take one for the team.

Anyway, I was overthinking. Jackson probably didn't give two hoots about which scenes I found hot. Chances were he was too busy having wild sex with supermodels or his girlfriend, if he had one.

What was I saying? *Of course* Jackson had a girlfriend. There was no way a man like that could be single.

It wasn't just about how he looked. That alone would get the women flocking. But it was also how kind he was.

When he mentioned that he used to get his mum paracetamol, a hot water bottle and chocolate when she got her period, my heart melted.

The men in my family never showed any sympathy for me or Mum when we had our periods. I still remember when I was doubled over on the sofa as the pains ripped through me and Dad told me to stop complaining. He said women had their 'thing' every month and I should be used to the pain by now.

Arsehole.

I was so embarrassed when I had to tell Jackson that I still lived at home with my parents. I saw the disgust in his eyes. But I was sure that was because he remembered how awful they were rather than the fact that he was judging me.

Talking of things that he remembered, I couldn't believe it when he mentioned the bookmark stash I used to carry. And what my favourite biscuits were. Although my stomach sank a little when he said he preferred more *exciting* biscuits.

That was just another reminder of how different we were. Jackson liked fun, exciting stuff, whereas I stuck with things that were ordinary and boring, which basically summed up my life.

Whilst I stayed in Shamwick, Jackson went off to one of the most prestigious universities in England and probably had a wild time. Then he got a big, fancy job in the City, living it up in London. I on the other hand hadn't done anything interesting. I was still 'plain Jane'.

If Jackson thought my biscuit choices were boring, imagine what he'd think if he knew I hadn't had sex. I groaned internally as I shelved the last book.

When I walked back to the meet-cute desk, I saw Theo come in.

'Hi, how are you?' he asked.

'Good, thanks. You?'

'Fine. Jess asked to see you in the office. I can take care of things here.'

'Oh, okay,' I said, wondering what she could want to see me about. I knew she'd had a meeting with Jackson about the cafe opening, so maybe it was related to that.

'Hi!' Jess said as I stepped in the office.

'Everything okay?' I asked.

'Yeah! All good. Take a seat,' she said. This sounded serious. A million thoughts raced through my mind before I told myself to calm down and just listen to what she had to say. 'How are you feeling this morning?'

'Much better, thanks.' I still felt awful about telling that white lie.

'I wanted to talk to you about last night.'

'Oh?' I frowned.

'I just wanted to make sure you were okay. I know the conversation got a bit… X-rated, so I just wanted to check that it didn't make you… uncomfortable. You're an important part of the team and I never want you to feel pressured into talking about or revealing stuff about yourself that you don't want to.'

'Um.' My eyes widened and my mind raced as I tried to think of how to respond. 'Yeah. Okay. Thanks,' I stuttered, thinking it was nice of her to check on me. Then wondering if she'd guessed that I was a virgin based on my reluctance to talk about sex. Oh God. I really hoped not.

'I mean, I'd consider myself pretty liberal,' Jess added, 'but even *I* found it awkward.'

'You *did*?' I frowned, thinking that topic would be right up her street. I'd walked in on Theo and Jess kissing in the office on more than one occasion and something about the way they couldn't keep their hands off each other told me that they had a very active sex life.

'Yeah. I don't have a problem with talking about sex. It's just, I'm still trying to adjust to being a boss. Up until I'd opened this place, I'd only ever been an employee, so it's hard to remember that I have to set boundaries. It would've been so easy to get carried away with that conversation, but that would've been disrespectful to Theo. Imagine I'd said, "Theo and I love fucking on the beach", hypothetically speaking, of course, and then Celeste saw him and mentioned it, he might get embarrassed. Actually, he probably wouldn't care, but still.'

'I understand,' I said, wondering if her comment about them banging on the beach really was *hypothetical*.

'So, yeah, the point I'm trying to make is that I want everyone that works here to be comfortable. And if there's anything you ever want to talk about, professionally or… otherwise—y'know, one-to-one rather than in a group in a busy pub—my door is always open.'

'Th-thank you,' I said, wondering once again if she suspected something.

Although I'd be mortified if she did, I appreciated the fact that she hadn't made me feel like a loser.

'That's all I wanted to say.' Jess got up and headed to the door. 'Theo's okay covering the library if you fancy taking an early lunch?'

'Okay, thanks.' I nodded as she left the office.

I was about to leave too, then remembered I'd promised to give Jackson my copy of *Office Delight*.

When I fished it out of my drawer, embarrassment washed over me. I knew I'd added loads of tabs, but I hadn't realised it was this many.

There was nothing I could do about it now, though. I found a Jiffy bag, stuffed the book inside, got my jacket and handbag, then made my way to the bookstore.

Luckily when I arrived, Celeste was serving a customer. If she saw how much the book had been annotated, she'd probably snatch it away and start reading all the steamy bits I'd highlighted out loud, which would be even more mortifying.

'Hi!' Jackson smiled as he saw me walking towards him.

A jolt of electricity shot through me. How was it possible that he looked even more attractive than when I'd seen him just a few hours ago?

The sleeves of his shirt were rolled up to his elbows, exposing his muscular forearms. As I took in the sight of the thick veins and sprinkling of dark hair, I was overcome with the urge to reach out and stroke his arms to see if his skin was as smooth as it looked.

'You okay?' Jackson's face crumpled, then I realised I was just standing there, staring.

'Um… I… I came to give you this.' I handed him the Jiffy bag. 'It's the… book.'

'Thanks.' He smiled again and butterflies flooded my stomach.

As he peeked inside, another wave of embarrassment hit me. There was no way I was going to stick around and watch the inevitable look of horror spread across his face when he pulled out the book and saw all of the tabs.

'I've gotta go. Enjoy!' I raced out of the bookshop, down the corridor and out of the library, making a beeline for the beach.

The moment the salty sea air flooded my nostrils, I exhaled.

I'd given Jackson the book. It was done. It'd be fine. Whatever he thought about my overenthusiastic highlighting, I just had to focus on the bigger picture. If reading my copy helped him bring my new favourite author to our library, it'd be worth it.

A gentle breeze tickled my cheeks. It was too cold to take my shoes off today and walk on the sand, but I didn't mind because the sun was still shining and the sky was a beautiful shade of blue.

As I strolled along the beach, my thoughts turned back to my conversation with Jess.

It was kind of her to check in on me, but I also felt bad that she'd had to. Despite what my parents thought, I was a grown woman. I should be able to handle these situations. And if I wanted to have sex, I should stop pussyfooting around and just do it.

For ages I'd wondered whether it was as mind-blowing as everyone said it was. I imagined it had to be, right? Sex played an important part in my favourite romance novels and it seemed to play an important part in real life too.

People were always talking about sex. Take last night at the pub. The whole conversation was dominated by it.

People paid money to have sex.

People fell head over heels when the sex was great. And people went through the pain of break-ups and divorce when people cheated by having sex with someone else.

Sex was powerful.

It had the ability to make or break relationships.

They say that money makes the world go round and

whilst that could be true, it seemed like *sex* made the world go round too. So the fact that I hadn't even tried it yet made me feel like I was really missing out on life.

I'd love for a man to ravish me and fuck me on a desk or sofa like Rocco had done to Virginia in *Office Delight*.

At this point, though, I'd be happy to be screwed on top of a dustbin.

After striding over to my favourite bench, I sat down and pulled my phone out of my bag.

I was tired of just thinking about sex, reading about it, or hearing people like Celeste and Jess talk about it.

I was tired of wondering how it'd feel.

Once I'd unlocked my screen, I selected the App Store.

No more holding out for Mr Right.

No more fantasising about a colleague who'd never be interested in me.

No more waiting and passively hoping an opportunity to lose my virginity would drop into my lap.

It was time to finally take action and experience sex for myself.

It was time to download Tinder.

14

———

JACKSON

I flopped onto the sofa. It'd been a long day at the library.

After my meeting with Jess about the cafe opening, I'd dived straight into planning the event.

The library was now closed for three days so that the bulk of the building work could be done. With all the drilling and banging, it'd be too noisy and messy to keep it open.

Theo used to work in property development, so thanks to his contacts, he was able to hire a team that could get the work done super quickly so we could officially open the cafe next weekend and start bringing in more cash. But the fast turnaround also meant that I didn't have much time to get the event organised.

I spent most of the day creating posters and fliers on the library's laptop so that I could get them printed up and distributed around town.

Then I spoke to Jess's friend Sarah to fill her in on our plans. She was based in the Midlands and had a full-time job but helped out with the library's social media whenever she had time, so she'd promised to start plugging the opening online ASAP.

And once Celeste had arrived around lunchtime, I'd met Maddie to discuss the biscuits and cakes we could have for the event.

Luckily Maddie said she'd planned to create some anyway because they'd been a big hit when she'd baked some for the library's opening.

After that, I'd contacted a company about ordering some library merch, then drafted an email to D.D. Desire and her agent to pitch her visiting the library as part of her promotional tour.

Jess had made it crystal clear that I needed to find a way to bring her here, so I couldn't let her down. I really wanted to make this library a success. Not just because I needed the job, but because I saw how much joy it brought to the members, customers, Jess, Theo and of course, Jane.

I'd only seen her briefly this afternoon when she came to drop off her copy of *Office Delight*. She literally handed it to me, then raced out of the bookshop.

Strange.

She wasn't joking when she said her copy was annotated. There were hundreds of multi-coloured tabs sticking out of the edge of the book. And inside, multiple sections had been highlighted within an inch of their lives in different colours. Actually, it was probably easier to say what *hadn't* been highlighted instead of what had.

There didn't seem to be any notes to say what each colour tab or highlight meant, but I was sure I'd work it out.

Ideally I would've wanted to have read the book before

contacting D.D. Desire, but luckily Jess was able to tell me what she loved about the book (without spoilers) and from there I was able to write a paragraph that made the email sound more personalised and passionate.

If Jane hadn't been so busy this afternoon, I would've asked for her thoughts too, but every time I passed the hall, she was with a member and I had to make sure the email got sent before the end of the day.

Although I was shattered, it felt good that I was making progress. The role was originally supposed to just be part-time, but since they'd hired me, apart from last Sunday when the library was closed, I'd worked every day.

Obviously I wouldn't get paid for this Monday and Tuesday when the library was closed, but I still planned to do some stuff in my own time.

Tomorrow was Sunday, so I planned to work on the event and make a shortlist of merch items we could order to present it to Jess next week.

And if I could keep my eyes open for long enough tonight, I'd like to start reading *Office Delight* so that when I followed up with D.D. Desire's agent I sounded like I knew what I was talking about.

Just as I was about to think about what to make for dinner, my phone rang.

When I saw that it was Marcus, my heart rate picked up. I'd messaged him earlier to see if he had an update on the video.

'Hey,' I answered. 'How's it going?'

'Good, just knackered.'

'Same,' I said.

'Yeah? I thought you just sat around reading books all day and staring into the hot librarian's eyes!' He laughed.

'Not funny!' I tried to stifle a chuckle. 'It's not as intense as working in M&A, but there's still a lot to do. We're opening a cafe next Saturday and I'm organising the event. Plus my boss signed off on a silent reading party the following week too.'

'Whoa. That's not a lot of time.'

'I know. But the sooner we open, the sooner we can generate extra revenue, so the builders are pulling out all the stops.'

'What kind of marketing are you planning?'

'Social media, posters, leaflets, that kind of thing. We don't really have a marketing budget, so everything has to be done on a shoestring.'

'I hear you. Do they have a newsletter?'

'Don't think so.'

'That's a low-cost form of marketing too. You should start collecting email addresses so when it opens, you can email to let everyone know. And include a special offer or something.'

'They should already have the members' email addresses, so I'll look into that.'

'And run a competition on social media with a prize—something simple like a book bundle so you can get non-members to sign up and expand your reach.'

'That's a great idea! I'll talk to Sarah about setting that up.'

'Who's Sarah?'

'She's the woman who does the social media remotely. She's a friend of Jess's.'

'Got it. So…' He paused. 'I put the video live this morning.'

'Yeah?' My heart started thumping in my chest. 'And? How's it doing?'

'It's early days, so not much to report yet.'

'Have I had any views, followers or subscribers?'

'It's not even been up for twenty-four hours yet, so give it time. I'm going to set up a couple of social media accounts to help drive traffic there. Don't worry. I'm on it.'

'Thanks, man. I feel bad about you doing all this work for me, though. Especially when you're so busy yourself right now.'

'I'm not doing it for you. I'm doing it for your mum. She was always good to me.'

I swallowed the lump in my throat. Mum loved Marcus. She said he was like the second son she never had.

'I appreciate it. What can I do to make things easier for you and help get this off the ground quickly? I don't have much time to get the money together.'

'I know. If you really want to speed things up, there's two things you can do.'

'Name them,' I said as I got up and headed to the kitchen to make a start on dinner.

As I flicked on the light switch and took in the sight of the room, my stomach sank. I hated coming in here. It reminded me of how much work had to be done to this place.

The beige cupboard doors were so dated. Both the wall and floor tiles were chipped and there was damp in the corner by the back door. No wonder this place hadn't sold yet.

It'd been on the market for a year. When I realised Mum would have to go into a home, how much it was going to cost and that she couldn't get any financial support, I didn't have a choice.

I hoped that by selling the house, I could use the money to pay for Mum's care. But Shamwick had been a shithole when we'd moved here almost twenty years ago and since then it'd only got worse.

It wasn't like Sunshine Bay, which was the kind of idyllic place that everyone wanted to move to. Shamwick was where you came to live if you were desperate.

So trying to sell a house which needed a lot of work done, in an area which was about as desirable to live in as a sewer, was proving to be a challenge to say the least.

'First up,' Marcus said, snapping me out of my thoughts, 'you need more content. People need to know that your video wasn't just a one-off. They need a better feel for your brand and what to expect from it. And that's hard to do with just one video.'

'Okay, I hear you. The library's gonna be closed for a few days, so I'll have more time. I can fit those around my visits to see Mum.'

My stomach tightened. It felt kind of sick that I'd be going to visit Mum, then I'd be coming home to shoot videos of myself dry-humping cleaning tools. But it had to be done.

'Good. Try and do at least half a dozen.'

'That many? Okay. And the second thing?'

'You're not gonna wanna hear this, but you'll earn money much faster if you get your dick out.'

'What?' I shouted. 'I thought you said I could earn money *without* getting naked.'

'You can. But it'll take longer. People will be more willing to subscribe and pay more if they know they're gonna get to see your cock.'

'No.' I shook my head, even though I knew he couldn't see me. 'It's already difficult enough doing this wearing a shitty G-string. Putting my cock on the internet is taking things way too far.'

I knew lots of people stripped for money and that was their choice. Each to their own and all of that. I didn't mean to sound judgy, but Dad would be so disappointed. Mum too. She didn't work her arse off, make so many sacrifices or help me get a place at Cambridge so that I could flash my dick online. I didn't want to let either of them down.

'I hear you and I respect your decision, but you asked me what would help, so I'm just telling you. Listen, do some more videos with the G-strings and let's see how it goes. Okay?'

'Okay. And thanks again.'

'Thank me when you start earning decent money. I better go. But I'll update you when I have more news.'

'Cool.'

'Talk soon.'

As I ended the call, I blew out a breath.

My head felt like it was being squeezed in a vice. I was under so much pressure.

Pressure to find the money to pay Mum's care fees.

Pressure to sell this house.

Pressure to help the library generate more income so that I and the whole team could keep their jobs.

It was a lot.

And I didn't know how to deal with it.

So after I'd set some pasta to boil on the stove, I went into the hallway, reached inside my jacket pocket and pulled out Jane's copy of *Office Delight*.

When reality became too much, reading was the one thing that helped me to feel better.

And right now, I needed some escapism more than ever.

15
———

JANE

'It looks amazing!' I stepped back and admired the cafe, which was finished last night.

Like the rest of the library, the large, airy room had a pink-and-white colour scheme.

The rich scent of freshly brewed coffee and sweet pastries filled the air and as I took in the sight of the pretty glass display counter, my mouth watered.

It wasn't just the traditional cakes and pastries in Sweet Treats that were impressive. What immediately caught my eye was the display of bookish-themed cupcakes and biscuits.

Some cupcakes had a colourful 3-D bookstack on top, which almost looked too pretty to eat. Others had a mini open book resting on the pink, white or yellow icing with different messages like 'I Love Spicy Books' or 'Romance Rocks'.

The biscuits also had romance-related quotes like 'Good Girl' and 'Book Boyfriends Are the Best', and the extra-large cookies had longer sayings—for example, 'I

Like My Coffee Steamy, Just Like My Books'. I loved the heart-shaped biscuits with pretty red icing too.

I could see that Jess and Maddie had put a lot of thought into choosing the furniture. There was a mixture of pink-and-white painted wooden tables, and light grey chairs. I didn't even need to sit in them to know that they were comfortable. They weren't those hard wooden seats that hurt your bum after two minutes. *Nope*. These ones were spongy and cushioned with a circular arc shape to support your bottom and your back, so you could immerse yourself in a great book whilst enjoying some coffee and cake in comfort.

There were also cute window seats with a view of the pretty row of shops opposite us, so if customers wanted to take a break from reading, they could people-watch instead.

Shelves lined one wall with a display of popular books available to buy, including our book of the week, and the other walls were decorated with framed quotes about love and romance.

Yep. Love & Lattes was even more perfect than I'd imagined.

'We still have some little bits and bobs to do this morning,' Maddie said, 'but hopefully we'll get it all done before the big opening at lunchtime.'

'I'm sure we will. And these are fantastic!' I picked up the stack of glossy leaflets on the table and turned to face Jackson.

During the three days that the library was closed, I'd missed him.

I knew it didn't make sense. After all, I'd gone years without seeing Jackson, but during the short time he'd been working here, I'd grown to like the ritual of seeing him. Even if we hadn't got to spend much time together this week.

When the library reopened on Wednesday, Jackson had asked for my help with choosing the merch items shortlist to present to Jess. He'd said that as I was the expert, he'd really value my opinion on what kind of things romance book lovers would enjoy.

Naturally I told him that a selection of bookmarks were a given, as well as a tote bag. I also suggested stickers and T-shirts would be good too.

Jackson seemed so grateful for my suggestions. As I talked, his eyes sparkled with enthusiasm causing my whole body to light up. Truth was, that was how my body responded whenever he was around. Especially when he saw me and his face broke into a smile. God, I loved his smile. And I liked talking to him (when I wasn't getting tongue-tied, of course). He was just so…

Gah.

I was becoming obsessed. I really needed to find a man outside of work instead of fixating on one that could never be mine.

The whole Tinder hook-up plan had fallen flat before I'd even created my profile.

When I'd got home that night, I'd seen my brother scrolling through Tinder, complaining about the 'mingers' that were clogging up his inbox and how he was only interested in 'fit birds' with 'big knockers'.

Listening to how he spoke about women made me want to throw up. And then it occurred to me that if I went on any of the dating apps, my poor excuse of a brother would be on them too. If he ever saw me on there, he'd go straight to my parents, and because of their double standards, all hell would break loose.

So that was that. Dating apps weren't an option. If I wanted to lose my V-card at some point this century, I had to find another way.

Anyway, I didn't want to think about that, or my family, right now. Being at my parents' felt suffocating. Like all of the happiness and joy was being sucked out of me. But thankfully I was here, at my happy place. As soon as I stepped into the library, it was like I came back to life.

Spending time with like-minded people like Jackson and of course Jess and Theo was like a breath of fresh air.

The positivity and happiness within these walls were infectious. That was why it was so important that we made this cafe opening a big success.

'Thanks.' Jackson smiled and just like always, my stomach fluttered. 'Glad you like them. Hopefully we'll get some sign-ups for the first silent reading party next Friday night too.'

'I'm sure we will,' I gushed.

'What do you think?' Jess said as she came into the cafe with Theo. As happy as I was to see them, I was also a little gutted as I was enjoying chatting to Jackson.

'I absolutely love it!' I replied. 'And the sign looks brilliant too. I'm amazed you were able to get it made so quickly.'

'You can thank this gorgeous man for that! He literally knows everyone in the trade, so he clicks his fingers and shit gets done.'

'That's not entirely accurate,' Theo said. 'I'd never click my fingers. Not my style.'

'True,' Jess laughed. 'You two came up with so many

good names it was hard for me and Maddie to choose, but I think Love & Lattes suits this cafe perfectly.

'Agreed,' Jackson said. 'Jane's suggestions were brilliant.'

'It was a *team* effort,' I said, thinking how sweet it was of him to give me all of the credit. 'And I'm sure it was you, Jackson, who suggested Love & Lattes.'

'You two work well together.' Jess smiled. 'We're expecting a good turnout, but I reckon the majority of people will come tonight, which means it's gonna be a long day.'

'We're ready for it!' Jackson said enthusiastically.

'That's the spirit!' Theo added.

A few hours later the cafe was all set up. Maddie had added an extra batch of mini bookish cupcakes in a variety of flavours, including chocolate, vanilla, coffee and red velvet, to give to guests who ordered a coffee or drink.

Guests gushed not just about how pretty the cafe was but also how delicious the cakes, biscuits and coffee were, which was exactly what we wanted to hear.

At around five, just as it was starting to get dark, we closed the cafe to have a quick tidy-up and get everything prepared for the evening opening celebrations, which were scheduled to start at seven.

'Need an extra pair of hands?' Jackson asked as I helped Maddie and Tamsin, who would be the main person manning the cafe, clear away the last of the coffee mugs and plates.

'We should be fine, right, Maddie?'

'Yeah. Once we're done here, me and Tamsin will get the next batch of biscuits and cakes and bring them over.'

'Okay. If you need anything, just shout,' he said before leaving the cafe.

'We will.'

Ten minutes later, Maddie and Tamsin had headed off to Sweet Treats and I was setting out leaflets on the tables promoting our new offers and the first silent reading party.

Just as I bent down to take more leaflets out of the box, a loud crash made me jump out of my skin. When I looked up, I saw a brick flying through the air before plummeting to the ground.

What the hell?

Seconds later, I heard footsteps and Jackson raced into the room.

'What was that? I heard…' His eyes flicked to the window, then to the floor where the brick had landed. 'Shit!' He raced over and placed his hands on my shoulders. 'Are you okay? Are you hurt?'

I heard him talking and I saw him in front of me. I even felt the heat from his palms, but for some reason, I couldn't speak.

'What happened?' Jess ran into the room, quickly followed by Theo.

'Someone threw a brick through the window!' Jackson shouted.

'What the fuck?' Jess's eyes bulged. 'Jane?' She walked quickly towards me. 'Jane,' she repeated. 'Talk to me. Are you okay?'

'Maybe you should sit down.' Jackson released his hands and pulled a chair behind me. I instantly missed the heat of his palms. 'Here.' He gently guided my body towards the chair. 'Sit down for a second.'

'I'll make some tea.' Jess rushed behind the counter.

'Jane.' Jackson's voice sounded again, softer this time.

'I…' I attempted to talk. 'It just came out of nowhere. I bent down to get more leaflets and then…'

'I'm going to look outside,' Theo said. 'Whoever did this will be long gone, but it's worth a try.'

'Be careful,' Jess called out.

'I'll be out in a sec,' Jackson said. 'I need to make sure Jane is okay.'

'I… I'm fine,' I said.

'You're in shock.' He took my hand and squeezed it gently. I was about to tell him that it felt really nice but caught myself, just in time.

'Maybe.' I nodded slowly. 'But what are we going to do? The evening celebration is starting soon. We need to get everything ready!' I jumped up.

'We'll cancel it,' Jess said calmly as she brought over a steaming mug of tea.

'No!' I raised my voice, which I didn't do often. 'There's too many people coming. We can't let them down. And we need the money.'

'Your safety's more important than money,' Jess insisted.

'I couldn't see anyone out there,' Theo said as he returned to the cafe. 'But I've called the police. This was a deliberate attack. Call me paranoid, but I think someone's trying to sabotage the library. This is the second time something has happened.'

'What?' Jackson said. 'Someone's done this before?'

'Not a brick, no. But a few weeks ago, just before you

started, we had a leak on the roof. Bill said it looked like someone had deliberately tampered with the tiles and damaged the roof. We both suspected it was foul play, because causing a leak like that wasn't easy, but didn't have any proof. And now this? It's too much of a coincidence.'

'But who would do something like that?' I asked.

I remembered Jess had said Theo thought the roof leaking was suspicious, but I didn't realise he meant someone had deliberately sabotaged it. I thought maybe the tiles the builders had used weren't the ones they'd paid for or something a lot less sinister.

'Someone with a grudge against the library,' Jess added.

'What, like another library? Or a bookstore?' My brow furrowed. That sounded a bit drastic.

It couldn't be another cafe in town that was worried about the competition because Sweet Treats was the main cafe slash bakery in Sunshine Bay and Maddie was a partner in Love & Lattes. Plus everyone in this town was so lovely.

'No.' Theo blew out a frustrated breath. 'Someone like my father. He's not happy that Edwin sold the building to Jess to open a library. And he hates that I resigned from working at his company to work here instead. If he drives us out of the library and we had to sell, the land would be free for him to buy to build his luxury apartments, just like he always wanted.'

'And I suppose he thinks that then you'd be forced to go back to work for him too, right?' Jackson said.

'Correct.' Theo nodded. 'My brother Ben said he's convinced that it's only a matter of time until I come running back with my tail between my legs. And although Father wouldn't admit it, I've heard on the grapevine that he's lost a lot of business since I left because many of my contacts aren't happy working with him.'

'So he has a strong motivation for the library to fail,' Jackson added.

'That's right.'

'Shit,' Jess said. 'I know your dad's a monumental dick, but would he really stoop *this* low?'

'When it comes to business, he's ruthless. Father would stop at nothing to get what he wants.'

'So what can we do?' Jess said, concern in her eyes.

'I'd love to march down to his office right now and give him a piece of my mind, but we don't have any proof, so I don't think we'll get anywhere that way. Hopefully the police will be here soon and we can see what they say. In the meantime, I'll make a call and get some cameras installed.'

'But what about tonight?' I asked.

'I don't know.' Theo sighed. 'Maybe we should cancel, like Jess said.'

'I really think we should go ahead,' I insisted. 'If your dad is trying to sabotage the library, he'd love us to cancel and upset customers and members. He'd want us to fail. Which is exactly why we have to go ahead.'

'That's actually a good point.' Jess stood up straighter. 'If he wants to fuck with us, we have to show him we won't be defeated.'

'Yes!' I said, feeling a surge of energy race through me.

'I was kind of in agreement about cancelling,' Jackson said. 'I wouldn't want anyone else to get hurt. But you're right, Jane. The show must go on. I can keep watch outside whilst the event is on to make sure no one comes back, but we'll still need to find a way to get everything cleaned up and ready in time for tonight.'

'That won't be a problem.' Theo smiled. 'This is Sunshine Bay. The town famous for its *community spirit*. Isn't that right, Jess?'

'Yep!' She smiled like a light bulb had just gone off in her head. 'I reckon we can round up a few people who'd be more than happy to help...'

16

JACKSON

'That should be everything!' Glenda, the lady who apparently ran the B&B, smiled as she swept up the last of the shattered glass on the floor.

'Looks as good as new,' Edwin said. Theo told me that he was the guy who used to own the building.

I couldn't believe how quickly everything had happened.

Within fifteen minutes of Theo calling Edwin, about half a dozen local residents rushed over to the library, armed with brooms, vacuum cleaners and other cleaning products, asking what they could do to help get the cafe ready for the evening opening celebrations.

And less than an hour later, the cafe was almost as good as new.

The local glazier couldn't fix the window straight away as he was out of town, so once me and Theo had boarded up the window, Jane and I found some thick card and some colouring pens, then made some bookish signs to make it look pretty.

The police also came quickly, which blew my mind. If this was London or even another town like Shamwick, we'd be lucky to see them by the next day. But I supposed crime happened so rarely in Sunshine Bay that they had to come and see how such an anomaly had happened.

Jane seemed better too, thank God.

I was on my way back from the toilets when I heard the loud smash, and when I saw the window, then the brick, and realised that Jane was in the cafe all alone when it happened and could've been hurt, it felt like I'd been stabbed in the gut.

It was crazy, considering we'd only started talking again a few weeks ago after being apart for years, but the thought of anything bad happening to her made me feel physically sick.

I should've stayed to help her. Maybe if I was there this wouldn't have happened, or I could've protected her somehow?

I didn't know who had done this, but when I found out, they'd pay for putting her in danger.

One thing I knew for sure was there was no way she'd be walking home alone tonight. Yeah, maybe Theo and Jess were right: it could be Theo's dad targeting the library. But what if it was someone trying to hurt Jane?

I couldn't see how, though. It was impossible not to like her. But I wasn't taking any chances.

'Thanks so much for your help.' Jess gave Glenda, Edwin and the other residents whose names I hadn't memorised yet hugs and kisses.

'I still can't believe it,' Maddie said. 'Stuff like this doesn't happen in Sunshine Bay.'

'And we'll all be on high alert to make sure it doesn't

happen again,' Edwin said. 'When one business is attacked, they attack us all.'

'Too right!' Glenda said defiantly.

'The police are investigating and I'll be doing my own investigation too,' Theo said. 'In the meantime we'll have cameras installed outside tomorrow. Don't worry. We'll do everything we can to keep everyone here safe.'

'Okay.' Maddie nodded. 'Well, now that everything's tidied up, shall we get the second celebration started?'

As the last guest left the library and I locked the main door, I breathed a sigh of relief.

We did it.

There was an even bigger turnout than at lunchtime and everyone was safe.

'All clear outside, Big T,' Theo's brother Ben said as he entered the cafe. 'Well, *hello*…' He walked over to Jane and stretched out his hand. 'I don't believe we've had the pleasure of being introduced. I'm Ben. Although, the ladies like to call me Big Ben.' He smirked at her, and I ground my jaw.

'Oh!' Jane smiled and my chest tightened. 'You're Theo's brother, right?'

In the end, I didn't have to keep watch outside. Ben was over from the US, so he'd come to help out instead.

I'd only spoken to him briefly, and although he seemed decent, I could tell that he was a massive flirt. Like Theo, he was a handsome motherfucker, so the last thing I wanted was him coming on to Jane.

Not that I had any claim to her, but didn't mean I had to like it.

'I sure am.' He ran a hand through his short dark hair. 'I'm the youngest Eaves brother. And the hottest.' He grinned.

'And clearly the most modest.' Jane raised an eyebrow.

'Just speaking the truth. I can tell you with absolute certainty that out of all my brothers, I'm the most experienced. But I can see you're a woman who likes scientific proof to back up bold claims, so anytime you'd like to find out more about my skills, just say the word.'

'Thanks, but I'm okay,' Jane said, her gaze flicking in my direction. As she flashed me a warm smile, I exhaled, relieved that she didn't seem to be falling for his charms.

'Suit yourself,' he shrugged, clearly unbothered, then went to stand with Theo.

'That seemed to go well,' Jane said as she walked towards me.

'It went brilliantly!' Maddie said. 'We sold out of all of the cupcakes and literally have three biscuits left!'

'We sold a lot of books too,' Theo added. Celeste had gone back to uni, so he'd helped man the bookshop. 'We'll need to do a new order on Monday.'

'Amazing!' Jess said. 'If only every day could be like this. Thanks for all of your help, everyone.'

'I second that,' Theo said. 'I know we were all a bit shaken up after the incident earlier, so I appreciate you staying to help the show go on.'

'No worries!' I said. 'We're a team. Do you want some help clearing up?'

'Most of it's done,' Maddie said.

'Yeah,' Jess added. 'Go home and get some rest. Same

for you, Jane. Enjoy the rest of your weekend and see you on Monday.'

'Okay, thanks, you too. I'll head off now, then,' she said.

'Wait!' I called out as she went towards the door. 'I'll walk you home,' I said quickly. 'See you on Monday, everyone.'

'Night, Jackson,' they chorused.

I stepped out into the corridor with Jane.

'It's okay. You don't need to,' she said.

'Jane.' I stood in front of her. 'If there's someone throwing bricks through the window, it means it's not safe. We need to take extra precautions.'

'I don't want to put you out.'

'You're not. We both live in the same town, so it's on my way. Even if it wasn't, I'd still do it. I'd feel better knowing you're safe. You don't want me to be up all night worrying about you, do you?'

'Course not.'

'So I'm walking you home, okay?'

'Okay.'

After we'd got our stuff from the office, we set off to the station.

'I still can't believe what happened,' she said.

'I know. This is the kind of shit I'd expect in Shamwick. Not in Sunshine Bay.'

'Exactly. I hate living in Shamwick.' She wrinkled her nose.

'Same.'

'At least you got to escape for years before you had to come back. Apart from the summers I worked at a library in Hastings and the year I was at the bookstore in London, I've been stuck there my whole life.'

'Huh?' I frowned. 'What about when you went to uni? Didn't you move out then?'

'Never went to uni.' She lowered her voice.

'What?' I stopped in my tracks. 'But you always wanted to go to UCL. Studying English lit there was your dream.'

We used to spend hours talking about the day we'd get to escape to uni. Jane always knew what she wanted to study. She loved books, so always said that it'd be more like doing what she loved every day rather than actually studying.

She even researched the books that she'd heard the undergraduates studied as part of the curriculum and started reading them in her spare time so that she could get a head start. That was when we were fifteen, so three years before she'd even be able to go to uni. *That* was how passionate she was about it.

'Well, dreams don't always come true.' She sighed heavily.

'What happened?' I said as we continued walking.

'I couldn't go. Dad decided to take over the corner shop and said I had to stay and help. Of course I was upset, but he made it sound like it'd only be a short-term thing and I didn't want to let him down, so I just thought I'd go the next year instead, but then my parents refused to help.'

'You're joking?'

'No.' She hung her head. 'Said they weren't going to waste money on me studying rubbish. That university was for toffs and I was getting ideas above my station.'

'But they knew how much you wanted to go!' I said,

anger bubbling in my chest. 'How much you loved studying and reading.'

'They didn't care.' She shrugged. 'And they only gave me a pittance for working in the shop all day. Told me I should be grateful because I got a roof over my head and food in my belly for "free", so working at the shop was the least I could do. So I stayed.'

Hearing that made me feel sick. I always knew her family was toxic and her dad was an arsehole, but what he'd done was plain evil.

Parents should want to support their child's ambitions, not stifle them.

Dad was a professor of mathematics at a top London university and when he was alive, he'd done everything he could to help me grow and succeed. Even when he was busy, in the evenings he'd sit and help me with my homework, or teach me something new.

He bought me every book I ever needed and more. I never wanted for anything. But he wasn't a pushy parent that was only interested in me becoming top of the class. He showered me with love and at the weekends I used to like riding my bike in the park with him at my side.

And even when we lost him, despite having to work multiple jobs to keep a roof over our heads, Mum still took an interest in me and how I was getting on at school. She encouraged me to apply for the scholarship which led to me securing a coveted place at Cambridge to study economics.

My parents were always my biggest cheerleaders. So to hear how shitty Jane's parents were to her made me so fucking mad.

'I'm so sorry you had to go through that. But you

know, if you're still interested, it's never too late. You could still get your degree. There are options. You could do it part-time, for example.'

'Can't,' she said quickly. 'Dad's going to… my family's going to need me, so I won't have time. And anyway, I'm working at the library now, which is a dream, so I don't need the degree.'

I was going to add that she didn't need to do it as a means to get a job. Because it'd always been her dream, she could do it to give her that sense of achievement. But I didn't want to push her. At the end of the day it was her life.

We walked inside the station. The next train was leaving in seven minutes, so we didn't have long to wait.

Once we got on the train, Jane sat down and I took the seat opposite.

'So, I started reading *Office Delight*,' I said, hoping that talking about the book I knew she loved would lift her spirits.

'Yeah?' Her face instantly brightened. 'What do you think so far? Where have you got up to?'

'I didn't get to read as much as I would've liked because…' My voice trailed off. 'I… I had other stuff to do.'

I'd spent the days we'd had off from the library visiting Mum and churning out multiple videos to send to Marcus.

There was no real change with Mum. Both days I'd gone to see her, she didn't recognise me. I attempted reading some of her favourite books, but I knew she couldn't follow the story. And everything else I tried to interact with her didn't work either, so in the end I just sat there and watched her stare out of the window.

When I'd got home in the evening, the last thing I'd wanted to do was start grinding in front of a camera, but I had to. My lack of enthusiasm must've come across, though, because not long after I'd sent the first batch of videos to Marcus, he called me back and said I needed to redo them and bring some 'fire' to my next attempt.

I called it a night, then banged out three new videos in the morning, which Marcus gave the green light.

Between seeing Mum, making the videos, chasing up the estate agents to see if they had any viewings lined up, cleaning the house and going shopping, I was too exhausted to read.

'Oh, right. But where did you get up to?' Jane repeated her question.

'I think chapter three? Virginia's just started working for Rocco.'

'You're so lucky!' she sighed. 'I wish I could read that book for the first time all over again. I can't wait to see what you think when you get to read more!'

'I'll keep you posted. I was hoping to read some more tonight, but I'm not sure if I'll have the energy.' I yawned, quickly covering my mouth.

'I know what you mean. I want to carry on reading my new book, but I'm shattered.'

'How do you decide what to read? With a whole library and bookshop dedicated to romance, there's so much choice. I have no idea what I'll read once I finish *Office Delight*.'

'I'm a mood reader,' Jane said. 'I have a massive TBR, so when I've finished a book, I just ask myself what I feel like reading. Sometimes I want something short, so I'll pick up a novella, sometimes I feel like a steamy sports romance and other times I might want some romantic suspense.'

'What are you reading now?'

'A cowboy romance.'

For the rest of the journey, Jane told me all about her book and how she'd stayed up way past her bedtime last night devouring it, so she absolutely couldn't do the same again tonight.

We got off the train and started walking towards her house.

'I'll be fine from here,' she said when we got to the bottom of her road.

'I said I'd walk you home, so I'm taking you to your door. I need to make sure you get inside safely.'

'I really appreciate that, but…' She paused. 'It's better if you don't. It's my—'

'*Your family,*' I interrupted. 'If your dad sees me…'

'I'm sorry.' She winced.

It may have been over a decade since we'd last seen each other, but it looked like some things hadn't changed.

When we were at school I was never 'allowed' to come to her house or knock at her door, and now, even though we were in our thirties, it was exactly the same.

'It's not for me to tell you what to do, but you're a grown woman, Jane. You can't let your dad or your family keep controlling your life like this. It's not right. You should be able to do what you want and be friends with who you want. They can't keep treating you like a child.'

'I know, I know. You're right. It's just until I save up

enough to leave and rent my own room. Until then, I have nowhere else to go, so I have to toe the line.'

My stomach clenched. I hated that she had to live like this.

If the circumstances were different, I'd say that she could rent the spare room at Mum's house.

It wasn't exactly a palace, but I knew Jane wouldn't judge and I'd feel a lot better knowing she was safe and well. But it was too complicated.

Doing that would mean I'd have to tell her about Mum.

Plus now that I had to film these videos, it'd be awkward. And what if somehow she found out? It was too risky. I needed to keep my work and private life separate.

'Right,' I said. 'I get it. I hope you get out of there soon, though. It can't be healthy to be in an environment like that.'

'Believe me, I know.'

'Text me when you get in, okay?'

'Okay. And, Jackson,' she said.

'Yeah?'

'Thank you.'

'You're welcome.'

As I watched her walk to her house, open the front door, then slip inside, my chest tightened.

One day I'd help her get out of that place.

She was too good for that family.

If her dad continued to control her and make her sad, I'd have to do something.

We might not have seen each other for years, but I still cared about Jane. A lot.

And now that I was back in her life, I wasn't going to let anyone hurt her.

17

———

JANE

My alarm sounded and I switched it off.

It was Monday morning and I hadn't slept well again.

I'd kept replaying the moment that I saw the brick flying through the window on Saturday night. It was almost like it'd happened in slow motion. I was frozen with shock because it was the last thing I expected.

Everything was still so confusing. Was someone targeting the library or were they aiming for me?

That didn't really make sense. As far as I could remember, I hadn't upset anyone. I was an eternal people pleaser. I always tried to avoid rocking the boat, so maybe Jess and Theo were right. It was someone targeting the library.

The fact that it might be Theo's dad was awful. But I more than most people understood what it was like to have a father who was rotten.

I was glad that we'd ignored his attempt to make us fail and gone ahead with the evening. It was a huge success and seeing the relief on Jess's face made everything worth it. I knew she was under a lot of financial pressure.

Another reason I didn't sleep well was because I was thinking about Jackson.

When he raced into the room and saw what had happened, genuine concern was etched on his face. He really cared. He wanted to make sure I was safe.

Throughout the evening, he kept checking on me, and when he offered to walk me home, of course I wanted to accept, but I knew he was tired and he'd already been so kind, so I didn't want to put him out.

Although talking about not going to uni was painful, I was touched that he'd remembered how important it used to be to me.

And I loved when we talked about books. I was so happy when he'd said he'd started reading *Office Delight* (and relieved when he didn't tease me about all the tabs). Then when I told him what I was reading, he listened intently. I felt like even if I gushed about the book for hours, he wouldn't mind.

Jackson made me feel like I could be myself. That was why it was so hard to tell him it was best that he didn't walk me to the door.

What I said was true, though. I didn't want to drag him into any family drama. If Dad saw him, he'd go mad and make my life here even more hellish than it was already.

No. I just had to toe the line.

I reckoned that if we kept doing these events at the library, we should be financially stable, and hopefully in a few months, once I knew my job was secure, I'd have enough for a deposit and the first two rent payments and could start looking for a place.

It wouldn't be easy, but I just needed to hold on for a bit longer.

After I'd showered, dressed and picked up my bag, I crept down the stairs, hoping I could avoid bumping into Dad. But just as I got to the bottom step, he came to the kitchen doorway.

'Jane. Get here. Now!' he snapped.

I sighed, then headed to the kitchen.

'You called,' I said flatly.

'You need to take a day off work tomorrow. We're going to get some family photos done for my campaign. The voters will want to see that we're a happy, stable family.'

'That's a joke,' I muttered.

'What did you say? Speak up, girl!'

'Nothing.'

I wouldn't be going. Not just because it was too short notice, but because there was no way I was going to lie for him.

'I've also arranged for Ricky to stand in as your boyfriend, so people don't think you're some sad cat lady.'

My jaw dropped.

Was he serious?

Of course he was.

'Best you take the whole day off, in case we can get the local paper to do an interview too.'

'No.' The word flew out of my mouth.

'What do you mean, *no*?' He clenched his jaw. 'I've told you what I need you to do and that's it. Whilst you're living under my roof and eating the food *I* pay for, you will do as I say.'

Anger fizzed in my stomach.

I hated this man so much.

I thought about what Jackson had said last night about standing up to my dad. He was right.

The idea of me doing a photoshoot with this man, smiling like we were all one happy family and pretending to share his archaic, toxic, disgusting views made me want to puke.

Yes, I was living under his roof, but I paid my way. I wasn't staying for free. And I was only here because I was desperate.

Sleeping in this house was one thing, but publicly declaring that I supported a bigot was a step too far.

'No,' I said, louder this time, but still avoiding his gaze.

'Are you defying me?' He ground his jaw.

My heart thundered against my chest. I'd never disagreed with him in person before and the shock was written all over his face.

'I said I'm not doing it!' I raised my voice, trying to stop my hands from shaking. 'I… I'm going.'

I raced towards the door.

'Jane!' he bellowed. 'Get back here, *now*!'

His heavy footsteps followed behind me, but luckily I was able to sprint through the door before he caught up.

I continued running, terror coursing through my veins and didn't stop until I'd reached the station.

My heart was racing dangerously fast. It was thundering before, but now after running the mile and a half here without stopping, I was gasping for breath. But I had to keep going. I didn't know if he'd come after me, so after taking my pass out of my bag, I rushed through the gates and to the platform, where luckily a train was waiting.

I dived into the closest carriage just as the doors were about to close, then flopped onto the seat, relief washing over me.

As my mind replayed what had happened, my chest tightened.

I couldn't believe he'd asked Ricky, my brother's awful deadbeat friend, to pretend to be my boyfriend. I wondered if he'd offered to pay him?

Just the fact that he was going to lie about me being coupled up and get someone to act as my partner was another reason he couldn't be trusted to hold a position of power.

God.

How did my life become like this?

Fat, salty tears rolled down my cheeks. And once they started falling, more followed until I was sobbing like a baby.

I turned to face the window, in an attempt to stop the other passengers from seeing me, reached into my handbag for a tissue and took off my glasses. As soon as I'd wiped away the tears, more fell.

The driver announced that the next stop was Sunshine Bay.

After putting my glasses back on, I dragged myself from my seat, feeling the eyes of the other passengers burning into me. As soon as the doors opened, I hauled myself off the train, then went through my bag again, hunting for another tissue, but I'd used them all up.

'Jane?' I heard my name being called and instantly recognised the voice without having to turn around.

It was Jackson.

At first I was happy. If ever I needed a friend and someone who could instantly lift my mood, it was now.

But then I remembered that I'd just spent the whole train journey crying and must look an absolute state. So the last person I wanted to see me at my worst was him.

'Jane!' he called out again and then before I knew it, he was standing in front of me. 'Oh my God. Are you okay? Have you been crying?'

Right on cue, another giant tear rolled down my cheek and my head dropped to the ground.

'Fuck!' Jackson gasped. 'What's wrong? What happened?' He reached forward and gently swiped his thumb over my cheek to wipe away the tear.

The sensation of his thumb against my skin made my whole body come alive.

'Talk to me.' He softened his voice. 'Come on. We don't have to open the library for another half an hour. Let's go for a walk on the beach. Okay?'

I nodded.

We walked in silence, and as I watched the waves gently roll towards the shoreline, my shoulders relaxed a little.

'It's so peaceful here, isn't it?' Jackson broke the silence.

I nodded again. He was right. Everything about this town was soothing. I wished I could live here instead.

Although I was feeling calmer, I still wasn't ready to talk. But at least I'd stopped crying. Jackson had some kind of magical ability to instantly put me at ease.

'Shall we sit?' Jackson gestured to the wooden bench.

I followed him and sat down, being sure to leave enough distance. I could already feel myself being drawn to Jackson and now wasn't the time to think about how attractive I found him. I needed to figure out what the hell I was going to do about my situation.

'So...' he said softly. 'Do you want to tell me what's wrong?'

This time, I shook my head.

I gazed out to the sea. Sometimes in the mornings when I came here I'd spot a boat in the distance, but today there was nothing. Just the deep, dark blue water stretching to the horizon.

'I hate seeing you cry,' Jackson said. I quickly raised my hand to my cheek. I hadn't even realised that thinking about staying at my parents' house less than a minute ago had made me start crying again. 'I know you're not ready to talk yet, so can I give you a hug? Whenever I felt sad, that's what my mum used to always do and it was like medicine. It instantly made me feel better. Do you want to try?'

Hearing that he wanted to hug me made my heart instantly bloom.

A hug was what I desperately needed right now. I felt so sad that I'd take a hug from anyone, but the fact that it was Jackson offering was the cherry on top.

I knew I shouldn't, though. I liked Jackson too much to be that close to him without my feelings getting out of control, but I was too sad, too broken to refuse.

I nodded, then looked up at Jackson. Our eyes locked and after a few moments, Jackson leant forward slowly, then wrapped his arms around me.

Oh. My. God.

This wasn't just a hug.

This was *everything*.

The warmth from his solid chest.

The feel of his muscular arms wrapped around my back.

His intoxicating scent.

Feeling his heart beat.

This was the most amazing thing.

Ever.

I wanted to stay here, in his arms, forever.

Right now, I felt safe. Cared for. Like someone actually had my back.

As I sat here, the sea breeze tickling my skin, a wave of happiness washed over me. I couldn't remember the last time someone had hugged me. Like, *really* hugged me. Not just a quick friendly hug, but a long, lingering embrace.

This year? No. Last year? In the last decade?

Maybe never.

It didn't matter, though, because I already knew that nothing could ever top this.

Jackson pulled away slowly and I instantly missed his warmth. He looked me in the eyes and I couldn't drag my gaze away.

I thought he was amazing before, but now, I didn't need a mirror to know that I was looking at him like he'd just invented cake and ice cream.

'Thank you,' I whispered.

'Did it work? Do you feel better?'

'Yes. Much better.'

'Good.'

'It was my dad,' I said, dragging off my glasses before my gaze dropped to my lap. 'He… he wants me to… he wants to become a local MP and he wants me to do some stupid photoshoot and interview playing happy families. But I can't do that! I don't want to be associated with him and his views. But I… I don't know what I'm going to do. I don't know how to get out of it.'

I started to blubber like a baby. I didn't even tell him the bit about my dad hiring my brother's friend to be my boyfriend. I couldn't. My emotions were already all over the place. I knew it was good to let everything out, but at the same time I was embarrassed. Jackson must think it was so pathetic that a grown woman like me was being ordered around by her dad.

Any minute now he was going to tell me to woman up, stop being so stupid and pull myself together.

But instead, without saying a word, he leant forward, wrapped his arms around me again and stroked my back gently.

'It's going to be okay,' he whispered. 'You'll get through this. I promise.'

Hearing his kind words made me sob onto his shoulder even more.

I didn't know how many minutes had passed, but eventually, I stopped crying. Probably because my body had no water left for tears.

Jackson still continued stroking my back in a soothing circular motion and my heart rate slowed. So did my breathing.

This time, I pulled away slowly, then gasped when I saw that his shoulder was completely soaked.

'I'm so sorry!' I said.

'Why?'

'Your shoulder! It's covered in tears and probably snot. God!' I winced.

'It's just a shirt.' He smiled. 'I have others. Don't worry about it. Normally I have a pack of tissues, but I forgot them today, so you're welcome to use my shirt instead.' He smiled, then reached up and wiped my damp cheek, just like he'd done at the station, and once again my body reacted to the heat from his thumb.

'Thanks for listening and not calling me a baby.'

'I'd never do that.' He shook his head. 'Look, I get it. I know it's not easy to escape when someone is so controlling and your options are limited. And I totally understand why you feel so conflicted. I respect you for being brave enough to tell him no. For staying true to yourself and your beliefs.'

'Thanks,' I said.

As we looked into each other's eyes in silence, so many thoughts raced through my mind.

First, how grateful I was for his kindness. Before he'd seen me at the station, I'd felt so low and genuinely hadn't known how I was going to get through the day. But now, I felt calmer.

Second, I thought again about how much I loved his dark, sparkly eyes. They were literally the most beautiful eyes I'd ever seen.

Third, I considered if it'd be weird to kiss him. Not on the lips, of course, I wouldn't want to make him uncomfortable. It was just that saying thank you alone didn't seem like enough. Maybe a cheek kiss conveyed more emotions?

In the end, I leant forward, my heart thundering against my chest, and this time, I wrapped my arms around him.

'You have no idea how much you've helped me or how much I appreciate your kindness. Thank you again.'

'You're welcome,' he whispered.

Just as I started to wonder how long I could keep holding him before I had to pull away, the alarm sounded on my phone.

'Shit!' I sprang back, put my glasses on, then looked at my watch. 'I need to open the library in five minutes. We're going to be late, I'll never be able to walk there in time!'

'Give me your keys.' Jackson held out his hands.

'What? Why?' I asked.

Jackson hadn't been given keys yet as he'd only recently joined. I was sure that'd change soon, though.

'We won't make it if we walk, but I'll get there in time if I run.'

'Oh. Okay. Thanks.' I trusted Jackson and I was sure Jess and Theo wouldn't mind. After reaching in my handbag and finding the keys, I handed them to him.

'See you there!' he said, sprinting off into the distance.

I'd always believed that men that swooped in and saved the day only existed in books or films, but Jackson had just proved that heroes really did exist.

If only fairy-tale endings happened in real life too.

18

———————

JACKSON

What a day.

After I clicked send on an email to Jess with a list of event ideas I wanted to organise, I leant back in the office chair and exhaled.

The day wasn't even over yet, but it'd been full on.

When I woke up and saw a message from Marcus saying that the new videos he'd posted were doing 'okay', but that I hadn't had many more subscribers, I already thought the day hadn't got off to a good start.

Then on the train I'd received a message from the estate agent cancelling the viewing that was scheduled for tonight—the first one I'd had for weeks.

That message was quickly followed by an email from Mum's care home, chasing up on the overdue payment.

At that point it was barely past eight in the morning and I thought things couldn't get worse. Then as I'd got off the train, I saw Jane and my mood instantly lifted.

I recognised her straight away. She was wearing a dark blue Lycra pencil skirt which clung to her curves.

And of course, her beautiful brown hair was tied up in a bun.

But then I noticed that it was looser than normal. And her posture and body language were different too.

Instead of radiating happiness and confidence like she always did in the library, Jane's shoulders were slumped and her head hung low. Somehow she didn't seem like herself.

When I'd called out and she hadn't answered, I'd raced to catch up with her, and when I'd seen her crying, it was like someone had taken a knife to my chest.

Even though she didn't open up until we got to the beach, I instantly knew the person who'd upset her was her fucking dad.

There weren't many people I hated in this world, but he was definitely at the top of my shit list.

What kind of father made his daughter cry?

When she said it'd be okay for me to hug her, relief washed over me. I just wanted to make her feel better.

But I wasn't prepared for how good it was going to feel.

Damn.

That hug was everything.

I loved feeling her heartbeat, the rise and fall of her chest as it pressed against mine and breathing in her sweet scent.

And I loved the way she held me like her life depended on it.

In those moments I felt like I was actually doing some good. I didn't feel like the deadbeat son who'd had to leave his job and couldn't afford to pay for his mum's care. I felt needed. Wanted. *Useful*.

But then thoughts I had no business having, like wanting to kiss Jane and stroke her hair or do whatever she needed to make her feel better, kept finding their way into my head. And that wasn't good.

The woman was upset. She needed a friend right now. Not someone who wanted to get into her knickers.

That was one of the reasons I pulled away, because as much as I'd ordered my body to behave, I was finding it difficult not to be affected by being close to her.

I was happy that the hugs seemed to help, though. The library had opened on time, and when I'd checked on Jane after lunch, she'd seemed okay.

Speaking of which, now that I'd completed my main tasks for today, I should check on Jane again and give her something I'd bought earlier to cheer her up. It wasn't much, but I hoped it'd bring a smile to her face.

After making a cup of tea in the office, I pulled a plate from the cupboard, opened the two packets of biscuits, arranged a selection from each onto the plate, then made my way to the library hall.

There were about a dozen members reading on the sofas and a couple perched on the comfortable window seats with their noses buried in books.

'Hi,' I whispered as I stood in front of the meet-cute desk.

Jane's head bolted upwards. She was so engrossed in whatever she was reading that she hadn't heard me come in.

'Hey.' She smiled and my heart swelled.

'Just checking how you are,' I said, then gestured for her to come outside into the corridor so we could talk without disturbing the members.

'I'm okay.' She nodded.

'Good. I brought you some tea and a little surprise.'

I handed her the plate, which I'd covered with a paper napkin. When she lifted it off, her face broke into a huge smile.

'Rich tea and digestive biscuits!' She beamed. 'My favourites! Thank you!'

Jane threw her arms around me and the gesture took me by surprise. Looked like we were friends who hugged now.

And I was definitely here for it.

'You're welcome,' I said, pulling away before my body got the wrong idea again.

We stood there, staring at each other in a trance.

God, she was beautiful.

I'd thought the same thing earlier on the beach. Even with tears staining her cheeks, she was stunning.

'I'd better get back.' She broke the silence.

'Yeah. Me too,' I said, knowing that it was for the best.

A few hours later, it was home time. Seeing as the viewing had been cancelled, I wanted to see Mum, but I couldn't. They'd only ask about the money.

'See you tomorrow.' Jane walked in the office and picked up her handbag and jacket.

'You're going home?' I asked.

'No choice. For once, I wish I was working the late shift, but after what happened yesterday, Jess has taken all of those with Theo, which means more time spent at home tonight.' Her shoulders slumped.

I had to say something. *Do* something to make her feel better.

'D'you know what you need?' I said.

'To win the lottery so I can buy my own place?' A small smile touched her lips.

'Well, yeah, that'd be nice too, but I was thinking you need a night out. Obviously not in Shamwick. I don't want to completely ruin your evening, but a night out right here in Sunshine Bay. You hungry?'

'A bit.'

'I've always wanted to try that fish and chips shop. Want to come with me? My treat!'

I was flat broke. The fifty pounds I had in my wallet was supposed to pay for my travel, lunch and dinner for the rest of the week, but this was an emergency. Jane needed me.

'Um, yeah!' She grinned. 'I mean, if you're sure?'

'Course!' I said.

Once we'd said bye to Jess and Theo, we headed over to May's Fish and Chips. I'd heard lots of people raving about this place, so I was looking forward to seeing if it lived up to the hype.

'Mademoiselle.' I opened the door and gestured for Jane to go inside.

'Why, thank you, kind sir,' she joked.

This was good. We'd only just arrived and already she seemed happier.

As the scent of freshly fried fish surrounded us, my mouth watered.

The restaurant had matching pine tables and chairs. There were silver metal fishes on the blue wood-panelled walls and the specials of the day were written in colourful chalk on a big blackboard.

'Hello, you two!' A lady with white skin and long blonde hair tied into a ponytail walked towards us, flashing a warm smile. She was wearing a blue-and-white striped apron and jeans. If I had to guess, I'd say she was in her forties. 'Lovely to see you, Jane. I'm Candace and you're Jackson, right?' She turned her gaze to me.

'Good to meet you, Candace, and yeah, I'm Jackson. How did you know?' I frowned.

'You're the talk of the town!' She smiled. 'All the women are gushing about you. They're calling you the new Theo! That or bus number two.'

'Huh?' My frown deepened.

'Bus number two!' she repeated as if the meaning was obvious. 'Y'know! It's like you wait ages for one bus and then two come at once.' I still didn't follow. 'But in this case, Sunshine Bay goes years without having any hunks and then all of a sudden two come along at once. First Theo, now you!'

'Ah… right. Erm, thanks?' I wasn't sure if I should be flattered that the town were talking about me.

'Sorry! That's objectification, isn't it? You're more than a piece of meat!' She chuckled. 'You'll have to forgive us. It's a small town and we don't get many newbies, so when we do, it's all anyone can talk about!'

'No worries,' I said.

'And we hadn't realised that you were already off the market!' She smiled and my face crumpled again. 'I see The Romance Library's already working its magic! Follow me. I've got a lovely table for two over here. Should I get a candle—y'know, to make it more romantic?'

As Jane and I took our seats, the penny dropped.

'No.' I shook my head. 'This isn't a date.'

'Oh, no?'

'No!' Jane and I chorused emphatically.

'Oh!' Her hand flew to her mouth. 'My mistake!'

'We're just friends,' Jane added.

'Right. Okay… Jess and Theo used to say the same thing…' She winked. 'Let me get you the menu.' As she left, Jane winced.

'Sorry! That was so awkward!' She shook her head.

'Why are you sorry?' I asked.

'Because here you are, taking me out to cheer me up, and now all the women in Sunshine Bay will be devastated when word spreads that you've been snapped up.'

'Ha!' I laughed. 'I'm sure they'll cope.'

I had zero interest in any of those women. I was off the market, but not because I was attached.

If my circumstances were different, there'd only be one woman I'd consider dating. And she was sitting right in front of me.

I doubted she was interested anyway and I still didn't even know if she was single.

'Here you go.' Candace returned with the menus.

'I'll just have cod and chips,' I said.

'Same,' Jane agreed.

'And drinks?' Candace asked.

'Tap water's fine,' I said. I hated that I had to think about saving money, but I didn't have a choice. Although Jess had asked me to start working full-time hours, I didn't know how long that would last and it still wasn't enough to cover Mum's fees. I needed to save every penny I could.

'That's good for me too,' Jane said.

'You can get a proper drink if you like?' Just because I was trying to conserve my limited funds, I didn't want to deprive Jane. I said I'd treat her and I meant it. Jane deserved whatever she wanted.

'No, no. After eating all those biscuits earlier, best not to have any sugary drinks.'

'Two cod and chips and glasses of tap water coming right up!' Candace said, then left.

'Thanks again for those biscuits. That was really kind of you.'

'You're welcome. I left them in a tin, so there's more whenever you want them.'

'I'll definitely take you up on that! So, I got you something.' Jane reached in her bag and pulled out four packages wrapped in brown paper and handed them to me.

'What are these?' I frowned.

'Those are your four blind dates.'

'Huh?'

'It's a bookish thing. Blind Date With a Book is when you have a book wrapped up so you don't know what it is. All it has is a clue on the front. When you're ready, you pick the book that matches your mood based on the clue, then unwrap it to find out what the book is so you can curl up with your "date" and start reading.'

'Ah, right. Got it.'

'You said the other day that you didn't know what you'd read once you finished *Office Delight*, so I bought you four books that I loved and thought you'd enjoy too.'

'Wow. Thank you.' I smiled. She must've bought them from the bookshop when I was either in the office or at lunch.

I looked at the first package, which said, 'Open when

you're feeling festive and want a romantic Christmas adventure'.

The second said: 'Open when you want an emotional book that will break you, but put you back together again in the most beautiful way'.

On the third secret package it said: 'Open when you want a romantic adventure that will make you laugh and warm your heart'.

And the final package said: 'Open when you need something short and very sweet'.

My heart swelled. I couldn't believe she'd done this for me. I knew that Jane was trying to save every penny she had to start renting her own place, so the fact that she'd spent her money on me, put so much thought into what books to get me and gone to the trouble to wrap them up and write these clues meant so much. I was excited to find out what books she'd chosen.

'As soon as I start reading them I'll let you know. Speaking of books you love, I read more of *Office Delight*,' I said, eager to hear her reaction.

'Yeah?' Jane almost jumped out of her seat with excitement.

'Yeah. And it's pretty steamy.'

'It is!'

'But that Rocco is a bit of dick sometimes, no?'

'He's an alpha-hole at the beginning, yeah.'

'*Alpha-hole*?' My face crumpled.

'It's a romance term for an alpha male who's also a bit of an arsehole.'

'And women like that?'

'In a book it's okay. As long as he redeems himself and the grovel is good,' Jane said.

'I'm guessing "the grovel" is the technical term for a hero's apology in romance novels, right?'

'Yeah. It's when he begs for forgiveness and tells the heroine how she's changed him for the better. When you start reading a book about a hero like that, you kind of know that he won't be an arsehole for the whole novel, so somehow that makes it more acceptable. Having a man who's domineering and in control is… kind of…' She blushed. '*Hot.*'

'So when he orders her to get on her knees and suck his cock, that's… hot?' I frowned.

When I'd got to that part whilst I was reading the book on the beach at lunchtime and I'd seen that Jane had highlighted that section and put asterisks in the margins, I'll admit, it sent a jolt of electricity straight to my dick.

Then I shamefully started picturing Jane on her knees with her lips wrapped around my cock, so I had to shut the book. I couldn't risk embarrassing myself by getting hard in a public place in broad daylight.

Judging by how many tabs Jane had sticking out from the rest of the book, it was only going to get hotter, so it was best that I didn't pick that book up again until I was at home, in bed alone.

'Um…' She blushed again. 'Yeah. It kinda is.'

'So you don't think it's demeaning to Virginia?'

I always tried to be respectful when I slept with women and couldn't imagine *ordering* them to blow me.

'I hear what you're saying. And on the surface, I'd agree with you. But remember, Virginia isn't under any obligation to say yes. If she doesn't want to do it, she could tell him to sod off.'

'But maybe she feels obligated, because Rocco's her boss and she's just started a new job?'

'Ordinarily, yes. But it's obvious there's a mutual attraction there. She wants him just as much as he wants her. And actually, in that situation, it's *Virginia* who's in control. Rocco is desperate for her. She's the only woman he wants. The only woman who can give him what he truly needs, so actually in that scene, *she's* the powerful one. *She* has the control. Like when she starts… y'know, when she…' Jane's eyes dropped to the plate.

'When she slides him in her mouth,' I said, finishing her sentence because I sensed she was embarrassed.

'Yeah, when she does *that*, she realises how much he wants her. How at that moment she could probably get him to do whatever she asked. She's the one calling the shots.'

'Hmmm.' I nodded. 'Good point. I hadn't thought about it that way.'

'That's why I love talking about books with other people. Everyone picks up on different things. When I was reading *Office Delight*, I loved discussing my favourite scenes with Jess. She did the same with Theo.'

'Like a book club discussion,' I added.

'Exactly! I'm looking forward to our first silent reading party on Friday. I bet everyone's going to love talking about books during the breaks and at the end of the night,' Jane gushed.

'Two cod and chips.' Candace appeared and put the plates on the table.

'It smells so good! Thanks,' I said.

'Tastes even better!' Candace said. 'Enjoy!'

It didn't take long for us to polish off our food.

In between bites, we talked more about *Office Delight*,

then Jane updated me on the cowboy romance, which she planned to finish tonight.

The conversation flowed so easily. We went from one subject to the next whilst Candace kept us topped up with water.

When she came over with the bill and I looked around, we were the last two people left in the restaurant. I'd been so fixated on Jane, I hadn't even realised. The time had flown by.

'What time do you close?' I asked.

'About twenty minutes ago.' Candace smiled.

'Shit. I'm so sorry.' I jumped up.

'We didn't mean to keep you,' Jane added.

'It's fine! You two were getting on so well, I didn't want to interrupt. When you see two *friends* staring into each other's eyes for hours, it'd be criminal to break them apart.' She smirked.

Had we been staring into each other's eyes?

I mean, of course I thought Jane was fucking beautiful, but I hoped I hadn't given her or anyone else the wrong idea.

'We should go.' I stood up. I reached into my wallet and pulled out the money to cover the bill.

'Wait. Let me pay half,' Jane said.

'No.' I put my hand over the money. 'I've got this.'

'*Awww*, paying for the meal too. So *romantic*.' Candace smiled mischievously again.

'That's really kind, thank you,' Jane said. 'I had a difficult day, so Jackson's just being a good friend and helping to cheer me up.'

'How lovely,' Candace said.

'The food was fantastic. Thanks for everything.' I

edged towards the door before she started making any more suggestive comments about me and Jane being more than just friends.

'You're welcome! Hope to see you both again soon. Enjoy the rest of your evening together.' She winked, then strutted off to the kitchen.

'She's so cheeky!' Jane said. As we stepped out onto the street a gust of wind hit us and Jane shivered.

'You cold?' I asked.

'A bit,' she said. 'That's the thing with being so close to the sea. The evenings are a bit chilly. If I'd known I was staying out so late I would've brought a scarf or a thicker jacket. Thanks again for tonight. I had a brilliant time.'

My heart swelled. Mission accomplished.

Jane shivered again.

'Here.' I whipped off my jacket and placed it over her shoulders. 'This will keep you warm.'

'I can't take your jacket! What about you?'

'I'm good. I've got plenty of hair on my chest to keep me warm.'

'Have you?' she asked, then her face dropped. 'Sorry! I shouldn't be asking about your naked chest.'

'I was the one who mentioned it, don't worry. And, no, I was only joking. I don't have any hair on my chest.'

'Oh… er… good to know.'

Jane's eyes fixed on mine and she swallowed hard.

We held each other's gaze. I imagined Jane running her hands over my chest. Then my mind pictured my chest pressed against hers, like it was this morning, but skin to skin.

I wondered how it'd feel to run my hands over her breasts.

To suck on her nipples.

To…

Shit.

'Do you know what time the train leaves?' I said, trying to drag my thoughts out of the gutter.

These fantasies about Jane were becoming way too frequent. In the beginning, I noticed they happened whenever I spent a lot of time with her. Back then they were limited to admiring her body and how beautiful and smart she was.

Then I'd thought about her when I was making my videos and things started escalating. It seemed like there was rarely a time I *wasn't* thinking about Jane.

Thanks to reading *Office Delight*, I hadn't been able to stop imagining her sucking me off and now me burying my tongue between her legs.

And I still thought about how much I'd love to take her up against the bookcases.

If ever I got the chance, I'd start by…

'In twenty minutes, I think,' Jane said and I snapped out of my thoughts.

Jesus.

What the hell was wrong with me?

'Uh, okay. Cool,' I said, quickly pulling back the sleeve of my shirt to look at my watch. 'We've got plenty of time.'

For the rest of the walk, Jane was silent. I hadn't realised at first because I was so busy chastising myself for allowing my fantasies to get so X-rated. Jane was a great girl. She would be horrified if she knew I was imagining all the different ways I wanted to fuck her.

I needed to keep my distance.

I knew Jane was going through shit at home and I was glad that taking her out tonight helped to cheer her up, but I needed to find other ways to help her that didn't involve spending more time with her. Especially outside of work.

From now on, I'd just stick to general conversation in the library. We could talk about books, but I needed to avoid discussing the sex scenes like we did at dinner. Because reading about the kinds of things that Jane found hot just made me imagine us acting those things out. *Together*.

Which was definitely a *me* problem.

Just because Jane liked when a man—no, a book character—told the female main character to *get on her knees and take this dick like a good girl*, it didn't mean she wanted a man to do that in real life.

And it definitely didn't mean she wanted to do that with *me*.

'Are you okay?' I turned to face her and saw the lenses of her glasses were misty and tears were rolling down her cheek. Shit. Had I done or said something? I hoped she hadn't somehow realised what I was thinking and got upset.

No. It couldn't be that.

'What's wrong?' I asked.

'I can't go home,' she said. 'I… it's going to be awful. Dad will be so mad and…'

I stopped and stood in front of her. Jane's hands were shaking and terror was written all over her face. My chest instantly tightened.

'Does he ever hit you?' I clenched my fist.

'No.' She shook her head. 'He doesn't, but…'

'I get it.' I nodded. 'He doesn't need to. He makes the

atmosphere hostile. The way he controls you is still a form of abuse. It's not right that you have to deal with that. Listen, would it help if I come home with you and tried talking to him?'

'No!' Her head shot up and her eyes bulged. 'Thank you, but that'd only make it worse. I don't know what I'm going to do!' She started crying.

'Don't you have somewhere else to go. Like a friend or a boyfriend…' My words hung in the air.

I'd wanted to find out so many times whether she was dating but it didn't seem right to ask. Bringing it up now wasn't exactly good timing either, but the priority was to get her somewhere safe.

'I don't have one,' she sobbed.

Relief washed over me that there wasn't a man in her life and then I chastised myself. This wasn't about my feelings for her. It was about keeping her safe.

'And friends?'

She shook her head and then started sobbing so much she was practically hyperventilating.

I'd never seen her like this before. She was even more upset now than when I saw her this morning.

A pain ripped through my chest. I couldn't bear seeing her like this. It was fucking awful.

'Come home with me,' I blurted out.

'What?' Her eyes widened with shock.

Shit.

That was a bad idea.

A very, very bad idea.

What the hell had I just done?

19

JACKSON

I'd just finished telling myself that I needed to keep my distance from Jane. So inviting her to stay overnight at my place was one of the stupidest ideas I'd ever had.

My life was already complicated enough without adding to it.

But the way she was freaking out was killing me.

I couldn't stand seeing Jane upset and I couldn't let her go back to that controlling narcissist. It'd be like leading a cute puppy to get slaughtered.

'What about your girlfriend? Won't she mind?'

'I don't have a girlfriend.'

The fact that Jane had asked me that question was interesting. Had she been wondering if I was single just like I'd done about her, or did the thought come into her head for the first time just now?

'Oh.' Her brow furrowed like she was surprised. 'I hate to put you out, but I don't know what else to do.' She lifted up her glasses, then wiped her eyes and cheeks with the back of her hand.

'It's okay,' I said. 'Tomorrow we can ask around town. See if anyone has a room they can rent you.' I had to make it clear that this was just an arrangement for tonight.

'Yeah.' She nodded.

We spent most of the train journey in silence. I was mentally working out how to bring her home without telling her about Mum and making sure she didn't somehow find out about the videos.

It should be okay. I'd woken up extra early to clean the house because I thought I had a viewing.

'You're in the same house?' Jane said as we turned down my street.

Wow. Although she'd never been inside because her dad and brother watched her like a hawk and Shamwick was full of gossips, she still remembered the road I lived on.

'Yeah.'

'Will your mum mind me staying?' she asked and my stomach dropped.

'No. She's, er… away.' I put the key in the door and stepped inside.

'Oh, okay. Has she gone anywhere nice?'

I dropped the keys on the hallway table and tried to gather my thoughts.

'If you wait in the living room, I'll just change my sheets so you can have my bed and I'll sleep on the sofa,' I said, quickly changing the subject.

'No!' Jane shook her head firmly. 'Thanks, but you've already done enough for me today and you're helping me out massively by letting me stay, so *I'm* sleeping on the sofa. No arguments. I just need a blanket and I'll be fine.'

'But I'm not sure how comfortable it is.'

'It'll be fine! My bed at my parents' is awful, so I'm sure this is much better. *Please.*'

'Okay,' I relented reluctantly.

It didn't seem right to let a woman sleep on the sofa when there was a bed in the house. Mum's room was off limits. It'd been stripped of most of her belongings as they'd been taken to the home to make her feel comfortable, so if Jane went inside, she'd instantly know something wasn't right.

'Back in a sec.'

I raced up the stairs, checked Mum's door was shut, then pulled out some stuff from the linen cupboard.

Jane would probably need something to sleep in too. I went in my drawer and took out a T-shirt. Maybe she'd prefer a shirt? I pulled one off a hanger and added it to the pile.

'Here you go,' I said, returning to the living room. 'Fresh sheets, towels, a blanket and a duvet in case you get cold in the night and I thought you'd need something to sleep in, so I brought you a T-shirt and a shirt. Choose whatever's comfortable. There's obviously shower gel and toothpaste in the bathroom. I'll check if I have a new toothbrush. Anything else you need?'

'No, all of this is amazing. Thanks again. I've got a toothbrush in my toiletries bag.'

'Cool. Wanna use the bathroom first?'

'You sure?' she asked.

'Yeah. I'll make up the sofa whilst you're in there.'

'Jackson.' She looked up at me and my heart raced. 'Honestly, I don't know how to thank you.'

'Don't worry about it. That's what friends are for, right?'

I didn't know if I mentioned the whole friends bit for her benefit or mine. Definitely mine. I needed a reminder to keep my dick under control.

'Yeah. Hopefully one day I can return the favour somehow…' She bit her lip and blushed.

Did she mean…?

Nah. I pushed the thought that there was some kind of innuendo in how she was offering to return the favour out of my mind.

Jane would never say something like that. She was sweet and pure. Unlike my dirty mind.

She didn't need to do anything, sexual or otherwise. I was genuinely doing this to help her. It was the right thing to do, that was all.

Jane pulled a toiletries bag out of her handbag, picked up the towels and the T-shirt, then walked towards the door.

'Bathroom's the first door on the left at the top of the stairs.'

'Thanks.' She nodded.

I made up the sofa, went to my room, then realised I'd left my bottle of water in the kitchen.

Just as I left my room to head downstairs, Jane came out of the bathroom.

Her wet hair was down and it almost reached the middle of her back. I hadn't realised how long it'd grown because it was always tied up.

Jane wasn't wearing her glasses, so I had a clear, unobstructed view of her big, beautiful brown eyes and fuck. She was wearing my T-shirt.

As I took in the sight of her creamy skin and the way my T-shirt skimmed her bare thighs, my dick thickened.

Especially when I thought about the fact that she couldn't be wearing any underwear underneath.

Jesus.

The thought of Jane's bare breasts and pussy being so accessible sent my mind into overdrive.

'Oh!' She looked up. 'Didn't see you there! No surprise, really, with my eyesight.'

'Sorry, I didn't mean to scare you.'

'You didn't.'

My gaze dropped to the T-shirt again. Her nipples were now poking through the fabric.

Was she cold or…

Nah. I dismissed my thoughts again and quickly dragged my gaze back up to her face before she caught me looking at her like a pervert.

Our eyes locked and once again my mind drifted. I imagined stepping forward, scooping her up and carrying her to my bed, where I'd lay her down and…

For fuck's sake. This really had to stop. Jane was here because she was upset about going home. She wasn't here to be ogled.

'You… how was the shower?' I stuttered.

'Great! I feel so much better. Anyway, bathroom's free. I'm going to bed. Sleep well.'

'You too,' I said, warning myself not to look at her arse as she walked away.

Too late…

Shit.

Jane had told me to sleep well, but something told me that I was about to spend most of the night dreaming about her.

20

JANE

As I slowly opened my eyes and took in my surroundings, confusion washed over me.

Where am I?

Then it all came back to me. I was at Jackson's.

I still couldn't get over how kind he'd been to me. Hugging me on the beach, running to open up the library, bringing me my favourite biscuits, taking me out for dinner. Then literally saving me by inviting me to stay.

Jackson was top-tier book boyfriend material.

Not that he was my boyfriend, of course.

When Candace had said she thought we were a couple, I'd been mortified. He had been too, which was obviously why he'd set the record straight so quickly.

I'd done the same, telling Candace we were just friends because I didn't want to embarrass Jackson or make things any more awkward because I assumed he had a girlfriend. I was so shocked when he said he didn't.

I mean, yeah, he'd never mentioned having one, but look at him.

How was someone like *him* still single?

He was unbelievably kind and caring too. So much so that he even worried about whether Rocco, a fictional male character, was disrespecting Virginia by telling her to get on her knees and give him a BJ.

When he mentioned that scene, my whole body sparked. I'd reread it dozens of times, wishing that I had the power to drive a man that I liked that crazy with desire.

If Virginia wasn't massively attracted to Rocco and into the whole dirty talk thing, or if he was pressuring her to do something she didn't want to, then of course it'd be creepy. But I knew they were so hot for each other.

And because I'd already read the whole book, I also knew that it wouldn't be long before Rocco was on his knees, returning the favour to Virginia and then some.

In fact, Rocco went down on her a lot more than she did for him and those scenes were even hotter. They'd lived rent-free in my head for weeks. Now that I thought about it, I'd even written some comments in the margins. *Cringe*. There was no way that Jackson wouldn't read those.

Having a man go down on me was one of my ultimate fantasies. But I'd also thought about what it'd be like to do that to a man.

When I read about blow jobs in romance novels, there seemed to be a lot of licking, sucking and head bobbing, but I had no idea if you were supposed to follow a particular technique and, if a guy was big, how to fit it in without gagging.

And what did a dick taste like? Some characters swallowed the man's semen, but I also wondered how much came out and what that tasted like too.

Embarrassment washed over me. It was shameful that I didn't know the answers to these questions at my age.

When I'd come out of the shower yesterday and seen Jackson in the hallway, for a second I'd wondered what it'd be like if he picked me up and carried me to his bedroom.

Even though I had zero experience, I'd get on my knees for him in a heartbeat. I'd almost accidentally said as much when I'd thanked him and said that one day I hoped I could *return the favour*.

Thankfully he hadn't realised what I meant. Anyway, even if he did, it wouldn't exactly be a tempting offer. What man would want to get their dick sucked by a woman who had no idea what she was doing? I'd probably end up scraping or biting him with my teeth.

Maybe I should practise on a banana to see if I left any teeth marks.

I was supposed to be working out a way to get some experience, but with all of the stuff going on at home, I'd been distracted.

My alarm went off, pulling me out of my thoughts. I was dying for the loo, so quickly raced up the stairs.

Just as I was about to touch the bathroom door handle, the door opened and I came face to face with Jackson.

Oh. My. God.

I said that I came face to face with Jackson, but what I really meant was that I came face to face with his chest.

His *bare* chest.

I could tell from the way his clothes clung to his body that he was muscular but I'd never imagined *this*.

Gone was the slim, boyish chest I'd seen whenever we

went to swimming classes at school. And in its place were perfectly defined pecs, abs and *everything*.

It was so impressive that I wanted to reach out and touch it to see how it felt.

This was the kind of chest that hot underwear models had. Not *real* people. Not people I knew and went to school with.

My eyes followed a drop of water as it trickled down his chest, along his abs, until it disappeared beneath the white towel wrapped around his waist.

I swallowed hard as desire coursed through me.

Underneath that towel was Jackson's dick.

And I bet it was magnificent.

Not that I had anything to compare it to, of course. But I bet it was like the ones I read about in romance novels: long and thick.

A fantasy of me dropping to my knees and wrapping my lips around it flew into my head. I bit my lip and my nipples instantly hardened. I could already feel the wetness pooling between my legs as I pictured him gripping the back of my head and pushing himself deeper into my mouth. Just like Rocco did to Virginia.

'S-sorry,' Jackson said.

My eyes flicked up to his face for a second, but as beautiful as it was, it wasn't Jackson's face I wanted to admire right now.

Don't look at his chest.

Don't look at his chest.

Don't look...

My gaze dropped to his chest, where it lingered for a few seconds before quickly moving back up to meet his eyes, which were the colour of charcoal.

We stared at each other for I don't know how long. I was hypnotized. I couldn't draw my eyes away from him.

'I should…' He broke the silence and took a step back to create some distance. 'I… we should leave soon.'

'Yes!' My voice came out high-pitched. '*Totally*. I… I'm sorry. I didn't know you were naked. No, that came out wrong,' I babbled. 'It's not like you're standing here with your bits out. Although technically you are, naked underneath, *that*…' I gestured towards his towel, then swallowed hard when I saw the outline of a very large, very hard-looking cock straining against the fabric.

Wait.

He was *hard*.

Had *I* made that happen?

No. Must be that morning wood thing men got. I thought that was just when they woke up, but what did I know?

'I…' My brain turned to mush as I started to imagine what Jackson's erection would look like. 'I should've knocked.'

'It's fine,' he growled. His voice was even deeper than normal, which was hot. 'I should go.'

He stepped forward, his body now just inches away from mine.

'Yeah.' I swallowed again before realising that I was blocking the doorway. 'Sorry!' I stepped back in the hallway to give him room to get out.

'Meet downstairs in about half an hour?' he said.

'Okay.'

I raced into the bathroom and locked the door behind me.

Bloody hell. I'd never been so turned on in my life.

Thanks to the desire racing through me right now, I literally felt like my blood was on fire.

Jackson's chest.

Jackson's hard dick poking out from the towel.

I wished I could've touched it.

A pain shot through my bladder and I remembered that I needed to wee.

After plonking myself on the toilet and emptying my bladder, I went to wipe myself.

I was soaking. Looked like I needed another shower.

I looked over at the showerhead. The urge to use it to relieve myself was strong.

Typically, if I ever felt the *need* (usually after reading something spicy), I would use my hands in bed. But I could never fully relax, because I wasn't allowed to have a lock on my bedroom door, so the only place I knew I was really safe to touch myself was in the shower.

I'd take my phone in with me and play music to drown out any noise, just in case the shower stream didn't cover it.

But even though I wanted to, it wouldn't be right to do that in Jackson's house. And I'd left my phone downstairs.

The vision of him standing there in a towel was going to play on repeat in my head until the end of time.

No. I shouldn't.

I tried to distract myself by thinking about other things. I took in the sight of the faded avocado-green tiles which matched the bathroom sink and toilet.

Then my eyes drifted to the shelves, where there was a bottle of shaving gel, and body lotion in dark packaging. I couldn't see any of his mum's products. Everything on display was very clearly Jackson's. Maybe his mum preferred to keep her stuff in the cupboard under the sink or in her room.

I got off the toilet seat and washed my hands. But when I looked at myself in the mirror, my rock-hard nipples were poking through Jackson's T-shirt. I lifted the fabric up to my nose and inhaled. It smelt like him. Fresh and spicy.

I rubbed my nipple with one hand and the other trailed along my thigh, then dipped between my legs. As my fingers skimmed my throbbing clit, a moan escaped from my mouth.

Then I knew I didn't have a choice. I had to touch myself in the shower.

Immediately.

My head was spinning. My body was aching.

If I didn't find a way to release the pressure building inside of me, I wouldn't be able to concentrate at work today.

I stepped into the shower, turned it on, adjusted the setting on the showerhead, then held it in front of my pussy as I replayed the image of Jackson in just his towel.

But this time I created my own fantasy.

This time, when he stepped forward, Jackson's towel dropped to the floor and he really was standing there naked.

Then he peeled his T-shirt off my body, and this time, *he* dropped to his knees and buried his head between my legs.

As I ran my fingers over my clit, I imagined it was Jackson's tongue. The water pressure added to my arousal and before I knew it, I felt the ripples of pleasure building.

'Yes,' I panted, circling my sensitive spot and bringing

the shower head closer. Desperate for more friction, I increased the pressure of my fingers rubbing against my clit. 'Oh, Jackson, yes… just like that. More.'

The wave ripped through me like a tsunami and I cried out before sliding down to the base of the shower and slumping against the wall.

Wow.

I hadn't realised how much I'd needed that.

'Jane?' Jackson knocked at the door. 'I thought I heard you call me. You okay?'

Crap.

'I'm fine,' I replied quickly, trying to catch my breath. 'Just finishing in the shower.'

Literally.

Shame washed over me. I couldn't believe I'd just masturbated in Jackson's shower.

What was wrong with me?

He'd heard me call his name. Imagine if he knew what I was doing.

My attraction to Jackson was totally out of control.

And I had no idea how to stop it.

21

—————

JACKSON

If I thought Jane looked fucking incredible in my T-shirt, then the sight of her walking around the library dressed in my shirt set my blood and my dick on fire.

When Jane realised she didn't have any clean clothes to wear to work, she asked if I minded if she wore my shirt.

Mind?

Of course I didn't.

It was one of the sexiest things I'd ever seen.

As I stood at the entrance of the library hall, I couldn't take my eyes off her.

My shirt completely dwarfed her. It was so big it reached her knees. Underneath she was wearing the spare pair of tights she apparently kept in her bag and had my belt around her waist. And I can't explain why, but seeing her in my clothes made me hard. Just like when I thought about her last night.

As I suspected, I couldn't sleep. I spent most of my

time in bed replaying the vision of her in my T-shirt as she came out of the bathroom.

I couldn't get it out of my head, which is why I woke up early to take another shower, because my fantasies about Jane had gotten so out of control that I had to release. I thought that once I'd exploded in my hands and showered off, I'd be able to get through the day.

But then when I stepped out of the bathroom and I saw Jane standing there, wearing my T-shirt again and looking hotter than hell, I knew I was back to square one.

Then something strange happened.

Jane looked at me.

She didn't just glance at me, then look away like she normally did. Her gaze roamed from my chest all the way down to my dick as she undressed me with her eyes.

I kid you not.

At first I thought I was imagining things, but *nope*. She definitely checked me out, then of course, when I realised, I got hard.

And I know for a fact that she knew I was turned on.

I thought she'd be horrified, but she just stared, then bit her lip like she was imagining something.

Now I could be wrong, but I think she was imagining me naked.

Before I would've said there was no way that'd happen. But when she started stuttering about me being naked and mentioned my 'bits', I thought it was actually a possibility.

Anyway. It didn't matter.

I'd said it before and I'd say it again: I couldn't go there. Not after last time. Not with all of the shit I had going on in my life.

I didn't have time to think about whether Jane liked me or not. I needed to spend that time and energy working out how to get myself out of my shitty financial situation.

My phone vibrated and I pulled it out of my pocket.

It was Marcus.

MARCUS

> Sorry, mate, but these videos aren't working. I know you're not gonna like it, but if you want to make money, you're gonna have to get your dick out.

> I've been looking at what videos are most popular on this website and the ones where there's proper full-on nudity perform better.

> I'm not working late today (thank God), so send me some new videos by seven thirty-ish and I'll get them edited and uploaded tonight.

As I read the messages, I swallowed hard. I really, really didn't want to strip on these videos, but I was out of options. It wasn't like I was expecting to get hundreds of thousands of subscriptions and become a millionaire overnight, but I'd hoped we'd be doing better than we were. And I knew these things normally took time, but that was a luxury I didn't have. We'd tried different videos and nothing was sticking.

When Marcus had first suggested I strip, I'd told myself I couldn't do it because I didn't want to disappoint my parents and dishonour Dad's memory. But now I realised that if I didn't do it and Mum lost her place at the home, I'd be letting her down, which was something Dad definitely wouldn't have wanted.

I had less than two weeks to bring Mum's account up to date at the care home, so I had to try.

It was just a dick, right? No big deal. Half of the population had one. And at least I wouldn't be showing my face, so apart from Marcus, no one would know it was me.

I finished work by five, so if I left on time, I could probably film a few videos before seven thirty.

As long as I didn't have any distractions.

I shoved my phone in my pocket, then looked up and saw Jane staring at me from across the other side of the library.

I waved, hoping she hadn't seen me leering at her five minutes ago. She smiled, then came over.

'Everything okay?' Jane whispered as she stepped into the corridor.

'Yeah. Just wondered if you'd spoken to the B&B lady about getting a room there for tonight?'

If I needed to film, I definitely had to be home alone. But at the same time, I needed to make sure that Jane would have somewhere to stay.

'I did and she said normally she has at least one room free, but there's a wedding nearby, so she's fully booked.'

'Shit.'

'Jess said I could've crashed at hers, but Theo's brother Ben's staying there at the moment. They're never sure whether he's going to come home or sleep somewhere else, so it's a bit tricky. But she's asked Edwin to see if he knows anyone. Hopefully I'll hear something later.'

'Okay. Keep me posted,' I said.

'Will do. And thanks again for the shirt. I really like it!' She smiled.

'It suits you.'

It definitely did.

Although I'd be lying if I said I wouldn't prefer to see how she looked without it.

'Jackson.' I turned round and saw Jess approaching. 'Can I have a word?'

'I'd better go,' I said.

'See you later,' Jane replied.

'Yeah,' I said, already mentally counting down the minutes.

I should be focusing on speaking to Jess, but I couldn't resist watching Jane walk away.

Fuck. I had it bad.

Snapping out of my thoughts, I turned and followed Jess to the office.

'I'm just about to call my friend Sarah and thought you might want to speak to her too about the social media.'

'Okay, great.'

Jess dialled the number, then put it on loudspeaker.

'Hey, you!' Jess said. 'How's it going?'

'Okay,' Sarah sighed. I'd only ever liaised with her on email, so it was good to put a voice to the messages.

'What's up?'

'Just the usual. Feeling stuck. I hate my job. I hate this town. It's boring.'

'I'm so sorry. You know I'd hire you in a heartbeat to do our social media full-time if I could. Things are tough right now, though.'

'I know. I'm just having a bad day. I know it's not the worst place to live. I've got a lot to be thankful for. It's just there's no inspiration whatsoever. How am I supposed to fulfil my dream of writing a romance novel when I'm living in a dump like this?'

'So you're going to do it, then?' Jess's eyes widened. 'Sarah, I've got Jackson with me.'

'Hey, Sarah!' I said.

'Oh, hey, Jackson. Nice to put a voice to the emails.'

'I was just thinking the same.' I smiled. 'So you're a romance author? Sorry. I hope it's okay to ask.'

'I'm a *wannabe* romance author. It's something I've always wanted to do, but never told anyone in case they laughed at me.'

'She only told me a couple of weeks ago,' Jess said. 'I told her she should go for it. If anyone knows about romance books, it's Sarah. She reads tons of them.'

'It's the only excitement I get!' Sarah laughed. 'I'm still waiting for you to set me up with one of the sexy Eaves brothers.'

'Ben's still around.'

'Dammit. I wish I could get down there. But I've got so much on at work and a load of boring family events I have to go to. My life sucks so hard right now!'

'Well, on the plus side, you're doing a great job with the social media. Do you want to fill Jackson in on your plans and then we can speak later about other stuff?'

'Okay.'

Sarah told me about the posts she had planned to drum up some more bookings for the silent reading party this Friday. Plus she said she planned to create and post some TikTok videos and Instagram reels to promote the autumn-themed books we were selling.

'That all sounds great,' I said. 'If there's anything I can do to help, like taking photos of the books, just shout.'

'Will do,' Sarah said. 'Good luck tonight.'

'Thanks,' Jess said and after I said bye to Sarah and Jess hung up, I wondered what was happening this evening. Maybe it had something to do with the attack on the library.

'Are you still okay to keep doing full-time hours?' Jess said.

'Definitely.' The extra money would come in handy. 'I meant to ask, has there been any update with the investigation? Are the police any closer to finding out who smashed the window?'

Just like he'd promised, Theo had arranged to have cameras installed outside, but we still had to stay vigilant.

'Not yet. That was kind of the next thing I wanted to ask: are you able to work late tonight? Theo's going to see his dad to ask whether he hired someone to sabotage the library and I want to go with him. I've already asked Jane and I don't want to leave her alone.'

Ah, so that must be why Sarah had wished her luck.

'Sure,' I said without hesitation. I had to film more videos and if I worked late I wouldn't be able to meet Marcus's deadline, but there was no way I was putting Jane's safety at risk. But I couldn't put Mum's future on the line either. Shit. 'Actually, Jess, what time do you need to leave?'

'By five.'

'I had some stuff I needed to do this evening, but if I could go home after lunch, get it done and be back by four thirty, would that be okay?'

'Course!'

~

A few hours later I was on my way to the station. My phone rang.

'Hey, you got my message, right?'

'Yeah,' Marcus said. 'But I thought I'd better brief you properly to help you get this video right.'

'Okay.'

'So when you're filming, you need to tease them. Don't just whip your dick out right off the bat. Build up to it.'

'Yeah, I get it, man. Like if I was going to have sex.'

'Exactly. We want to work them up. Make them desperate to see it.'

'You sure you're not getting a kick out of this?' I raised an eyebrow, even though he couldn't see me.

'I love you like a brother, but you're not my type. Nothing against dudes who are into dudes, but I'm a certified pussy lover.'

'Good. Because you're not my type either.' I laughed.

'I know. You prefer librarians called Jane.' He chuckled. 'How are you two getting on, by the way? Still on your best behaviour?'

'Trying to be.' I blew out a breath. 'She stayed over last night.'

'What?' Marcus shouted, nearly causing my eardrum to burst.

'No! Not like that! She's going through some shit with her parents. You remember what I told you about her dad.'

'The racist twat who controlled every move she made?'

'Yep.'

'Be careful, man. That could get messy.'

'I know. It was just a one-off. She's trying to find somewhere else to stay.'

'Good. I know you like her, but after what happened with—'

'I know, I know.' I cut him off.

The last time I'd fucked someone at work, I'd ended up losing my job. If I hadn't got involved and let my dick rule my decisions, I wouldn't be forced to strip online now. That was why I definitely couldn't get involved with Jane.

'Where are you?'

'I'm at the station. I'm heading home now to do the… stuff,' I said, looking around me to check no one overheard.

'Cool. And wear the apron I sent you.'

'Okay,' I sighed.

'And you need to get hard. The bigger you can get, the better.'

'This is getting too weird, I'm hanging up now.' I winced. Marcus and I had known each other so long we could talk about anything, but him giving me a boner pep talk was pushing the boundaries of our friendship too far.

'See you and your cock later, baby!' He laughed, then hung up whilst I tried to fight the urge to puke on the platform.

Once I was on the train, I reached into my jacket pocket and pulled out *Office Delight*.

I was barely halfway into the chapter when I spotted a huge section that had sticky tabs, was heavily highlighted and had notes in the margin.

When I kept reading, I started to understand why.

Rocco had called Virginia into his office, told her to sit

on the leather sofa and spread her legs. This time, it was Rocco that was on his knees as he tore off Virginia's soaked knickers with his teeth, then ate out her pussy until she screamed his name.

Fuck.

I'd told myself I shouldn't read this book outside of the house and I should've taken my own advice. This book was steamy as hell.

My gaze moved to the margins and I brought the book up closer so I could read what Jane had written.

SO HOT.

Was written in CAPS and underlined.

And when I saw what else was written and circled, I swear I almost came in my pants.

MY ULTIMATE FANTASY.

That was Jane's ultimate fantasy?

For a man to go down on her? But that was kind of... standard. Surely one of her exes must've done that to her?

No. It must be the tearing off the knickers with his teeth part that she fantasised about. Or the sofa.

Either way, that was an easy fantasy to check off the list.

If my circumstances were different and Jane gave me the chance, I'd fucking devour her pussy. On a bed, on a sofa, anywhere she damn wanted.

The driver announced that Shamwick was the next stop. I put the book in my pocket and thanked the powers that be that my jacket was loose and covered my crotch because now I couldn't stop thinking about going down on Jane.

By the time I burst through my front door, I was harder than steel.

I raced straight up to my bedroom, got everything set up for the video, stripped off, oiled up, then put on the fake leather and spandex apron.

It was like a normal apron, except for a square section over the crotch which opened so I could slide my cock out.

Still high on desire, I set the timer on the video, and when filming started, I ground my hips, thrust and stroked my dick in front of the camera like my life depended on it.

I imagined that Jane was on the bed, watching me, her legs spread wide open, touching herself because she was so turned on.

That vision almost sent me over the edge, so I knew it was time. After I unzipped the crotch section, oh-so-slowly, I peeled it away to give the camera a full-frontal view of my cock, then slid my hand over it. Back and forth. Back and forth. Building up the speed and increasing my thrusts.

I did this over and over until I knew I was about to come, then I paused to give Marcus time to edit the shot, stopped filming, then continued fucking my dick with my hand.

'Jane. Oh. Fuck. Yeah. Oh… fuuuckkk…' I growled as I exploded into the tea towel on the bed.

Jesus fucking Christ.

I couldn't remember the last time I'd come so hard.

And if that was how hard I came just thinking about Jane, I couldn't even begin to imagine how good it would feel if I fucked her for real…

22

JANE

'So sorry.' I approached one of the members snuggled up under a blanket on the window seat. 'The library's closing in fifteen minutes. Would you like to check that out?'

'Definitely! It's just getting good, so probably best I take it home...' She smiled mischievously. I hadn't read that novel, but I knew it was spicy.

After I'd checked out the book and the last few members had left, I walked around the library hall, straightened the cushions, folded up the blankets, then neatly placed them back on the various sofas and chairs so that everything was ready for the morning.

It'd been so busy today I hadn't got a chance to read even a page of my latest book at lunchtime. I was desperately trying to see if anyone had a room I could crash in, but no joy.

Looked like I'd have to go back to my parents' tonight.

This afternoon I received a text from Mum. She was replying to the text I'd sent last night to say I wasn't coming home. Apparently Dad wouldn't be at the house tonight because he had 'meetings' to get funding for his campaign.

I didn't know what kind of 'meetings' required an overnight stay, but I wasn't going to ask. I think it was her way of telling me that the coast would be clear if I wanted to come back tonight.

Of course I was relieved, but that was only a temporary solution. I'd have to face Dad sooner or later.

Even though I knew I could go back tonight, I didn't want to. I wished that I could just spend time with Jackson. Have dinner together like we did last night. Then go back to his place and… I shook my head. Just because I liked him didn't mean he liked me.

Although the towel erection thing did make me wonder if he did.

No. Of course he didn't.

If I couldn't spend time with him tonight, I'd spend the evening with my latest book boyfriend instead. I'd stay here for an hour or so, then get the train to my parents'. The less time I spent there, the better.

'You ready to go?' Jackson walked into the library and I swear my knees almost buckled at the sight of him.

'I, er… I was actually going to hang out here for a bit.'

'You avoiding going home? I thought you said your dad wasn't gonna be there tonight?'

When Jackson came back this afternoon, the first thing he'd asked was whether I'd found a place to stay, so I gave him an update.

'No, it's not that. Sometimes I like to curl up and read here at the end of the day. It's really peaceful and these sofas are like sitting on a cloud, so that's what I was going to do for an hour before heading to my parents'. It's okay, though, I know you must have stuff to do, so I can make my own way back.'

'I'm not leaving you, Jane,' he growled and his commanding deep voice sent a tingle down my spine. 'It's safer if you don't go home alone until we find out who's been sabotaging the library. If you want to sit and read here, that's fine, as long as you don't mind some company?'

'You want to stay and read with me?' My eyebrows shot up.

'Unless you have any objections?'

'No! Of course not. I just didn't want to interrupt your plans.'

'I don't have plans for tonight. I got the stuff I needed to do done when I went home this afternoon, so I was just going to read more of *Office Delight*, which I can do here.'

'Okay!'

'You pick the comfiest sofa and I'll get the tea and biscuits, then we can get stuck into our books. Deal?'

'Deal, but I've had a long day, so instead of tea, why don't we have something a bit stronger. There's still a couple of bottles of Prosecco from the cafe opening which Jess said we could share. What do you think?'

I didn't know what had come over me. A cuppa, biscuits and a book were much more my style than sipping Prosecco whilst reading, but maybe I wanted to do something more dangerous for a change.

Okay, okay, I know that drinking one glass of Prosecco would hardly be considered *dangerous* for most people over the age of thirty, but that was exactly my point. I didn't want to keep doing the same things anymore.

Yesterday, I'd done something different. I'd said no to Dad for the first time ever. And I'd gone out for dinner with Jackson and stayed over at his house. Most people did that kind of stuff in their teens. But when it came to my personal life, I was at least a decade behind my peers. I still hadn't had sex for God's sake.

So, yeah, as sad as it sounded, tonight I was going to let my hair down a bit, drink a glass of fizz and sit on the sofa and read with a guy that I fancied like crazy and try to enjoy the experience.

And maybe see what happened next…

23

———————

JACKSON

'Want a top-up?' Jane asked, holding the bottle of Prosecco up over my glass.

We were on the sofa in the library hall. Shoes off, feet and bodies under a blanket as we read our books.

Jane was at one end of the sofa and I was at the other, but there was still less than a metre's distance between us, so I was finding it difficult to concentrate. Especially as Rocco had just gone down on Virginia.

Again.

This time in the back of his limousine.

Just like the first time he'd eaten her out, this section was tabbed, highlighted, and circled, with asterisks in the margins, emphasising that this was something Jane definitely approved of.

A jolt of desire shot to my dick as I imagined Jane spread wide open and me licking her like she was my favourite ice cream.

'Go on, then,' I said, even though I knew this was a bad idea. Alcohol plus reading a steamy book, plus sitting with the woman you'd been attracted to since forever alone in an empty library surely equalled bad decisions, but somehow, I couldn't say no.

'Oh, I keep meaning to ask. Did you hear back from D.D. Desire yet or her agent?' she asked, topping up my glass before pouring herself another and draining the bottle dry.

Damn, we finished that fast. I hadn't even noticed. How many glasses had we had? Two? Three?

'No. Nothing. I've followed up a few times, but the agent's phone just rings out. I've sent two more emails and haven't had a reply to those either.'

'That's a shame.'

'Yeah. But I'm not giving up. And it also gives me more time to finish the book.'

'How are you finding it now?'

'It's great.' I sat up straighter, turned to face her, tucked my knees under my chin, then pulled the blanket up. Jane did the same as she pushed her glasses further up the bridge of her nose. 'He's been going down on her, a *lot*.' I smirked.

'Yeah. Rocco likes to do that…' Her cheeks flushed.

I thought about the part where Virginia was trying to get to know Rocco better after they'd hooked up a few times; she innocently asked him what his favourite food was and he replied "your pussy".

Damn.

'It's good that it's written from the female gaze,' I said, trying not to think about how Jane would taste. 'That's what I like about romance novels. They celebrate a woman getting pleasure, and I know a lot of women enjoy receiving oral sex even more than having intercourse, so it makes sense that the author has focused a lot on that. Don't you think?'

'Y-yeah.' Jane took a large glug of her Prosecco. 'She writes those scenes so well, it almost makes me feel like it's me that's experiencing everything, not Virginia. Then again, I have no idea whether it's written realistically or not, seeing as I've never had a man do that to me.'

Jane's eyes bulged as she realised what she'd just said.

'Wait, what?' My face creased, then distorted into what felt like a thousand different expressions. 'Did you just say that a man has never gone down on you?'

Nah. I must be hearing things.

'Yeah.' She dropped her gaze to the book resting on the blanket. 'Never.'

My jaw dropped.

That was fucking criminal.

Insane.

Nuts.

Incomprehensible.

There weren't enough words in the dictionary to describe how crazy that was.

What man in their right mind would have a woman like Jane in bed with them and not want to give her pleasure?

What man wouldn't want to taste her sweet pussy?

I'd give up food for days. I'd starve myself voluntarily if the reward was to spend one night feasting on her.

I'd give anything to be the first man to bury his head between her legs. I'd lick her over and over until she screamed my name.

Jesus.

I was supposed to be keeping my attraction for her

under control, but hearing that a man had never pleasured her with his mouth made me want her more.

Jane was fiddling with the blanket and I realised that she was embarrassed about her confession. I needed her to know that it wasn't her fault.

'I'm sorry, Jane. On behalf of the entire male population, I apologise. Some men can be so fucking selfish.' I shook my head. 'Please tell me that they at least satisfied you in other ways?'

My heart thudded against my chest, waiting to hear her response.

'Nope,' she sighed loudly, then took another glug of Prosecco. 'Never had an orgasm from a man. Never had a man go down on me. And never...' She drained her glass dry. 'Never had sex.'

'What?' My brows shot up to the ceiling.

No. Fucking. Way.

This time I was definitely hearing things.

Did she just say...?

Is Jane a...

Virgin?

I could believe that a man would be too lazy to satisfy a woman, but I found it impossible to believe that Jane, the most beautiful woman I'd laid eyes on, had never had sex.

I mean, we were thirty-one.

Yeah, she'd lived in Shamwick her whole life, which was hardly the dating capital of the world, but even so. She'd lived in London for a year.

I knew she was shy and softly spoken when she didn't know people, but she must've been inundated with offers. At bars, on the street, on the train, even at the bookshop she worked in.

I didn't get it.

'I know, I know. I'm a weirdo.' She let out a heavy sigh. 'Now you can laugh at me. Just like they did at work. And you can start asking if *Jane the Virgin*, the TV show, which I've never seen by the way, was named after me. Go on, then! Laugh!' Her eyes began to water. 'Tell me I'm sad for being thirty-one and a virgin. That I'm so hideous that no man will ever want me! Tell me I'll end up like Steve Carell's character in *The 40-Year-Old Virgin*. That I'll become an old, lonely cat lady, just like my dad already thinks I am.'

'No,' I said softly, moving closer to her and taking her hands in mine. The sensation of holding her palms felt incredible, but I had to push those thoughts away. I needed to focus on making her feel better. 'I'm not going to laugh at you. Am I surprised? *Yes*. But not because I think you're weird. But because I'm stunned that a woman as beautiful and sexy as you doesn't have an army of men beating down your door.'

'What?' Her head shot up. She looked at me, confusion etched all over her face. 'You don't mean that. You're just saying that to make me feel better.'

'No. What I'm saying is the truth. I honestly don't know how any man has chosen to miss out on the opportunity to be with a woman like you. Whoever you decide to give yourself to, whether that's in ten days or ten years, will be a very, very lucky man.'

She stared at me in silence.

'You…' She paused. 'You think a man would be *lucky* to sleep with me?'

'One hundred per cent.' My dick twitched, literally begging for the opportunity, before I warned it to calm down. 'Being a virgin is nothing to be ashamed of. There's nothing wrong with waiting for the right time and the right person. You shouldn't be embarrassed about who you are. The right guy will understand that.'

'I hope that's true,' she said. 'Sometimes I just wish I could get it over and done with. I always thought it would happen, y'know? It wasn't like I was holding out for religious reasons or anything. Well, I think in the beginning it was because I was scared.'

'Scared?' I asked. 'Why? Because you thought it would be painful?' I stroked her hand gently. Her skin was even softer than I'd imagined.

'That too, but mainly because my parents put the fear of God in me.'

I ground my jaw. Her fucking parents. Did they have any idea how much they'd messed with her head?

'What did they tell you?' I tried to keep my voice level so she didn't know how much anger was bubbling inside of me.

'Do you remember Tracy Tennant?'

'Yeah. You two were friends, right? She lived on your road.'

'Remember she got pregnant at fifteen?'

'Yeah.'

'Well, when my parents heard, they freaked out. They went on and on about how disgusting it was, how her life was ruined, and told me that's what happened to "dirty girls who gave in to temptation". They told me that "those kinds of activities" should only be done by adults when they were married and were ready to procreate. They banned me from speaking to her. Said she'd corrupt me.'

'You're fucking kidding me?'

'No. I felt so bad. Everyone on our street gossiped about her. She never left the house. In the end her family moved away and I didn't even get to say goodbye.'

'That's fucked up.'

'Yeah. So it was just kind of drummed into me that I shouldn't ever do it because if I got pregnant, I'd bring shame on the family. I saw how people were towards Tracy and I didn't want that to happen to me. I hardly had any friends as it was.'

'You had me.'

'Only partly. Only in class. Because Dad and Wayne were always watching me like a hawk. I wasn't allowed to go out and definitely wasn't supposed to hang out with boys. That's why I could never meet up with you. And then you went to a different college and we didn't stay in touch—'

'Because of your family,' I finished her sentence.

'I know it sounds pathetic.' She hung her head again.

'But I always thought that when I went to uni, I'd finally be free to let my hair down a little and, y'know… of course that didn't happen. Then I got stuck in Shamwick and never left.'

'What about when you worked in the library in Hastings or when you lived in London?'

'I tried dating, but then because sex had been built up so much in my head, I was nervous, so I wanted to take things slow. And inevitably, guys that I did date got tired of just kissing. They wanted to take things further. They weren't willing to wait and so… in the end it would just fizzle out. I thought it was finally going to happen earlier this year with a guy I was dating from work, but then it all blew up in my face.'

'What happened?' I asked.

Based on what she'd said earlier, it seemed like they'd teased her or something, but I wanted to hear the story for myself.

'When he asked me out I couldn't believe my luck. He was handsome, charming and he loved books.'

'I bet that was a massive green flag.' I smiled.

'Yeah, at first. He mainly read sci-fi, so I wasn't familiar with that genre, but I still liked the fact that he was a bookworm. We went on a few dates, like to the cinema or for a drink, that kind of thing, and we'd kiss. Whenever he tried to touch me up I'd freeze. So I had to tell him I wanted to take it slow because I wasn't ready. I could tell he wasn't happy, but he agreed. This went on for a couple of months and I thought we were fine. I still didn't feel ready, but I thought I just needed a bit more time.'

'That's fair enough.'

'But then one night, I was at home, reading a book, and it was kind of hot and I went to touch myself and I thought, what am I doing? I don't have to do this. I have a boyfriend who will do this to me. By that time I think we'd been dating for three months and I finally felt ready. So I got dressed and headed back to work. I thought I'd surprise him. Tell him I wanted to go home with him to have sex. But when I got to the bookshop, my colleague said he wasn't there. She said she thought he'd gone out. I should've known from the way she stuttered that something was wrong.'

'Why do I not like the sound of how this story is going?'

'I said I'd just pop to the loo whilst I was waiting for

him to come back, but she followed me, saying I should wait at the till instead, which I thought was strange, but when I stepped into the toilets I realised why. I heard someone having sex and when I saw a familiar pair of brown trainers at the bottom of the toilet stall, I knew it was him.'

'Shit.'

'My colleague called out my name, probably to warn them I was there. I was mortified. I wanted to run, but he casually stepped out of the cubicle, zipping himself up, before I got a chance. And he wasn't even sorry.'

'What?'

'He said it was *my* fault, for giving him blue balls, and that because I was so frigid, he had to go elsewhere. "What the hell's wrong with you?" he said. "It's been three fucking months! Anyone would think you're a virgin or something!" He laughed and I froze. "Wait," he said. "Don't tell me you're a virgin! You're in your thirties! That's fucking *hilarious*!"' A tear rolled down Jane's cheek and my heart broke for her.

'I'm so sorry.' I wiped her tear away. Jane took off her glasses and rubbed her eyes.

'The toilets weren't too far from the shop floor, so by that point, word had spread. Some other colleagues came to see what the commotion was and they all heard *every-thing*. I ran out of there, crying my eyes out. I was so embarrassed that everyone knew and that he'd cheated so blatantly. I took the next day off sick, something I never did. And when I came back, everyone kept laughing, making jokes, calling me Jane the Virgin.'

'That's so childish.' I shook my head, trying to under-stand how people could be so cruel.

Both Jane and I used to get bullied at school. You'd think shit like that would change when we were adults but it looked like no matter what age they were, some idiots just got a kick out of seeing other people suffer.

'I hoped it would die down once they got bored, but it didn't. That's why I had to leave. It was too hard. And I couldn't find any other jobs and I was already finding living in London super expensive, so I moved back to my parents'. That's when I saw the ad for a job at the library.'

'Shit. I'm pissed that you had to go through that, but I'm glad that it led to you working here. Not just because it's clear that you were made for this job, but also because it meant I got to see you again.' I released one of my hands and brushed away another tear that had rolled down her cheek.

Our eyes locked and at that moment, I desperately wanted to lean forward and kiss her. I wanted to show her that she deserved more than the way that idiot had treated her.

She deserved a man who would spend hours, days, weeks, hell, his whole life worshipping her.

She deserved a man that would get on his knees without asking and understand that the opportunity to feast on her was an honour and a privilege.

Jane deserved a man who would take his time with her in bed, putting her pleasure, satisfaction and joy ahead of his own. Who would do everything he could to make her feel like the most special woman in the world.

Because she was. Jane was special. Precious.

I wasn't lying when I said that any guy would be lucky to have her.

If the circumstances were different, I'd gladly throw

my hat in the ring. I'd happily accept the chance to be her first.

But now I knew everything Jane had been through, I was more certain than ever that man couldn't be me.

After waiting so long, Jane would want the fairy tale. A man that could commit to a relationship. Not a man who was so desperate for money that he'd just spent the afternoon filming himself flashing his dick to put on the internet for money.

No.

Now that I'd crossed that line, there was no going back.

24
——

JANE

W ow.
    I'd done it.

No, not *that*.

My virginity was still well and truly intact, but I'd told someone about it. Voluntarily.

At first when I let it slip that a man had never gone down on me before, I was horrified, but once I'd started talking about it, I couldn't stop. And actually, now that I'd spilled my guts about that and the reason I left my last job, I felt like a weight had been lifted off my shoulders.

Never in a million years would I have thought that the person I'd tell would be Jackson, but now that I had, I saw that it made sense. He was so easy to talk to.

The way that he listened and didn't judge was so sweet.

When he took my hands in his, I felt like my body had been set on fire. But once I'd managed to calm myself down, I began to relax again. It felt so natural that after a while, I didn't even remember that our fingers were intertwined until just now when he took one hand away to wipe my cheek.

God. This man. He was *everything.*

Jackson was exactly the kind of man I'd want to take my virginity.

I wondered if…

If I asked him, would he…?

We'd been staring into each other's eyes in silence for ages.

And he'd called me beautiful.

He'd said that any man would be lucky to have me. That it was *the truth.* So, maybe…

'Jackson,' I said, my heart thundering against my chest. 'Y'know, you said that any guy would be lucky to… pop my cherry, I-I wondered if… if you… would you… could that guy be *you*?' I swallowed the lump in my throat and as Jackson's face fell, I instantly knew I'd made a mistake by asking.

Crap.

I should've learnt my lesson after last time. I shouldn't ever consider getting involved with someone at work. *So stupid.*

'Jane,' he said softly and my stomach plummeted. 'That's not a good idea. We work together and… things are just… complicated for me right now.'

'Don't worry. I get it.' I jumped up from the sofa and slid on my shoes. 'I'd better go to my parents'. It's late.' I scooped up the empty Prosecco bottle and glasses. 'I'll sort these out first.'

'Jane. Don't be upset. I…'

'It's fine!' I rushed off to the cafe's kitchen, washed up

the glasses, then put the bottle of Prosecco in the recycling bin before rushing to the loo.

I whipped off my glasses and rubbed my eyes. They were red and bloodshot from a combination of tiredness and tears. No wonder he didn't want to do anything with me. Jackson was just being kind when he said those things. I was stupid for believing he'd ever be interested.

Probably just as well, really. I wasn't even prepared. I was wearing my usual boring white cotton underwear, and although I kept everything downstairs tidy, I'd always thought that if I was going to lose my virginity, maybe I'd go and get a Brazilian.

I had no idea whether it was 'normal' to be all bare downstairs or not, but I guessed that men preferred it if they were going to be feasting down there. But what the hell did I know?

Anyway, considering Jackson had just rejected me, it wasn't important.

Once I'd been to the loo and washed my hands, I stepped outside and saw Jackson standing in the hallway holding my handbag and jacket.

'You forgot these. And like I told you earlier, I'm walking you home.'

'Okay,' I said. 'But please forget about what I just asked you.'

'But, Jane, I…'

'Please, Jackson. I'm really embarrassed and I don't want to talk about it.'

'Okay.' He nodded.

I was supposed to be preparing an email to inform our members about our silent reading party this Friday, but my mind kept drifting back to last night.

Luckily Jackson had kept his word not to talk about what had happened and we walked to the station in silence. When we got on the train, we read, and then once we got to my street, he stood and watched as I went inside.

I went straight into the bathroom, then to bed and made sure I left early this morning to avoid bumping into anyone. Then I'd gone for breakfast at Sweet Treats until it was time to come to work.

So far I'd avoided Jackson, but it was only a matter of time before I saw him.

When one of the volunteers relieved me for my break, I went to the office. Jess was in there with Theo and thankfully there was no sign of Jackson. He must be in the bookshop.

'How did it go with your dad yesterday?' I asked Theo.

It was the first time I'd seen them both properly all morning and I'd been patiently waiting to find out if there'd been any developments.

'He denied it.' Theo rubbed the back of his neck. 'He said he was a busy man and had better things to do with his time than throw bricks through windows like a thug.'

'He was so smug about it too.' Jess scowled. 'Said the library was destined to fail before it even opened and that it was sure to go under soon without him even having to lift a finger, so all he had to do was sit back and wait for it to happen and when it did, he'd be happy to snap it up. The bastard even predicted he'd get it at a bargain rate because by that point we'd be so desperate to sell.'

'No way,' I gasped.

'That's my father.' Theo shook his head. 'Ever the cold, ruthless businessman. He hasn't changed.'

'I'm so sorry,' I said. I genuinely was. I knew what it was like to have an awful dad.

'So we're back to square one.' Jess blew out a frustrated breath. 'The police still don't have any leads, so we just have to hope that changes and, in the meantime, keep an eye out.'

'Don't worry.' Theo stood up, walked behind Jess and rubbed her shoulders. He was always so affectionate towards her. She was so lucky. 'We'll find whoever did this. How about I take you out tonight?'

'Thanks, but I'm doing the late shift,' Jess said.

'I don't mind staying late!' I jumped in.

'You stayed late yesterday!' Jess said.

'It's okay, honestly.'

'Seriously, Jane, I don't know what I'd do without you,' Jess said softly and I knew she meant every word. It was nice to feel wanted.

'You're welcome.'

The day flew by. I'd sent out another email about the silent reading party and already received multiple RSVPs to confirm they'd be attending.

Basically, guests paid to come and sit and read together in our events room. The ticket price included a glass of Prosecco and nibbles and they could either bring their own book, check one out from the library or buy one. The idea was that we made money on the tickets and the extra drinks and snacks we anticipated they'd buy. I was already looking forward to it.

'My last customer just left,' Jackson said. When he'd heard I was working late, he'd volunteered to stay late too so that Theo could take Jess out, which was kind. Still felt awkward about last night, though. 'You all clear in here?'

'Yeah. I was just about to organise the blankets and stuff.'

'Do you want to stay and read for a bit?' he asked.

'In silence?' I said, hoping he understood that I didn't want to discuss my pathetic request for him to take my virginity.

'If you want.'

'Okay, then.' I nodded. Excitement fizzed in my stomach and I told myself to calm down. I'd definitely be drinking tea today. There was no way I could risk embarrassing myself two nights in a row. 'I'm just going to the loo.'

'Cool. I'll lock up.'

When I returned to the library, Jackson was already sitting there with *Office Delight* on his lap and there were two mugs of tea and a plate of rich tea biscuits on the table in front of the sofa.

My stomach flipped. I didn't know how he did it, but somehow he just always knew what I needed.

After picking up my book from under the meet-cute desk, I walked over to the sofa in silence, toed off my shoes, and slid under the blanket next to Jackson.

'Thank you for…' I pointed to the tea and biscuits.

'You're welcome.' He started reading again, then stopped. 'Look, I know I agreed not to talk about last night, but I just need to get something off my chest because it's been eating me up inside all day.' Jackson turned to face me and I fought the urge to meet his gaze.

'Jane, I need you to know that it genuinely isn't about you. I meant everything I said. If the circumstances were different, I'd jump at the chance to... to be with you. You're smart, kind, and fucking gorgeous. I've always liked you. Even when we were kids.'

'What?' My head bolted up. He seemed genuine, but it didn't make sense. There wasn't a single guy that was interested in me at school and I couldn't blame them. I'd dressed like a nun and worn braces and hideous thick-rimmed glasses.

'I was crazy about you! There were so many times I wanted to ask you out, but I never had the guts. And when I finally plucked up the courage to ask you to the school dance, your brother must've sensed I liked you and warned me off.'

'Seriously?'

'Deadly.'

'I had no idea.' I shook my head with disbelief. 'I wasn't allowed to go anyway, because Wayne told Dad there'd be alcohol there and Dad said drinking leads women to make bad decisions.'

Jackson shook his head with disbelief.

'Doesn't matter now. Anyway, the point is, I don't want you to think that you're not desirable or feel like I rejected you because I'm not interested, because that's not the reason why. One of the reasons I can't get involved is because we work together. I did that in my last job and I ended up having to leave.'

'What?' My eyes bulged, thinking how similar it sounded to my situation. 'What happened?'

Jackson inhaled deeply.

'I got involved with a woman at work that I shouldn't have. From the start I knew it was a bad idea. She made it very clear that she was interested, and I can't lie—I was flattered. She was smart and attractive. There wasn't a guy in the office who didn't want to be with her. After being the nerdy ugly duckling that girls used to laugh at at school and college, it felt good that out of all the guys in the office, I was the one she wanted. But I'd always believed in the motto: don't shit where you eat. And as big-headed as it might sound now, by the time I got that job, I didn't have a problem finding women to sleep with, so it didn't make sense to complicate things by having sex with a co-worker.'

'So what changed?' I asked softly.

'We were at a work party and like always at these things, there was a lot of alcohol. Normally I'm pretty sensible, but that night we were celebrating a successful deal and I overdid it. Next thing I knew, I was dancing with her, then she led me outside and suggested we go up to her room.'

'Was the party in a hotel?'

'Yeah. They had a restaurant downstairs and rooms upstairs, so a lot of people planned to stay overnight because they knew it'd be easier. Anyway, I was alert enough to say what I'd been saying for months: hooking up wasn't a good idea. But she persisted and I was weak. She said it'd be a one-off. That her father, who owned part of the company, was about to set her up with a husband, so she wanted one last hurrah before she settled down.'

'Her father had found her a husband?' My face crumpled. 'Sorry. That's not the point. Carry on.'

'I thought it was strange too, because she was so ambitious. I always thought she was the kind of woman who called her own shots, but her father was known for being a ball-breaker, so I didn't question it. The thing I focused on most was the fact that she'd said that it could only be a one-off. That seemed like a win-win. I'd get to sleep with a hot colleague, then we'd go back to normal. I thought we were on the same page. We slept together, I left and thought that was that. But then on the Monday morning, she called me into her office, locked the door and said she wanted to do it again.'

'No!' My jaw dropped.

'Yep. I told her that we had an agreement. That it was just a one-off. She said she didn't remember that conversation, which was bullshit because she wasn't drunk. I wouldn't have slept with her if she was. I'd drunk too much, but I was alert and sober enough to remember what we'd discussed. But she said that if I didn't want her to tell her father that I'd touched her, I needed to do whatever she asked.'

'Wow. That's awful.'

'It was.' Jackson adjusted his position in the sofa. 'And I told her so. I walked out and went to my superior. I wanted to get ahead of the situation.'

'Good idea.'

'I thought it was. But instead of taking it seriously, he just called me a *lucky bastard* and said the whole office would give their right arm for a roll in the hay with her, so I should stop whingeing.'

'Oh my God!'

'Yeah. Anyway, she wasn't happy that I'd turned her down and called me into her office the next day to see if

I'd "seen sense yet", and when I told her I wasn't changing my mind, she was furious. She repeated what she'd said before: that if I didn't do what she asked, she'd ruin me. At first I thought it was an empty threat. She was just some entitled woman who was used to getting what she wanted and would move on when she got bored, but she didn't. She kept her promise. Whenever anything went wrong, I don't know how she did it, but I'd get the blame. She didn't just make my work life hell, she'd turn up at my apartment too. Once she turned up naked.'

'What?' My brows knitted together.

'She wore a coat but was naked underneath. She'd found out where I lived and tried to force herself inside. As well as stunts like that, she'd also call my phone at two in the morning on repeat, so I always had to keep it switched off at night. When I blocked her, she'd just call from a different number. I changed my number twice, but it didn't make a difference because the office needed my number on file and so did my clients, so it wasn't difficult for her to get hold of it.'

'Surely that was some sort of data protection breach?' I shook my head with disbelief.

'Probably. And when I was in the office, she'd grope me—she was always smart enough to do it when someone was looking away. I started dreading going to work because I never knew what she was going to do next. When she became my boss, things got worse. Whenever I tried to report it internally and go over her head, I was either laughed at or warned off. Marcus suggested going to the police, but by that point, she'd already warned me that if I tried to fuck with her I'd lose. "All I have to say is that you came on to me and wouldn't take no for an answer.

Who do you think they'll believe? A petite woman like me, or a big, imposing man like you? Your reputation with the ladies definitely won't help your case." She grinned, and that was when I knew I was fucked.'

'What a cow!' I said. 'Women like that ruin things for the true victims of sexual harassment who are brave enough to come forward.'

'Exactly. That was what I said to her and she said she didn't care. That she always got what she wanted. She made every day at work a living hell. And in the end it all became too much. It brought back all the bad memories from being bullied at school. But this time it was worse because no one in the office had my back, like you did at Northwood.'

'Oh, Jackson,' I said, a lump forming in my throat. I remembered how bad the bullying had got sometimes. They called him such awful names, start singing Michael Jackson songs whenever he walked in the room and used to taunt him about his braces and broken glasses when he couldn't afford to get them fixed and had to use Sellotape. Luckily he qualified for a voucher from the NHS to get some new ones.

I always did whatever I could to stick up for him, but I didn't exactly have any clout myself.

'No one could understand why I didn't just fuck her and do whatever she wanted.'

'That's so wrong.'

'They didn't see it like that. I thought when I started working out and bulked up, no one would ever be able to make me feel shitty again like they did at school. But I was wrong. In the end I had to decide whether I wanted to keep working in an environment that was messing up my head or leave and keep my sanity. I'd been saving up to buy my own place and had a chunk of money, so I decided to resign. I thought she'd be happy because she'd won. But she said she wasn't done with me yet and if I went through with it, she'd make sure I never worked in finance again.'

'Could she do that?'

'Her dad was influential, so yeah. At the time, I didn't care. I was done. I was mentally exhausted. And like I said, I had money saved up, so I thought I'd be fine to take time out for a few months whilst I worked out my next move. But it was only when I left that I realised how much what had happened had affected me. I went to stay at my mum's for a week and never left. And then… anyway, long story short, some things came up.' Jackson avoided my gaze and shifted on the sofa. 'So the money, it… er, it didn't last as long as I'd hoped and when I tried to apply for jobs in the same sector, I started getting panic attacks and I realised I needed to try a different path.'

'I'm so sorry. Do you still get them now?'

'No. Thankfully, I haven't had one for a while.'

'That's good.'

My heart broke for Jackson. I hated that he had to go through that.

I wondered where all his savings had gone and what he meant by 'some things came up'. It seemed like there was more to the story, but I didn't think it was the right time to ask. He'd already opened up a lot.

'So yeah, that's one of the reasons why I'm apprehensive about getting involved with someone else from work.'

'I understand. And thanks for telling me. I know it can't have been easy. But, Jackson, you know I'd never do something like that to you, right?'

'I know, I know. It's just… it's better to keep things professional. The point is, I need you to understand that it's not that I don't want to. Yesterday when you told me that a man had never gone down on, you don't know how tempted I was to lay you down right here and rectify that. But you'd been drinking and…'

'I haven't been drinking tonight,' I jumped in.

What the hell?

I couldn't believe I'd just said that.

'So if you wanted to… you could.' I blushed. *What was I just saying about not embarrassing myself again?* I didn't know what was wrong with me. Talk about a glutton for punishment. 'Sorry.' I dropped my gaze to the floor. 'Forget it. It was insensitive of me to ask, especially after what you just told me.'

Just as I was about to consider whether I should get up and leave after putting my foot in it and not respecting his feelings, I felt the heat from his fingers as he lifted my chin.

My gaze flicked up, and when I looked at him, Jackson's eyes were the colour of charcoal.

'That's what you really want?' he growled. 'You want me to spread your legs and lick your pussy, on this sofa?'

'I'm sorry.' I winced. 'Like I said, it was wrong of me to ask. The last thing I want is to make you feel uncomfortable like your ex-colleague did.'

'You're right. You're nothing like her. I'm sorry, I shouldn't have… I know all women aren't the same.' He paused and I could tell he was thinking. 'You didn't answer my question. I asked if you want me to spread your legs and lick your pussy.'

'Oh, I, er…' My brain froze and my eyes widened. I

still wasn't sure if he'd really just asked me that or if I was dreaming.

'Jane. If you really don't want to upset me, answer my question.'

'I…' I hesitated, still feeling guilty that what he'd said was exactly what I wanted. 'Yes,' I whispered.

'And if I did that, would it make you feel better? Would it make you believe that you really are desirable?'

I paused for a few moments, wondering if this was a trick question.

'Um…yes.' I nodded.

Jackson held my gaze and I could literally hear the wheels turning in his head again.

My pulse rocketed and tingles raced between my legs.

No way.

Was he seriously considering it?

Even after what he'd just told me about his past and not wanting to get involved with someone at work again?

I held my breath, waiting for his response.

Could this really be happening?

After years of longing, wishing and hoping, was I finally about to have my first proper sexual experience?

Either way, it looked like I wouldn't have to wait long to find out…

25

JACKSON

I couldn't believe I was contemplating whether to go down on Jane.

My colleague.

My friend.

My childhood sweetheart, who I'd recently discovered was *a virgin*.

Fuck.

This was another very, very bad idea.

Especially after what had happened the last time.

But like I'd just said, not all women were the same. This was different, right?

This was *Jane*.

I knew her. I could trust her. She wasn't going to tell lies, blackmail me or do whatever she could to ruin my life when I told her I didn't want to take things further like Alicia had done.

Jane didn't have a bad bone in her body.

She was the kind of person who'd gently scoop up a spider in a glass and take it outside rather than kill it. Jane would rather be irritated by a fly buzzing around her than swat one like most people.

Alicia and Jane couldn't be more different.

It was a relief to tell Jane what happened.

After Jane shared what happened with her ex, I thought about telling her that I'd also had a bad experience of getting involved with a colleague, but put it off.

But I saw the disappointment in her face when I turned her down and I needed her to know it wasn't because I didn't want her.

I'd never wanted anyone more.

Anyway, this wasn't about me and my needs. This was about Jane.

Seeing her upset was my kryptonite. I couldn't stand the fact that she felt like I'd rejected her because she wasn't desirable.

It didn't seem to matter how many times I told her that wasn't true, the words weren't sinking in. And like the saying goes: *actions speak louder than words.*

I couldn't let my mistakes with Alicia and her vindictive actions affect how I acted towards Jane. That wouldn't be fair.

If I went down on Jane, if I did that one small gesture, it'd boost her confidence. It'd finally make her see just how desirable, powerful and beautiful she really was.

I could do that.

It was no big deal.

Mum and Dad always taught me that if you were in a position to help someone in need, as long as it wasn't illegal and wouldn't cause others harm, you should.

At the time, I'm sure they had different things in mind

than performing oral sex on a co-worker, but the principle was the same.

Right now, Jane's confidence was at rock bottom and if I fucked her with my mouth, I knew that I could give Jane her first orgasm from a man *and* her first oral sex experience.

After that, she'd feel more confident and she could go out there and find someone else to take her virginity.

That was too important for me to mess with, so it'd just be oral sex. No kissing or penetration. After all, having a man go down on her was her ultimate fantasy, right? And we were on a sofa. Plus the library was her favourite place, so it'd be a perfect experience for her.

It wasn't a good idea on paper, but my gut told me I should do it. This time it would be different. It'd be fine.

'I really want to taste you, Jane.' I continued holding her gaze. 'But if I do this… if I drop to my knees, right here, right now, and feast on your pussy, it could only be a one-off. We wouldn't be in a relationship. There'd be no kissing, no cuddling or sex afterwards. I'm not going to take your virginity. It's too important. Save it for someone who really means something to you. I'd only be doing this to prove that you *are* desirable, sexy and beautiful. Because I want you to know how good it feels to have an orgasm given to you by someone else. Okay?'

'Okay.' She nodded quickly. 'But only if you're sure?'

'I'm sure. But once I do this, we shouldn't talk about it again. I don't want it to come between us or ruin our friendship. Do you think that's possible?'

'Yes.' Her eyes were the size of saucers.

I knew she was excited, but I still had a chance to back out of this.

It wasn't too late.

But when Jane bit her lip, then brushed her finger over her nipple before trailing her hand down to her stomach and beneath her skirt, I knew I was too far gone.

I threw off the blanket and leapt off the sofa.

Then dropped to my knees in front of her.

This was probably going to be a big mistake, but *fuck it*.

I was going to do it anyway.

26

JANE

O*h. My. God.*
I couldn't believe it.

Jackson had offered to go down on me.

He was on his knees in front of me.

Bloody hell.

I'd wanted to have sex for years. That was obvious.

But one of my biggest fantasies was to have a man go down on me. On a sofa.

I didn't know why. Maybe because it was more risqué than a bed?

Maybe it was because I'd read about it in different romance novels.

Whatever the reason, and as lame as it might sound to other people, that was what I'd always wished for.

And now there was a chance that this was about to actually happen.

In my favourite place in the world: a library.

Not just in any library. At the library I worked in.

Holy crap.

This was so naughty. So forbidden. So *hot*.

There was no way I wasn't dreaming.

A mixture of excitement, anticipation and fear rippled through me.

I had no idea what to expect or what to do.

Should I offer to go and wash first?

Should I take my tights, knickers and skirt off or would he do that?

And when should I open my legs?

I racked my brain, trying to remember what the heroines did in the millions of scenes I'd read in novels like *Office Delight* before the hero went down on them, but drew a blank.

'Stop thinking and relax,' Jackson growled, clearly reading my mind. 'I'm going to take off your tights first, okay?'

'O-okay,' I said, struggling to get the word out.

'Lift your bum up a little.'

After I did as he asked, Jackson placed a blanket underneath me. That was a good idea because I was already soaking and I didn't want to soil the sofa.

Keeping his eyes fixed on me, Jackson slid his hands slowly up my thighs. The heat from his palms instantly sent a bolt of electricity through me.

As his hands got closer to my pussy I lifted my hips up.

'Oh God,' I cried out. He hadn't even touched me *there* yet and I already felt like I was losing my mind.

Avoiding touching between my legs, his hands found the top of my tights and began to roll them down me, *oh-so-slowly*. When he reached my toes, he rolled them off.

My heart thundered with anticipation, as I wondered what he was going to do next.

'If you didn't have to walk home, I'd rip that skirt off you right now,' he growled again, then leant forward and pushed the fabric up around my waist.

I was glad I'd worn one of my Lycra pencil skirts again today so it was easier to move.

The cool air hit my bare legs. I couldn't believe I was lying on the sofa with my knickers exposed and Jackson knelt in front of me.

It was then that I'd realised that yet again I had on a pair of plain white cotton knickers. If I'd known that Jackson was going to do this, I would've gone shopping for something more exciting and I…

My train of thought came to a grinding halt as he trailed his fingers up my legs, skimming the edges of my knickers repeatedly but never touching me where I needed him most.

Jackson did this repeatedly and it was driving me so wild I thought I was going to explode then and there.

'*Please*,' I begged.

'No,' he said. 'You've waited a long time for this, I'm not going to rush it.'

His fingers skimmed the top of my knickers, then dipped beneath them.

Just as I thought he was finally going to touch me, he pulled his fingers away.

He teased me repeatedly and just when I was about to scream out in frustration, he leant forward, bit the top of my knickers, then dragged them down with his teeth.

'Oh my God!' I panted. 'That's so… hot!'

This was what Rocco did to Virginia in the book.

Then I realised—he'd read that scene. He was recreating it. *For me.*

He dragged the knickers down past my ankles, leaving me completely bare down there, then looked up, his eyes meeting mine.

'Holy shit, Jane,' he said. 'I knew your pussy would be beautiful, but Jesus.' My eyes bulged. Turned out I didn't need to worry about getting a Brazilian. Jackson seemed to like how I looked down there. 'Spread those legs for me, please, so I can feast on you.'

I spread them as wide as I could, desire rocketing through me.

He swiped a finger in between my legs.

'Oh, Jackson!' I cried out, my hips jerking up off the sofa as I watched him pull his finger away, then lick it clean.

'Fuck. You taste amazing. I'm going to eat you now, but before I do, I just need to check again that you're sure you want to do this. If you want me to stop now or at any time, just tell me, okay?'

'I'm sure. *Please, Jackson.* I want you to… please eat me.'

He leant forward and licked me from my opening up to my clit.

'Oh my God!' I screamed.

Jesus fuck. I'd never felt anything like this in my life. He'd only licked me once and already I was losing my mind.

As he began lapping at me, I gripped the back of his head.

Bloody hell.

This was… wow.

Now I understood what all the fuss was about. This was fucking incredible.

I looked down at the sight of Jackson's head between my legs and couldn't believe this was really happening. He was feasting on me like he hadn't eaten for days and I was his favourite meal.

I pushed his head deeper into me. I never wanted this to end.

He started circling my clit and I cried out again.

'Don't stop!' I shouted. 'Fuck! It's happening! It's…'

Jackson picked up the pace, circling me as the wave started building within me. Not even my vibrator got me off this fast.

But that made sense. A piece of plastic couldn't compare to the hottest man in the universe fucking you with his tongue whilst you were spread wide open on the sofa at the library that you worked at.

This was so thrilling that it was a million times better than any sex scene I'd read in a novel.

When Jackson slid a finger inside me whilst he continued lapping at me, I knew I was at the point of no return.

'Shit, fuck, bloody hell!' I cried out, unable to control anything anymore.

As Jackson licked my clit in circular motions, my orgasm rocketed through me.

'Oh, oh, oh my Goddddddd!' I screamed, digging my nails into his back, my body shaking from the explosions happening from within me.

I felt it everywhere. From the tips of my toes all the way up to my head.

I rarely raised my voice, but I was powerless to stop the feral sounds that flew from my mouth.

I crashed back onto the sofa. As crazy as it sounded, I swore I saw stars circling over my head and my throat was hoarse from the screaming.

I felt incredible right now. So relaxed. So high. So satisfied.

I squeezed my eyes shut, my heart still racing at a hundred miles an hour.

Jackson gave me one final long, slow lick.

I opened my eyes and when he removed his head from between my thighs, I saw that my juices were all around his mouth.

'So?' he said. 'How was that?'

'That was… out of this world,' I panted. 'I have no words. It was amazing.'

'Good. So now you've ticked three things off your list: first orgasm given to you by a man, first oral sex experience and ultimate fantasy fulfilled.'

I froze.

'How did you know that was my *ultimate fantasy*?'

'You wrote it in the margins…'

'Oh God!' I winced. 'I'm so embarrassed.'

'Don't be.' He smiled. 'Glad I could be of service.'

'You've been *more* than helpful. I'll remember this forever.'

'Mission accomplished, then.'

'Would you like me to, er…' I looked down between his legs. Jesus. His erection was enormous. It looked like he had a baseball bat down his pants and it was seconds away from bursting through his jeans. 'I've never given a blow job before, but…'

'No.' He shook his head. 'This was about you, but thanks for offering.'

Jackson stood up, and seeing his boner from this angle made it look even more imposing. I wasn't even sure how I'd get half of that in my mouth, but after the way he'd just made me feel, I'd give it a good try.

'I'm going to… go to the bathroom.' He started to walk away.

'I should clean up too,' I said, climbing off the sofa.

'Okay. I'll go to the old toilets upstairs so you can have some privacy in the ones down here.'

'Thanks.'

As Jackson left, I flopped back on the sofa. I was still buzzing. I wished I could lie here a little longer to recover.

I wished Jackson would run back into the room and tell me that he enjoyed going down on me so much that he wanted to do it again.

But we'd agreed.

It was just a one-off.

As amazing as it was, it wouldn't happen again.

It couldn't. Especially after what he'd been through with that woman at work who went back on her word.

I should be grateful that he'd even offered to do it in the first place.

And I really was. The word *grateful* didn't even begin to cover how thankful I was that he'd given me this incredible, otherworldly experience.

But although I knew I shouldn't be greedy and want to repeat what just happened, a small—okay, a very big part of me was still hoping that maybe, just maybe, Jackson would remember that I was different and change his mind…

27

JACKSON

Holy. *Fucking. Shit.*
I stared at myself in the toilet mirror, still trying to get my head around what had just happened.

I am so fucked.

I knew that eating Jane out wasn't my smartest idea. I knew that I was probably going to enjoy it, but *sweet Jesus*. That was fucking *incredible*.

Her scent.

Her taste.

The way her body responded to my touch.

The way that she screamed my name as her orgasm ripped through her.

It was a miracle I hadn't exploded in my boxers.

I deserved a medal for my self-restraint. Seriously. I wasn't sure I'd ever been so turned on in my life.

I was still rock hard now.

Although it was true that I was doing it to help Jane, I'd be lying if I didn't admit that I'd got just as much from that as she did.

As I replayed the moment where she'd come, my dick strained against my jeans again. And then she'd asked if I wanted her to suck me off.

Sweet Jesus.

Just imagining Jane's lips wrapped around my cock was too much. I raced into the toilet cubicle, quickly unbuttoned my jeans, yanked down my boxers and gripped my dick.

Jerking off at work was something I never wanted to do, but I couldn't last any longer.

I frantically moved my hand back and forth over my cock, imagining it was Jane's mouth, and seconds later, I blew my load.

A guttural sound flew from my mouth.

'Fuuuck!' I groaned, my heart still thundering against my chest.

I needed that.

After I'd cleaned up, I washed my hands, went to the storage cupboard to get the cleaning tools, then went to the library.

Jane wasn't there. She must be still in the toilets.

After plugging in the small steam cleaner into a nearby socket, I picked up the blanket. It was soaked with Jane's juices and I resisted the temptation to lift it to my face and bury my head in it.

Like I'd said to Jane, it was just a one-off. We'd both got something out of it, now it was time to go back to normal.

I dropped the blanket on the floor. I'd take it home and wash it.

Once I'd taken the plates and mugs to the cafe's kitchen and put them in the dishwasher, I returned and started polishing the table before using the steam cleaner to go over the sofa.

It wasn't because I believed what Jane and I had just done was dirty. It was just a respect thing. As hot as it was for me to lick out my crush's beautiful pussy on a sofa at work, even though I'd placed a blanket beneath her, it was still common courtesy to clean up properly afterwards.

Our members didn't want to sit on a sofa with sex juices. The only evidence I wanted to leave of what had just happened was in our memories.

And trust me. The memory of my head between Jane's thighs wouldn't be one that I'd ever forget.

Now I totally understood what Rocco meant when he said Virginia's pussy was his favourite food. I'd only gone down on Jane once and she was already the most delicious dish I'd ever tasted.

'You're cleaning?' Jane's voice sounded from behind me.

'Yeah.' I turned to face her as I ran the steam cleaner over the sofa again. 'It's kind of my thing.'

'Since when?' She frowned.

'Since, I dunno.' I shrugged. 'Maybe the last year and a half? I find it calming. It gives me a sense of satisfaction. It's like, you start with a mess or something disorganised and you clean it and suddenly everything is so much better. It's like instant gratification.' I shook my head. 'I sound like such a saddo!'

'No, you don't,' Jane said softly. 'I totally get it. It's like when there's a pile of dishes in the sink and you think it looks terrible and then you start to wash them and the pile gets smaller until, *voila*! It's all done, the sink is empty and everything's sparkling and you realise you did that. You made it better. It's an achievement.'

'That's exactly it.' I nodded.

'I mean, a busy mum or dad with a houseful of kids probably doesn't feel like that. It's probably just one task out of a million others that they have to do, but still, I understand. Loads of people love ironing or cleaning. Just like people love cooking. Just because it doesn't sound particularly sexy doesn't mean there's anything wrong with loving it.'

My chest bloomed.

Jane got it.

She always understood me like no one else seemed to.

Yeah, she could still be high on the orgasm, but I swear there wasn't a fake bone in Jane's body. She was genuine. If she said those words, I knew she meant them.

I was glad I'd fucked her with my tongue.

She was right, cleaning something did feel like an achievement.

But right here, right now, one of my great achievements was giving her pleasure.

Now she could get on with her life and find some guy to give her virginity to with more confidence.

But as I thought about another man peeling her clothes off, seeing her bare, laid out on a bed in front of him and then sliding his cock into Jane's beautiful pussy, a sharp stabbing pain ripped through my chest.

I know what I'd said before, but after feasting on Jane, I didn't want another man to be her first.

I didn't want another guy to taste her, to feel her.

I knew that we'd agreed to make this a one-off.

I knew that I shouldn't be thinking about being with her again, but I couldn't help it, because the more I thought about it, the more I realised there was only one man who should take Jane's virginity.

Me.

28

JACKSON

'I love them!' Jess said as I showed her the laptop screen resting on the bookshop counter with the merch design proofs. 'I can't even pick a favourite. They're all so amazing!'

The designer had created tote bags and mugs with The Romance Library's logo as well as fun quotes like 'Reading is a workout for the mind, so when I say I'm going to the gym, I'm really going to the Romance Library.' Another option was 'Buying books and reading them are two separate hobbies.' There was also 'Sorry, I can't talk. The friends are about to become lovers.'

'I love them all too. The bookmarks and stickers have already been printed and will arrive tomorrow morning in time for the silent reading party. But because the tote bags and mugs take longer and are more expensive, we need to choose maybe two, maximum three options to start with.'

'We should go and ask Jane,' Jess said. 'Actually, it's gone five, so your shift's ended. Theo can man the library, so tell Jane she can go home now too. I'll cover things here.'

'Okay,' I said.

I hadn't seen Jane much today, at least not in person. But she'd occupied almost every thought in my head since yesterday. My brain alternated between replaying memories from last night and creating new fantasies of how it would feel to be inside her. I needed to get a grip.

Anyway, Jess was my boss and she'd just asked me to get Jane's opinion on the proofs and tell Jane she could leave early, so I was only doing what she'd asked.

As I walked through the main library hall door, Jane was just stepping away from the meet-cute desk. When she spotted me, her face broke out into a huge smile and my heart inflated like a hot-air balloon.

'Hi!' She came over and we stepped out into the corridor. 'H-how are you?'

'Good, yeah. You?'

'Amazing!' She grinned, then held my gaze.

Fuck. Right now I just wanted to carry her back over to that sofa and spread her legs.

'I...' My brain froze. I was the one who'd told her that I didn't want things to get awkward between us, and yet here I was getting tongue-tied. 'Jess wanted your opinions on these merch designs. What do you think?'

My eyes drifted down to the laptop. I held it up so she could see the screen, which still had multiple windows open with the different designs.

'Oh my God, I love them all!'

'Do you have a favourite?'

'It's hard to pick, but I definitely like the one about the friends becoming lovers...'

Jane bit her lip and her eyes locked on mine. I could be wrong, but as well as talking about the design, I got the feeling that she was referring to something else… *us*.

'Thanks for your feedback,' I said, my brain overruling my twitching dick. It didn't matter that I wanted Jane. I couldn't go there. I'd already gone too far. It was for the best. 'Jess also said that you could leave now. Theo will take over.'

'Now?' Her face dropped. 'But it's only just gone five. I was looking forward to working late so I could sit and read here in peace. I had a run-in with my dad this morning and I'm not in a hurry to go back home.'

'What happened?' I ground my jaw.

'Hi, you two.' Theo appeared. 'It's time to go home. I'm taking over in the library, so I'll see you both tomorrow.'

'Oh, okay,' Jane replied flatly. Most people would be happy to be told they could leave work early, but I understood why she wasn't feeling enthusiastic. 'Thank you. See you tomorrow.'

'I have to put this in the office,' I said, closing the laptop.

'I better get my things too.'

'So what happened?' I asked as we stepped into the office.

'In a nutshell, he said he hadn't forgotten about my "little outburst" and that the photoshoot had been postponed, but I wasn't off the hook. And seeing as I was working all these extra hours, I could start paying more to stay there because he needed the money to help with his campaign.'

'Wow,' I said. There was a lot more I wanted to say, but it wouldn't be polite.

'Exactly. So you can understand why I'm not in a hurry to spend the evening there.'

'You could come and read at my place if you like?'

As soon as the words flew out of my mouth, I regretted them. After last night I should be keeping my distance, not inviting her into my home. Again. It was hard enough the last time, and then I'd only imagined and fantasised about how Jane tasted. But now I knew from first-hand experience, I'd found it hard to think about anything else.

'That would be amazing! Thank you!'

Too late to change my mind now.

After Jane got her bag and jacket, we walked to the station, then got the train, all whilst exchanging stories about our day.

I put the key in the door and stepped inside Mum's house. The good thing about being into cleaning was that the place was always tidy.

After taking off my jacket and shoes, I gestured to the living room.

'Want something to drink and some snacks to eat whilst you read?'

'Yes, please!' Jane's eyes widened like I'd just offered to take her on an all-expenses-paid trip to the Caribbean.

'Okay. Make yourself at home and I'll be back in a sec.'

Once I'd washed my hands, I put the kettle on, and whilst it was boiling, arranged some biscuits on a plate. Luckily I'd bought a pack of digestives when I went shopping. Not because I was planning on inviting Jane round here or anything. Just for… I don't know, really. I saw them and thought of her and somehow they ended up in my trolley.

These days it was hard to remember a time when I *wasn't* thinking about Jane.

I pulled out a tray, then arranged several little bowls on it. In the first I tipped out some nuts. Then I opened a bag of popcorn and filled up the second bowl. Popcorn was one of my favourite reading snacks because it didn't leave residue on my fingers like crisps did.

What else? *Of course*, I said to myself. I opened the cupboard and reached for the bar of chocolate I saved for 'emergencies'. I tried to eat healthily, so treats like that definitely had to stay out of sight so I didn't get tempted. I added it to the tray.

If I had marshmallows, those would've been great too. Maybe next time.

Next time?

Nah. There definitely couldn't be a next time.

After putting some carrot sticks into the final bowl, I added the tea and plate of biscuits to the tray, then carried it out to Jane in the living room.

She was already curled up on the sofa, her legs up, multiple cushions behind her and her head buried so deep in the book that her glasses were in danger of sliding off her nose.

When she realised I was there, her head jerked up, then when I rested the tray on the coffee table, her eyes popped.

'Oh, wow!' she gasped. 'When you said you'd bring me snacks, I thought you meant a bag of crisps or some biscuits. I wasn't expecting *this*! This is a reading snack platter of dreams. Thank you!'

Seeing how happy and grateful she was that I'd just

arranged a few things on a tray for her made my heart swell.

'You're welcome. I'll leave you to it.'

'You're not joining me?' Her face fell.

I wanted to. I really did. The thought of cosying up on the sofa with Jane made every part of my body light up. Including my dick. So, no. I definitely couldn't join her.

If I sat on that sofa with Jane tonight, I couldn't guarantee that I wouldn't ask her to spread her legs for me again, but this time it'd be to fuck her.

Shit.

This was out of control.

I knew I wanted to sleep with her, but the way I wanted to fuck her wouldn't be appropriate. I wanted her so bad that I'd need to do it hard. She was a virgin. Her first time needed to be gentle, and after craving her for so long, I didn't think I'd be able to hold back. I'd be too rough. The last thing I wanted to do was hurt her.

'I, er, have some stuff to do, upstairs.'

'Course. Sorry. You didn't know I'd be intruding on your evening.'

'You're not intruding. I'm happy to have you here.' *Yeah. Way too happy.* My dick twitched again. 'Enjoy the snacks.'

I raced up to my room, then closed the door.

Just as I was about to hide the tripod and the cleaning props that were neatly arranged in the corner, my phone rang.

'Hey, M,' I said, pleased to hear from Marcus. I'd messaged earlier to see if he had any updates and he said he'd call me back.

'Dude!' he shouted down the phone. 'It's happening!

Your video's taking off! I told you! I told you once you got your dick out things would improve and I was right!'

'Wait, what?' I sat down on the bed, trying to take it all in. 'When you say it's taking off, do you mean I'm getting loads of views or subscriptions?'

'Both!' he shouted, his voice dripping with excitement. 'If it keeps going like this, you'll be able to pay at least a big chunk of your mum's fees this month! Check your phone. I've just sent you a screenshot.'

I moved the phone from my ear, touched the screen and opened the image.

'Holy shit!' I yelled as I tried to take in the amount of views and subscriptions we'd racked up. I zoomed in on the image, just to make sure I wasn't seeing things.

'And this is just the beginning, bro, I'm telling you! I'm not surprised it's doing so well. Your cock is fucking huge, you lucky bastard! I mean, I don't get any complaints, but if I had an anaconda in my pants like that, I'd be swinging it about every chance I got. That's a freaking pussy magnet! If I'd known you were packing that in your trousers, I would've suggested you started showing it in the videos from day one. No wonder they're lapping it up! How soon can you make more? Can you do something tonight?'

'Er…' Shit. 'Maybe later? I've kinda got someone here right now.'

'No way! You've brought someone home? That's major! Glad that monster dick isn't going to waste. Who is it?'

'It's not like that.'

'Wait.' The line went silent. 'Is it your sexy librarian?'

Busted. I hated that he knew me so well.

'She's just here to read.'

'*Read?*' He laughed. 'Is that what they're calling it these days?'

'It's not—' Just as I was about to continue protesting, despite knowing I'd gone down on Jane last night and hadn't stopped thinking about it ever since, Marcus screamed down the phone.

'No way! I've just sent you another screenshot!'

'Oh my God!' I roared as I took in the amount on the screen. The subscription revenue was now enough to pay half of Mum's fees. With what I earned from the library, I was close to being able to cover a whole month's care. I still had two other months' payments that were overdue, but this was going to help massively. 'This is amazing!' I cried out again. '*Fuck yeah!* Thanks, man. For everything. You don't know what this means to me!'

'I do, bro. And you're welcome. Now go and celebrate with your *friend.*'

When I hung up, I jumped off the bed and punched the air triumphantly.

It felt like a massive weight had been lifted from my shoulders. Not knowing how I was going to pay Mum's fees had been so stressful. But now, I could finally see a light at the end of the tunnel, I felt fucking fantastic.

Just as I was about to start dancing around the room, there was a knock at the door.

'Jackson? Are you okay?'

I practically skipped over to the door and opened it. When I saw Jane standing there looking sexy as hell, my body temperature rose by what felt like thirty degrees.

Her face was flushed, her lips were parted and the top

few buttons of her blouse were undone, giving me a glimpse of her soft creamy skin.

'Hey!' I smiled. 'I'm absolutely fantastic!' I picked her up off the floor, lifted her into my bedroom and spun her around.

'Oh!' she said. 'That's great! I just heard you shouting, so wanted to check.'

As I continued spinning her in the air, her sweet scent flooded my senses. Fuck.

'I just got some good news and I'm so fucking happy right now!'

'Yay!' she cheered. 'I'm really pleased for you!'

I loved that she was so enthusiastic even though she had no idea why I was in such a good mood.

Right now I felt high. I was never into drugs, but I'd imagine that how I was feeling had to be a similar kind of buzz.

Adrenaline raced through my veins and I felt so light that if I took my feet off the ground I'd float in the air. I was dizzy with joy, I was…

'Jackson, we're gonna…' Jane called out and just as we landed on a heap on the bed, I realised what she was about to say.

'Sorry!'

We both burst out laughing.

'Don't be sorry.' Jane turned on her side to face me and I did the same. 'I'm just happy to see you so happy!'

'Thanks,' I said. 'You're always so kind and under-standing.' I reached over and brushed away a strand of hair that had fallen from her bun onto her cheek when I'd spun her around like a lunatic.

'So are you.' She smiled. 'I don't know many men

who'd put together such an epic reading snack tray. And I don't know any other man who'd go down on a friend so magnificently to help her lose her oral virginity and experience her first non-solo orgasm either…'

She bit her lip, and just the mention of me eating her out set my blood on fire.

'I could pretend that I was a saint and did it purely for you and got no pleasure from it, but that'd be a lie. The truth is, Jane, I fucking loved eating your pussy and I haven't been able to stop thinking about it.'

'Yeah?' She grinned mischievously. 'Me too. And that's not the only thing I've been thinking about.'

Her gaze dipped a little like she was embarrassed.

I should leave it at that. I shouldn't ask her what else she'd been thinking about, but I couldn't help it.

'Tell me,' I growled. 'What else were you thinking?'

'About how good it would feel to have your… cock inside me.'

'Fuck, Jane.' I winced.

'Exactly.' She laughed. 'That's exactly what I'd like, Jackson. I'd really like you to fuck me.'

'Jane…' I swallowed hard as I tried not to let what she'd just said affect me. 'I… I really, really want to. You have no idea. I've been thinking about that too. I think you're a fucking goddess.' I traced my finger over her lip, and as a groan slipped out of her mouth, my dick turned to stone. 'But I'm just not sure that I'm the right person for you to lose your virginity to.'

I wanted to, of course. But this wasn't about me.

'You're the perfect person. I don't want to go to a bar and hook up with a stranger. I don't want to sleep with someone who'll make me feel stupid or incompetent or laugh at me because of my inexperience. I want to do it with someone that I trust. Someone that I'm crazy attracted to. And I trust *you*. I feel comfortable with *you*. And in case it wasn't obvious from the way I screamed your name last night, I really fancy you. I've always fancied you. I liked you at school, but now… wow. You're… you're like, the hottest guy I've ever seen.'

God. Damn.

My eyes bulged and my dick was straining in my jeans so hard, I was convinced that it was about to burn a hole through the fabric.

'You liked me?'

'Of course I did.'

Shit. She meant it.

Jane liked me before I got a decent haircut or nice clothes and started working out.

That meant everything.

'We work together,' I said weakly, struggling to find reasons not to fuck her right here, right now. 'Remember what I told you? I dated someone at work before and it ended badly. It cost me everything.'

I knew that argument was lame, because like I'd said last night, Jane was different. But I needed to say something to stop myself from giving into what I really wanted. And that was to go all the way.

I was trying to do the right thing, but it was getting harder and harder to resist temptation.

'I know. And you know what happened to me and why dating someone from work isn't a great idea for me either. But I wouldn't suggest we do this if I wasn't sure I could trust you. And I hope you know you could trust me too. If you like, I can sign an agreement. I don't think Jess or

Theo would mind, but I'll sign something to say it was consensual, I'll even say I begged you if you want!' She chuckled and the sound made my chest swell.

'I don't want to hurt you.'

'It'll be just sex,' she insisted. 'We can just do it the once. Just so I can get rid of this virginity noose around my neck.'

'I don't just mean emotionally. I don't want to hurt you physically. I'm not saying this to sound like an egotistical prick, but my dick… I'm not exactly small, so for your first time you'd be better off with someone else.'

'So someone with a micropenis?' She smiled.

'Maybe…'

Based on the reaction women had had when they saw me and Marcus's comment earlier, it was safe to say that I was probably bigger than the average guy.

I knew a lot of women thought they wanted to be fucked by a man with a huge cock, but the reality was for some it was too much. It could be uncomfortable. So it wasn't going to be ideal for a virgin.

'This might sound dumb and contradictory, but it's not so much your penis that I'm interested in—I mean, obviously I need it to help me solve my *problem*. But what I'm saying is, it's the man attached to the penis that I want tonight. So it doesn't matter whether you have a micro or jumbo dick, I want to lose my virginity with *you*.'

Shit.

Hearing that pushed me close to the edge.

I was so close to kissing her right now.

This close to finally giving in and doing what I'd wanted to do for what felt like forever.

'Please, Jackson.' She looked me in the eyes, then

reached out and ran her hand over my chest. 'Please can you fuck me?'

Game. Over.

Did I just say I was close to giving in?

The woman who lived in my dreams, who I fantasised about, had just pleaded with me to have sex with her. And I wasn't about to let her down.

If Jane wanted me to fuck her, that was exactly what I was going to do.

29

———

JANE

Bloody hell.
    This could be it.
Jackson's eyes darkened.

My hand was resting on his delicious firm chest and his heart was beating at what felt like a million miles an hour. Just like mine was.

I didn't know what I'd expected to happen when I'd come to his room to check he was okay. But I'd never for a second thought we'd end up on his bed, staring into each other's eyes, *hopefully* just moments away from having sex.

'Jane,' Jackson growled, his voice low, deep and so sexy. 'I'm going to kiss you now.' He edged his head closer to me, his warm, sweet breath tickling my face. 'And then… let's see, but if at any point you want me to stop, just say.'

'Kiss me,' I panted. I was so desperate for him, I could hardly breathe.

Jackson held my gaze for a few seconds, as if to give

me time to change my mind, then crushed his lips onto mine.

'Oh God,' I moaned as our mouths collided. The kiss was frantic and hungry, like all of the pent-up wanting and longing was coming out at once and we were desperate to taste each other.

As I parted my lips, Jackson slid his tongue inside, and as it thrashed against mine, another groan of pleasure slipped out.

Jackson climbed on top and when I felt his hardness pressing against me, I swear a dam burst in my knickers.

He really did feel huge. But call me a sadist, even though I knew it would be painful, I still couldn't wait to feel him inside me.

Jackson's mouth trailed along my neck, then moved down to the exposed skin where my blouse was unbuttoned.

He slid his hands beneath me and attempted to undo the buttons, still peppering kisses over me.

When his attempts failed, he lifted off me and I instantly missed the feel of his lips.

'Sorry, the buttons are really fiddly,' I said, struggling for breath.

'No, *I'm* sorry, because I need you so badly that I can't waste time with buttons, so I'm gonna have to rip this off you, okay?'

'Okay,' I panted, tingles racing through me.

Jackson placed his hands between the gaps, then in one swift move ripped the blouse open.

Holy shit. That was hot.

'Jesus.' Jackson looked down at me. I was lying here with my bra exposed, my chest heaving with anticipation.

'You're fucking beautiful. I can't wait to suck on your gorgeous tits.'

He reached behind my back and unclipped my bra like it was the easiest thing to do in the world.

My bra dropped and he snatched it off my chest, tossed it over his shoulder, then leant down slowly before taking my nipple in his mouth and taking a long, slow suck.

'Oh God.' My hips jerked off the bed. 'More, please.'

'Seeing as you asked so politely.' He smirked.

Jackson moved his head over to my other breast, then sucked on the other nipple, before circling it slowly with his tongue.

Every time his mouth made contact it was like a bolt of electricity shot through me.

Just when I thought the pleasure couldn't become more delicious, Jackson moved his hand up my skirt, slowly trailing up my thighs before he gently ran his fingers over my pussy.

'Your knickers and tights are soaked,' he said into my breasts. 'Shall we take them off and see just how wet you really are for me?'

'Yes,' I panted again.

He lifted his head from my chest, slid down the bed and pulled my skirt, knickers and tights down to my knees, then paused.

Ordinarily I'd feel exposed and self-conscious about the fact that a man was staring at my naked pussy. But this wasn't just any man. This was *Jackson*. And he was staring between my legs like he was admiring the most beautiful piece of art he'd ever seen. Just like he had last night.

Desire and awe filled his eyes.

'Such a pretty pussy.' He swiped his finger slowly over my clit, down to my entrance, then back again and I bucked against his hand. Jackson then brought his finger to his lips and licked it clean, just like he had the first time he'd gone down on me.

'Mmm, you taste so good, Jane. I love how wet you are for me.'

'Please.' I reached up and placed my hand on his dick. Bloody hell. He was rock hard. 'Put it inside me. I want it.'

'Not yet.' He moved my hand away gently. 'We need to get your body ready to take my cock.'

'I *am* ready!' I cried out. 'Do you have any idea what a turn-on it was when you brought me that snack tray?' I was so desperate for him I swore I'd explode if he didn't enter me soon.

'We'll see about that.'

This time, Jackson slid my skirt, knickers and tights from my knees, past my ankles and onto the floor.

'You have no idea how incredible you look.' He shook his head. 'I don't even know where to start. I want to fuck you, I want to eat your pussy and I want to suck on those delicious tits all over again. I wish I could do them all at once. Spread your legs for me,' he instructed, and I did as he asked. 'Wider. I know you want me inside you, but I need to make sure you're satisfied tonight, so first I'm going to make you come with my tongue, because it might be harder for you to climax with penetration the first time, okay?'

'Okay.' I squeezed the words out of my throat. Jackson leant forward between my legs, spread my lips, then flattened his tongue against my clit.

'Fuck!' I cried out, jerking off the bed at the sensation.

As his tongue lapped at me, my whole body pulsed with desire. I squeezed my toes and tried not to wriggle beneath him but, my God, it was difficult. He was giving me so much pleasure, I didn't know how much more I could take.

Jackson began circling my clit, then slid two fingers inside of me, causing me to cry out.

'I fucking love how wet you are. You're almost ready for me.'

'Oh God, yes! Right there,' I said, pushing his head deeper into me. 'Oh God, Jackson, I can't… I…'

The wave built, rising higher and higher and higher until…

'Jackson! Jackson!' I screamed, lifting my hips off the bed as my orgasm ripped through me.

My chest heaved, my head spun and I struggled for breath.

I squeezed my eyes shut, convinced that I wouldn't have enough energy to open them again for hours whilst I recovered from that orgasm. That was until I heard the sound of a belt unbuckling and my eyes flicked open faster than you could say *horny virgin*.

When I looked up, I saw Jackson undoing his jeans, and suddenly a fresh wave of adrenaline washed through me.

For a second I thought that because he'd made me come, he might change his mind and not follow through with the 'real' sex part, but from the fire in his eyes and of course the fact that he was undressing himself, it looked like my wish to feel Jackson inside of me was still firmly on track.

'Would you mind if I…' I mumbled.

'You want to undress me?' He smirked.

'Yes,' I replied quickly.

I'd dreamt of seeing Jackson naked so many times and I wanted to savour the moment.

Using every ounce of energy I had, I pulled my body up off the bed and leant forward.

Nervously, my hands rose to Jackson's waist and I gripped his jeans.

'Wait. Let me stand up. It'll make it easier.'

He leapt off the bed, then stood beside me. After turning to face him, I gripped the waist of his jeans, then slowly pulled them down his muscular thighs. As I saw the enormous tent his cock had created in his boxer shorts, I swallowed hard.

This was it.

I was about to come face to face with a real dick.

My eyes followed the strip of curly black pubic hair which led to the main attraction. After taking a deep breath, I started tugging at his boxers.

I'd barely rolled them down more than a few inches before his cock sprang free.

Oh. My. Good. Lord.

I gulped as I got a full, uninterrupted view of Jackson's dick.

I had no words.

He wasn't lying when he said he wasn't small. And when I'd seen the outline last night at the library and compared it to a baseball bat, I hadn't been far off. This was absolutely *huge*.

'Still think you can handle this?' Jackson lifted my chin and looked me in the eyes.

'Yes.' I nodded, even though the truth was I really

wasn't sure I could. A weapon like that would probably dislodge my insides.

'Can I…' My hand hovered between his legs.

'Be my guest.'

I wrapped my hand around it and moved it up and down, slowly. It was long, thick and surprisingly smooth, like velvet.

Jackson's dick jerked in my hand and I loved the sensation. I moved my hand back and forth, building up the rhythm.

'Fuck, Jane. I love the feel of your hand on me, but if you keep doing that, you're going to make me come. I need to see if I have a condom.' He reached into his bedside drawer and rooted around. 'Shit!' Jackson groaned. He reached in his wallet, then blew out a frustrated breath. 'I don't have one. I wasn't expecting to… it's been a long time for me.'

'I have one.' I smiled.

'Yeah?' His eyebrows shot up.

'In my toiletries bag. It's been in there for months. Just in case. Remember, I was a Girl Guide, so I learnt the importance of always being prepared.'

I had to put it inside one of my sanitary towels just in case my parents went through my things. Yep. That's how intrusive they were. But I knew they'd never look there.

'I'm not sure having a spare condom in your bag just in case you wanted to get fucked was what the Girl Guides had in mind when they taught you that motto'—he smirked—'but I'm glad you have one anyway. Want me to get it?'

'Please. Just bring up the whole bag.'

'Will do. But I'm going to need you to keep yourself

warmed up whilst I'm gone. Touch yourself, like you would if you were alone. I need you to stay wet for me.'

'Okay,' I said as Jackson raced out of the room.

As I lay back and ran my hands over my breasts, I felt weird. I didn't know if I'd ever spread out on a bed completely naked before and touched myself.

Doing that at my parents' was a hard no for obvious reasons. And even if I'd done it in the room I rented in London, it would've been under the covers, just in case.

I'd been taught that masturbation was a shameful act for so long that I was still embarrassed to do it, but tonight, I felt different. I felt free.

I slid my hand between my legs. Jesus. Jackson didn't need to worry about me staying wet for him. It was like an ocean down there. I'd never been so horny in my life.

As I swiped my finger over my clit, a tingle raced through me, but it didn't compare to Jackson's touch.

I scanned his room whilst continuing to pleasure myself. As I took in the sight of the different weights on the floor and the pull-up bar attached to the wall, which was decorated with faded dark blue striped wallpaper, I imagined Jackson working out, sweat dripping down his muscular body…

'Oh God,' I moaned.

'Fuck.' Jackson stepped into the room and stood there, his eyes roaming between my legs. My immediate reaction was to stop. Even though he'd asked me to do it, I still somehow felt like I'd been caught in the act. 'Keep going, baby, I love watching you touch yourself.'

He came closer, put my handbag on the floor, then stood in front of me, his eyes fixated on my pussy whilst he stroked himself.

'Do you see how hard you've made me, Jane?'

'Yes.' I nodded.

'I want you so bad. Are you ready for me?' Jackson slid his finger between my legs and I instantly removed my own.

'Yes,' I panted.

As I turned to reach inside my handbag and pull out my toiletries bag, Jackson continued stroking my clit.

With shaking hands, I fished the condom out from the sanitary towel.

'How many do you have?' he asked.

'Just one,' I replied.

'You want to put it on?'

'I don't know how to,' I said, looking at his dick, which was already leaking precum. 'I don't want to rip it.'

God. That would be just my luck. I finally get the chance to have sex and then fall at the final hurdle after ripping the condom.

'How about I open it, then you roll it on?'

I nodded and Jackson carefully ripped the foil packet, then held the condom up.

'Let me start you off,' he said gently, rolling it onto the tip of his dick. 'Now your turn. Just roll it all the way down.'

I sat up and used my left hand to hold his dick in place at the base whilst I rolled it down slowly.

'Now lay down for me,' Jackson said in a calming voice. 'We're going to take it nice and slow and I'll be as gentle as I can, but I'm pretty sure it's going to hurt. If it gets too much, just tell me to stop and I will, okay?'

'Okay.'

Jackson climbed on top of me and pressed his lips on

mine. As I tasted myself, I got a delicious reminder of the fact that he'd already made me come with his tongue, which turned me on even more.

This time the kiss was less frantic. It was gentle and intense, and as his tongue softly tangled with mine, he rolled my nipples between his fingers, then started rubbing his cock against my entrance.

The sensation of it slipping and sliding between my legs was delicious and I rocked against him, loving the friction.

Suddenly the kisses turned wild and hungry again as his thrusts became more urgent.

My glasses slid further and further down my nose and I felt my bun loosening.

Jackson paused and whipped off my glasses before grabbing his cock and rubbing it harder against me. Then he lined it up against my entrance.

'I'm going to fuck you now,' he panted into my mouth.

'Please, do it.'

I spread my legs and Jackson fed his dick inside me.

'Oh God,' I cried out as he breached my entrance. A sharp, stinging pain hit me. I knew it was going to hurt, but it still took me by surprise.

'I know it's not easy, but try to relax.'

'You're so big. Is it all in now?'

'No, baby. That's just the tip,' he said. *Fuck. There's more?* 'If you want, we can stop and try again when we have some lube. Might make it easier for you to take me. If I'd known we'd be doing this tonight, I would've got all the supplies. Maybe we should do it another time. I can plan it properly. Make it extra special for you.'

'No! I don't want to plan. I'll be even more nervous

than I am now. I want to do it. Without overthinking. Please don't stop. I can take it.'

'Okay. I need you to spread your legs wider and breathe. Deep breaths, in and out.'

I did as he said as he stretched me wide, feeding himself deeper.

As I looked up and saw the god that was on top of me, pushing his long, hard dick inside me, inch by inch, tingles erupted in my veins.

This was the moment I'd waited for, for so long.

My body had yearned for this. Ached for this.

I'd dreamt about a man filling me up for years and now that it was finally happening, I shouldn't be focusing on the pain—I wanted to focus on the incredible pleasure.

I could do this.

'Go deeper,' I panted. 'I want to feel all of you. Just do it. Quickly.'

Surely it was like ripping off a plaster, right? The faster he buried himself in me fully, the quicker it'd stop hurting.

'You sure?'

'Yes. Forget that it's my first time. Fuck me like you would if we'd just met.'

Jackson's eyes darkened and then a mischievous grin spread across his face.

'If that's what you really want.'

'It…'

I didn't even get a chance to finish my sentence before Jackson thrust into me. Hard.

'Jesus Christ!' I cried out.

'You okay?'

'Don't stop!'

'Yes, ma'am!' He laughed, pounding into me.

I dug my nails into his back as my body adjusted to being filled up in the most delicious way.

Yes, it was painful, but it was good pain, if that made sense. I liked the sensation of being stretched to the hilt and the friction of Jackson pummelling in and out of me.

'Put your leg on my shoulder,' Jackson commanded. 'Just one for now. I'm gonna go deeper.'

Jackson started circling my clit whilst he continued pumping in and out of me and my eyes practically rolled into the back of my head.

I understood it now.

Now I knew why people talked about sex so much. Why people loved reading about it, but more importantly, why they loved actually doing it.

I'd never felt sensations like this before in my life.

'Jesus,' Jackson groaned, 'you're so fucking tight, Jane. I love it. I need to make you come now before I do. I'm so fucking close.'

'Me too,' I panted.

Jackson continued thrusting, harder, deeper, faster.

The bed shook. My hair completely unravelled from the bun as my head kept hitting the soft headboard. Jackson picked up speed, stroking my clit as he circled his hips.

My body moved in sync with his as the warning signs that another orgasm was imminent raced through me.

'Oh God,' I said. 'Oh God... oh, oh, I'm close, keep going... oh fuck, fuckkkkk!' I screamed as what felt like a thousand bombs detonated inside me.

Jackson continued thrusting and then his body stilled as he came. He thrust a few more times before collapsing on my chest.

I didn't know how long we stayed there, our bodies slick with sweat, chests heaving, hearts racing. But eventually, Jackson lifted off me.

'I need to take off the condom,' he said. 'I'll pull out slowly, okay?'

As soon as he was out, I instantly missed the feel of him. Suddenly I felt hollow. It was crazy. That was only the first time I'd had a man's dick inside me, yet I felt like I was suddenly missing a vital organ.

As Jackson went to roll off the condom, he winced.

'What's wrong?' I asked.

'There's blood. I thought there would be, but are you okay? Was I too rough?'

'No. Don't worry. I'm fine. I have periods every month, remember? I can handle a bit of blood.'

'Wait here.' Jackson rolled the condom into a tissue, then walked out of the room.

When he returned, he was juggling a towel, a flannel, a bowl of water, a bottle of water and some paracetamol in his hands.

He laid them all on the bed, then handed me the water and paracetamol.

'Here. Just in case it's painful. I don't know if it'll help or not, but…' He shrugged his shoulders, then knelt down between my legs. 'Lift up, then open your legs a little.' I did as he asked as he slid the towel beneath me. 'I'm going to clean you up.'

After dipping the flannel in the water, he gently wiped between my legs. At first it stung a little, but then I was fine. As I watched the way Jackson was taking care of me, I almost melted all over again. There was no way I would've got this kind of aftercare if I'd slept with some random guy from a bar.

'There,' he said. 'You okay?'

'I'm great, thank you.'

Jackson patted me dry with the towel, folded it over to cover me, dropped the flannel in the bowl, then put it on the floor.

'Now, unless you have any objections, I'd like to hold you.'

'I'd really love that,' I said, my heart fluttering.

Jackson came back on the bed and lay on his side, facing me, then wrapped his arms around my back.

'I can't believe I actually did it!' I blew out a breath.

'You did!' Jackson planted a soft kiss on my lips.

'I've *finally* lost my virginity. At the tender age of thirty-one!'

'Your age doesn't matter.' Jackson stroked my cheek. 'What matters is whether it was worth the wait…'

'Definitely.' I smiled. 'It was incredible. I've heard some horror stories about people losing their virginity. Like how disappointing it was. But how many people can say that their first time was amazing, with the hottest guy in the UK—well, quite possibly the world—*and* that they got an orgasm at the end of it?'

'I'm glad you enjoyed it. I did too. It was an honour and a privilege to be your first, so thank you. You were fucking amazing. And the way you took my dick was… wow.'

'Did I take it *like a good girl*?' I sniggered.

'That's a quote from *Office Delight*, right?' He smirked.

'Yep. And many other romance books.'

'You certainly did. You sure this was really your first time?'

'Positive.'

'Well, you're a natural.'

'Not yet, but maybe with practice I could be. It's a shame this was just a one-time lesson.'

'Yeah.' His gaze dropped for a few seconds before he looked at me again.

I knew I should be grateful that he'd helped me lose my virginity and should be satisfied with that.

But as I scanned Jackson's gorgeous body, all I could think of was that now I'd had sex with him once, I wanted to do it again…

30

JACKSON

As daylight pierced through the gaps in my bedroom blinds, I squinted.

The scent of strawberries and cream wafted in the air, and as I came to my senses, I looked down and saw the top of Jane's head on my chest. In an instant, the memories of last night came flooding back.

We had sex.

And it was fucking incredible.

It all happened so quickly. One minute I was speaking to Marcus, jumping around my room, celebrating the fact that a video had finally taken off and I wouldn't have to worry about paying Mum's fees, then the next, I was burying my cock inside the woman I'd liked since I was a teenager.

Damn.

Geeky sixteen-year-old Jackson would be so proud of adult Jackson right now. Actually, scrap that. If someone had told me back then that I'd get to sleep with Jane and be the first guy to fuck her, there was no way I'd ever believe it.

I meant what I'd said to her yesterday, though. She was amazing. I was worried about hurting her, but she took my dick like a champ. That was no easy feat because even women who were more experienced found it difficult at first.

And even though I'd been apprehensive about being her first because, let's face it, after she'd waited so long, her expectations would be high, so it was a lot to live up to, now I was glad that I'd done it. Not just because of how much I'd enjoyed it, but because I was able to give her the care and attention she deserved.

Yeah. Now that the mission had been accomplished, she could go out into the world with more confidence and find a boyfriend.

I'd said this would be a one-off and this time, I really meant it.

Jane stirred, opened her eyes, then looked up at me.

God, she even looked beautiful in the morning.

'Hey.' I stroked her hair. I loved seeing it down.

'Morning,' she said sheepishly.

'How did you sleep?'

'Like a baby.' She smiled.

'Good. How are you feeling?'

'Like I've been impaled on a giant cactus, but it's all good!' She laughed.

When we'd eventually got off the bed last night, we'd showered, then I'd brought the tray of snacks up, which we'd both demolished.

We'd planned to read together in bed after we'd taken a little nap, but we both fell asleep.

'Well, if you need anything to help with the pain, like more paracetamol or something, let me know. We have about'—I lifted my wrist up in the air to check my watch —'fifty-eight minutes before we have to leave for work.'

'So soon?' She sighed. 'Normally I can't wait to get to the library, but this morning I wish we could just stay in bed.'

. 'I hear you,' I said. I felt exactly the same. I knew that once we left this bed and this house, that'd be it. There'd be no more kissing Jane. No more tasting her. No more touching her. No more fucking her.

What a damn shame.

Jane rolled onto her back and propped herself up higher on a pillow.

'I'd happily lay on your chest for fifty-eight more minutes, but I've got shoulder ache!' She laughed. 'I should go and brush my teeth.' She put her hand over her mouth self-consciously.

'You're fine,' I reassured her.

'Plus, you probably want to do a morning workout or something.' She gestured to the large weights on the floor near the door.

'Nah. I already had a good workout last night.' I smiled.

'Me too! Speaking of which, what's with the tripod? You're not into filming yourself having sex, are you?' She laughed, and my stomach bottomed out.

Shit. I'd meant to hide that when I came upstairs, but then Marcus had called and I'd got distracted.

There was a pile of cleaning tools I'd used for the videos too.

Thank fuck that apron was in the wash and those damn thongs were safely in my drawers.

'Sorry.' Jane's face fell. 'I was just joking. I didn't mean to offend you.'

'You didn't,' I said quickly. 'It's just that the house is, er, on the market, so I was… I took some photos.'

'Oh.' She frowned. 'I thought the estate agent took photos with one of those cameras which makes the rooms look ten times bigger than they really are.'

'Yeah… they took some too, it was just…' My mind went blank. This was why it wasn't a good idea to have Jane here. And this was another reason why she couldn't come back here again. Even if I wanted her to.

It was already awkward when she asked when Mum was coming back. I really didn't like lying to her.

'Want some breakfast?' I said as I leapt off the bed, guilt washing over me. Changing the subject seemed like a better option than outright lying.

'Oh, okay. Yeah. Please,' Jane said. I could tell she'd noticed the abrupt subject shift. 'Just some tea and toast will be fine.'

'Cool. Give me five minutes, then the bathroom will be all yours.'

I quickly left the room, slipped into the bathroom, closed the door, then leant against it.

It's fine.

Jane had just seen a tripod. She hadn't even mentioned the cleaning stuff, which was good. It was no big deal.

When she'd asked if I filmed myself having sex, she hadn't realised just how close her joke was to the truth. But even so, there was no way she'd be able to make the leap from that to guessing that I used them to create naked videos online.

I mean, it wasn't like Jane was into watching internet porn.

If she wasn't even 'allowed' to keep spicy romance novels in the house and had to hide condoms in her sanitary towels, there was no way she'd risk watching a naked guy swinging his junk around whilst he stroked himself with a pink feather duster on her phone at home. She'd be too worried about her dad or brother finding out. She wouldn't watch that at work either.

Jane was more likely to have her head stuck in a book than watching me play with the head between my legs on the internet.

I was worrying over nothing.

As long as we stuck to the agreement that having sex was a one-off, my secret was safe.

And I had to make sure I kept it that way.

31

JANE

'Morning!' I chirped as I walked into the office, desperately trying not to wince with every step I took.

I wasn't joking earlier when I said that I felt like I'd been impaled by a cactus. But I wasn't complaining. With every sting came a fresh reminder of my incredible night with Jackson and all discomfort was temporarily forgotten.

'Good morning to you too!' Jess smiled, then held my gaze. 'You seem happy today!'

'Aren't I always?' I cocked my head to the side.

'Yeah, course! It's just, today you seem… *extra* happy. You've got a kind of glow. Y'know, like if you'd just had a facial… or… no. I know what it is. You've got that freshly fucked, post-orgasm glow. The sparkly eyes, the flushed cheeks, the…' My eyes bulged and Jess's face fell. 'Sorry! Still trying to remember to keep those workplace boundaries. Didn't mean to overstep.'

Whilst Jess was focused on her apology, I was rooted to the spot, shocked that she knew that I'd had sex. Especially when it had happened last night. It wasn't like me and Jackson had been banging in the bogs five minutes ago and I'd just returned to the office.

Did I really look different?

I felt different, and actually, she was right. When I was getting ready for work earlier, I did notice that my cheeks were flushed. I had an extra sparkle in my eyes. My hair was all over the place and I looked, I dunno… *wanton*. If someone looked up 'just been fucked' in the dictionary, I swear there could've been an image of me.

And when I walked to the station with Jackson, I definitely had an extra spring in my step.

Both things were completely understandable. The weight of a thousand elephants had been lifted off my shoulders, and I'd challenge even the grumpiest person on earth not to walk around grinning like an idiot after one night with Jackson.

'It's okay. You're… you're not wrong.' The corner of my mouth twitched, then my face broke into a full-blown smile.

I was bursting to tell someone and Jess was the only proper female friend I had right now and I knew I could trust her.

Theo was manning the library and Jackson was working with one of our volunteers in the bookshop, so I was safe to talk.

'Yeah?' Jess said.

'Yeah. It's a bit embarrassing to say, so please don't laugh, but last night, I… I finally lost my…' I was embarrassed to say it out loud.

'Your *virginity*?' Jess said softly and my jaw dropped.

'How did you know?'

'I didn't. Not for sure. I just… it was a guess. You seemed really uncomfortable when Celeste was talking in the pub and you said you had period pains, but I remembered you'd had your period the week before because you'd asked me for a pad or a tampon, so I thought maybe there was another reason why you felt awkward. I mean, it could've been that you just didn't like talking about sex, which is totally fine. And I don't want you to think that I'm some creepy boss who tracks your menstrual cycle or anything.' She winced. 'Like I said, it was just a guess.'

'Your guess was so accurate you should play the lottery.' I smiled.

'Maybe I should!' She laughed. 'So… if you don't mind me asking, how was it?'

'Amazing!' I said. 'Well worth the wait!'

'I'm so happy for you! At least you had a good experience. My first time was on the back seat of some guy's grotty car and it was over in about thirty seconds. Actually, now that I think about it, I'm being generous. Fifteen seconds is more accurate. So it was a total anticlimax. Ha! *Climax!* That obviously didn't happen. That guy couldn't have found my clit even if I gave him a map and step-by-step directions.'

'Oh.' I winced, thinking how lucky I was that my first time was much more enjoyable and that Jackson had given me an orgasm both before and during sex. 'Sorry to hear that.'

'Thanks, but doesn't matter anymore. The amount of orgasms Theo gives me has more than made up for it!' Jess laughed, then slapped her forehead. 'Boundaries! Please don't tell Theo I said that.'

'Your secret's safe with me.' I smiled.

'So, who was the lucky guy that got to pop your cherry?' Jess asked.

'Er…' I stuttered.

Just as I was working out whether or not I should tell Jess who I'd spent the night with, the door opened and Jackson walked in.

Oh. My. God.

It'd literally only been about fifteen minutes since I'd said bye to him in the corridor, but my stomach was flip-flopping like it had been fifteen weeks.

My eyes widened, my lips parted, my nipples instantly hardened and tingles raced between my legs.

He was so gorgeous. I couldn't believe his beautiful face was buried between my legs last night.

I couldn't believe that we'd slept together.

I still couldn't believe that I'd slept with anyone, let alone *him*.

'Hey.' Jackson smiled at me.

'Hi.' I smiled back.

Our eyes locked and we stared at each other in silence.

'Ohhhhhh…' Jess said as if she'd just solved a cold case. 'Say no more…'

I snapped out of my thoughts and turned to Jess, who was grinning like a Cheshire cat.

She knew.

I supposed I shouldn't be surprised considering I was giving Jackson love heart eyes.

'Er, hey, Jess.' Jackson walked over to her. 'I was just coming to tell you that the silent reading party event is sold out tonight!'

'That's amazing!' Jess jumped up from her seat. 'Thank you!'

'It was a team effort. Jane prepared and sent out the emails to our members and Sarah's been blasting it on social media.'

'But it was *your* idea,' I added. 'And you did the posters and leaflets that everyone's been sharing around town. You were fantastic.' I beamed at him, another flashback of last night racing through my head.

'Are we still talking about Jackson's marketing skills?' Jess chuckled and I realised I was swooning again.

'Y-yes!' My voice shot up.

'Sure, okay…' Jess grinned mischievously. 'Great teamwork, you two. Is everything else prepared?'

'Yeah,' Jackson said. 'The bottles of Prosecco are chilling in the fridge, the batches of biscuits will be brought over later and I'll make sure all of the bookshelves are fully stocked.'

'The extra cushions and blankets came yesterday, along with the beanbags I ordered, so we're all sorted with comfy seats too.'

'Perfect!' Jess said. 'I can't wait.'

'It's going to be brilliant!' I added.

'Anyway,' Jackson said, 'I better get back to it. Just thought I'd come and, y'know, say hi.' He faced me before turning back to Jess. 'And, er, give you an update. See you later.'

'Bye.' I waved like a lovesick teenager and almost put my hand to my heart as he disappeared out the door.

'OMG!' Jess squealed. 'You two are *adorable*! I really should start playing the lottery because I told Theo that you two would get together!'

'What? I…' I stuttered. I'd never thought that Jess would object to us getting involved, but I still felt weird saying anything because it was all so new. And of course it wasn't anything serious.

'Don't worry! This isn't like a normal workplace, which I think we've already established based on our conversation before your lover walked in!' Jess smirked. 'I'm happy for you both. Like I said to Theo, it's like the perfect romance story: friends reunited after years apart and fall in love. Mrs Davis would be so chuffed!'

'Oh, no!' I said quickly. 'It's not like that! We're not *together.* Jackson was just… helping me out. I really wanted to lose my virginity and he was kind enough to do that.'

'*Wow! What a saint!*' She laughed. 'Most men would be absolutely *horrified* about being the first man to take a dip in a sweet, innocent, virginal pussy, but brave Jackson valiantly stepped forward and accepted the difficult challenge. I'm sure he hated every blissful second.' Jess erupted into a fit of giggles.

'Well, yeah, he seemed to enjoy it too, but it's true. It was kind of him.'

'I'm only pulling your leg! I can tell Jackson's a good guy, so I'm not questioning his motives, but I'm just reminding you that taking a woman's virginity, especially someone as beautiful and amazing as you, would hardly be a hardship. I'm not a man, but I'd put money on that being up there as a lot of men's ultimate fantasy.'

'Maybe. But anyway, it was just a one-off.'

'*Sure, sure.*' Jess nodded and her grin told me very clearly that she didn't believe me.

'It's true! We won't be doing it again, so please don't mention it to anyone. I mean, obviously I know you'll tell Theo, but please don't say anything to Celeste when she comes back or any of the locals. I've seen how quickly news spreads here.'

The last thing I wanted was for Jackson to think I'd gone back on our arrangement. He had his reasons for not wanting anything serious, and even if it was a fantasy of his, I didn't want him to think I didn't respect his wishes.

It would be so embarrassing if he had to sit me down and remind me that he wasn't interested in dating me. Cringe.

'Don't worry. Your secret's safe with me. But out of interest, why won't you be doing it again? You two would be great together.'

'Lots of reasons,' I sighed.

'Well, I hope you're not holding back on your urges because of me. I don't mind. I know you'll both be professional. This isn't *Office Delight*! There's no forbidden workplace romance issues here!' She laughed. 'Remember I always said that Mrs Davis hoped that The Romance Library would become a place where people could find love, so I'm not about to stand in your way.'

'It's not just the working together thing. Jackson's not interested in something long-term. He's got a lot on his plate.'

'Like what?' Jess frowned.

'I'm not sure…' My voice trailed off.

Every time I tried to find out more about his life outside of work, he shut down or changed the subject.

I knew he'd opened up about what had happened with his last job, but I got the feeling there was something else he wasn't telling me.

'Maybe he'll change his mind. Be patient.'

Even if he did, it wouldn't be that simple. It wasn't all

about Jackson. I had some stuff I needed to resolve too. Like finding my own place.

My parents would hit the roof if they ever found out that I'd slept with Jackson. But if I started dating him, World War III would break out.

I knew with absolute certainty that they didn't approve of interracial relationships. And now that Dad was doing his stupid local MP campaign thing and believed that he had to present the perfect family life, he most definitely wouldn't be happy with me dating a black guy.

Personally, I didn't understand why it bothered them. All that they should care about was whether I was happy and if the man I was dating was good to me, but that was far too logical for my family.

That was why my focus had to be on getting away from them. Even though Jackson wasn't going to change his mind about us becoming a couple, it didn't matter. I needed to be free to do whatever I wanted and date whoever I wanted. I was getting really tired of the control my family had over me. Especially the way my dad butted into my life.

Take last night.

Whilst Jackson was in the bathroom, I thought I was being courteous by messaging Mum to tell her I wouldn't be coming home. But five minutes after I'd sent the text, Dad started calling. Obviously I ignored the call. It was almost midnight and I was still in a blissful haze after Jackson and I had had sex, then demolished every scrap of food on the tray he'd prepared. But then Dad had sent an angry text asking where the hell I was.

I didn't reply. Instead, I switched the phone off. I didn't want anything to ruin my perfect night.

And there was no way I could've gone to my parents'. The night that Jackson went down on me, when I got back to their house, I was paranoid that someone would take one look at my flushed, happy post-orgasm face and know I'd been tongue-fucked.

Luckily everyone was already in bed, but I'd had to wash my tights and knickers by hand too because I was convinced they'd somehow smell my juices and know what I'd been up to. And that was just after having oral sex. So given what me and Jackson had got up to last night, I knew it was better to stay over.

Now that I thought about it, I should probably turn my phone back on. Maybe I'd do that later. I was at work after all.

'It's okay. I'm happy with it just being a one-off thing,' I said, trying to convince myself as well as Jess. 'I need to focus on finding somewhere else to stay and we've got a lot to do here. I don't want to get distracted.'

'If you say so.' Jess raised an eyebrow.

It was true. I needed to focus.

But I also knew that if Jackson offered me the chance to have another ride on his dick, whether I had to deal with work, finding a flat, or facing the wrath of my ignorant family, the truth was, I'd say yes in a heartbeat.

32

JACKSON

As I sat at the front of the library hall and saw fifty guests with their heads buried in different romance books, my heart swelled.

We were only an hour into our first silent reading party and it was already a big hit.

Originally, we'd hoped to get thirty guests, but we'd exceeded expectations and I could tell from the massive grin on Jess's face that she was happy.

Even though the ticket price included a glass of Prosecco or hot drink, guests had already bought extras in the cafe, which would be great for boosting the library's profits.

Guests were allowed to bring their own books, but we were running special offers on some bestsellers tonight, so we'd sold a shitload of those novels too.

And people were loving the merch. They'd bought a ton of stickers and bookmarks. The tote bags and mugs would be ready in time for the next event and I reckoned they'd sell well too. Things were really starting to take off.

My phone pinged. Shit. I thought I'd put it on silent. As I pulled it out of my pocket and glanced at the screen, my eyeballs nearly flew out of their sockets.

'Fuck!' I shouted. Everyone's heads snapped up from their books.

'Sorry.' I winced. 'Jess, Theo, Jane—can I borrow you for a second?' I whispered. Once we were safely out in the corridor, I held out my phone. 'I think you'll all want to see this.' I pointed to the email that had just come through from D.D. Desire's agent.

'Oh my God!' Jess squealed before remembering she had to keep her voice down.

'Wait.' Jane's eyes popped. 'D.D. is coming *here*? To do a signing? *And* a reading?'

'Yep!' I grinned, then read the message again, just to double-check that it was real.

Dear Jackson,

Thank you for your patience. I'm thrilled to confirm that D.D. would absolutely LOVE to visit The Romance Library for a signing. She has also suggested that she do a reading from Illicit Delight.

We're still working out dates, but it's likely D.D. will be available to visit on a Sunday afternoon in around four weeks' time. I'll confirm the exact date and time shortly so that you can start promoting the event.

Looking forward to it already!

Yours sincerely,

Veronica x

'That's incredible!' Theo said. 'Well done, Jackson.'

'This is the best news ever!' Jess jumped up and down repeatedly. 'Thank you sooo much! Right, Jane and I better get back. Although I doubt I'll be able to concentrate on anything right now. I'm so excited!'

'Me too! You've made our week, Jackson.' Jane gave me a warm smile and my insides lit up.

I felt like I'd just invented water. They were all so happy and grateful. And knowing that I'd played a part in their joy made pride fill my chest.

'This really is fantastic news.' Theo slapped me affectionately on the back. 'Everything's going well tonight too.'

'Yeah, I'm really pleased with it.'

'When Jess told me you planned to hold a party in the library, at first I thought she meant a rave!' He laughed. 'I'd seen stuff about these bookish gatherings in other countries but never realised it'd be so popular here too.'

'Book lovers obviously love reading, but I think there's something cool about doing it in a social setting with other bookworms. Maybe it's because they know that in the breaks they can chat about what they're reading with someone who'll be interested. It's a good way to switch off from scrolling on social media and do something social, without being too social if that makes sense!' I chuckled. 'They don't have to worry about having to make awkward conversation because they already know they've got stuff in common.'

'So true. I love the idea of people coming here and making friends. Thanks for organising it. It's only been a few weeks since you've joined us, but we're already starting to see an increase in profits thanks to these events and the marketing initiatives you've implemented in the bookshop and cafe, and now we've got this mega signing to look forward to. Anyway, I wanted you to know how much we appreciate you.'

'Thanks.' My face broke into a smile. It was good to know that I was making a difference. And even better to hear that my efforts were appreciated. 'I'm really enjoying working here.'

'Glad to hear it. Anyway, we're going to need more Prosecco and teabags. I had no idea readers got so thirsty! For speed, I was thinking I could get the Prosecco from the pub because Barbara will give me a discount, whilst you get another box of teabags and some biscuits from the supermarket. We've sold out of all of the bookish ones Maddie made.'

'Course. I was just gonna bring more books from the shop to sell in the library during the next break.'

'Okay, great. I'll help you with that first.' Theo nodded.

We started walking towards the bookshop, but just as we stepped inside, the whole building plunged into darkness.

'What the…?' I said loudly.

'Must be a power cut,' Theo replied.

I reached in my pocket, pulled out my phone and switched on the torch. Theo did the same.

'You okay, Ellen?' I called out as I spotted our volunteer behind the till, her eyes wide.

'What happened?' she asked.

'Power cut,' I said.

'Hmmm, I'm not sure…' Theo called out. I used the torch to scan the shop and spotted him with his face pressed against the window. 'The streetlights are on. And the lights are on in the shops across the road too. I'm going to take a look in the electricity cupboard downstairs. Maybe a switch has tripped or something.'

I really hoped it was something we could fix quickly. There was a hall full of people who'd paid good money to come and read, which they couldn't do in the dark.

'I'll come with you.'

'We need to let Jess know we're on the case first, though.'

When we got to the hall, people were holding their phones in the air to light up the room like music fans did at concerts and the hall wasn't quiet anymore. The sound of nervous chatter buzzed in the air.

'What happened?' Jess said.

'We're going to check the electricity cupboard to find out.'

Theo and I raced down to the basement, eager to get the lights back on ASAP. If guests didn't enjoy themselves tonight, they wouldn't fork out to come to another event and we needed all the money we could get.

When Theo reached the electricity cupboard, it was already open.

'Fuck!' he shouted.

'What?' I said, wondering what was wrong, but as I got closer I understood his reaction.

'This was exactly what I feared.' He sighed. 'There hasn't been a power outage. Someone deliberately cut the electricity.'

Shit.

33

JACKSON

It'd been just over a week since someone had tampered with the electricity and we were still no closer to finding out who it was.

After Theo and I discovered what had happened, he'd called the police whilst I'd phoned Edwin, who'd once again saved the day by arranging for a load of residents to bring over as many candles as they could to light up the library.

Luckily, Maddie was working late at the cafe, so she was able to fill up multiple jugs with freshly brewed tea, which we handed out to guests for free whilst we tried to make the room bright enough for them to read.

In the end we just about pulled it off and the majority of guests were understanding, which was a relief.

The real test would be when we announced the next event. I had everything crossed that people would forgive us and still attend.

Theo had stepped up security, putting cameras in the

corridors and inside the bookshop and basement. He wasn't taking any chances.

None of us could understand who'd want to harm the library. Theo's dad was the obvious suspect, but after he'd denied it, he'd been ruled out.

I really hoped that whoever it was would get bored and stop soon because it was putting a lot of extra stress on Jess and Theo's shoulders.

I was worried and so was Jane.

Jane.

Just saying her name made my body light up.

We hadn't spoken much since the event.

Jess had insisted that Jane do the earlier shifts so she was never locking up or alone at the library. I'd been working the late shifts with Theo. During the day it'd been crazy busy, so we hadn't got to catch up then either. Especially as I was working alone in the bookshop most days, with Jess or a volunteer relieving me for my breaks.

But things would be different today.

Jane and I had agreed to work late today to give Jess and Theo time to go and follow up on the only other person they could think of who might have something to do with the attacks on the library: Jess's ex.

Although he didn't go into detail, Theo said that Jess's ex was against her reading romance novels and they'd had a bad break-up. Would that be enough of a reason for him to throw a brick through the window, cut the electricity or attempt to ruin the books by creating a hole in the roof? They seemed to think so.

The police hadn't come up with any leads, so I totally understood why Theo and Jess felt that it was worth paying her ex a visit.

I stepped inside Mum's care home with a spring in my step. Not only was I excited about getting to visit her, I was also relieved because for the first time in months, I wasn't worried about walking into reception or seeing the manager, Hilda.

Up until recently, whenever I visited, my heart would be pounding in my chest because I was worried about being summoned to the office to discuss my overdue invoices.

But not today. For the first time in what felt like forever, Mum's account was up to date. And it was all thanks to the videos, which had gone viral.

When Marcus had called before Jane and I had sex, it was already doing well. With all of the excitement of being with Jane, then what happened at the event the following night, by the time I got home, I was too exhausted to check my messages. But when I did the next morning and saw how much it'd blown up, I couldn't believe my eyes.

It was insane. And it kept growing.

That was when Marcus had suggested I film more. Then he'd come up with an idea to take requests and create different subscription tiers. People who paid more got to make a request for what cleaning tool they wanted me to dance with next in a video.

It was fucking genius.

Those were the videos I'd filmed this morning. Marcus did all of the liaison with the subscribers and sent over a list of instructions. I knew I wouldn't get time to do them once I got back from the library and I wanted to see Mum before my shift started. So I got up extra early, cleaned the house, then got in front of the camera.

It still took me a while to get into doing them and I still

felt kind of embarrassed. But the bottom line was, I'd earned enough to pay the bills that had been hanging over my head and the relief was priceless. So if I had to swing my dick around and create sexy videos to make sure Mum got the care she needed, that was what I'd do.

Knowing that everything was anonymous because I wasn't showing my face on camera definitely made things easier.

'Hey, Hilda!' I said enthusiastically.

'Mr Campbell.' She nodded in acknowledgement.

'Did you receive the payment safely?' I asked.

'We did, thank you. Next one will be due in two weeks.'

'No probs!' I said confidently. With the extra subscriptions and my salary at the library, I was close to being able to pay for all of that too.

Ordinarily I'd say money didn't buy happiness, and I knew that first-hand after the stress I was under in my last job, but right now, having this extra cash really helped.

'Your mother is expecting you.'

'How is she today?'

'Good.'

'Great! I'll go and see her now.'

I walked along the corridor and when I got to Mum's room, I knocked on the door.

She was sitting by the window, which looked out onto the gardens. It was a decent view. They kept the grounds well maintained, so the residents could sit outside or stare at the colourful floral arrangements from their room, which Mum liked to do.

'Hi, Mum.' I walked in. My heart thumped against my

chest and I crossed my fingers, hoping that today she'd remember me.

'Jackson!' Her face lit up. 'How are you, son?'

'I'm good!' I said enthusiastically as I walked over and wrapped my arms around her.

She remembered who I was. This was great.

I'd lost count of the amount of times that she either didn't remember me or got me mixed up with Dad, which was heartbreaking.

'How's work? Are you eating?' she said. 'Got to keep your strength up for your big City job! Don't make them work you too hard. It's important to make time for family.'

So she thought I still worked in finance.

This was always the difficult part. I never knew whether or not to go along with what she thought or correct her.

'I'm at the library now. I've got a new job. It's really fun. I get to talk to lots of people about romance books.'

Mum used to love reading romance novels, so knowing one of her biggest passions had been ripped away from her was one of the hardest things to see.

Both of my parents were always big readers. And even when Dad passed, Mum was never without her romance books. She'd read them on the bus to her many jobs and if she got an evening off from work, which didn't happen often, she'd prefer to sit and read instead of watching TV.

But now, she could barely read a Post-it note.

Mum couldn't read books anymore because she couldn't follow the story. And even if she'd read something a few minutes earlier, she wouldn't be able to remember what happened.

Seeing the kind of books that she used to devour in the

library and bookshop that I could've bought for her to read but knowing that she couldn't do that or simple things like write her name anymore broke my damn heart.

'How's work in London, son?' Mum repeated.

Shit.

I knew it wasn't good to correct her or make her feel bad for forgetting, so I decided it was best to go along with it.

'Everything's good. Do you want to go for a walk, in the garden?' I stood up and held out my hand, but Mum didn't take it.

That meant she just wanted to keep looking out of the window. So that's what we did. For an hour, we sat there together.

Occasionally she'd speak. Usually to ask me the same question, and I answered the best I could and smiled in the right places, despite my heart shattering.

This was such a cruel disease. I still didn't understand how my vibrant, smart mother couldn't even do the things that used to be so easy for her. It was like she was a shadow of how she used to be and it was so tough to watch.

Eventually, I hugged her goodbye and told her I'd be back soon. It was unlikely that she'd even remember this visit, but I'd still keep coming to see her. Because it mattered. Even if me being there made her feel happy for just a few seconds or minutes, it was worth it.

As soon as I stepped through the library's doors, my shoulders relaxed. This place was my sanctuary.

The cherry on top right now would be to see Jane before I started my shift. I missed our chats.

Although I'd been busy at work and making videos

over the past week, I still thought about Jane. All the damn time. I hoped that we'd get to spend some time together later once the library closed. I didn't want the fact that we'd fucked last week to get in the way of our friendship.

Things with Mum were bound to get harder, not easier, and I could really use a friend. I wasn't ready to talk about Mum yet, but when I was, I knew Jane would understand. She was always a good listener.

It wasn't just her empathy that I liked. There was something about her that made things better.

When she smiled at me, it was like she turned on a happy switch in my body. And, no, I wasn't talking about the happy switch in my boxers, although, yeah, based on the night we spent together, she did that too.

It was more than that. Whenever Jane was around, I felt comfortable. Accepted. Happy.

Instead of heading straight to the office, I made a detour to the library hall to see Jane, but she was with a member.

I hovered by the door for a while, hoping to catch her attention, even just to wave at her. *Anything.*

Going to see Mum was always difficult. I could really use a hug right now.

After a couple of minutes, I left. She was busy and I had to plan the next event.

'Hey, Jackson,' said Jess as I stepped into the office. 'Are you okay?' Her face creased with concern.

'Yeah, fine,' I said. It wasn't a complete lie. Although I was still sad about my visit to see Mum earlier, now I was at the library, I was feeling a bit better. 'How are you?'

'I'm good. Dreading my visit to see my ex later, though, to be honest.'

'I can imagine,' I said. 'At least Theo will be there.'

'Yeah. That's a good and also a bad thing.'

'Oh?' I frowned.

'Theo's not a fan of my ex after what he did to me.'

'Did he hurt you?' I ground my jaw. Jess was a good person and I hated the idea of anyone doing anything bad to her.

'Physically, no. Mentally, *definitely*.'

Jess went on to explain that he hated her reading steamy romance books and when she refused to get rid of them, he burned her entire collection.

Actually set fire to them.

What kind of fucked-up person would do that?

No wonder he was a prime suspect. Anyone who could do something that shitty was capable of anything. The guy should be locked up.

'Fuck. What an arsehole. I'm with Theo. I don't blame him for wanting to punch your ex's lights out.'

That was exactly how I felt whenever I heard about the things Jane's dad did or said to her. If he ever upset Jane again, I couldn't be held responsible for my actions.

'Yep. My ex was a monumental shithead, so I'm not looking forward to coming face to face with him again. But I need to go. I have to look him in the eye and find out whether it's him that's doing all of this.'

'I hear you. I hope you get to the bottom of this soon. Let me know if I can do anything to help.'

'You're already helping by filling in tonight. Thanks again.'

'No worries,' I said, picking up the laptop. 'If you need me, I'll be in the bookshop.'

∾

I couldn't believe it was almost closing time. There'd been so much to get through today. Checking the stock, ordering stock and sending out the email newsletter for the next event.

After the last customer had left the bookshop, I finally got the chance to go and see Jane.

Excitement raced through me. It felt like it'd been months since I'd spoken to her properly, not just over a week.

When I saw a guest leaving the meet-cute desk, my pulse quickened. Jane was finally free.

'Hey!' I said.

'Hello, stranger.' She smiled.

'It's been a while.' I stood in front of her, grinning like a teenager who'd just met his celebrity crush in real life.

Our eyes locked and we stared at each other in silence.

As well as coming to speak to Jane, I'd come to ask her something, but now I couldn't remember what. All I could think about was how much I wanted to touch her. To hold her. To kiss her.

And more.

'That was the last guest.' Jane broke the silence, pushing her glasses up the bridge of her nose.

'You going to your parents', or do you want to hang out, here?'

I'd considered inviting her back to mine, but I couldn't say Mum was still away. Plus, the sex thing was a one-off and if she came home with me, that'd be putting temptation right in front of us.

No. It was safer to read here.

'Yes!' Her eyes widened. 'I'd love that.'

'By the way, I read two of the blind date books *and* I finished *Office Delight*.'

'No way!'

'Yep.'

'I want to hear what you thought!'

'Cool. I'll lock up. You okay to get some tea and biscuits and then we can talk about it?'

'Course!'

A wide smile spread across my face. There weren't many people that would want to stay late at their workplace voluntarily. I hated doing that at my old job, but I'd be happy to chill here all night with Jane.

I went back to the library hall, where Jane was already curled up on the sofa.

A flashback of her lying naked in my bed popped into my head and I pushed it out again.

It was just a one-off, I reminded my brain.

If my dick could talk, it'd ask whether it really had to be.

This was the battle I'd been fighting since we'd had sex last Thursday night.

It was now the following Saturday and I still hadn't managed to get my desire under control.

'Party Rings and Jaffa Cakes!' I grinned as I looked down at the plate.

'Yep. I've been saving them. Just in case.' She smiled and my heart swelled. Her buying my favourite biscuits wasn't going to help me keep my feelings under wraps.

'Thank you.'

'So!' Jane fixed her gaze on me as soon as I walked

into the room. 'Tell me all about *Office Delight* and the blind date books you read.'

'In a minute.' I sat beside her and tried not to be affected by her delicious strawberry scent. 'First, I need to hear how you've been. Are you still at your parents'?'

Jane's body language immediately changed. Her shoulders dropped and she hung her head.

'Yeah. Still there. I've been looking and there's nothing. I thought I'd found somewhere in a town about forty minutes away, but a few hours before I went to see it, I got a call to say it'd been rented. There's so few properties and the ones that are available are either too expensive or aren't safe, either because of the location or the condition of the property. One I went to see had so much damp I was surprised it hadn't been reported.'

'Shit.' My chest tightened. I hated that she was going through this. I'd start looking myself to help her tomorrow. 'I'm sorry.' Guilt washed over me. I wished I didn't have to hide the video stuff from her and Mum's condition. Then she could stay with me.

If I waited a few more weeks so I saved up enough money to clear next month's payment, hopefully then I could consider asking her.

'Don't apologise! It's not your fault. It's okay for now. I've been able to keep out of Dad's way and his photoshoot has been put off for another couple of weeks, so it's only when that comes around and I tell him I'm not taking part that things are really going to kick off.'

'Well, if it ever gets too much, you call me, okay?'

'Okay. Now, please! Tell me your thoughts!'

'First I'll tell you about the blind date books.'

'Which ones did you read?'

'So I went for the short and sweet one first, which was *The Exception to the Rule* by—'

'Christina Lauren,' Jane said, finishing my sentence.

'That's it. And I loved it. All the emails were really cute. Then I read the one which said to open it when you want a romantic adventure that will make you laugh and warm your heart, which was *The Love of My Afterlife* by— wait, I know this one: Kirsty Greenwood.'

'Correct!'

'It was brilliant. I loved the premise. It was really unique and the ending warmed my heart, just like you predicted.'

'I'm so glad you enjoyed them!'

'You're excellent at book recommendations. I can see why you're a librarian.' I laughed.

'So, I'm dying to know your thoughts on *Office Delight*!'

'Well.' I slid my shoes off, lifted my legs up onto the sofa, then angled my body to face her. Jane tucked her legs under her chin and leant forward, her eyes wide with antic- ipation.

I fought the urge to take her head in my hands and kiss her. Instead I told myself to focus on answering her question.

'Spoiler alert… I loved it!'

'Yes!' she cheered.

'I mean, at first I was like, this Rocco dude is a giant, what was the romance lingo again? *Alpha-hole*?'

'Yep!' She nodded.

'Yeah, so at first he seemed like an arrogant twat, but when I learnt more about his character and backstory and saw how much he loved Virginia, he wormed his way into

my good books, excuse the pun. And the grovel was good,'
I said, using another one of the romance phrases Jane had
taught me when we'd had dinner at the fish and chips
restaurant.

'I know, right!'

'It was funny, romantic and I'm not gonna lie: it was a
bit emotional in parts too. The ending was cute. And the
spice… *damn*!'

'It's hot, isn't it?'

'That's putting it politely,' I said, thinking about all the
different ways Rocco had fucked Virginia and wishing I
could do the same to Jane.

Focus. Focus. Fucking focus.

'I liked when Rocco had Virginia up against the desk
and the wall…' Jane said, her cheeks flushing.

'Yeah.' I smirked. 'I noticed, from the way that almost
every page of that chapter was highlighted.'

'*Oi!*' She hit my arm playfully.

'What? No judgement. But if you don't like people
dog-earing pages, how come you don't mind underlining
and annotating your books?'

'It's totally different! It's not intentionally damaging a
book, it's making it my own. When I annotate a novel, it's
a sign of love and appreciation. I'm documenting my
favourite sections. I'm showing which parts I connected
with emotionally and my reactions. What made me laugh,
what made me cry, what made me…' She bit her lip.

'It was a great chapter. I enjoyed it too…' My voice
trailed off and our eyes locked again.

Shit.

I was trying to focus, but all I could think of was
pinning Jane against the meet-cute desk. Or wall.

Then again, now that she wasn't a virgin anymore and knew how amazing sex could feel, she could've met someone else already.

Jane was smart and sexy. Like I'd always said, any guy would be lucky to have her and I wasn't the only man on earth, so it wouldn't take long for her to be snapped up.

'So how about you? Have you found someone to take you against a desk or wall since we, *y'know…*'

That just slipped out. I had no right to ask her. It was none of my business. But I couldn't help myself.

'No.' She shook her head. 'I know I've only had sex once, but you've ruined me. No one else is going to compare to our night together.'

My eyes widened and I admit, hearing that made me feel ten feet tall.

'You don't mean that.'

'I do. In case it wasn't obvious. I really like you, Jackson. I think about you. A *lot*.'

'Yeah?' I cocked my head. 'What kind of things do you think about?'

'When I'm… in the shower holding the jet against my…' Her voice lowered like she was embarrassed to say the word.

'You think about me when you're holding a showerhead against your pussy?' I filled in the blanks.

'Yes,' she said softly and my dick jerked.

Fuck. Me. I was trying to keep my cool, but she was making it difficult.

'And at night. When I touch myself,' she added.

'I think about you too,' I said quickly. 'I have fantasies about all the different places I'd like to fuck you.'

Jane swallowed hard, then bit her lip.

My cock was now straining against my jeans. I wanted her so much right now.

'I think about that too,' she said softly. 'Last night I dreamt that you… never mind.' Jane dropped her head.

'What?' I lifted her chin. 'Tell me.'

'I dreamt that you had me up against the bookcase. Right over there.' Jane pointed.

'Yeah?'

'Yeah.'

I'd been thinking about that since I first saw her again, but hearing Jane saying she'd had the same fantasy activated a switch in my brain. And my cock. There was no going back now.

'Talking of a bookcase, I was looking for a book earlier and I couldn't find it.'

'What book?' Jane frowned.

'It was the new one by Susie Tate.'

'It's definitely there.' Jane frowned. 'I literally saw it two hours ago.'

'Can you show me?' I got up, then held out my hand.

'Course.' She jumped up and took my hand.

I knew I'd missed the feel of her palm in mine, but it was only when our fingers intertwined that I realised how much.

Jane led me over to the bookcase, then went straight to the section.

As she bent down to get it with her back to me, I stood behind her.

'Here it is!' She spun around.

'I have a confession,' I said. 'I knew the book was there. That wasn't why I asked you to find it.'

'Oh,' she said. 'Why did you?'

'Because you just said you've been thinking about me when you touch yourself. Then you told me that your fantasy is to be fucked against a bookcase and I don't know why, but it's like, whenever you tell me you need something, I can't help doing whatever I can to make it possible.'

It was true. The same thing happened when I knew someone going down on her on a sofa was her fantasy.

The same thing happened when she asked me to take her virginity.

And now that she'd told me that she wanted to do it in the library, how could I refuse?

I'd tried everything to forget about that night we spent together, but I couldn't.

I'd missed Jane. Not just the physical, but spending time with her. Talking to her.

And I'd been thinking. Maybe we could make this work.

Things were going well with the videos, and with the money I was earning at the library now I was working full-time, I'd be able to pay for Mum's fees for at least the next month or two, which was amazing. So I wasn't under so much financial pressure.

Jane had mentioned that Jess and Theo knew that we'd hooked up and were fine about it, so I didn't have to worry about things blowing up at work. So maybe we could enjoy ourselves a little bit. Not anything serious, but just enjoy spending time with each other and see where it went.

'You want to have sex, *here*?' Jane's eyes bulged.

'Only if you want to.'

'So you're just doing this to help me?' She raised her eyebrow.

'I'd be lying if I said this was entirely selfless. I can't stop thinking about you. I want to be inside you again. And you're a love librarian, so surely being fucked against a bookcase is a rite of passage, right? I reckon it's occupational research and I'd be *very* happy to volunteer my services to help you. So the only question now is whether you'd like to accept.'

'You're seriously asking if I'd like you to take me against a bookcase like I've read and fantasised about so many times?'

'Yep. Consent is important. Especially considering we're co-workers.'

'I appreciate you checking, but in case it wasn't obvious, the answer is a very clear, extremely enthusiastic *yes*.'

'Good,' I growled. 'That's all I needed to hear…'

34

———

JANE

Before I had a chance to catch my breath, Jackson pushed me up against the bookcase and our lips collided.

Jackson kissed me like his life depended on it. The kiss was urgent and frenzied. As his lips roamed hungrily over mine, I felt so desired. It was as if I was the only woman that could satisfy him and that thought made my body pulse with need.

'Oh God,' I moaned as he plunged his tongue into my mouth. 'I want you.' I lifted my leg and wrapped it around his back.

Jackson trailed his mouth along my neck, causing goosebumps to erupt over every inch of my skin.

'Is this your favourite blouse?' Jackson asked, his mouth still on my neck.

'No,' I panted. 'Why?'

'Because it's got those difficult buttons again and I might have to destroy it.'

'Do it,' I said.

Jackson found a small opening, then ripped it open with his hands.

So hot.

After reaching behind my back, he skilfully unclipped my bra, then pulled it off with his mouth.

My bra tumbled to the floor and as the cool air hit my chest, my nipples instantly hardened.

'Look at you, standing here against the bookcase with your beautiful tits out,' he growled. 'What would you like me to do to them?'

'Suck them,' I said. 'Please.'

'Always so polite.' He smiled.

Jackson dipped his head and took my nipple in his mouth, sending shockwaves through me.

Whilst he sucked at my sensitive bud, his hands roamed down to the hem of my skirt. He pushed it up around my waist, then tugged at the top of my tights and knickers.

'You're wearing too many clothes,' he said, lifting his head, then moving his attention to suck on my other hard nipple.

'So are you,' I said through a ragged breath before taking off my glasses, which had steamed up, resting them on a shelf, then moving my hands to his belt.

I could feel his long, thick cock straining against his jeans and was desperate to set it free.

It took a few attempts to unbuckle his belt because with Jackson's delicious tongue licking and sucking my nipples, it was hard to keep my fingers steady. But eventually I succeeded.

I dragged his jeans down his thighs. It'd been over a

week since I'd last seen or felt his dick and I was desperate to know if it was as amazing as I remembered.

Dropping my gaze between his legs, I quickly pulled down his boxer shorts. As his cock sprang free, I gasped.

Yep. As I wrapped my hand around him, then began moving it back and forth, I could confirm that it felt just as long, thick and velvety smooth as it'd been in every fantasy I'd had since he'd taken my virginity.

'Fuck, Jane,' he grunted. 'If you keep touching me, I won't last. And this is supposed to be about your fantasy, not mine.'

Jackson dropped to his knees and slid my knickers and tights further down my legs.

'Take these off and spread your legs,' he commanded.

Lifting one leg and then the other, I let Jackson slide them past my ankles and on the floor.

I couldn't believe I was standing here up against the bookcase, basically naked. The only thing I had left on was my skirt, which was still wrapped around my waist.

'Want to take this off too?' I pointed to the skirt.

'Nah.' Jackson looked up at me. 'Adds to the excitement.'

'Yeah,' I said. 'Like you're so desperate for me you don't have time to take it off because you need to fuck me quickly before we get caught.'

'Is that what happens in your fantasy?'

I nodded.

'Hmmm.' Jackson smiled. 'I like it. And in your fantasy, do I also do this?'

I was about to ask what he meant when he dipped his head between my legs, spread my lips, then licked me from my entrance to my clit, oh-so-slowly.

I cried out and my head pushed back, hitting the books on the shelves behind me.

'Yes,' I moaned. 'More.'

Jackson continued lapping at my clit as I gripped the back of his head, pushing him deeper.

'I'm already close,' I said, 'but I want you inside me. Please.'

Jackson lifted his head, smiled, then stood up.

'Is my love librarian ready to get fucked against the bookcases?'

'Yes,' I panted, my heart thundering in my chest.

Jackson reached into his jeans, which were still around his knees, pulling out his wallet and then a condom.

'I bought some the other day. Just in case… want to put it on?'

'Okay,' I said.

After carefully tearing the corner, I slid it out of the pack, but then I frowned, not sure which way to roll it on. When I figured it out, I wrapped my fingers around him with one hand, then slid the condom down with the other.

That wasn't so *hard*.

'Sure you're ready?' Jackson said, sliding his fingers between my legs.

'Definitely.'

'Wrap your leg around my back again,' he commanded.

After lining himself up between my thighs, Jackson slid his cock between my legs without entering me. The sensation of him slipping and sliding over my clit drove me insane with desire.

'I need you,' I pleaded. 'Put it in. *Please.*'

Just when I thought I was about to pass out with desperation, Jackson slammed into me.

'Fuck!' I cried out.

It took me by surprise so much that my knees buckled and my elbow knocked against the books.

'You okay?' he asked.

'Yes!' I gripped his waist as I tried to adjust to the feeling of his huge dick inside me. 'Don't stop.'

Jackson did as I asked and continued thrusting.

I wasn't gonna lie. At first it was painful. Not as much as the first time, but there was still a sharp, stinging sensation. But then when I looked down and saw his cock sliding in and out, desire rocketed through me.

Here I was getting fucked against a bookcase and living out yet another fantasy.

I moved my hips against his and it wasn't long until we found the perfect rhythm.

Just when I thought it couldn't get any better, Jackson slid his fingers between my legs and started stroking my clit.

'Jesus!' I screamed. 'Oh my God!'

And then he dipped his head, took my nipple in his mouth and sucked it hard, all whilst he pounded into me.

Whoever said men couldn't multitask clearly hadn't experienced Jackson's ability to use his cock, mouth and hands simultaneously to give me pleasure.

We were now fucking so hard that even though the bookcase was secured to the ground, I was sure it started to shake.

As my elbows and arse crashed against the books, several tumbled onto the floor around us, but I didn't care.

Even if I ruined a hundred novels, right now, I'd

happily pay for every single one to be replaced, even if it meant I had to stay at my parents' for longer. I wasn't going to let anything get in the way of me experiencing what I knew was going to be the best orgasm of my life.

Admittedly, my experience of receiving orgasms was limited, but I was convinced that even if I'd had hundreds before, this would still come top.

Jackson was now circling my clit as he slammed into me, harder. Faster. Over and over again. As I gripped his bum cheeks, pushing him deeper, I knew I was powerless to stop the fire burning inside me.

He crashed his mouth onto mine and as our lips moved frantically over each other's and I tasted myself on him, I hurtled closer to the edge.

This man wasn't just fucking my brains out—earlier, he'd also feasted on my pussy, again, like I was his favourite meal.

I wasn't plain Jane the boring virgin anymore.

I wasn't Jane the librarian who worked in a romance library but had never had her own romance.

Tonight I was Wanton Jane.

The sexually liberated woman who got her pussy eaten out on a library sofa. The wild woman who let her sexy co-worker fuck her against a bookcase.

Right now, I felt like the sexiest woman alive.

'Jackson!' I moaned as I felt my orgasm building. 'I-I can't hold on. I'm gonna…'

'That's it, baby.' He pounded into me, filling me up deeper than I even thought was possible. 'Come for me.'

My breathing went ragged and then broke into full-blown erratic panting.

'Jackson!' I squeezed my eyes shut. 'Oh… oh, Jackson!'

My orgasm erupted like a volcano.

My body shook as tingles ripped through me. And my head flew back so violently that it sent dozens more books crashing to the floor.

Jackson continued pumping into me.

'Jane,' he groaned. 'Fuck. Fuck. Fuckkkkk!' A feral sound shot from his mouth as he exploded inside me.

After a few more thrusts, his body stilled and he dropped his head on my shoulder.

Our chests heaved against each other's. I was desperate to lower my leg. It hadn't had this much of a workout since… I didn't know when, but I didn't have the energy to move a single muscle.

I had no idea how much time passed with us resting against the bookcases, trying to catch our breaths, but eventually Jackson lifted his head.

'That was…'

I opened my eyes and looked up at him. He was staring at me like I was the woman who invented orgasms.

'Yeah,' I said, sure that my eyes were big love hearts right now. 'Absolutely incredible.'

'Just absolutely incredible?' He raised his eyebrow. 'I was gonna say *phenomenal*. That's better than incredible, right?'

'Debatable,' I said. 'Okay, how about absolutely phenomenally incredibly out of this world? Would that cover it?'

'That's more accurate!' Jackson laughed and the sound made my heart flutter. 'I should take the condom off.'

'Okay,' I said, lowering my leg. As he pulled out, I instantly missed the connection. It was like when Jackson was inside me, I felt whole, but now I felt hollow. 'I should get cleaned up. And then, we'll have a lot of cleaning up to do…' I signalled to the floor, which was littered with my underwear, a ripped blouse, buttons, dozens of books and my glasses, which miraculously were still intact.

Jackson pulled out a pack of tissues from his pocket, handed two to me, wrapped the condom in another, then wiped himself before pulling up his boxers and jeans.

'Later. First let's rest. Come on.' He took my hand and led me to the sofa. He released my palm, picked up a blanket, spread it over the sofa, laid down, then patted the space beside him. 'Lie with me.'

'I should get my clothes,' I said. 'I'll get cold.'

'I'll keep you warm.'

I got on the sofa and sank into him, resting my head on his chest as he wrapped one arm around me, then used the other to lift the blanket to cover us both.

This was bliss. I could stay here forever. The sound of his heartbeat, the warmth from his body, his delicious woody scent, the softness of his skin… everything was perfect.

This was what dreams were made of.

The first time we'd had sex was fantastic.

The second time was—how had I described it? *Absolutely phenomenally incredibly out of this world.*

And even though yet again I knew I shouldn't wish for more, I couldn't wait to find out what the third time would be like…

35

JACKSON

I kissed the top of Jane's head and wrapped my arms tighter around her.

When I'd said that was phenomenal, I was massively downplaying things. Even her description didn't cover it. That was hands down the hottest sex I'd ever had.

I loved everything about it. Eating her out against the bookcase, stripping her naked, fucking her as the books crashed on the floor around us, when her pussy tightened around my cock, then she screamed my name again, and of course when I exploded inside her.

For the past week, I'd tried to convince myself that the reason it had felt so good the first time was because of the thrill of doing something I shouldn't combined with knowing I was the first man to bury my dick in her sweet pussy.

Jane could've chosen anyone to take her virginity, but she'd chosen *me*.

But now we'd done it again, I knew for sure it was

more than that. Yeah, there was the thrill of fucking in the library, which was forbidden. But everything felt more intense and so much better because of our history and the fact that I was finally having sex with the girl I'd crushed on for years at school.

It was difficult to put it into words, but Jane did something to me. I was hypnotized.

Some people got addicted to drugs or alcohol, but my addiction was this woman.

I was falling for her. *Hard.*

'Jackson,' Jane said softly.

'Mmm?' I stroked her hair, which had fallen out of her bun and was hanging around her shoulders.

Jane's glasses were either on the bookcase or on the floor, which meant I had an uninterrupted view of her pretty brown eyes.

'Can I ask a question?'

'Course.'

'I know I'm supposed to act cool about this, but we both know that I've never been one of the cool kids.' She laughed.

'That makes two of us,' I chuckled.

'Yeah, so, originally you said this was a one-off and obviously we've done this twice now, so… what does this mean? Is this just a hook-up or have you changed your mind? Do you want us to be together?'

Shit.

Before we'd had sex, I'd asked myself the same question. And I'd thought that maybe this *could* work. But I still wasn't sure if I was ready for something serious. I took a deep breath.

'I want to be with you. I'm just…' I was about to say

that I was going through some stuff, but I knew that if I did, she'd ask what, and I wasn't ready to tell her. 'I just… it's been a while since I've been in a proper relationship.'

'I'm hardly an expert, but maybe it doesn't have to be so complicated. We already know we get on well, we enjoy spending time together, we have loads in common and there's obviously a strong attraction, so surely as long as we're honest with each other and we communicate, we'll be able to get through anything, right?'

Good point.

I always felt better when I was with Jane and I'd never felt more connected to a woman in my life. But she'd also spoken about the importance of honesty, and it felt wrong to start a relationship without telling her about Mum and the other stuff I was going through.

We'd had the perfect evening. I'd just fulfilled another one of her fantasies. I could tell by the way that she was looking at me that she was on cloud nine and didn't want to pop her happy bubble by talking about depressing stuff. Mum was ill and there was no way to sugar-coat that.

Although things were looking up financially, I still had bills coming out my arse and had a long way to go before I pulled myself out of my mess.

And then there were the videos. What woman would be happy knowing that her boyfriend was flashing his dick to strangers online for money? Precisely zero.

Jane would already have an uphill struggle once her parents found out about us. They never thought that someone like me would be good enough for her.

Before, I would've disagreed. But now I'd started to sell my body for money, I was kind of proving them right.

This was messy as fuck. I had more baggage than an airport terminal.

'I don't know, Jane. I've got… there's things I need to…' I was about to tell her, but her face fell and I chickened out.

'Jackson.' She paused. 'I really like you. And I get that you're worried about getting into a relationship. But the thing is, even though Jess is cool about us being involved and clearly I enjoy having sex with you, it's not something that I should keep doing unless I know it means something. I need reassurance that it's not just a fling. The more that we do this, the more I'm going to fall for you, and I don't want to get my heart broken.'

'I know.' I stroked her cheek. 'I hear you. And I'd never want to do that. You're more than just a fling. I really want you to be my girlfriend. I want us to be together—'

'Really?' she jumped in, her eyes sparkling with happiness.

'Yeah.'

I meant every word.

I also meant to continue my sentence and add 'but I can't because my life's a mess right now' to the end of it, but when I saw how happy Jane looked, I couldn't do it.

'Oh my God!' she squealed, then wrapped her arms around me. 'That's amazing! I'm so happy!'

Of course I was going to tell her about Mum. I wanted to. And I'd pluck up the courage to confess about the videos too. I was sure once Jane heard why I had to do it, she'd understand. So did it really matter whether we made it official now or in a couple of weeks?

As soon as the time was right, I'd lay it all out there.
Put all my cards on the table.
I'd tell her everything.
Just not tonight.

36

JANE

The past two and a half weeks had been a whirlwind of joy.

I couldn't remember the last time I was so happy.

And it was all because of Jackson.

My *boyfriend*.

That night after we'd had sex at the library and I'd asked if he wanted us to be together and he'd started stuttering, I thought he was going to say no. I felt so connected to him, but I couldn't shake the feeling that there was stuff he was holding back.

But I needn't have worried. It wasn't because Jackson was keeping secrets. He was just afraid of getting into a relationship, that was all. Like I'd said, though, as long as we communicated, we'd be fine.

Jess was the only one who knew it was official between us, but apart from telling Theo, I'd sworn her to secrecy. It was still early days, so I didn't want the whole town finding out.

That was why during working hours we tried to keep

our distance. But as soon as we were alone, we couldn't keep our hands off each other.

If we were working the late shift together, we'd either make love on the sofa (always covering it with a blanket, which Jackson would wash at home) or against the wall (once again, thoroughly cleaned by Jackson afterwards), and when Jackson was sure his mum would be home late, we'd slept together in his bed too.

Last weekend his mum was away again, so I'd stayed over. I knew my parents were getting suspicious of all my late nights, but I didn't care. I was having too much fun.

I'd even successfully given Jackson multiple blow jobs. The first time was at the library about a week ago. I'd wanted to do it for a while and after Jackson had gone down on me against the bookcase, I'd fantasised about doing the same to him, but just like Rocco had asked Virginia, I wanted him to ask me too.

'You want me to order you to get on your knees?' Jackson had asked.

'Yes,' I'd panted. 'Ask me to… to take it.'

A smile had touched his lips.

'Now, I'm only saying this because you highlighted it in the book. Not because I'm being disrespectful, okay?' he'd started.

'Say it,' I demanded.

'Jane. Get on your knees and take this dick like a good girl,' he'd growled and I almost came on the spot.

I didn't know why I found it such a turn-on, but I did.

I pulled down his boxers, grabbed his dick and then wrapped my lips around it. I didn't really know what I was doing at first, I just moved it in and out, taking care not to bite him, and soon I got into a rhythm and it was fine.

The first two times, Jackson pulled out before he came, but the third time when we were at his mum's place, I offered to swallow.

Yep. Sweet, innocent Jane the Virgin had officially left the building and been replaced by Wanton Jane the cum-swallowing seductress.

So that was my sex life. In terms of work, things were also going well at the library. Although Jess and Theo didn't get to confront Jess's ex (apparently he'd been on holiday, so wasn't there on the two occasions they'd tried to visit him), there'd been no other threats to the library.

Since the electricity had been cut, we'd hosted two more silent reading parties, which had run smoothly, and Theo said profits were up, so hopefully our jobs were safe.

And Glenda had said if I wanted to move into the B&B at the end of next week, she'd give me a room for a special rate, so I could finally move out. All I had to do was hold on for a little bit longer at my parents' and I'd be free.

Life really couldn't get any better.

'I'm off,' I said to Jess as I put my scarf around my neck. It was the first week of November now, so the temperature had dropped.

'Have a nice evening. Oh! You still on for drinks with Maddie and Kara on Friday night?'

'Definitely! Can't wait! Enjoy your evening too and see you tomorrow.'

As I left the library, I pulled out my phone. Jess and Theo were doing the late shift, which meant no after-hours sexy library time with Jackson. So because we couldn't chill alone at his place tonight, we'd agreed to go for a walk on the beach.

He'd gone ahead of me and had just messaged to say

he was at the far end, which was much quieter than the section closest to the main part of town, so we'd have more privacy.

Because Jess had let us leave early, the sun hadn't set yet, which was perfect. I hoped we'd get to watch it together.

As my boots sank into the soft sand and I watched the waves rippling against the shore, I smiled. Sunshine Bay really was beautiful. I couldn't wait to live here.

Realistically I couldn't stay at the B&B forever, but even if it was for a month or so, it'd be better than my current accommodation.

Just think: Jackson could come and stay, it'd only take minutes to get to work and I could go for beach walks every morning or whenever I wanted. It was going to be amazing.

'Excuse me, miss. Do you know how to do CPR, because you just took my breath away.'

My head snapped away from the sea and I saw Jackson standing there, smiling.

'Did you just use a cheesy chat-up line on me?' I raised my eyebrow, trying to look serious, but knowing I was about to burst out laughing.

'Yep!' He grinned. 'Did it work?'

'Hmmm, not sure…' I tilted my head.

'I have more if you need convincing? How about, "good thing I have my library card, because I'm *totally* checking you out!"?'

'Oh my God,' I groaned. 'That was terrible!'

'What?' Jackson clutched his chest as if he'd been wounded. 'You're not even giving me credit for the fact that it was a library-related chat-up line?'

'Nope!' I grinned.

'*Cold!* Okay, what about… "if I could rearrange the alphabet, I'd put *U* and *I* together"?'

'Stop!' I winced, shaking my head but still unable to wipe the grin off my face.

'No, no, wait! I've got it: "If you were words on a page, you'd be *fine* print!" Convinced yet?'

We both burst into a fit of giggles.

'Those were all *terrible* chat-up lines. Lucky for you, you don't need any smooth words to impress me.'

'No?' Jackson wrapped his arms around my waist and my body melted.

'Nope.'

'Good to know…'

Jackson pressed his lips on mine and as we kissed, the rest of the world fell away.

There were no sounds. Nothing else existed.

All I felt was the softness of his mouth and the sensation of his heart beating against me.

My head grew fuzzy and my whole body tingled, not just with desire but sheer contentment.

And I knew why.

I loved this man. With all my heart.

I wasn't lying when I said that I wanted to make things official because I was falling for him.

The truth was, the years we'd spent together at school already made him have a special place in my heart. Even though we hadn't seen each other for years, I'd still kept space for him.

So with all of the time we'd spent together since he'd come to work at the library, it didn't take much for those feelings to resurface.

And then when you added in the sex, how patient and caring he'd been, the way he looked out for me and how he rocked my world, it was easy to see why I'd fallen head over heels for Jackson.

I wasn't sure when I should tell him. I'd never told someone I loved them before and didn't want to scare him off. His actions told me he felt the same, but I couldn't know for sure.

'Mmm.' Jackson pulled away slowly. 'I could seriously kiss you all day.'

'No objections from me.' I snaked my arms around him and we deepened the kiss.

It was such a shame we couldn't go back to his place. It wasn't just about having sex. I'd be happy just to lie in his arms for the rest of the night.

'You dirty dogs!' a woman's voice called out.

We sprung apart and when I looked round, I saw Celeste standing there, grinning.

'Oh, er, hey, Celeste!' I smoothed down the front of my skirt nervously. 'What are you doing here? I thought you were at uni?'

'It's reading week, so I'm back home. I was just on my way to see Jess to ask about doing some extra shifts, but thought I'd have a walk first. This beach is one of the few things I love about this tiny town. I certainly wasn't expecting to see you two *snogging*! How long's this been going on?'

'Not long,' I said. 'We're keeping it to ourselves for now, so if you wouldn't mind not saying anything, we'd really appreciate it.'

'If I was banging this hottie, there's no way I'd be keeping it a secret! I'd put it on billboards!' She turned and winked at Jackson.

'We don't want the town gossiping,' he added.

'Some of the residents here do love to gossip! Anyway, I'll leave you two shag buddies to it. And if you ever fancy having *fun* together, I'm your girl! See you around!' She blew us a kiss and strutted away towards the town centre.

'Shit.' I winced.

'It's not such a big deal.' Jackson shrugged. 'The important thing is that Jess and Theo know and are cool with it. And it could've been a lot worse. She could have walked in on us fucking in the library.'

'Oh God!' My eyes widened. 'You're right! We're lucky the cameras Theo installed are only in the corridors and not in the library hall—otherwise we'd be in *big* trouble. And could you imagine if someone like Celeste was looking through the footage? She'd probably post it online or something!' My blood ran cold just thinking about it. 'It's one thing having sex in a library when no one's around, but the last thing I'd want is to have a video of my naked bits on the internet.'

Jackson's face fell. He was clearly as mortified as me about being exposed publicly.

'I don't think Celeste would do something like that,' he said.

'Yeah, you're probably right. I only said that because I remembered her asking if I wanted to watch a video she'd made of her having sex with some guy at uni, which shocked me, because sex is something private.'

Says the girl who did it in a public library.

What I meant was that it wasn't for other people to see. I wouldn't invite the town to come and watch us or do it in front of a crowd.

Of course, Celeste could do whatever she wanted. Each to their own and all that, it just wasn't something for me.

Jackson stayed quiet and I suddenly felt bad, like maybe he thought I was sounding judgy.

'Obviously it's up to her,' I added quickly. 'What I was trying to say is that I wouldn't want you to share videos of me online or with anyone. And I wouldn't share pictures or videos of you naked to a colleague either. That's intimate. My body's for your eyes only and vice versa, right?'

'Y-yeah,' Jackson said, his gaze flicking towards the sea. 'Wow! Look!' He pointed and I took in the sight of the sky. It was orange with streaks of pink and yellow.

'It's so beautiful. I love watching the sunset!'

'Let's sit and watch it together.' He pointed to a wooden bench nearby. 'I bought snacks. And a blanket.'

'You had me at snacks!' I linked arms with him as we walked to the bench, then sat down.

'Thought so! I know the way to my lady's heart.' He placed a soft kiss on my cheek and my heart melted. I adored that he'd just called me *his lady*. I really did love him.

'You do! So come on, then. What kind of snacks are we talking?'

'Do you even have to ask?' He reached in his rucksack and pulled out a packet of rich tea biscuits and then another of chocolate digestives.

'*Chocolate* digestives? Wow!'

'Seeing as you're into having sex in the library and snogging on a public beach, I thought you might want to live life a little more dangerously and add chocolate to your digestives.' He smirked.

'Oooh, I dunno…. That might be a little too wild, even

for me!' I laughed. 'I might be partial to recreating my favourite sex scenes from romance novels, but don't be fooled. I'm always going to be plain Jane who loves digestives and rich tea biscuits.'

It was true. I just had to hope that Jackson didn't get bored when he realised that I wasn't that adventurous in life or with my biscuit choices.

Jackson reached over and stroked my cheek.

'I was only joking,' he said softly. 'They didn't have any plain digestives left, so that's why I got these. Not because I think you need to change what you like. You and your taste in biscuits are perfect just the way they are.'

Hearing those words made me dissolve faster than a biscuit in a hot mug of tea.

Jackson didn't want me to change.

Just when I thought I couldn't love him any more, he proved me wrong.

After pulling out a blanket and placing it over my lap to keep me warm, Jackson put the packets of biscuits on the bench, took out a flask, poured the hot tea into two small mugs, handed one to me, then wrapped his arm around my back, pulling me closer to him.

As I rested my head on his shoulder and watched the sunset with my favourite person in the whole world whilst enjoying my favourite treats, a wave of happiness washed over me.

Before Jackson, the only time I'd felt these kind of happy butterflies was when I was lost in a romance novel. But tonight I wasn't reading someone else's love story.

I was living my own.

37

———

JANE

'See you tomorrow.' I smiled at Jackson as we stopped at the corner of the road near my parents' house.

The temptation to kiss him was so strong, but I resisted. It was now Thursday, so there was only eight more days until I moved into the B&B. It didn't make sense to rock the boat by putting on a show for the neighbours. We just had to hold on for a bit longer and then we'd be free.

'Goodnight, beautiful,' Jackson said. 'I'll wait until you're inside.'

'Thanks.' I smiled again. I loved how he always did that.

It was almost midnight. We'd worked the late shift and once we'd locked up, we'd managed to read for a whole hour before the sparks started flying again and we ended up sleeping together.

Lately, sex with Jackson had been different. It wasn't always the wild, frenzied fucking we'd done in the beginning. It was slower and more sensual. Like making love. The connection between us felt deeper.

I was so far gone for him it was crazy. Now I finally understood that giddy feeling I read about whenever the main characters fell for each other.

Just like sex, I could now one hundred per cent confirm that falling in love definitely lived up to the hype. The butterflies, the feeling of floating on a cloud, the warm intoxicating sensations that flooded me whenever I saw Jackson were real.

It was so hard to drag ourselves away from that sofa, but we didn't want to miss the last train, so after we'd finished snuggling, we'd cleaned up, then raced to the station, only making it with two minutes to spare.

Now, though, it was back to reality. The one good thing about coming back late was that I didn't have to interact with anyone. Especially if I left the house early in the morning too. So far I'd gone three days without seeing any of my family and that was just the way I liked it. If I could keep this up until I moved out next week, that'd be perfect.

After pulling my keys out of my pocket, I opened the front door as quietly as I could, then closed it gently behind me.

Just as I was about to climb the stairs, from the corner of my eye, I saw something move in the darkness.

'Finally decided to come home, did you?' Dad's voice boomed from the living room and I almost jumped out of my skin. 'You've been treating this house like a bloody hotel!'

He flicked on the lamp and when I turned to look, he had a face like thunder.

'D-Dad,' I stuttered, my heart thumping against my chest. 'Why are you sitting there in the dark?'

'Where have you been?' he shouted, his face getting redder by the second.

'Out,' I said.

'With that black man?' he snapped.

My stomach plummeted.

How did he know I was with Jackson? Had he seen him waiting for me to go inside the house?

'Do you mean *Jackson*? The man that I work with?'

'I don't care what his name is! Answer the question. Were you with him?'

'Yes,' I replied. I hadn't done anything wrong.

'And he's the one you've been with… he's the reason you've been coming home late every night?' He ground his jaw.

'Sometimes I have to work late.'

'Don't give me that crap about *working*!' he spat. 'You've been staying out late and not coming home because you've been with *him*! Have you…? Did you have *sex* with him?'

'That's none of your business!' I swallowed hard.

Now he looked like he was about to explode.

'No, no, *no*!' he screamed, leaping out of the chair. 'My pure, sweet, innocent daughter has been defiled by a… bl…'

'A *what*? A black man?' I crossed my arms and narrowed my eyes. That was the second time he'd referenced Jackson's skin colour. 'What's your problem? What does it matter what colour he is?'

'I don't agree with it.'

'That's racist!'

'I'm not racist, I just think people should stick with their own!'

'I cannot believe you said that!' I shouted, my blood boiling hotter than a kettle. Then again, this was my bigoted dad, so I shouldn't be surprised. 'We're all human beings! We're living in the 2020s not the 1920s! England is a multicultural country. We're free to date whoever we want. Jackson's colour shouldn't matter. You should be happy that I've found someone I love!'

'You *love* him?'

Shit. I didn't mean to tell my dad how I felt before I'd even confessed my feelings to Jackson, but it had just slipped out. I wasn't embarrassed, though. I needed Dad to know that this was serious. And I needed him to stop being such an ignoramus.

'Yes, I love him! He's amazing. He's smart, kind, caring and honest. Jackson's the perfect gentleman and he treats me like a queen. That should be enough.'

Dad put his head in his hands and staggered backwards towards the chair like he'd just heard I'd been found guilty of murder, not that I'd shared the good news that I was finally happy and in love.

'I knew I was too soft on you! I should've been stricter. Then this wouldn't have happened. This is going to ruin my campaign before it's even begun! How could you do this?' he yelled. 'Imagine what people will say!'

'Oh, I don't know! Maybe they'll be happy I've found someone who makes me happy, adores and treasures me and will think *that's* more important than the colour of his skin. Radical, right?!' I said sarcastically.

'You're to stop seeing him, immediately! Before

anyone else finds out. You'll come straight home after work and you'll start dating Ricky. Hopefully he hasn't heard about your indiscretions and will still agree to make you look acceptable. If anyone finds out my daughter is a whore, I'll never be elected!'

I blinked quickly, trying to take in what I thought I'd just heard.

Did he just…?

No.

Dad was an arsehole, but he wouldn't have gone that far. I must've misheard.

'Did you just call me a whore?' I said, my eyes wide with shock.

'You heard what I said! You're a disgrace to this family. Sleeping around. Coming home at all hours of the morning! It's disgusting!'

'No! *You* are disgusting!' Anger bubbled inside me. I was so angry that it felt like I had fire in my veins. 'You're a disgusting, bigoted, ignorant, poor excuse for a human being and I'm ashamed that you're my dad!'

'Watch your mouth, girl!' He raced towards me, pushing his face just millimetres away from mine. The stench of alcohol and his stale breath flooded my nostrils and I jolted back.

Mum rushed down the stairs, terror written all over her face.

'Don, please,' she pleaded.

'Stay out of this!' he snapped, then pointed at me, his hand shaking with anger. 'You will apologise to me, right now! I will not tolerate this disrespect in my house. You'll do what I say, otherwise you're out!'

'You know what?' I put my hands on my hips. 'Fuck you. And fuck your stupid, toxic house! I'd rather sleep on the street than be anywhere near you for another second.'

I scooped my bag up from the floor, stormed to the front door, opened it, then slammed it shut before sprinting down the street.

Tears streamed down my cheeks and my heart thundered against my chest. I had to get as far away from that house as I could.

It was only when I saw the main road in the distance that I realised I had no idea where I was going.

After stopping to catch my breath, I fished out my phone and dialled Jackson's number.

He answered after two rings.

'Jane? You okay?'

'No.' My tears continued falling. I yanked off my glasses and wiped my eyes with the back of my hand. 'I… can I come over? I couldn't take it anymore, Jackson. He was waiting for me when I got home and we had a massive argument. He knows about us and I…'

'Where are you?'

'I don't know. A few streets away. Near the main road.' I looked for the sign, then told Jackson the street name and the number of the house I was in front of.

'Don't move. I'm coming right now.'

When I put the phone down, I started sobbing and shaking.

I couldn't believe what had just happened.

There was no way I was expecting Dad to have waited up for me.

My stomach twisted as I thought about all those

horrible things he'd said. His disgust towards Jackson. What he'd called me. He was just vile.

Normally, I'd never have argued back. I just swallowed his toxic words and walked away.

But tonight, after decades of biting my tongue and pushing my words back down, never saying what I wanted to, everything just bubbled to the surface. No, it didn't bubble. It exploded.

Tonight was the last straw.

Everyone had their limits. Including me. If you keep goading and pushing someone, even a person who was normally a mild-mannered people-pleaser like me was going to lose it. And I just did.

I didn't know who I was in there.

If someone had predicted that I would tell my strict, super controlling dad to fuck off, I would've said they were mad.

But that was what I'd just done. And do you know what? I wasn't sorry about it. He deserved to be put in his place for a change.

I wasn't pushover Jane anymore. Working at the library and doing something I was actually good at had boosted my confidence. The support and appreciation I received from Jess and Theo had also made me feel better in my skin.

And then there was Jackson.

The affection and kindness he'd shown me made me feel like I mattered. He saw me. He understood and accepted me. And I felt stronger for it. With him by my side I felt like I could move mountains. That was probably why telling an idiot like Dad to sod off wasn't as terrifying as it would've been a couple of months ago.

It was actually liberating.
Yep.
I'd found my voice.
And now, I intended to use it.

38

JACKSON

As I dragged on my clothes and raced to the door, my heart thundered against my chest.

That fucking arsehole.

I swear to God, if he'd laid a finger on the woman I loved, I'd fucking end him.

After slamming the door shut, I sprinted down my street. It would take at least ten minutes for me to get to her. If I could've, I would've got a taxi, but when I checked, the nearest one was fifteen minutes away and I couldn't wait. I had to get to Jane. I needed to make sure she was safe.

I loved her so damn much it fucking hurt.

There were so many times this week that I'd wanted to tell her. I almost had a few days ago when we were on the beach, watching the sunset, drinking tea and eating her favourite biscuits.

Even though the conversation after Celeste caught us was difficult, the moments afterwards were so perfect. Her head was resting on my shoulder whilst we looked out to sea. I was about to say those three words, but then I stopped myself.

I knew that before I said them, I had to tell Jane everything. Then she could decide whether she still wanted to be with me or not.

When she said that she wouldn't want anyone else to see my body, I felt sick. I hated the thought that she didn't know what I did online.

Plus, if I told her I loved her first, maybe she'd feel guilty or compelled to stay with me and I didn't want that.

No.

The right thing to do was lay my cards on the table, give her time to process, then take it from there.

I wondered how much her dad knew—and how he'd found out. We'd been pretty careful. Yeah, Celeste had seen us on the beach, but I doubted she had any links to this town or Jane's parents, so it didn't make sense.

How Jane's arsehole dad found out was irrelevant right now. All I cared about was making sure Jane was okay.

One thing was crystal clear: she'd be staying with me from now on.

I was going to tell her about Mum and the videos now anyway, so all the barriers that had meant I had to keep Jane at arm's length before would be gone. I'd finally be able to give Jane all of me. There'd be no more secrets.

I turned down the corner and saw Jane crouched on the pavement, leaning against a wall.

Using every last ounce of energy that I had, I sprinted over and scooped Jane up in my arms.

'You came,' she cried into my shoulder.

'Of course I came.' I held her tight and kissed the top

of her head softly. 'I'd run to Scotland to get you if you needed me. Might take a few days… okay, maybe weeks, but I'd still do it. I'd run anywhere to get you.'

For some reason, that made her cry harder.

'Thank you,' she sobbed.

I continued carrying her for a few streets, then when she felt better, she climbed down and walked beside me, her arm linked in mine.

When we got home, I led Jane to the sofa and sat her down.

'I'll make you some tea,' I said, wrapping a blanket around her. 'You're freezing. I need to get you warmed up.'

Once the tea was made, I carried it in to her with a plate of biscuits.

After she'd finished, I took her hand.

'So, are you ready to tell me what happened?' I asked.

'It was awful!' Jane sobbed before telling me everything.

When she said that her dad had called her a whore, I wanted to race over there, kick down the door and knock him out. But Jane needed me. And when I heard what she'd said back to him, a grin erupted on my face.

'Yes!' I cheered. 'That's my lady! He deserved to be told to fuck off after what he said. I'm so proud of you!' I pulled her into me, then squeezed her tight.

'Thanks. It was a long time coming.'

'Definitely. But you did it. The man needs to learn he can't speak to people however he wants and get away with it. You can stay here for as long as you need, okay? I want to make sure you're safe.'

'What about your mum? Won't she mind? Where is your mum?'

My stomach clenched.

I took a deep breath.

It was time.

I had to tell Jane the truth.

'She's not here…' My face turned to stone. 'There's something I need to tell you.'

'Sounds serious.' Jane's face creased.

'Yeah. It is…'

'Oh, no!' Her head dropped. 'I'm really sorry, I know this sounds awful, but I can't take any more bad news right now. Can it wait until later?'

'I…' I paused. I really needed to tell her. I'd already held back for too long. She deserved to know the truth. 'I'd prefer to tell you tonight.'

'*Please*.' She squeezed my hand. 'If it's something that's super urgent or life threatening, then of course, I'll listen. I want to be there for you. Like you've been for me. But if it can wait eight hours without making any difference, I'd really appreciate it if you told me later. Would that be okay?'

I thought about it. Technically it wouldn't make a difference if I told her now or when we woke up. Obviously I wanted to get it off my chest. The sooner she knew everything, the better I'd feel. But this wasn't about me. This was about Jane. And I could see that she was already broken. Telling her now would only make things worse.

She'd asked me to wait, so I would. Just until the morning.

'Okay.'

'I'm really tired. Can we go to bed now?'

'Sure.' I nodded. 'Whatever you need.'

And so I carried Jane upstairs, wondering if when I told her the truth, I'd ever get the chance to hold her in my arms again.

39

JANE

After writing a quick note for Jackson and leaving it on the pillow, I picked up my bag and crept out of his bedroom, down the stairs, then out the door.

It was almost seven in the morning and I was on my way to meet Mum.

When I'd got up to go to the toilet about an hour ago, I'd checked my phone and as well as some vile messages from Dad, there were dozens of concerned texts from Mum, checking I was okay.

The most recent ones said that she understood why I was upset and that if I met her this morning, she'd bring me some clean clothes and some other bits and pieces in case I needed to stay away for a few days.

A few days? I was never stepping foot in that house again. But I needed my clothes, so I agreed to meet her.

Like me, Jackson tossed and turned a lot last night, so I doubted he'd got much rest. And before I left he finally seemed like he was in a deep sleep, so I didn't want to wake him.

Plus, there was a chance he'd try to discourage me from going. I completely understood why. He wanted to protect me. And I loved him for that.

The way he ran to get me last night was one of the kindest things anyone had ever done for me.

When he said he'd run to get me from Scotland if I needed him, I believed every word.

Jackson was amazing.

He'd carried me when I felt like I wasn't strong enough to walk.

He'd held me when I cried.

He'd brought me tea and biscuits.

And he'd understood when I said I couldn't listen to any more bad news.

I'd felt terrible putting off whatever he wanted to tell me. But I had said that if it really couldn't wait, then I'd listen. As soon as I got a break today, we'd talk. But first I had to get this done.

'Hiya,' Mum said when I walked towards her at the station.

It'd crossed my mind that when I hadn't replied to his texts, Dad had asked her to message me. Saying she wanted to meet to give me clothes could've been a lie. That was why I suggested we met at the station. If Dad turned up and there were other people around, he wouldn't make a scene.

'Hi,' I said, scanning the entrance to see if there was any sign of him.

'He's not here,' she said, reading my mind. Mum handed me a bag. 'I've put in some blouses, skirts, tights, underwear and toiletries.'

'Thanks.' I took the bag. 'Look, Mum…'

'I'm sorry, Jane. Your dad's… set in his ways. He's not good with change. To him, you're still his little girl. So when a friend saw you with that man a few times late at night at the station and told him, he was upset.'

'So what if I was with Jackson? We could've just been friends. But now we're together and I don't care if that makes Dad *upset.* He's an ignorant dinosaur! How can you stay with him?'

Sometimes Mum openly agreed with him and other times when Dad spouted his nonsense, she'd either just sit there or busy herself in the kitchen, so I never truly knew where she stood.

I'd always thought it was because she didn't like confrontation. I didn't either. And maybe that was why, up until I'd started working at The Romance Library, I was also afraid to speak up.

But now I realised that silence wasn't always good.

By saying nothing, we were both guilty of enabling his actions.

I knew why I'd kept schtum. I was scared that he'd be angry that I disagreed with his archaic views. But mostly, scared he'd kick me out of the house and I'd have nowhere to go.

Not anymore, though.

'I don't agree with everything he says.' Mum hung her head. 'But for all his faults, I still love him,' she sighed.

Although it was hard for me to understand what there was to love about Dad, I knew that Mum wouldn't be the first woman to fall for a bad man and she wouldn't be the last.

'The thing is, Mum, his opinions aren't just awful, they're

dangerous. Someone like him really shouldn't be allowed to be in a position of power. So if you support his campaign, you're condoning his views and his actions. I've spent too long turning a blind eye to his toxic views, but I can't do it anymore. I'm sorry. Thanks again for the clothes. Bye.'

I walked away from her, willing myself not to cry.

Although I was upset, I was also proud of myself for finding the strength to say what I thought, to Dad last night and to Mum this morning.

Knowing that there was a chance I might not ever see either of them again was hard, but I'd done the right thing. It was painful now, but all I could hope was that in time, it would hurt a little less.

My phone beeped. When I checked the screen, I saw a message from Jackson.

JACKSON

I overslept! Just saw your note. You okay?

ME

Yeah, fine. Just met Mum. On my way to work now.

I'll be there ASAP. Might be a bit late, though. Can you let Jess know?

Will do.

Can we talk later?

Course.

See you soon, Beautiful.

My heart fluttered. *I love when he calls me beautiful.*

After I sent him a row of blowing kisses emojis, I put my phone away and pulled out my Kindle.

Time to get lost in another world.

~

'Are you okay to hold the fort with Jackson for the rest of the day?' Jess whispered as she stood in front of the meet-cute desk.

'Yeah, course.'

'I received this today, so I really need to nip this shit in the bud.'

Jess handed me a piece of white paper which had been folded in half. I opened it up and saw two sentences typed in bold caps in the centre of the page.

SHUT THE LIBRARY DOWN <u>NOW</u> OR YOU'LL REGRET IT.
THIS IS YOUR FINAL WARNING.

'Oh my God!' I mouthed, then jumped up and rushed to the corridor so we could speak. 'This is terrible! Have you told the police?'

'Theo's on the phone to them now. But I just called my ex's office and he's definitely there today. Obviously I didn't say who I was. Anyway, me and Theo want to go there now to have it out with him. But it's gonna take a while for us to get there and back.'

'Go! Me and Jackson will take care of things here.'

'Thanks. Now Celeste is back, I was hoping she could do a shift, but she's with friends in London today. I should be back for our drinks tonight, but don't wait for me. Just go ahead and I'll join you later.'

'Okay. Good luck.'

Jess raced off and I returned to my desk.

I really hoped they got to speak to her ex. From what Jess had told me, he sounded like a nasty piece of work. What he did to Jess's books was horrendous. The bastard probably hated the fact that she had moved on and was doing so well, so he was trying to bring her down. Here's hoping that they found a way to get him to confess and the police locked him up.

My phone vibrated.

JACKSON

Did Jess tell you what happened?

ME

Yep. It's awful.

I know, right?! I probably won't be able to get away for lunch to talk now, so can we speak tonight instead?

By the time Jackson got to work, I was already serving members, so couldn't chat. And when I got a break, he had a delivery he had to deal with. So we'd agreed to speak at lunch, but now it was clear we wouldn't be able to go out today. Jess and Theo needed us.

Can't tonight. Going to the pub with Jess, Maddie and Kara.

Oh yeah. I remember you mentioned that. Okay, cool.

'Excuse me, can I check these two books out?'

I looked up and saw a member clutching two dark romance novels.

'Of course!'

I quickly fired off a reply to Jackson, telling him I had to go and we'd speak later.

The rest of the day flew by. Luckily Tamsin from Love & Lattes made us sandwiches for lunch, so we had something to eat. And she closed the cafe briefly to cover the meet-cute desk whilst I had a loo break too.

After seven, Jess and Theo returned. Jess looked drained.

'How did it go?' I asked.

'It's not him.' She blew out a frustrated breath. 'Theo and Jackson are gonna stay until eight, so we can head to the pub now.'

Once I'd grabbed my coat and bag, I said a quick goodbye to Jackson, who was happy to tell me how much he loved the third blind date book that he'd just finished: the romantic Christmas adventure I'd picked, *Five Gold Rings* by Kristen Bailey. I was glad he was enjoying my recommendations.

I left the bookshop, found Jess and then we left.

'So what happened with your ex? How do you know it's not him?'

'He said he had no idea what I was talking about. But when I told him about the library, he said it sounded like a place for sad, desperate women and even if he knew it existed, he wouldn't humiliate himself by going inside it. He thought it was in the red light district, like a sex shop!'

'Sounds like he's still an arsehole.'

'Definitely.'

'I'm surprised Theo didn't punch him.'

'I asked him to wait in the car. It was something I wanted to do by myself. It was the first time I'd seen my ex since I left, so I needed to prove to myself that I was strong enough. That I was able to stand up to him.'

'I get it,' I said, thinking about how I'd done the same to Dad. It was important to show those bullies that we weren't afraid anymore.

'So, yeah. We're back to square one. Anyway, I want to forget about it for tonight and have some fun.'

'Yes!' I cheered, thinking the same. It'd been an intense twenty-four hours for me too, so I was looking forward to letting my hair down.

When we got in the pub, Maddie and Kara were already there.

With Celeste.

Shit.

I hadn't seen or spoken to her since she caught me and Jackson kissing on the beach. I really hoped she hadn't said anything.

'Hi!' Maddie said.

'Hi!' I gave her a hug.

After I'd greeted Kara, then Celeste, who gave me a wink when we hugged, we ordered drinks, then sat down.

Bob brought over two bottles of wine with some glasses, then Kara filled us in with how things were at the salon, Maddie shared how happy she was with Love & Lattes and Celeste spoke about how she was dreading going back to uni.

'But enough about work stuff!' Celeste said. 'What have I missed since I've been away? Done anything outrageous? Anything to add to the crazy places you've had sex list that we spoke about last time?' She grinned, then turned to face me.

On the one hand, I felt a sense of relief. The last time we were all here, I was single and a thirty-one-year-old virgin.

I had absolutely nothing to contribute to the 'wildest places I'd had sex' conversation. I'd never done anything exciting in or out of the bedroom.

But since then, so much had changed.

Not only had I lost my V-card with the hottest man ever created, I'd also had sex on a sofa at work, multiple times, been fucked against a bookcase in a library and had a man go down on me there too.

And now that man was my amazing boyfriend.

Talk about going from zero to sixty.

If I told Celeste all the things I'd been up to, I doubted she'd believe it. But even someone as sexually experienced as she was would be impressed. Not that it was a competition, but it was wild, even by her standards.

But of course, I wouldn't talk about what I'd done with Jackson. Our sex life (still hard to believe that I actually had one) was private. And even if it wasn't, as close as I was to Jess, I was hardly about to admit that we'd spent multiple nights fucking all over the library. She was a cool boss, but *that* would be pushing it.

So yeah, it felt good to finally *belong*. Not to be an outcast like I was before.

At the same time, though, this conversation made me nervous because Celeste knew about me and Jackson and I was worried she'd spill the beans.

'Nothing new to report!' Maddie replied. 'Been too busy running two cafes.'

'Same!' Kara added. 'Not the cafe-running, obvs! Just with work. We had another big wedding party last weekend.'

'Oh yeah!' I said. 'Glenda said they were all staying at the B&B.'

'That's right.' Kara nodded.

'I'm moving in there next week,' I said, keen to steer the conversation away from Celeste's sex-related question.

I knew Jackson had let me stay last night and he'd said I could stay for as long as I needed, but I didn't want to impose. His mum might not be happy with it, so maybe it was best that I went and stayed at Glenda's as planned.

'That's great!' Kara said.

'I was really happy there,' Jess added. She'd said the same thing when I told her that Glenda had given me the green light to stay at the B&B.

'Hopefully I will be too.'

'And will *Jackson* be staying over there with you too?' Celeste smirked and my stomach twisted.

'Jackson?' Kara said.

'Uh-huh…' Celeste grinned mischievously. 'I caught the two of them snogging on the beach the other day!'

My eyes bulged and I gave her a WTF glare before taking a large glug of my wine. We'd asked her not to say anything.

'You're with *Jackson*?' Maddie gasped. 'You're a *very* lucky lady!'

'I know, right?' Celeste replied, which I used as an excuse to avoid responding. 'That's what I said! I'm having to rely on the internet to get my rocks off. There's literally no one decent left at uni.'

'What are you watching? Porn?' Kara asked.

'Yeah, sort of. But it's not your average porno with a couple shagging. I've been watching this guy, who's *sooo* hot! Sounds really random, but he takes his clothes off whilst he's cleaning and he touches himself with whatever he's using.'

'What?' Jess laughed.

I never thought I'd be relieved to hear Celeste talking about her favourite pornos, but right now I was. The more time she spent talking about that, the less she'd focus on me and Jackson.

'Yeah! So like, the first video I saw, he was basically touching himself whilst he was wearing an apron. But the apron had a bit cut out, so at the end, he whipped out his dick, which is *huge*, and basically starts wanking! Oh my God. When he did that, I came so hard! It's definitely a favourite for my wank bank!' She cackled. 'And now he takes special requests.'

'What kind of requests?' Kara frowned.

'Basically, if you subscribe to his platinum package, you can choose what he should touch himself with next!'

'Have you done that?' Maddie's eyebrows shot up.

'Course I have!' She rolled her eyes like it was obvious that she would. 'I asked him to use rubber gloves, but sexy black ones whilst he lathers up his body with a sponge.'

'Did he do it?' Kara asked, her eyes wide with excitement.

'Yep! Haven't seen it yet, but when he replied he said the video will be up this weekend!'

'OMG!' Jess said.

'Yeah. It's *so* cool. Now I'm wondering how much it'd cost to spend the night with him.'

'You'd *pay*?' Kara's jaw dropped. 'What, is he like an escort too?'

'Hell yeah, I'd pay! Don't know, but it's worth asking. With a monster dick like that, whatever he charged would be worth every penny!' She cackled again.

'Is it really *that* big?' Kara asked.

'*Totally!* Hang on.' She pulled out her phone. 'I'll show you the video.' After tapping away, she spun her phone around, then pressed play.

'Oooh!' Kara cooed. 'He's got a great body.'

I couldn't see the screen very well, so I leant in closer, just as the guy unzipped the pouch on his apron.

As he pulled out his dick, Jess, Celeste, Maddie and Kara gasped with shock, then squealed with delight.

'Wow! He really is *huge*!' Maddie said.

But whilst they were laughing and swooning, I frowned.

That background looked familiar. I recognised the faded blue striped wallpaper.

And it wasn't just the wallpaper that looked familiar.

The dick that Celeste had just helpfully zoomed in to admire more closely looked familiar too.

My stomach bottomed out.

I could be wrong, but that looked very much like Jackson's dick.

It was a similar length and thickness.

Yeah, it was possible that there was another guy somewhere else in the world that had the same skin colour and same-sized penis, but the same wallpaper that Jackson had in his bedroom too?

That was too much of a coincidence.

And Jackson loved cleaning.

And OMG.

Now I remembered that the morning after we'd first slept together, there was a tripod and a load of cleaning tools in his room too.

He'd said it was to take pictures to help sell the house, but at the time I thought that sounded strange.

I wasn't a gambler, but I'd bet good money on the fact that was Jackson in the video.

I always felt like he was hiding something, and I was right.

He agreed that our bodies were for each other's eyes only.

Now I knew for certain that he'd lied to me.

And I needed to know why.

40

JANE

I walked to the station in a trance.

Jackson was an online stripper.

My boyfriend was an internet porn star.

I was still trying to get my head around this bombshell.

To say that pretending I was fine in the pub was diffi-cult would be an understatement.

When I realised that it was Jackson in the video, I knew I couldn't leave straight away. Everyone would've guessed it was him or at least known something suspicious was going on.

So I'd sat there, pretending to enjoy the sight of my so-called boyfriend thrusting his hips back and forth, grinding in front of the camera, then flashing his dick for the whole world to see, whilst my heart was breaking as I struggled to understand what would lead him to do that and, most importantly, why he hadn't told me.

Whilst my friends ogled Jackson's cock, I'd made a mental note of the website so I could look at his profile in more detail later, and I'd also noticed that the video was recent.

Did that mean this was something he'd only started recently too?

How long had he been stripping?

Years? Months?

It was clear that he was still doing the videos now, though. Celeste had said so. They'd been speaking privately and he'd told her the video of her request was going up this weekend. Did that mean tonight or tomorrow?

Was that what he was doing this evening? Filming more videos for other women?

And how far did he go with his subscribers?

Celeste had said that she'd like to pay for him to spend the night with her. Would he fuck her too if she paid him enough?

Bile rose in my throat. I felt sick.

I should've known that someone as sexually gifted as Jackson would never be satisfied with sleeping with a woman as inexperienced as me. I wasn't enough for him, so he had to get his kicks from wanking online.

How many hundreds or thousands of people had seen my boyfriend's dick?

My head was swimming. A million different thoughts clouding my head at once. It didn't take long for the tears to start falling.

I pulled off my glasses. God. I felt like I'd cried more this past month than I had in years.

So this was what heartbreak felt like.

All of those love songs were right. This hurt like hell. It was as if someone had got a machete and slashed my insides, then scooped out any signs of remaining organs slowly with a knife wrapped in barbed wire.

My chest ached.

It was like a thousand elephants were trampling all over my heart whilst wearing spiky ten-inch heels.

How could Jackson do this to me?

I'd begged him not to break my heart.

He'd promised me that he wouldn't, but he'd lied.

I tucked myself away in a seat at the back of the train carriage away from the handful of other passengers so that they couldn't see me crying my eyes out.

It was no big surprise that I nearly missed my stop. The last thing I was thinking of was keeping track of the stations.

As I stormed towards Jackson's house, all I could think about was how mortifying it was to watch him gripping his cock in that video as Celeste gushed about how huge he was and how much she wanted him to 'ruin' her with his 'monster dick'.

By the time I rang the bell, my blood was boiling. I didn't know if I'd ever been so upset.

If anyone had asked me several hours ago, I would've said my outburst with Dad was the angriest I'd ever been, but now I felt like if I opened my mouth, fire would shoot out.

I expected crap from my dad, but Jackson? I'd trusted him. I'd defended him to my parents. Told them he was a good, honest man.

I'd told them they were wrong to believe he wasn't good enough for me. And now look. He'd humiliated me. Just like my ex at the bookshop had done. Except this was a million times worse.

'Hey! You're back early!' Jackson smiled as he opened the door and leant forward to give me a kiss.

I hated the way that my stomach did that annoying flip-flopping. I was angry at Jackson. I couldn't be happy to see him.

'Did I interrupt your filming?' I spat as I pushed past him and stepped into the house. 'Need to get back in front of the camera to flash your dick to some more strangers online?'

Jackson's face fell.

'Jane…' He shut the door. 'It's not…'

'Please don't insult me by saying it's not what I think!' I shouted. 'I saw the video! Celeste took great pleasure in showing me a video of my boyfriend, wanking online!'

'She knows?' His eyes bulged.

'No, I don't think she knows it's *you*, but she knows all about your videos, that's for sure. Do you know how embarrassing it was to sit there listening to my friends talking about my boyfriend's dick and how much they'd like to have a ride on it?' My voice shook with a combination of embarrassment and rage.

It was only then that I thought that I hadn't checked whether or not Jackson's mum was home. I couldn't imagine she knew about the videos either.

I knew how shocked I'd been to find out, so the last thing I wanted was to upset her too.

'Please.' Jackson took my hand and attempted to lead me into the living room. I snatched my hand away. 'Jane. Let me explain.'

When I looked up at him, his eyes were watering and that made my heart break all over again.

I hated that I felt my resolve weakening so quickly. I was supposed to be furious.

But I knew that if I didn't find out why he'd done this, it'd keep spinning around in my head.

'You've got five minutes,' I snapped.

As I heard the words fall from my mouth, I almost gasped. A couple of months ago, I never would've had the strength to be so direct.

The old me probably wouldn't have said anything at all. I would've just been so grateful that Jackson had paid any attention to me in the first place. But I'd had enough of people treating me like a meek little doormat. All of these years of bottling up my feelings had caused me to explode. I couldn't stay silent anymore. I deserved to be treated with respect.

'Okay.' Jackson sat on the sofa.

I deliberately plonked myself on the armchair at the other side of the room. The last thing I needed was to be close to him. When he'd leant down to kiss me, he'd smelt of his delicious body wash, so I knew he'd just had a shower. Was it because he'd just wanked in front of the camera and had to clean himself up?

I'd drive myself mad if I didn't talk about this soon.

'Come on, then. Why did you lie to me?'

'I did it for my mum.'

'Your *mum*? Please.' I rolled my eyes. 'Are you going to tell me that your mum is some kind of evil madam who forced her son to make sex videos on the internet? I know a lot of time has passed, but I remember your mum, Yolanda. She was always sweet and lovely, so if you think you can blame her for this, you've got—'

'She's sick,' Jackson jumped in.

I froze and my stomach instantly plummeted.

'What?'

'She's… she had to go into care and I couldn't afford to pay the fees. They were going to kick her out if I didn't settle the invoices. So I needed to find a way to make money, fast. At first I tried escorting, but they wanted me to sleep with the customers and I couldn't do that. I didn't want to do the videos. I tried to do some with my clothes on, but it didn't work. So Marcus suggested I try showing my dick, which I didn't want to do either, but I was desperate. So I did it and, well, it worked. And I was able to pay Mum's bills.'

My jaw was on the floor.

I hadn't even thought too deeply about what would lead him to do the videos. I was so shocked and humiliated that I just thought about how *I* was feeling.

Never in a million years would I have thought that *this* was the reason.

'I didn't know.'

'I know.' He blew out a breath.

Now so much made sense. Why she was never at home. Why I never saw any of her clothes or shoes out anywhere. And why there was no sign of any female toiletries in the bathroom. At the time I'd reasoned that she was just ultra tidy and liked to keep stuff packed away in cupboards, but now I understood.

'What's wrong with your mum?'

'Alzheimer's.'

'Shit.' I squeezed my eyes shut. 'I'm so, so, sorry. How bad is it?'

'Not great. Most days she doesn't even remember who I am.'

My heart broke again. But this time for Jackson and his mum, not for me.

'Why didn't you tell me?' I said. 'I could've helped.'

'You had your own shit to deal with. I couldn't expect you to take on my burdens too. Marcus has helped me out, but I couldn't keep relying on him or ask other people. She's my mum. She took care of me. Now it's my time to take care of her.'

He rubbed the back of his head and I could tell this was difficult for him to talk about. I didn't fill the silence, though. I knew he needed time to talk about it at his own pace.

'I didn't find out about her condition until after I'd left my job,' he continued. 'And I thought I'd be okay with my savings until I found something else, but I just couldn't. The work stuff hit me harder than I thought and then finding out about Mum and seeing more and more of her slip away each day, it just all got on top of me and I knew going back into another high-pressured environment like I was in before would destroy me.'

'And that's why you applied for the job at the library?'

'Yeah. Everything I told you before was true. I needed something that wouldn't stress me out, that wasn't going to affect my mental health like my last job did. I wanted a fresh start. I knew that if I told people about Mum, they'd treat me differently. They'd ask me how she was. How I was doing. And there'd be nothing wrong with that. It's good that people care. But before I discovered the library, her illness consumed me so much. When I wasn't visiting her, I'd be worrying about her. How bad it was going to get. How I'd cope when…' His voice trailed off. 'I knew it wasn't healthy. I needed to occupy my time. I needed something to take my mind off my problems. And I needed to earn money to pay for her care. It's so expensive.'

When Jackson explained the costs I almost fell off my chair. He'd tried to get support, but was told his mum wasn't eligible. And with no one interested in buying the house, despite it being on the market for ages, his options for finding the money every month were limited.

'I can't believe how much it costs!' I said.

'Me neither.' He blew out a breath. 'So, yeah. The library became my refuge. When I walked through those doors, I was able to forget about my real life outside of those four walls. I could just be me. I wasn't expecting that you'd be working there. Obviously that turned out to be a blessing, but with everything that was going on, I just needed that safe bubble, y'know? I needed to keep my family stuff with Mum separate.'

'I understand what you mean by creating a bubble and the library being a refuge. Of course, what I went through with my dad doesn't compare to how hard it is for you to deal with your mum's illness. I can't even begin to imagine how you must be feeling. But I get it. For me, the library is the same. Every time I walk through those doors I feel safe. Like the rest of the world doesn't exist. It became a place where I could forget about my crappy family. That's why I stayed there so much after work. But once we got together, you still could've confided in me. *I* could've become your safe bubble. Remember what I said before? That as long as we talked about stuff and were honest with each other, we'd be fine?'

'Yeah.' He blew out a breath. 'Course I do. And you don't know how bad I felt keeping this from you. I wanted to tell you so many times, but didn't want to ruin things.

Yesterday I was determined to tell you. I tried. But you said you couldn't take any more bad news. And then today we didn't get the chance.'

So *that* was what he wanted to discuss.

'It's true. I did ask you to put it off until today. But you still could've said something sooner. I would've preferred that to being blindsided by Celeste.'

'I know, and I'm sorry. I'm not proud of what I've done. When my parents were working hard to secure my future and helping me succeed at school, they didn't do that for me to take my clothes off for money. But at the same time, I'm not ashamed of doing what I needed to do to give Mum the care she needs. If I'd taken another job in the City and it'd fucked me up, I'd be in no state to help her. So I did what was necessary,' he said defiantly.

I understood that. And the logical part of my brain understood his need to take care of his mum.

But at the same time, I still hated the fact that he'd lied.

No, it wouldn't have been easy to tell me the truth, but I needed to know that if in the future, there was something difficult, he wouldn't just hide it from me. I needed him to trust me. I needed to be able to trust him too. I might be inexperienced, but I knew that without trust and honest communication, we didn't have a relationship.

'Thank you for telling me,' I said, then went to the sofa, sat next to Jackson and took his hands in mine. 'I'm so sorry you're going through this. I really am. If there's anything I can do to help, just tell me, okay?'

'Just… I just need your support.'

'You have it. Always. But…' I took a deep breath. 'I'm going to need some time. I know you're going through hell right now, so I'm not going to add to that. But I just have to get my head around everything, because although I know you had your reasons, you still lied to me, Jackson. You still didn't trust me enough to tell me the truth and that's not a good basis for a relationship. Whatever happens, though, I'll always be here as your friend.'

'I want to be more than just friends, though,' Jackson said, his eyes filled with emotion.

It broke me to do this, but I didn't know if I was able to offer him more than friendship right now.

I was still trying to take in the news about his mum. We hadn't even spoken about half of the things that we needed to. Like whether he'd continue doing the videos. I doubted he had a choice with the fees he had to pay and I totally understood that.

It was Jackson's body, so ultimately it was his choice what he did with it. And knowing what I did now, I'd never want to stand in the way of him doing what he had to in order to keep his mum safe. But the truth was, I didn't know if I'd be able to deal with knowing that so many people were staring at my boyfriend naked.

And what would happen when someone found out? Secrets always had a way of being discovered and I knew that when this became public knowledge, it'd make things messy on so many different levels. With my family, work (especially if Celeste came back during the holidays) and amongst the residents of Sunshine Bay.

I knew I'd find that tough, so I needed to work out how much of a deal-breaker this was.

I meant what I said, though—even if Jackson and I had to break up, I'd still be there to support him. Whatever happened, I didn't want him to deal with his mum's illness alone.

'I want that too. But I've spent too many years not respecting my feelings. Keeping them bottled up. So I just need time. Okay?'

'Okay.'

'Maybe it's best if I don't stay here whilst I work things out.'

'What? But where will you go?' He looked at his watch. 'It's late now. I get why you wouldn't want us to share a bed, but I can sleep here and you can take the bed upstairs, so I know you're safe.'

When I looked at my watch, I saw that he had a point. I hadn't realised the time.

'Okay. You're right. It is late. But if I stay here, I'll take the sofa. You sleep in your bed. No arguments. And I'll find somewhere else to stay from tomorrow.'

'You don't have to leave. Stay. At least until you get the room at Glenda's next week.'

'No. I need some space to figure things out. It'll be harder if we're working *and* living together.'

Jackson nodded solemnly.

'I'll get you a fresh sheet and a duvet.'

Once he'd left, I dropped my head in my hands.

This whole situation was a nightmare.

I hated that his poor sweet mum was sick.

I hated that Jackson was hurting and going through so much pain.

And I hated that I didn't know what to do about our relationship.

I wanted to hope that things would work out.

But given all the stuff that we had to deal with, I really couldn't see how.

41

JACKSON

As I walked along the beach, I took a large sip from the flask of coffee I'd brought from home. I'd hoped that along with the fresh salty air, it'd help me feel more awake and clear my head. But I'd had so little sleep that even if I drank a gallon of caffeinated drinks, I wouldn't feel any better.

I still couldn't believe Jane had found out about the videos.

When she'd first asked if I'd been filming videos and I'd realised she knew, my stomach had bottomed out.

It must've been pretty shitty to have to listen to her friends talk about my body like that.

I could still see the look of betrayal and disappointment Jane gave me. And every time I pictured it, I felt like someone had punched me in the gut. She'd trusted me and I hadn't been completely honest with her.

Yeah, it was true that I'd said from the beginning that I wasn't looking to get involved. I'd told her repeatedly that I had too much on my plate to start a relationship. But then

I became weak. I gave into my urges and before I knew it, I was addicted to Jane.

As soon as I realised there was no going back, that I'd fallen in love with her, I should've told her everything. But I didn't want to ruin things. After so many months of sadness, Jane was a bright light, and being with her brought me so much joy that I couldn't bear to lose it.

Although I'd dreaded telling her the truth, now that she knew—everything, about Mum, the videos and my financial situation—I felt like a massive weight had been lifted off my shoulders.

The irony now was that by not telling her my secret and instead allowing her to find out the way she had meant that there was a good chance I was going to lose her anyway.

I couldn't blame her if she didn't want to be with me. Sex was still new for Jane, so to suddenly discover that I was an online porn performer was a lot to take in.

If Jane was taking her clothes off online to pay for her only living parent's care, how would I feel? I'd like to think that I'd understand and support her, but who knows? Until you're in that situation yourself, it's impossible to say for certain.

At least she'd said that whatever happened, she'd still support me as a friend. I needed that. Now that we'd been reunited after so many years apart, I hated the idea that I'd never be able to speak to her again.

After I'd given her the bedsheets last night, apart from saying thank you, she didn't speak to me. And when I woke up this morning she was already gone.

Now, though, it was time to go to work and face the

music. I hoped things wouldn't be awkward. But I had to be prepared for that.

'Morning,' I said to Jess as I walked along the corridor.

'Morning! How are you?' She smiled.

'Okay,' I replied, thinking that my boss didn't need to know I was feeling like absolute shit.

'Oh.' Her face fell. 'Jane looks just as miserable as you. Everything okay with you two?'

My face dropped. I had no idea how the hell I was supposed to answer that without lying.

'Nothing for you to worry about,' I said. 'But thanks. So I was thinking maybe we could have a catch-up later to talk about the signing tomorrow.'

Normally we were closed on Sundays, but it was the only day that D.D. had free in her schedule, so we were opening the library just for her.

'Yes!' Jess beamed. Swift change of subject successfully achieved. 'I'm so excited! I still can't believe that in just over twenty-four hours, my favourite author will be here, in our library!'

'I know, right?'

'Thanks so much again for arranging it.'

'You're welcome.'

'I'm hoping I don't fangirl too hard when I meet her.'

'Pretty sure that we'll *all* be fangirling. Well, I'll be fan*boying*, if that's even a thing!' A smile tugged at my lips. 'Anyway, we'll be in good company. That was one of the things I said when I was pitching to her agent. Everyone that's coming tomorrow is a massive fan, so she'll understand our gushing.'

'Yeah.' Jess nodded. 'Did the delivery of her books come in yet?'

'Arrived last night. The agent explained that they're being really strict with this release. They didn't send out any advance reader copies. We're actually one of the first places to get the book.'

'Amazing! I wish I could just sit and read it all day, but with everything that's going on, it's going to be difficult.'

'Sorry to hear that you didn't find out who's responsible.' I sighed.

'Thanks. Theo's arranged for his brother Ben and some other residents to come and help out tomorrow. They'll be outside, making sure there's no one suspicious hanging around and patrolling inside the building. The brick through the window and the electricity being cut both happened either before or during an event, so tomorrow we'll need to be extra vigilant. Especially as D.D. and so many other guests will be coming. We can't afford for anything to go wrong and we need to keep everyone safe.'

'Definitely.'

'I'd better run, but we'll catch up properly later, okay?'

'Sure. I'll be in the bookshop.'

'Great. Celeste is in today. I thought you might need to spend time in the office to deal with any final prep for the signing.'

'Cool.'

I could really do without working with Celeste, but it'd be helpful to have cover if I needed it.

It wasn't that I was worried about her finding out it was me in the videos, because realistically, she hadn't seen me naked, so she'd never know. It was just that sometimes she was full on. But hopefully now she knew I was with Jane, she'd tone it down a bit.

Was I still with Jane, though? That was the million-dollar question.

After I'd dumped my jacket and rucksack in the office, I went to the library to see Jane. When I got there, though, she was with a member and another lady was in the queue behind her.

I stood and watched for a while, captivated by her beauty and just how competent she looked. Jane was so good at her job. Whenever she talked about books, her passion was infectious.

Jane said something and the woman she was helping laughed. Their voices were low, so I couldn't hear what they were talking about, but my heart instantly swelled. Jane just had the ability to put anyone at ease. That was one of the many things that I loved about her.

Then it dawned on me. Jane didn't even know that I loved her. I'd almost told her last night, but held back. Saying those three big words after she'd just discovered I'd been keeping secrets from her would sound disingenuous. She'd think I was just trying to butter her up. So I didn't. But I really wanted to tell her. Jane needed to know how much she meant to me.

When I got to the bookshop, Celeste had just finished serving a customer and was handing over a bag full of books.

'Looks like that was a big sale,' I said once the customer left.

'Jackson!' Her eyes widened. She came out from the till, then threw her arms around me. I pulled back awkwardly, my hands still firmly at my sides. 'So good to see you. It's been ages!' She rested her hand on my arm and tilted her head to the side.

'Not really.' I frowned. 'I saw you on the beach the other day when I was with Jane, remember?'

'Oh yeah!' She squeezed my bicep and I yanked my arm away, causing her hand to fall. 'That was a surprise! Jane's sweet, but I thought a man like you would prefer someone a bit more adventurous…' Celeste winked.

'Actually, Jane's my dream woman.' I crossed my arms. 'I have zero interest in anyone else.' I held her gaze to make sure she got the message.

'Fair enough.' She shrugged.

'I can see you've got everything handled here, so I'm going to the office to work on tomorrow's event. I'll come back when it's time for your break.'

I turned away, then left.

Although I had no idea whether or not Jane wanted to continue our relationship, what I'd said to Celeste was true. Jane was my dream woman and even if she dumped me, I wasn't interested in Celeste or anyone else.

There was only one woman I wanted.

And all I could do now was hope that she still wanted me too.

42

JANE

'Excuse me, do you have any more of Lucy Score's backlist? I've already binged the Knockemout series and I finished the latest in the Story Lake series last night and I need more Lucy in my life!'

'I hear you!' I smiled, looking up at the member standing in front of the meet-cute desk. 'We're all big Lucy fans at The Romance Library. Have you tried the Blue Moon series or the Benevolence novels?'

'I looked, but I didn't see them on the shelves.'

'As soon as they come in, they go back out again. We need to order more. We should have stock in the bookshop though if you'd like to buy the paperbacks.'

'Can you show me where it is?'

After signalling to Jess that I was leaving the desk so she could take over if anyone needed help, I got up and headed out of the library.

The last thing I wanted to do right now was go to the bookshop. I'd gone there an hour ago to check whether the new delivery of Kennedy Ryan books we'd ordered had arrived and when I got to the door, I saw Celeste stroking Jackson's bicep.

Seeing her touching him made me sick. I couldn't get the idea out of my head that he'd made a sexy video just for her. Even though I knew why he'd done it, I still couldn't shake that feeling of jealousy.

I was up most of the night turning everything over and over in my head and I was still no closer to knowing what I was going to do. I'd even left Jackson's early so I could get to the library before it opened and start reading D.D. Desire's new book before the event tomorrow, but I couldn't even open it. And seeing how excited I'd been to read it, that said a lot.

'Here you go.' I gestured to the member. 'Celeste will show you all of the Lucy Score books we have.'

'I sure will!' Celeste's eyes brightened. 'Have you read *By a Thread* yet?'

'Yes!' the member replied excitedly. As I walked away, I heard them talking about how much they loved Drunk Dom in the book and smiled. But that smile faded when I saw Jackson walking towards me.

God, it'd be so much easier if he wasn't so bloody attractive.

'Hey,' he said, flashing a warm smile which unfortunately made my traitorous stomach fizz with excitement.

'Hi,' I attempted to say flatly.

'I came to see you earlier. But you were busy.'

'I stopped by the bookshop earlier too, but you and Celeste also seemed *busy* and I didn't want to interrupt her stroking your arm.'

Jackson's eyes widened.

'It wasn't like that,' he said softly.

Deep down I knew it was innocent. Celeste was tactile. She even stroked my arms sometimes. But because of those videos, my brain was inventing all kinds of stuff and it wasn't healthy.

'I know,' I said. 'But because of… I can't stop thinking about…'

'Jane.' He took my hand and walked towards the stockroom door. After unlocking it, he led me down the stairs.

'Why are we going down here?'

'Because I need to talk to you.' Once we were in the room, he stood in front of me. 'I know you're probably thinking all kinds of things, but I need you to know something important: I don't interact with anyone. Marcus does everything. He takes care of the liaison. He tells me what to film, so I never know who it's for. So please, don't think that when I'm filming, I'm thinking about Celeste or other women. The only woman I've ever thought about when I've made those videos is you.'

My eyes popped.

'You thought about *me*?'

'Yeah. It's the only way I could get hard. Even when I did the first one, not long after starting here, it was *you* that I thought about. I imagined you on the bed, watching me. And whenever I stop filming, it's your name I call out when I finish myself off with my hands. It's *you*, Jane. It's only ever been you.'

I was rooted to the floor. Stunned into silence.

I thought about everything he said, trying to process it all.

He wasn't messaging different women.

He wasn't thinking about them when he touched himself in front of the camera. He was thinking of *me*.

Jackson had always liked *me*.

Wow.

'Thanks for telling me,' I said.

'I want you to know everything. No more secrets. I promise.' As he stroked my cheek, I squeezed my eyes shut and my whole body tingled. I hated how easily I responded to his touch. 'So are we okay?'

'You'll still need to film the videos, right?' I asked, opening my eyes.

'Yeah.' He nodded.

'I understand why, but I have to think about whether I can deal with that. I need more time.'

'Okay. Oh, by the way, I'm reading the last blind date book, *Before I Let Go* by Kennedy Ryan. It's emotional, but brilliant. Thanks again for introducing me to so many amazing books.'

A small smile touched my lips. I was glad that he'd loved every book I'd recommended. I desperately wanted to chat to him about it like we used to do, but like I'd said, I had to work out the best way forward for us.

'That's good to know.' I nodded. 'I'd better get back.'

I quickly walked out the room and up the stairs. The closer I was to him, the harder it was to think clearly.

The day flew, especially with all the D.D. Desire event prep. I'd received so many emails asking if there were any tickets left and I felt so bad having to turn people down, but we were completely sold out.

As well as looking forward to the event because I was a huge fan, I was also excited because this had already given the library's profits a big boost. Everyone had to buy a ticket in advance, which included a copy of the book. Plus Maddie and her team were doubling down on making branded *Illicit Delight* biscuits and cupcakes that we knew would sell out.

Maddie had even come up with a menu of cocktails for the night and I reckoned they'd be a hit too.

Yep. Tomorrow was going to be epic.

I picked up my coat and bag and went to the bookshop. I didn't want to see Jackson, it was too difficult, but I needed to make sure he saw me leave, then get him to lock up.

'I'm going now,' I said as I stood by the door. His head jerked up.

'Aren't you coming back with me?'

'No.' I shook my head. 'I told you. I need time.'

'Where will you stay?'

'Don't worry about it. I've got somewhere temporary until I move to the B&B. I'd better go.'

I didn't wait for him to say anything as I knew he'd persuade me to come home with him.

Once I left, I went to May's Fish and Chips for dinner, then I headed back to the library.

When I'd said I had somewhere temporary to stay, I meant it. I'd brought my stuff to the library, which was where I'd sleep tonight. In the morning I'd ask Glenda if I could shower there. Hopefully she wouldn't mind. I just couldn't stay at Jackson's tonight.

After washing my face and brushing my teeth in the toilets, I changed into my nightdress, then got settled in on the sofa and picked up *Illicit Delight*. But before I even started reading the first page, my mind drifted.

I thought about all the times me and Jackson had sat on this sofa, reading together whilst drinking tea and eating our favourite biscuits. We'd chat about books and I'd laugh and smile until my cheeks hurt.

And then there was the sex. This sofa was where Jackson had gone down on me for the first time. Where he'd fucked me.

It was also the place where he'd listened sympathetically whilst I'd talked about my shitty family and what had happened in my last job. It was here that he'd opened up about why he'd left his career in the City too.

Without fail, whatever we'd done on this sofa, he'd always looked out for me.

Jackson had taken care of me. Walked me home. He'd always had my back, no matter what.

Once upon a time I'd always looked out for him too. When we were the outcasts at school that no one wanted to hang out with, we always knew we had each other. It was us against the world.

And that was how it should always be.

Jackson was my boyfriend. I knew we weren't married, but we were supposed to be in a committed relationship.

I'd told Jackson yesterday that relationships were about communication and honesty. And I still believed that.

But relationships were also about supporting your partner, through thick and thin.

Love was about not giving up without a fight.

Jackson was going through hell right now. He needed me. This was my chance not just to tell him that I loved him, but to *show* him.

Screw the videos. Fuck all the people that watched

them. They didn't matter. What mattered was that Jackson was with *me*.

He thought about *me* when he filmed them.

It was *me* he made love to.

Me he wanted to be with.

And I wanted to be with him.

I had to tell him that I loved him.

I needed him to know that whether he continued doing the videos or not, I'd support him one hundred per cent.

Reaching for my bag, I went to pull out my phone, then spotted that I had Jackson's jumper buried at the bottom. I couldn't even remember when I'd borrowed it. I held it up to my nose and inhaled. It smelt of him. Delicious and woody. I really wanted to see him.

After resting the jumper on my lap, I picked up my phone and checked the train times to Shamwick. There were only two trains tonight, and they were both cancelled.

Crap.

I launched the Uber app. They didn't have any drivers, so I tried calling another cab company, but there was an incident on the line going back into Shamwick, so they were booked up.

Walking there was possible, but at this time of night it wasn't safe. And something told me Jackson wouldn't want me to risk it.

So reluctantly, I got up, turned off the light, then closed my eyes, wrapping Jackson's jumper tightly around me so I could feel close to him.

And as I fell asleep, I promised myself that no matter what, I'd tell Jackson how I felt first thing in the morning.

43

JACKSON

As I stepped off the train and headed towards the crowded exit, my chest tightened.

Something didn't feel right.

I'd thought the same thing on the journey home. At first I'd just put it down to the fact that I'd gotten so used to staying late at the library in the evenings with Jane, locking up, then going home together that I was feeling weird because she wasn't here.

But it was more than that.

I missed her.

It also felt like I'd given up too easily.

Yeah, I understood that she needed more time to think, but I'd let her go without making sure that she had all of the facts.

Take today, for example. If I hadn't seen Jane in the corridor and led her down to the stockroom to talk, she would've spent the whole day thinking that there was something going on with Celeste and that I'd made that video knowing it was her who'd asked for it.

And I couldn't blame her. She wasn't to know any different unless I told her.

That was why, before she made a decision about our future together and whether or not we had one, Jane needed to know how I felt. Knowing that I loved her could change everything.

I turned back and walked to the opposite platform, passing a group of people who were asking the guard about some trains that had been cancelled. I didn't have time to stop and listen. The train I needed was delayed but was still running.

I'd decided. I was going back to Sunshine Bay to find Jane and tell her what I'd wanted to say for ages.

Even though I had no idea where she was staying, something told me it had to be somewhere local. If it wasn't the B&B, then maybe she was crashing at Maddie's or with Jess and Theo.

Wherever she was, I wasn't going back home until I'd spoken to her. Once she knew the extent of my feelings and how much she meant to me, she could take all the time she needed to make her decision. But at least then I'd know it'd be an informed one.

Earlier I'd said that I didn't know whether I'd support Jane if the shoe was on the other foot. But now I knew for sure that I would. I'd do whatever Jane needed. No matter what.

If she'd told me she'd make more money to pay for her loved one's care if I was in the video too, I'd do it. I'd work three jobs to help her. I'd do whatever it took, because I loved her. And when you loved someone, you'd move heaven and earth to help them even if it was outside of your comfort zone.

Don't get me wrong. I wasn't saying that I expected Jane to be cool with it or to go and work multiple jobs to help me pay for Mum's care. *No.* I was just talking about *me* and what *I* would do. Everyone showed their love in different ways and for me, just knowing that I could come home to Jane at the end of a long day would be enough.

The train to Sunshine Bay pulled into the station and as I got on, my heart raced. I was going to get my girl. Just like in the movies.

In an ideal world, knowing how much she was into romance novels, I'd plan some big gesture to show her how I felt like the hero often did. But there wasn't time for that right now. It was already late and I still had to find her. I hoped that when I did, telling Jane that I loved her would be enough to encourage her to give us a chance.

When I arrived at Sunshine Bay, I went to Sweet Treats first as the light was still on. Maddie was busy working late to get everything ready for the signing. Jane wasn't staying with her, so my next stop was Jess and Theo's house, but Ben opened the door and said they'd gone to the pub.

On the way there, I stopped off at the B&B to ask Glenda just in case. But as I suspected, Jane wasn't booked to stay there until next week.

'Hey!' Jess said when I spotted her in the pub with Theo.

'Hi,' I said. 'You don't know where Jane's staying tonight, do you?'

'No.' Jess frowned. 'I thought she'd be with you. Maybe she's gone back to her parents'?'

'I don't think she'd do that.' I shook my head. She was still coming to terms with all the shit that had gone down with her dad and if she needed to think clearly, that was the last place she'd go. Jane would want to stay somewhere calming.

A light bulb went off in my head.

I knew exactly where she was.

'You okay?' Theo asked.

'Yeah. I've just realised—she's probably at the library. I'm gonna head there now.'

'Actually, I was about to get my laptop. Mind if I come with you? Don't worry, I won't be staying, so you two can have your privacy.'

'Course,' I said. 'Let's go.'

'See you in a minute,' Theo said before kissing Jess softly on the lips.

I knew from the way he looked at Jess that he loved her. It was the same way I looked at Jane. Declaring my feelings was scary, because she might break up with me, but I was still determined to tell her.

'I really hope she's there,' I said as we crossed the road.

'Everything okay with you two?'

'We're just… I had some stuff I should've told her and I didn't and she found out and is upset. But I didn't get a chance to tell her how I really felt, so I want to do that now.'

'Ah, got it,' Theo said as we walked up the pathway towards the library.

'Yeah, so I…' My voice trailed off and I stopped abruptly. 'Hold on,' I whispered, holding out my arm to stop Theo from going any further. 'I think there's someone there.'

We took a few more steps towards the building, and

sure enough, we saw someone dressed all in black wearing a mask and holding some sort of container.

'Shit!' Theo said at the same time I realised what they were holding.

'It's a petrol can!' I whispered, watching in horror as the perpetrator sprinkled it around the exterior.

'I'm calling the police.' Theo pulled out his phone and started dialling 999.

'I'll go and stop them,' I said, racing towards the arsonist. But before I got there, they reached in their pocket and suddenly there was a flash of light as the match hit the ground and the fire ignited.

Theo was right behind me, talking to an operator as we sprinted to take the arsehole down.

'I need to get inside!' I shouted. 'I need to find Jane!'

'Go!' Theo shouted back. 'I'll take care of this bastard.'

I saw the person look up just as Theo dived on top of them, but I didn't have time to stick around. There was a chance that my lady was in that building and I had to save her.

After racing round to the front, I opened the door, then sprinted down the corridor towards the library hall.

'Jane!' I called out, snatching a fire extinguisher off the wall, just in case. The fire had been set close to one of the empty rooms, but it was only a matter of time before it reached the library. 'Jane!'

I burst into the room and when I saw Jane asleep on the sofa, I exhaled loudly.

She was here.

She was safe.

For now.

There was no time to lose. I had to get her outside.

I raced over, dropped the extinguisher, then scooped her up in my arms.

'Jackson?' She squinted.

'It's me, beautiful.'

'What happened?'

'Someone's set fire to the building. We need to get out of here.'

Jane's eyes widened and I could tell she was trying to work out whether she was dreaming. More like a fucking nightmare. I didn't have time to elaborate now, though.

After sprinting down the corridor with Jane in my arms, I flew out of the main entrance.

Several people were outside. Some were rushing towards the back clutching buckets of water, while others were armed with fire extinguishers.

Shit. The fire extinguisher. I'd put it down when I picked up Jane. It'd take time for the fire brigade to arrive and we needed to put the fire out ASAP. We couldn't lose the library. Jess and Jane would be devastated.

No way. Not on my watch.

'Wait here.' I put Jane down gently and took off my jacket, ready to put it over her shoulders. It was then that I noticed she had my jumper tied around her and my heart squeezed.

She was only wearing a thin nightdress underneath it, though, so she must be freezing. 'I'll be back in a minute.' I kissed her on the lips. 'I love you,' I said before racing back into the library, hoping I could stop the fire.

And hoping that I'd get to see Jane again.

44

JANE

It was like I was in the middle of a film. But not the feel-good romcoms that I loved. This was closer to a thriller. Actually, a horror movie would be a more accurate description.

I tried to take everything in.

I was staying at the library.

I fell asleep on the sofa.

Then when I woke up, Jackson was carrying me outside. Because he said someone had tried to set fire to the library.

Jackson saved me.

If he hadn't have carried me outside, I could've died.

Jackson.

Wait.

As I came to my senses, I realised that he'd gone back inside the building.

Snapping out of my trance, I bolted towards the doors, only realising once I felt the cold concrete beneath my feet that I didn't have any shoes on. I was wearing socks and my nightdress. *Didn't matter*. Jackson needed me.

'You can't go inside, love.' A man I recognised as one of the locals held his arm out to stop me passing. 'It's not safe.'

'But my boyfriend! Jackson's in there! I have to get him! I can't leave him! I have to tell him that I love him! I didn't tell him!'

I started sobbing uncontrollably. It was all coming back to me now. I'd wanted to go and tell him how I felt, but after I couldn't find a way to get to him safely, I'd decided to tell him in the morning and gone to sleep.

And now it might be too late.

I might've been dreaming, but I thought Jackson had told me he loved me before he went back into the library.

He loved me. And I loved him.

I couldn't leave him alone in the library.

I sprinted past the man and just as I got to the doors, Jackson ran out, clutching an armful of fire extinguishers.

'Thank God you're okay!' I threw my arms around his back, clutching him tightly.

'Jane! What were you doing? You can't go back into the building!' He kissed the top of my head. 'You could've been hurt.'

'So could you! I had to make sure you were okay.'

'I'm fine, beautiful. But I need to take these round the back and help Theo. He's restraining the person who did this.'

I quickly released Jackson, who raced away, and when I followed him, I saw Theo pinning someone dressed in black on the ground, whilst Jess and several residents were trying to put the fire out.

Jackson handed out the extra extinguishers and we all got to work.

Minutes later, multiple firemen appeared.

'Everyone stand back,' a fireman commanded and we cleared the area.

'The library!' Jess sobbed before racing over to Theo. 'I'm taking off the mask!'

'Maybe we should wait for the police,' he said.

'No!' Jess shouted. 'I need to know who did this!'

Jackson helped to restrain the perpetrator whilst Jess tugged at the mask. The person tried to resist, but Theo and Jackson held them still whilst Jess yanked off the black balaclava.

'*You!*' she gasped.

'You know him?' Theo asked.

'He's Mrs Davis's son!'

'Her *son*?' Theo frowned. 'But why? Why the fuck would you do something like this? Why would you want to burn down something that your mother dreamed about? This was her dying wish!'

'That bitch stole my inheritance.' He glared at Jess.

'What did you fucking say?' Theo lifted his fist, his nostrils flaring.

'Don't!' Jackson said, blocking Theo's hand. 'He wants you to hit him. Don't give this bastard the satisfaction.'

'Talk about my lady like that again and I'll fucking *end* you,' Theo growled.

'Fuck you!' he spat. 'The money my mother gave her for this stupid place should've been mine! I told you at the will reading that I wouldn't let you get away with it and I always keep my promises.'

'You've just fucked with the wrong people, arsehole,' Theo spat.

'Damn right!' Jackson added. 'No one threatens our library and gets away with it. Your mother obviously knew you didn't deserve the money, that's why you didn't get it. And money won't matter anymore, because you're going straight to prison.'

Two policemen hurried around the corner and their eyes widened when they saw the man pinned to the ground.

'That evil sod tried to burn down our library!' I shouted. 'He's a book murderer!'

'Yeah!' Jess said. 'What kind of monster tries to burn a place dedicated to love? Sicko!'

Jackson and Theo pulled the man to his feet and after the police read him his rights, they handcuffed him and led him away.

Whilst Jackson wrapped his arm around me and pulled me in closer, Jess collapsed on Theo's chest.

'I can't believe it,' she said, tears streaming down her cheeks.

'I know.' He rubbed her back. 'It could've been a lot worse, though. From what I can tell, the fire didn't reach the library or the bookshop. Because we acted quickly, hopefully there won't be too much damage.'

'What about the signing tomorrow?' she sobbed. 'We've got so many people coming! And Jackson worked so hard to get D.D. to come. And Maddie has made hundreds of biscuits and…'

'Don't worry, Jess,' I said softly. 'It's gonna be okay. We can fix this.'

'Yeah,' Jackson added. 'The important thing is that no

one was hurt. I'll send D.D. and her agent an email now to let them know what's happened and if it's not possible to go ahead with the signing, we'll get straight to work on notifying the guests and sorting everything out. Like Jane said, we're gonna be fine.'

'Why don't I take you over to the pub, get you warmed up?' I suggested to Jess.

'Good idea,' Theo said. 'Jackson and I will sort things out here.'

A few hours later, Jackson and I were in a taxi heading back to his place. When he'd come to the pub with Theo to collect me and Jess, Jackson said they'd done all they could for tonight, so the only thing we could do now was get some rest so we'd be ready to start trying to organise things first thing in the morning.

'What a night,' Jackson said as I rested my head on his shoulder.

'I know. I'm still trying to get my head around it all. Turned out that when Jess went to the will reading, Mrs Davis only left her son a chocolate bar and a mirror so that he could 'take a long hard look at himself' and he was furious. Jess remembered that he'd said she wouldn't get away with getting his mum's money, but at the time she'd just thought he was upset. She hadn't heard anything since that day, so totally forgot about him. She'd never for a moment considered that it would come to this.'

'It's crazy.' Jackson shook his head.

'It would've been so much worse, though, if you hadn't come to the library when you did. What made you go there?'

'I was trying to find you. I needed to tell you something important. I looked everywhere, then realised the library was the only place you'd be.'

'Thank God you know me so well.' I took his hand and squeezed it. 'What did you have to tell me?'

Jackson lifted my chin.

'That I love you.' He stroked my cheek.

Every atom in my body came alive. Butterflies danced in my stomach and I swear my heart swelled so much it was in danger of bursting.

Jackson loved me.

Although it was only the passing streetlights illuminating the car, I could still see his face clearly enough and the look in his eyes told me he really meant it.

'I told you before, when I carried you out of the library, but I wasn't sure if you heard because you were still waking up. I needed you to know how I felt, before you made your decision about us.'

'The thing is'—I smiled—'I wanted to come and tell you the same thing. But I couldn't get a train or a taxi, so I promised I'd do it in the morning, went to bed, then… well, we both know what happened next.'

'You wanted to tell me the same thing?' Jackson tilted his head. 'Can you clarify exactly what *thing* you're talking about?'

'You *know*!' My smile widened. 'But seeing as you asked for clarification, Jackson Joseph Campbell, I L-O-V-E you!'

'I'm sorry, what?' He smirked. 'I seem to have lost the ability to spell.'

'I said I *love* you!'

'Fuck!' He beamed like a studious child who'd just been told they were top of the class. 'Those are the sweetest words I've ever heard in my life. Did you hear that, mate?' Jackson tapped the driver on the shoulder. 'The woman of my dreams, the girl I've loved since I was a gangly, nerdy teenager, just said she loves me!'

'Congratulations!' The driver laughed good-naturedly.

Jackson pulled me into him and pressed his lips onto mine, and heat flooded my veins.

The kiss was gentle, but the intensity was enough to light up an entire city. Everything in the way that Jackson's mouth moved against mine told me that this was it. Jackson was the man for me.

But then again, I'd always known that.

'We're here,' the driver called out.

It still took several seconds for us to break the kiss. I didn't want it to end.

After we'd thanked the driver, we headed inside Jackson's place.

'So.' He took off his shoes. 'I know you said you were coming to tell me that you love me, but were you also coming to tell me that you'd made a decision about us?'

'Yes.' I took his hand and led him to the sofa. 'I wanted to tell you that I don't care about the videos. Do whatever you need to do to keep your mum safe and well. I'll support you, no matter what. I meant what I said. I love you. And I want us to be together.'

Jackson's eyes watered as he shook his head like he was trying to take in everything I'd said.

'Really?' he asked.

'Really!'

He threw his arms around me and squeezed me so tight I thought my bones were going to break.

'Thank you,' he whispered into my hair.

'No, thank *you*. Thank you for loving me, for supporting me. And for saving my life tonight. You're like a real-life book hero!'

Jackson pulled away slowly and smiled.

'Like a real-life book hero, eh? That's high praise. I'll take that!'

'It's true!'

'You wanna know something?' He brushed a strand of hair away from my face.

'Go on.' I pushed up my glasses.

'When I was coming to find you, I was worried because I thought I hadn't planned anything big for the moment I told you that I loved you. I thought that seeing as you were a romance book lover, I needed some kind of grand gesture to win your heart.'

'Well, grand gestures don't get much better than the hero saving the heroine's life! But just so you know, you didn't need to do anything flashy. You've already won my heart.'

'God, I love you, Jane Riley.'

'I love you too.'

'Right now, I'd love to carry you to bed, spread your legs and drop to my knees to show you just how much I fucking worship you, but we should probably get some sleep.'

'You're right,' I sighed. 'We've got a library and an epic book signing to save.'

45

JACKSON

'So, yeah.' I rested my phone between my shoulder and my neck as I sat on the armchair in Jess and Theo's living room, which was currently our temporary office, and explained the situation to D.D. Desire. 'That's what happened. The guy who started the fire is in police custody and he's confessed, so there's no other threats to the library. The building has been thoroughly checked and we should be fine to open again next week, but we understand if you aren't able to reschedule because of your prior commitments.'

'No way!' D.D. shouted down the phone. 'I'll *definitely* reschedule. I can't let the fans down. That motherfucker was trying to burn down a *romance* library! If he attacks romance, he attacks *all* of us! There's no way I'll give him the satisfaction of winning. The show must go on! I can do the signing next Sunday, will that work?'

'Um.' My eyes bulged. I hadn't expected her to agree so quickly. 'Yeah! Definitely! Next Sunday will be perfect.

This is going to be the best signing ever! Thanks so much, D.D.!' I said, jumping out of my seat.

'My pleasure, sweetie. And if there's anything else I can do to get the library back up and running, just let me know.'

'That's really kind, thank you. Looking forward to meeting you next Sunday.'

'Likewise. Bye, Jackson.'

'Bye. Take care.' I ended the call. 'D.D.'s coming to do the signing next Sunday!' I shouted.

Jane and Jess raced into the living room, their eyes wide with excitement.

'Seriously?' Jess said.

'She's really coming?' Jane added.

'Yes, and *yes*! She said, and I quote, "that mother-fucker was trying to burn down a romance library. If he attacks romance, he attacks all of us."'

'I always knew I'd love that woman!' Jess grinned.

'And she said she wasn't going to let the fans down. The signing's back on, baby!' I cheered.

Jane raced into my arms and gave me the biggest hug.

'Thanks so much for saving the signing, Jackson!' Jess said. 'I'm gonna call Theo and tell him the good news.'

Theo had been at the library since the crack of dawn with a dozen volunteers who'd all rallied round to help clean up the damage.

He'd also met with various fire officers, structural engineers and building control people to get them to check the extent of the damage. Normally this process took longer, but because Theo had so many contacts from his property development days, he was able to call in some favours.

Luckily, as we'd hoped, the damage wasn't as serious as it could've been and the books and the main library hall were intact, so we'd be able to reopen again soon, then go ahead with the signing.

All of the guests had been notified, and although they were obviously upset, they understood that it was out of our control.

I'd told everyone I'd be in touch once I knew more, so now I couldn't wait to tell them all the good news.

Today was the day.

The library had reopened. And thanks to the residents of Sunshine Bay, who'd helped to fix, repaint and restore all of the areas that had been damaged, it looked as good as new.

The cafe was well stocked with hundreds of branded biscuits and cupcakes, the themed cocktails had been mixed and we had piles of D.D. Desire's latest novel waiting to be signed.

'She's here!' Jess ran into the events room, where Jane and I had just finished double-checking the layout of the chairs. 'A flashy car just pulled up outside!'

'Amazing!' Jane beamed, mirroring her enthusiasm. 'We're all set here.'

'Ladies and Jackson.' Theo walked in. 'Allow me to introduce you to the one, the only D.D. Desire. Aka our favourite author!'

'Wow, what a welcome!' D.D. appeared from behind him. She had deep brown skin, short black hair and was wearing red lipstick and a tailored red trouser suit with white trainers that looked so fresh, I wouldn't be surprised if this was the first time she'd worn them. 'And that voice. *Yum!* You should narrate my audiobooks.'

'I'd be honoured,' Theo said. 'This is Jackson.' He gestured towards me.

'Jackson! So nice to put a face to the voice. And what a pretty face you have. What do they put in the water in this town? How are you two *both* so handsome?'

'Lovely to meet you, D.D.,' I laughed. 'I think I speak for all of us when I say that your books have not only been entertaining, but also very… inspirational.'

'Did your girlfriends want to jump your bones after reading them?' She smiled at me, then turned to Theo.

'Something like that…' I smirked.

'I got a lot of inspiration when I read the book too,' Theo added.

'Glad to hear it!'

'Speaking of our girlfriends, this is Jane, the best librarian ever created and my lady…' I said, then gestured to Theo.

'And this is Jess, my talented girlfriend and the founder of The Romance Library.'

'It's a pleasure to meet you both.'

'You're, like, my favourite author!' Jess gushed. 'I can't even pretend to be cool right now. Honestly, thank you sooo much! *Illicit Delight* was fucking amazing! I've already read it twice. My friend Sarah's also a huge fan. She's read it *three* times. She's gutted she couldn't make it today.' Jess had already put aside copies of D.D.'s books for her to sign so that she could send them to Sarah as a surprise gift. '*Office Delight* brought me so much joy. And it helped bring me and Theo together.'

'Oh *really*? I definitely want to hear more about that story after the signing…' She winked.

An hour later all the guests were seated. As D.D. read an extract from her book, the audience were captivated. I wasn't surprised. Jane and I had read it together during our nights at the library and we'd already recreated some of the scenes…

Once D.D. finished reading, the audience leapt to their feet and I swore they cheered and clapped for five minutes straight. It was well deserved. She was an incredible author.

We then invited guests to join the queue to get their books signed and have their photo taken with her.

The bookshop was packed with fans who'd flocked to buy special limited-edition copies of *Office Delight* and other novels. The biscuits, cupcakes and cocktails were also a huge hit and sold out, despite Maddie doubling the quantity she'd originally planned.

Everyone was having such a good time that D.D. ended up staying at the library two hours later than planned.

'That was brilliant!' Jess said as she locked the library doors. 'It couldn't have gone any better. Thanks so much, you two.' She wrapped one arm around Jane's waist and the other around mine.

'You're welcome,' we replied.

'Have you seen Theo?'

'He said he just needed to take care of something in the shop, but he wanted me to show you this.' I handed her a piece of paper.

'What?' Her eyes almost flew from their sockets.

'The first figure is my estimate for how much we've made from today's event.'

'No way!' she gasped.

'Yep!' I smiled. 'We're going to check all the figures again tomorrow, but we're pretty sure it's accurate. And the second figure is the amount we've received in donations to help keep the library open.'

'Donations?' Jess's face crumpled. 'From who?'

'We had a pretty hefty one from Liam Stone and Mia Bailey, who said they've been fans of this place ever since they opened the library and wanted to support you. Theo's billionaire friend Nico Chevalier was also happy to send over an eye-watering and life-changing cheque. D.D. Desire gave us a monetary donation and a shitload of signed books she claimed she had laying around her house that she needed to "clear out". And we've had dozens of bookworms and members who asked to donate because they said, and I quote, "what you're doing here matters." Everyone believes in The Romance Library, Jess. We're going to be okay!'

Tears rolled down her cheeks.

'Did Jackson tell you the good news, then?' Theo appeared and pulled Jess into him.

'Yeah,' Jess sobbed. 'I can't believe it! With that amount of money we can hire another team member. We could think about expanding the library upstairs. But most importantly, we can stay open!'

'Damn right!' I said.

'I'm so happy!' Jane squealed.

When Theo told me about the donations earlier, I was blown away. He'd explained that he never would've asked Nico or Liam for money because he considered them friends and didn't want to cross the line. But when they'd heard about the fire they'd both called Theo. When he told them how well the business had been growing with the new events and initiatives we'd implemented, they'd both offered to invest.

Theo said that even if they were his friends, they wouldn't have given us money if they didn't think the library was a viable business. They saw the library's growth potential and they believed in us, which meant a lot.

'There's something else D.D. donated that I want to show you.' Theo took Jess's hand and led her down the corridor.

'We'll start clearing up,' Jane said.

'That can wait,' Theo replied. 'I'd like you guys to see this too.'

We followed Theo. When we got to the library hall, he opened the door and my eyes widened. Electric candles lined the floor and one of the sofas had been moved to the centre.

'What's all this?' Jess frowned.

'Take a seat,' Theo said, gesturing to the sofa. He went to a table picked up a huge hardback, then handed it to Jess. 'This is a totally bespoke copy of *Office Delight* that I had created just for you.'

We all knew that was Jess's favourite book, so this was a big deal.

'Oh my God! It's gorgeous!' Jess gushed. 'Look at the gold foil and the gold edges! It's a work of art.'

'Open it,' Theo said.

Jess's eyes popped, then she gasped loudly.

When we looked closer, the inside had a square cut out

in the centre and a jewellery box had been neatly placed within it.

Theo dropped down on one knee.

No. Way.

Jane's head whipped round to face mine and wide grins spread across our faces as we realised what was about to happen.

'Jess.' Theo looked up at her. 'I've wanted to do this for a while, but when I heard that D.D. was coming to do a signing, I knew it'd be the perfect time. She's your favourite author, this is your favourite book and this library's your favourite place, so it just felt right. Just like our relationship. Whenever I'm with you, I feel like everything is right in the world. You're my best friend, my biggest supporter, my lover, my everything and I want to be with you for the rest of my life. Would you do me the honour of marrying me?'

'Yes!' Jess squealed with excitement before throwing her arms around Theo and kissing him.

'That's…' Jane's pulled off her glasses and wiped her eyes. 'That's so romantic.'

'It is.' I wrapped my arm around her waist and pulled her into me.

Theo slid the ring on Jess's finger, then she hugged and kissed him repeatedly.

'We're engaged!' she shrieked, flashing her left hand in the air.

We walked over and gave them both a big squeeze.

'Congrats, guys!' I said. 'You two are perfect together. We're so happy for you.'

'This is the best news!' Jane said. 'You deserve all the happiness in the world!'

'Thanks!' Jess said. 'I'm a very lucky woman.'

'And I'm a very lucky man.' Theo leant forward and kissed her. The kiss went from PG to X-rated pretty quickly.

'Er, we can see you've got some celebrating to do, so we'll leave you to it and we'll come in early tomorrow to tidy up…' I said.

Jess and Theo didn't reply. They were obviously focused on other things…

Jane and I quickly left the library hall, grabbed our stuff, then left.

'Looks like it'll be someone else getting busy in the library tonight!' Jane laughed.

'Yep!'

'They're the real deal. If we can be half as happy as them, we'll be lucky.'

'We're the real deal too. That's what I'd like with you, Jane: a lifetime of happiness together. I'm up for the whole shebang. Living together, marriage, whatever you want, Beautiful, it's yours. *I'm* yours.' I took Jane's hand in mine and kissed her slowly.

'I want all of that too. You're it for me, Jackson. You're *the one*.'

'I feel the same. I meant what I said before. It's always been you. Ever since we were kids. You're my past, my present and my forever love. And I never want to be without you.'

EPILOGUE
JANE

<u>Four months later</u>

'Mmm. This smells amazing!' I gushed as Barbara put a plate of roast chicken, roast potatoes, peas and Yorkshire pudding all covered in gravy in front of me.

'Wait until you taste it!' Barbara said.

'It's true. The Seaview Arms does the best Sunday roast,' Jess added as Barbara and Bob distributed the rest of the plates around the table.

I was in the pub with Jackson, Jess, Theo, Marcus and Sarah, who'd come down for the weekend.

We'd all got together for lunch to celebrate the sale of Jackson's mum's house, which was completed on Friday.

I still couldn't believe it'd finally happened. It'd been a busy few months.

When Jackson told Jess and Theo about his mum and

the challenges he'd faced with trying to sell his house to pay for her care, Theo immediately stepped in to help.

He came to look at the house, made some calls and literally a few days later, a team of workmen were there, renovating the kitchen and bathroom and giving the entire house a new lease of life with a fresh lick of paint.

The transformation was incredible. And Theo didn't ask Jackson for a penny. Said he'd called in a few favours and not to worry about it.

Theo also told Jackson to get rid of the estate agents he'd been using and arranged for another hotshot agent to list it instead. Jackson received an offer a few weeks later. In fact, the longest part of the process was the buyer arranging stuff from their end.

And now it'd been sold, Jackson finally didn't have to worry about his mum's care.

I'd been with him to see his mum, Yolanda, multiple times.

The first time was the day after the D.D. Desire signing. We were blown away because she seemed to remember me from all those years ago when she'd come into the school, which I thought was a great sign. But since then, she hadn't recognised me. It wasn't her fault. I knew that Alzheimer's was a cruel illness that robbed her of her memory, so I quickly got used to Jackson introducing me at the start of each visit. And when she was having a good day, I loved seeing her get excited every time Jackson told her that I was his girlfriend.

Jackson had continued making his videos to pay for Yolanda's care, and not only did he have my blessing, I'd become his director.

Yep.

Whenever he had a new batch of videos to make, I'd be right there not just watching him, but directing Jackson from behind the camera too.

I took great pleasure in telling him when I thought he needed to thrust his hips more vigorously, shake his arse more or change the pace of how hard he was wanking.

And, yes, watching him definitely got me going, because I knew that when he was stroking himself or doing his dirty dancing, it was *me* that he was thinking about.

As soon as I stopped filming, he'd pick me up and fuck me so good, which definitely made it worth it. And I wasn't bothered about the fact that other people saw his dick. I was proud and maybe a little smug too because I knew that they only got to watch him for a few minutes on a screen and fantasise about him. But I got to feel him and experience his incredible dick in real life, which was a massive thrill.

Now that the house was sold, technically Jackson no longer needed to make more videos. He hadn't decided yet whether or not to continue, but whatever he wanted to do, I'd support him one hundred per cent.

We'd also told Jess and Theo about the videos. We did it over dinner at their place and they almost choked on their food.

Jess said she had no idea that it was Jackson when Celeste showed us the video in the pub, but now that she knew she felt icky. Not because she was bothered about what he'd done (in fact, she was really cool with it) but because she said it was like watching your brother wank. Which was why Jess assured us that she would definitely *not* be checking out any more of his videos.

Theo agreed, but joked that maybe we could develop some new divisions of The Romance Library, suggesting that he could branch out into audiobook production and Jackson could film himself recreating spicy scenes from popular romance novels instead of just stroking himself with a feather duster.

That suggestion made us erupt into fits of laughter. But then Jess pointed out that for that to work, I'd also need to participate and as much as I was enjoying every single second of my fantastic sex life with Jackson (and recreating scenes from our favourite books), I preferred to do it off camera and not for the audience of thousands of strangers like Jackson had racked up.

It was crazy to think that it wasn't so long ago that I was still a virgin. That felt like a lifetime ago now.

These days Jackson and I couldn't keep our hands off each other. I didn't think there was a surface in his house that we hadn't made love on. And we still occasionally got up to no good at the library after hours too, of course always making sure that we cleaned up thoroughly afterwards.

Speaking of the library, after the success of the D.D. Desire signing, things really took off.

As well as the flurry of members that flocked to the library every day to borrow books, romance lovers came from far and wide to buy books from our shop too.

Jackson had built some great relationships with publishers and authors and negotiated deals where we got lots of signed copies and exclusive swag that readers couldn't get anywhere else, which encouraged them to buy from us instead.

The events were going from strength to strength too.

We hosted a weekly romance book club, ran silent reading parties every fortnight and had hosted two more author book signings, with more on the way.

Love & Lattes was also a big hit. Maddie and her team couldn't make the bookish biscuits and cupcakes fast enough. They'd become almost as big of an attraction at the library as the books, with visitors posting photos on social media and taking home the new gift boxes they sold, which of course were shaped like mini books.

Jess and Theo had hired two new part-time team members to help out in the library and the bookshop, which had been a lifesaver. Now they were busy looking at plans for expansion, including developing the first floor, and Jess said they also wanted to hire another full-timer too.

I was so glad that the library was now financially stronger and everyone's jobs were safe.

Speaking of safe, now that Mrs Davis's son had been locked up for his attacks on our library, we could all focus on growing the business instead of worrying about being sabotaged. Which was a massive weight off everyone's mind. If anything, it had made us even more determined to make the library a success. Like D.D. Desire eloquently put it, if someone fucked with The Romance Library, they fucked with all of us.

'This food is tasty,' Marcus said, tucking into his roast lamb. 'I can see why you like this place.'

I'd also met Marcus several times. I could see why Jackson had been friends with him for so long. He was a good guy and the way he'd helped Jackson out was amazing. I'd thanked him every time I saw him, but he said it was no big deal and that it was just what friends did.

'You're right,' Sarah said as she slid a forkful of her roast beef into her mouth. 'It really is delicious! What is it about Sunshine Bay? It's like everything here is perfect.'

'It's a pretty cool place to live,' Jess said. 'Wait until you try May's Fish and Chips!'

'If I didn't have to go back tonight, I'd be heading straight there after this. It's not fair,' she sighed. 'I wish I could live here too. I wish I could live anywhere but back home. It's so boring there. You guys are living the dream. You get to talk about books all day. If you wanted to, you could just sniff thousands of books for hours. You get to read books before they come out. You get to plan events for books. Aaargh! I'm so jealous!'

'Well… if you really want to live here and work with books all day, I might know someone who's looking for a new person to join their team full-time.'

'What?' Sarah's eyes bulged. 'Seriously? Work *here*? In Sunshine Bay? With you guys? At The Romance Library?'

'Yep!' Jess beamed.

'No fucking way!' Sarah shouted so loudly practically the whole pub turned around to see what the commotion was.

'*Yes*, fucking way!' Jess said. 'Me and Theo have got big expansion plans for this year, so we're gonna need an extra pair of hands to help Jane and Jackson out in the library and the bookshop, spend more time on the marketing and social media and get our online shop up and running. So what d'you reckon? Fancy joining The Romance Library team?'

'A million per cent, yes!' Sarah jumped out of her seat

so quickly she nearly knocked over her glass of Prosecco. 'Thank you!' She hugged Jess tightly.

'Obviously you'll get a good salary too. Theo can send you all the official details.'

'Don't tell Theo, but I'd work at the library for free! It's my dream job.'

'We absolutely won't hear of you working for free.' Theo shook his head. 'You helped Jess out so much with the social media when it was just starting out and never asked for a penny, so now the library's in a much stronger financial position, you'll be paid, just like the rest of us.'

'Amazing! Thank you!'

'You're welcome. We're also looking at bringing my brother Ben onboard too,' Theo added.

'So you'll finally get to meet him…' Jess raised an eyebrow.

Jess had told me that ever since she got together with Theo and Sarah found out that he had brothers, she'd been asking Jess to set them up. Looked like now she'd get the chance to do exactly that.

Like Theo, Ben was handsome, so I was sure she'd find him attractive. But from what I could gather, he was a bit of a ladies' man, so it'd be interesting to see how that worked out…

'It's great that you're hiring people that you know and trust.'

'Exactly. Sometimes it's good to keep things in the family. Not always, though…' His voice trailed off.

'I know exactly what you mean,' I said.

I hadn't seen either of my parents since I'd met up with Mum the morning after I'd walked out of the house. And I felt better for it.

Last I'd heard, Dad's campaign to get elected as a local MP flopped. Usually I hated to see people fail, but in this case it was a relief. The last thing a town like Shamwick needed was someone like him in a position of power, inflicting his toxic views.

To her credit, Mum had messaged a few times to check how I was. I always replied, but texting was as far as our relationship would go.

For years I'd tolerated them because I believed the stuff people said about the importance of family. In many cases that was true. But I'd realised that some people weren't willing to change. So to preserve my sanity and protect my mental health, I had to cut them out of my life. And that was okay.

I'd learned that family wasn't about being bound by blood. It was having people around you that truly cared about you and loved you.

Family were people that had your back, no matter what. Who didn't try and stifle your growth or manipulate you for their own gains like Dad did.

The famous saying that *friends are the family you choose* was true. Jackson, Jess and Theo and so many of the residents of Sunshine Bay were my true family. They were the relatives I'd always wanted, but never had. Until now.

The bond we had was much stronger than blood. It was real and everlasting.

'Where have you two moved to?' Sarah asked.

'We're staying in the B&B for a few weeks, then we're renting a house in town for a couple of months whilst the owner's away. After that, we're not sure. It's really hard to find accommodation in Sunshine Bay.'

I moved my hair back over my shoulders. Although I occasionally wore it in a bun, I'd been wearing it down a lot more lately. And when Jackson took me shopping to replace the blouses he'd ruined, I'd chosen some less conservative options. The days of worrying about what my parents would say about my clothes were long gone.

'Tell me about it!' Jess said. 'We're lucky the owner of our house decided to stay in the States for longer, but we'd still like to find somewhere permanent.'

'I'm sure something will come up soon,' Sarah said. 'I'd better start looking for myself too. I can't believe we're going to be neighbours! And if I'm here, I can help you plan the wedding too!'

I was still so excited that Jess and Theo were getting married. Hopefully one day that'd be me and Jackson, but there was no rush. We had our whole lives together to look forward to.

Once we'd finished lunch, the others stayed to have more drinks, but Jackson asked if I wanted to come for a walk with him on the beach.

The weather was still cold, but today was much milder than it had been the past few weeks.

'Still trying to get my head around the fact that the house is sold and this is where we live now.' Jackson took my hand.

'I know, right? It's like a dream. It doesn't matter how many times I walk on this beach, it still feels like I'm staring at a postcard. Minus the sun, of course.'

'I'm looking at the sun right now.' Jackson stroked my cheek and I laughed. 'What? Too cheesy?'

'Cheesier than a pizza with extra mozzarella.'

'I happen to love extra mozzarella on my pizza.' Jackson grinned. 'And anyway, I don't care if it sounds cheesy. It's how I feel. You're my sun, my moon, my stars, my everything.'

'*Awww.*' I kissed him on the lips. 'You're my everything too.'

'I mean it, Jane. I love you more than all of the Jammie Dodgers and Party Rings biscuits in the world.'

'Wow. That's a *lot*!'

'Yep. And I love you more than all of the digestives and rich tea biscuits in the universe.'

Jackson leant forward and pressed his lips on mine. And when he kissed me, fireworks erupted inside me.

I knew he meant every word.

I loved romance novels with all of my heart. I loved the warm, fuzzy, fluttery feelings they gave me. I loved the joy I felt when the couple got their happy ending.

But there was one thing I loved more, and that was Jackson.

After spending years living vicariously through the characters in my favourite romance novels, I'd finally got my own happily-ever-after.

And it was even better than I'd ever imagined was possible.

Want more?

Want to read about the amazing surprise Jackson arranges for Jane? Join the Olivia Spring VIP Club and **receive *The Love Librarian Bonus Epilogue* for FREE**! Visit https://BookHip.com/SXBKCGR to find out more!

Not ready to say goodbye to Sunshine Bay? Want to find out what happens when aspiring romance author Sarah and notorious playboy Ben start working together at The Romance Library?
Order book three in the series,
***The Romcom Writer*, now!**

ENJOYED THIS BOOK? YOU CAN MAKE A BIG DIFFERENCE.

If you've enjoyed *The Love Librarian*, **I'd be so very grateful if you could spare two minutes to leave a review on Amazon, Goodreads and BookBub**. It doesn't have to be long (unless you'd like it to be!). Every review – even if it's just a sentence – would make a *huge* difference.

By leaving an honest review, you'll be helping to bring my books to the attention of other readers and hearing your thoughts will make them more likely to give my novels a try. As a result, it will help me to build my career, which means I'll get to write more books!

Thank you so much. As well as making a huge difference, you've also just made my day!

Olivia x

The Romcom Writer

<u>The Love Hotel Series</u>
The One That Got Away
What Happens In Paradise
Too Hard To Resist

<u>Other Books</u>
The Match Faker
Losing My Inhibitions
Love Offline

<u>Box Set</u>
Ready To Mingle Collection

My Ten-Year Crush

Have you read my friends-to-lovers novel ***My Ten-Year Crush?*** Here's what it's about:

The first kiss wrecked their friendship. Could a second chance lead to love?

English teacher Bella isn't having much luck with her love life. No matter who she dates, no one seems to measure up to Mike: the ex-bestie she shared a drunken kiss with ten years ago, which led to the end of their friendship…

When Bella comes face-to-face with Mike at their university reunion, sparks fly. He's smart, funny and even hotter than before, and despite trying to fight her feelings, Bella still can't get him out of her head.

But after what happened the last time she stepped out of the friend zone, Bella isn't in a hurry to be rejected all over again.

Should Bella risk more heartache by telling Mike how she really feels? Could the attraction be mutual? Or is it finally time to put her past behind her and say goodbye to a second chance at love, forever?

My Ten-Year Crush is a fun, sexy, friends-to-lovers romcom about second chances and stepping out of your comfort zone. **Order *My Ten-Year Crush* now!**

AN EXCERPT FROM MY TEN-YEAR CRUSH

Chapter One

We all have those moments.

The moments when we agree to do something and regret it.

Like when you go for a run to support a friend who's started a new fitness regime, then it ends up raining.

When you say 'Of course I'll come out tonight,' when really, you wish you could just stay at home and chill on the sofa.

Or when a well-meaning neighbour sets you up on a date and you get the feeling it's going to be as successful as a trip on the *Titanic*.

Yep.

We've all been there.

In fact, I was there right now: sitting in a bar with Edwin, my neighbour's brother.

I'd met him briefly once before, and during our limited exchange, he'd seemed nice, polite and handsome.

My neighbour, Gina, was convinced we'd be great together and kept asking if I'd meet him. I said I'd let her know, but then last Sunday she'd knocked at my door, offering me a plate of freshly baked chocolate chip cookies. The sweet cocoa scent was intoxicating, so of course I'd accepted. But seconds later, she'd said, 'So, about that date with Edwin… is this Thursday okay?'

I couldn't exactly say no. She'd caught me when I was hungry. At the time, a quick drink with a guy who came highly recommended seemed like a fair exchange for satisfying my sugar fix.

There was no denying that just like when we'd first met, Edwin was good-looking. He had brown eyes and well-cut short dark hair and was dressed in a three-piece suit with a bow tie. Very different to the relaxed orange maxi dress and gold sandals I was wearing. But whilst he had the looks, so far, the jury was out on his personality.

He'd already asked me why I was single, which was one of my least favourite questions. I knew it was something most people wondered when they met someone new, but Edwin had asked it in a kind of 'what's wrong with you, woman?' way, which wasn't cool.

The red flag was well and truly raised when he asked if I'd had many boyfriends. I told him that question was too personal, so didn't answer.

And it wasn't just his personality. There was no chemistry either. I didn't feel that connection.

The thought of making up an excuse to get out of here had crossed my mind approximately fifty times in the last sixty seconds. But then the logical part of my brain reminded me that even though I hated dating, I had to keep an open mind. Plus, I couldn't just get up and leave. I'd only been here twenty minutes, so that would be rude.

Although I was certain that he couldn't be further from being *the one* if he lived on Mars, I'd promised Gina I'd give him a chance, because he'd been out of the game for a while, so I should at least try and stay for an hour out of politeness. It'd be fine…

'Yummy, yum, *yum*!' Edwin sipped the red wine he'd recommended we order, because apparently it was 'full-bodied' and had a 'silky texture', with 'an aroma of cherry wood, juicy berries…' and some other stuff I couldn't remember. Personally, I preferred to drink Chardonnay, but said I'd give it a go. 'This is absolutely *sublime*. Just like I knew it would be. The explosion of berries is like an orgasm on your tongue.'

Did he just…

'I'm sorry?' I frowned. 'What did you just say?'

'The wine.' He licked his lips. 'It's like an orgasm on your tongue. Not a small whimper of a climax. *No, no, no.* I'm talking about when you've had an unusually long dry spell and after months of waiting for a woman to accept your invitation to spend the evening together, you finally seal the deal, get to release and the explosion is cataclysmic. It's just boom! POW! *Whoosh!* Like a rocket! *That's* what drinking this wine feels like: the sweetest, juiciest orgasm on your tongue.'

'Right…' I took a sip and it tasted surprisingly like… red wine. Nothing spectacular and definitely not comparable to an *orgasm*. Admittedly, it had been a while since I'd had one, but I was pretty sure it was better than this.

'So!' Edwin sat up straighter in his seat. 'Are you ready?'

'Ready for what?' I frowned.

'For the date to begin.' Edwin rolled his eyes like it should be obvious.

'I thought it already had?'

'No, silly!' he scoffed. Edwin snapped open his black briefcase, then pulled out a stack of cards. Reminded me of the ones I used to help me revise for exams. He gave them a quick shuffle and cleared his throat. 'Where do you see yourself in five years' time?'

No way. I thought I was here for a date, not a job interview. I took a deep breath, wondering how my love life had come to this.

'Doing a career that I love and settled down, hopefully.'

'I see.' Edwin put the cards on the table, pulled out his phone and started typing. 'Ready-to-get-married-and-have-children. Exclamation mark. Good-sign. Exclamation mark.'

I quickly covered by mouth to stifle my surprise at the fact that he was actually taking notes and reading them out loud. And if that wasn't bad enough, somehow he didn't seem to realise that he was doing it.

'So you intend to work after you've had children?' He frowned.

'Yes. I'd like to. Even if it's part-time.'

'I see...,' he said with a disapproving tone before typing out, 'Career woman. Dot-dot-dot. Potential-question-mark.'

I sat there for half an hour as Edwin quizzed me on everything from where I'd gone to school to what A levels I'd studied, what my parents did for a living and my favourite hobbies. It was exhausting.

'And you?' I asked, attempting to make this date a two-way conversation. 'What do you like doing in your spare time?'

'No, no, no.' He wagged his finger. 'I haven't finished *my* questions. Actually, let's switch to the quick-fire round.'

Oh dear God. So now we'd gone from an interview to a game show? I was losing the will to live.

How could Edwin and Gina be so different? If she wasn't such a good neighbour, I would've attempted to make my excuses and left. I deserved a lifetime supply of home-made cookies after this ordeal.

'Ah, yes!' He selected the next card. 'This is always a fun one: Which way should the toilet paper go on the holder?'

What the…?

I scanned the room. I refused to believe this was happening. I must be part of a secret camera show. Ashton Kutcher was going to jump out at any second and tell me I'd been punk'd. It was the only explanation.

'Time is ticking!' Edwin tapped his fingers impatiently on the table.

'Over,' I answered. 'It should go over rather than under.'

Edwin gasped. 'That is incorrect.'

'Incorrect?' I huffed. 'Seriously, though: does it really matter?'

'Of course it does. Let's try another. Skiing in the Alps or relaxing on the beach?'

'Well, I've never been skiing, so I'd have to say beach…'

'This isn't going well…' Edwin tutted and waved his

finger again. 'Next question: What is your favourite television series?'

'That's easy. *Friends*. I used to watch it all the time with… with my old best friend.'

'Of all the television series you could have picked, you chose *Friends*? Dear oh dear oh dear.' He shook his head.

I'd just about managed to put up with being interviewed, but now he'd insulted *Friends*, he'd taken things too far. If I hadn't been before, now I was certain that Edwin was *not* the man for me. I'd felt it in my gut when the date had started, not to mention when he'd started comparing wine to bloody orgasms.

Forget the cookies. There weren't enough biscuits in the world to compensate for putting up with any more of his rubbish. Once I explained to Gina, she'd understand why this absolutely couldn't go any further.

'Bella, I'm sorry to break this to you, but I'm going to call this a night. I'm afraid you're just not a suitable candidate for me. You're just a bit too, you know…? Never mind.'

A bit too what? Actually, I'd rather not know.

Arsehole.

I should've left earlier, when I'd first realised this wasn't going to work.

Story of my life. Even when men waved more red flags than an overzealous football referee, I ignored the signs because I wanted to be kind and give them the benefit of the doubt. And then they dumped me without giving my feelings a second thought.

'Here.' He tipped a pile of coins onto the table. 'This is for my wine. I would've paid for yours too if I thought this could go somewhere. Should be enough. If there's any extra, you can keep the change. My treat!' He winked. 'Bye.'

And just like that, Edwin left.

I was rooted to the spot for a good thirty seconds. My cheeks burned with frustration. I wish I could have told him *exactly* what I thought of him and his stupid questions.

I needed to leave. Right now.

After handing my cash and Edwin's money (including the extra ten pence he'd so generously left) to the waiter, I rushed out of the bar.

I couldn't wait to get home and put this nightmare behind me. Although I wanted the date to end, I still felt like I'd been punched in the stomach. This was exactly why I hated dating.

I couldn't believe Gina had said he was a catch. If Edwin was the only fish left in the sea, I'd rather starve.

I'd told her my ideal man would have a good personality, not be an annoying snob. I was hoping to meet someone normal that I could have a decent conversation with. You know, chat about everyday stuff, like what was happening in the soaps, but also be able to talk about heavier topics too. Someone down to earth, who could make me laugh. Someone like M—

No.

Stop it.

What was wrong with me? I had to get a grip and stop comparing everyone to him. It had been a decade for goodness' sake. I'd cut myself off. Moved on. I was over him.

Thankfully, it didn't take long to get home. I opened the door, kicked off my shoes, hung up my jacket, tied my dark curly hair into a bun, then flopped down on the sofa.

My phone rang. Gina, who lived in the flat below

mine, had probably heard me come in and was calling to find out how the date went. Saying I thought her brother was a patronising dickhead wasn't going to be fun.

'Hi, B!' *Phew*. It wasn't her after all.

'Hey, Melody!' I breathed a sigh of relief. 'How are you?'

'I'm good. Thanks for the cool bracelet. You're such a luv, thinking of me like that. It really made my day!'

'Glad you liked it.' It was nothing extravagant. Melody always wore a million bracelets, so you could usually hear her jangling before you saw her. When I'd spotted the colourful beads on a stall in Camden Market last weekend, I couldn't resist getting it. She'd had a tough time lately, so I'd thought it might cheer her up.

'Anyway, what you up to?' she said.

'Just back from a terrible date.'

'Sorry to hear that, my lovely. Dating is pants.' *Exactly what I'd just been saying*. 'Let me guess: you deliberately picked someone crap who you knew wouldn't go the distance, so either butt ugly or a boring old fart.'

'What?' I gasped. 'I don't do that!' Yes, Edwin was boring, but I hadn't known that when I'd agreed to the date. I'd thought he had potential, and he was handsome.

Melody made my dating patterns sound so prescriptive and it really wasn't like that. I'd gone out with all kinds of guys over the years. I was an equal opportunities dater: I pretty much said yes to anyone who asked me. Tall, short, slim, big, good-looking, less aesthetically blessed.

Don't get me wrong: I was no supermodel, so it wasn't like I was inundated with offers. But whilst my friends shied away from the guys who were under six foot, even though I was five foot eleven, I didn't. Finding someone seemed impossible enough, so I couldn't afford to rule anyone out.

It made no difference, though. Sooner or later, they always found a reason to dump me.

I'd come to the conclusion that the perfect man for me just didn't exist. I was never going to meet anyone who ticked all three of my important boxes: great personality, chemistry and good looks.

It was like that saying. When it comes to choosing a service, there are three options: fast, cheap or good quality, but you can only pick two. So if something is fast and cheap, it'll be poor quality. If it's fast and good quality, it won't be cheap.

The way I saw it, the same principle applied to men. It wasn't possible to find one with the complete package. They'd either be hot with sizzling chemistry, but have zero personality. Or have a great personality, but there'd be no chemistry. If I could find a guy who had a great personality and good chemistry, I wouldn't be so bothered about his looks, but nope.

I'd only ever met one man with the complete package, but that hadn't ended well either. Because I'd discovered that even if by some major miracle a guy *did* have all three qualities, he still rejected me.

Which proved my original point: my perfect man didn't exist.

But I still wanted a partner, so rather than expecting to be swept off my feet and find the love of my life, I now considered dating a numbers game. It was a case of just persevering until I found someone to settle with who could tick a couple of boxes and was ready for something long-term. Realistically, that was all I could hope for.

'Say whatever you want, but I know you better than you think, B. Anyway, I was calling to check you were coming the Friday after next?'

I racked my brain trying to think what she was talking about. I'd known Melody for ages. We'd gone to university together, and although we texted and spoke often, we only saw each other a few times a year. Whilst I lived in South London, she was based miles away in Coventry, raising her daughter on her own, so it wasn't easy. I definitely didn't remember arranging to meet up.

'What's happening in two weeks?'

'The reunion!! Can you believe it's been ten years since we left uni! Crazy! So, anyway, Heather and a few of the others thought it would be cool to organise something. They said they'd sent you an invite?'

Oh. *That*.

'Erm, I'm behind on opening my post, so I must have missed it…' I crossed my fingers and prayed I wouldn't be sent to hell for telling a little white lie. I remembered seeing the invitation a few weeks ago, then putting it where it belonged: in the dustbin.

'No worries! It's pretty relaxed. You can still come. I'll just let them know. It'd be great to see you! They've hired a venue and everything. Tickets are really reasonable. Even includes a couple of drinks, a buffet and a DJ. It's going to be amazeballs! I've had my childcare booked for weeks. Can't wait!'

'I've actually got plans for that Friday…' My second lie of the evening. *Heaven help me*. Although, technically, staying at home could still be considered as having *plans*. If not, I'd find something to do. Plucking individual hairs

from my bikini line, walking across hot coals barefoot…
anything except going to the reunion.

'Oh really? What you up to?'

'Um, I've been invited to… I'm just busy… sorry. I'm sure you'll all have a great time, though! Maybe we can meet in a couple of weeks or something so you can tell me all about it.'

'Hold on! I'm coming!' Melody shouted. 'Sorry, I've got to go. Andrea needs me. Think about it, though, yeah? See if you can change these *plans* of yours.' Something told me she didn't believe me. Melody had always had some sort of sixth sense. I was glad the conversation was ending. I was rubbish at lying, so if she hadn't already guessed, it wouldn't be long before she realised I was telling porkies.

'Thanks for calling. And say hi to Andrea from me.'

'Laters!' Melody hung up.

As nice as it would be to see Melody, I definitely would not be changing my mind about going. It wasn't a good idea.

Not because of *him*. That had happened ages ago, so I was definitely over it. He'd probably forgotten all about that night too. Like me, I doubted he'd given it a second thought.

All the same, in the interest of avoiding any potential awkwardness, I'd leave that memory under lock and key.

Yep. Some things were best left in the past. Which was exactly where all thoughts of him belonged.

Want to find out what happens next? Buy *My Ten-Year Crush* today!

ACKNOWLEDGEMENTS

I'm so grateful to the following people for helping me to bring *The Love Librarian* to life:

- **My amazing husband**: for giving the best hugs, listening to my constant book talk and being one of my biggest cheerleaders.
- **Emma:** for beta reading this novel so conscientiously, providing such thorough and brilliant feedback and for the incredible support and enthusiasm you show my books.
- **Tammy:** for being such a wonderful beta reader and taking the time to give such detailed and fantastic feedback.
- **Mum:** for reading over the first draft and sharing your helpful thoughts.
- **Loz:** for your eagle eyes, which always spot things that I would've missed.
- **Lesley:** for sharing your experience of having a parent with Alzheimer's disease and taking the

time to read over my work to ensure that I handled the topic with care.

- **Jay:** for your super-helpful property/building expertise.
- **Rachel:** for the stunning book cover.
- **Eliza:** for your excellent editing skills.
- **Helen:** for your brilliant proofreading.
- **Dawn Li:** for being so talented and one of the kindest, loveliest people I've ever had the pleasure of knowing. Thanks for your support, patience and all that you did to help my website look so pretty from day one. I will miss you, my dear friend.
- **The members of the Romance Book Lovers Club and The Friendly Book Community Facebook groups:** for sharing your thoughts on what your dream library would include. I hope I've brought your vision to life!
- **The brilliant bloggers, Bookstagrammers, ARC readers** and **BookTokers** who read and wrote lovely reviews for this book. You rock!
- And **to YOU, my wonderful romance reader**. Thanks for buying, reading and supporting my love stories. I appreciate you so much and can't wait to write more romantic books for you to enjoy.

Lots of love,
Olivia x

ABOUT THE AUTHOR

Olivia Spring is the bestselling author of more than seventeen romance, romcom and women's fiction books. Whether you want to fake-date a hot Hollywood movie star in London, jet off to Paris with a handsome billionaire, enjoy some sun, sand and sea with a gorgeous Spanish DJ in Marbella or attend a castle wedding in the South of France, Olivia's books will help you to escape reality and transport you to a dreamy romantic location. No ticket or passport required!
Olivia was born and raised in London and divides her time between the UK and Spain.
When she's not writing new steamy romcoms, Olivia can be found reading on the beach, enjoying cupcakes and cocktails and seeking inspiration for her next book!

If you'd like to say hi, email olivia@oliviaspring.com or connect on social media.

TikTok: www.tiktok.com/@oliviaspringauthor

facebook.com/ospringauthor

x.com/ospringauthor

instagram.com/ospringauthor